Genteel Anarchists

by

S Ben Hawksworth

Grosvenor House
Publishing Limited

All rights reserved
Copyright © S Ben Hawksworth, 2025

The right of S Ben Hawksworth to be identified as the author of this work has been asserted in accordance with Section 78 of the Copyright, Designs and Patents Act 1988

The book cover is copyright to S Ben Hawksworth
Book cover design by Brian Jones
Cover images copyright to onfilm and PicturePartners, courtesy of iStock

This book is published by
Grosvenor House Publishing Ltd
Link House
140 The Broadway, Tolworth, Surrey, KT6 7HT.
www.grosvenorhousepublishing.co.uk

This book is sold subject to the conditions that it shall not, by way of trade or otherwise, be lent, resold, hired out or otherwise circulated without the author's or publisher's prior consent in any form of binding or cover other than that in which it is published and without a similar condition including this condition being imposed on the subsequent purchaser.

This book is a work of fiction. Any resemblance to people or events, past or present, is purely coincidental.

A CIP record for this book
is available from the British Library

ISBN 978-1-83615-113-5

"You open your heart knowing that there's a chance it may be broken one day and in opening your heart, you experience a love and joy that you never dreamed possible."

Bob Marley

CHAPTER ONE

"Oh, I do like to be beside the seaside, I do like to be beside the sea," Alex sang quietly to himself. He loved singing but admitted to the fact that his singing voice was not unlike that of a bronchitic bullfrog and not to be imposed on others. There was no audience today, so he allowed himself the luxury of croaking out a few lines. He had always intended to retire to the coast. More particularly, he had planned to retire to Kirksea, where he had spent so many happy childhood holidays. He fondly remembered the excitement of watching his dad packing the Ford Cortina with what seemed like half the contents of the family home. Alex still had cherished memories of the long drive over from Wakefield with his parents and sister Val. Each year they played the same game on their outward journey: the first one to catch a glimpse of the sea got the promise of an ice cream from Dad as soon as the tent had been erected at their camp site. Everyone knew that they would all get an ice cream anyway, but it didn't detract from the excitement of the game.

Dad had always taken a pride in selecting an appropriate location for the family tent, which he erected in a purposeful, almost military manner, with Mum dutifully holding tent ropes as instructed and accepting the minor rebukes for her ineptitude when Dad felt she had got it wrong. Once the tent was up, he would gaze around at his little 'stockade' with obvious pride while Mum took 20 minutes to boil the water on the camping stove to make the obligatory cups of tea, which the two of them would enjoy while sitting on their camping chairs. As he grew a bit older, Alex had been given the honour of helping Dad with erecting the tent. This was almost a rite of passage and one that could not be experienced by his sister, but he later learned that she had absolutely no ambition to be an expert in such a field and that she preferred to sit with her mum and derive some entertainment when things inevitably went wrong for the menfolk.

Once the tent was up, the children would set off to explore the harbour. While it was always referred to as a harbour, it was little more than a breakwater that gave some protection from the prevailing winds. It was a substantial stone structure that protected the point at which a small beck entered the sea. In this way, at high water, there was a safe anchorage point for the small fishing boats that were moored up there. Alex and Val were always keen to check the state of the tide. At high tide, they could swim in the deep water near the shore, but low water offered the excitement of rock pools or hunting for shrimps in the shallow sandy water further out. The first part of the visit was taken up with buying their ice cream 'rewards' and then touring the village to see what had changed. The same souvenir shop was there with its array of brightly coloured postcards outside. Reading the postcards was another ritual, particularly the naughty ones that often portrayed large ladies reprimanding their weedy husbands for some dalliance with a much younger lady in a skimpy bathing costume. As children, they had found these images outrageously naughty but often very funny. The fish and chip shop seemed to be open all day, with the alluring smell that drew in visitors. They obviously had their chippies in Wakefield, but they had restricted opening times, and the produce never seemed to taste as good as that eaten from paper on the harbour wall.

Even from a young age, Alex had been fascinated by the single pub in the village. Long before he could venture inside, he and Val would spend some time sitting outside with a bottle of lemonade and a packet of crisps while their parents went in for a drink. Alex's dad had been a miner, but he was never the stereotypical hard-drinking man and only ever drank on special occasions such as Christmas, and even then, he only ever drank in moderation. On the annual holiday, he allowed himself the occasional couple of pints, and Mum would have the odd port and lemon. On one particular holiday, the area experienced an exceptionally heavy freak storm, and even Dad's camping prowess couldn't cope with the deluge. The tent was shredded by the wind, and the water flowing down the field soaked all their belongings. It was so bad that the entire family had to retreat to the car for the night. Early the following morning, a group of locals came to their rescue and invited them into the pub for a hot meal. It was Alex's first venture into this magic realm of the pub, and he liked it. The Whelk Pot was an unusual pub, having been formed by knocking together three fishermen's cottages in the 1950s, largely to cope with the growing number of holiday makers. This offered a rather large saloon bar downstairs and a kitchen, while the upstairs contained accommodation for the landlord and his family.

In his late teens, Alex had been invited by his father to accompany him to the pub. On his first visit, he had sat with his half of shandy, trying to look inconspicuous but feeling proud to be there among the adult customers. It was in the Whelk Pot that he first experienced the surreptitious pleasure of drinking outside the fixed opening hours that were supposedly enforced at the time. In reality, the pub never entirely abided by the licensing laws; the nearest police station was some miles away, and the local constabulary were quite prepared to turn a blind eye to minor infringements as long as there was no trouble. Visits by senior police officers were generally well known in advance, and the landlord would be given discreet instructions by the local bobby to ensure that the pub looked empty outside of official licensing hours.

Alex was impressed by the way the local bobby went about his duties, and it was one factor that made him want to join the police later. As a young boy, he had avidly watched *The Sweeney* and *Starsky and Hutch*, and he fancied a life of excitement with fast car chases, arresting villains and impressing girls. His subsequent career did not provide a lot of these experiences. He had the misfortune of joining the police just before the miners' strike, and the subsequent social disruption caused a major falling-out with his father that never fully healed. The picket line violence between the police and the miners caused what, in many cases, were irreconcilable differences in families, and Alex sought to get away from the area where many of his former friends wanted nothing to do with him. He managed to secure a position in the Metropolitan Police and, for a while, experienced some of the drama that had at first attracted him to the job. After a short time, he realised that in order to get the promotion he needed to cope with the high property costs in the capital, it would be beneficial to gain experience in different aspects of policing and, before he really understood why, he found himself in the vice squad. He thoroughly enjoyed the colourful variety of sleazy characters he met and the fascinating glimpses of a thriving subculture it afforded him. Unfortunately, it was not seen as the best area to further his career, and ultimately he moved to the fraud squad. In his latter role, he played a small part in ensuring that some big-time criminals were prosecuted. It was a vital job, but it wasn't exactly chasing round London in fast cars, punching villains and shouting, 'You're nicked, sunshine'. Marginally disillusioned but having built up a good pension, he eventually left the force and looked to set up home in his childhood holiday village.

He had been in his new cottage for a fortnight now, having arrived towards the end of the summer season, and a chill September wind was blowing off the sea. As he walked along the deserted harbour wall, he disturbed a small flock of herring gulls, which flew off, appearing to screech abuse for being disturbed. Alex remembered the conversation he'd had with one of the older residents of the village who had suggested that the gulls were the returning souls of fishermen lost at sea. These particular lost souls must formerly have been particularly ill-tempered sailors as they wheeled noisily above his head before flying off. He stopped at the end of the harbour wall and, turning his back to the wind, looked towards the village. He had been well aware that the place would have changed in the last forty-odd years and that it would not be the place of permanent sunny holidays that he chose to remember from his youth. Many of his colleagues in London had warned him about looking at the past through rose-tinted glasses, and they had recounted tales of acquaintances who had retired to the seaside and been disillusioned and even depressed after their first winter there. Alex had listened to all the cautionary tales, but he had wanted to move back 'up north'. He had enjoyed his years in London, and the house they had lived in latterly had been in one of those many parts of the city that had once been villages and had kept some sense of local identity while protecting their privacy. He had settled with his wife and two young daughters in what was a relatively friendly community, but Alex had found that many of the people he came across in the central parts of the city seemed so obsessed with getting on with their busy lives that they had little time to communicate with each other and absolutely no time to talk to strangers. Indeed, it was almost deemed a criminal offence to even make eye contact with a stranger on the tube.

Alex had sought the more relaxed atmosphere of a small community. He had briefly considered moving back to the Wakefield area, but he knew many of his old friends didn't want to know him since he had been unfairly seen to be on the side of the scabs during the miners' strike. He had been back to his home town for his father's funeral, and it was obvious then that a few of the local people still remembered the strike and the part the police had played in breaking up the demonstrations. Later, after his mother had also died and Val had moved to Manchester, there were no strong family connections in Wakefield, which is why Alex had chosen to move to Kirksea. The fact that property prices were much lower there had undoubtedly been a factor, as had his divorce from his wife, Megan.

The divorce had been one of those rare truly amicable arrangements. They both felt that their marriage had run its course. Between them, they had provided a comfortable and loving family setting to bring up their daughters. Alex had tried not to let the irregular hours of his police work disrupt their family life, but it had caused tension at times. When Megan's own technology support business had taken off, she found the pressures of her work added to their matrimonial problems. After the girls had left home, it was Megan who first tentatively suggested a divorce, and she was relieved to hear that Alex also, albeit reluctantly, saw the sense in the move. It had been difficult at times as they effectively dismantled their marriage because they both still liked one another, but eventually it had been settled. The family home had been sold and other financial matters resolved, so Alex now found himself in an attractive cottage which had been bought for cash, and he still had some savings and his police pension to rely on. Even on a cold, windy September day, he had good reason to feel satisfied with his life.

Alex had completed all his domestic chores at home. Having eaten and cleared away after breakfast, he had put some washing in the machine and attacked the downstairs carpets with the vacuum cleaner. He didn't pretend that the house was as immaculately clean as his wife would have made it, but by new bachelor standards, he felt it was pristine, and he had managed to employ a local woman called Jean to come in twice a week and do a few of the domestic jobs just to keep on top of things. After a relatively busy start to his day, he felt that he deserved his walk around the harbour and even a trip to the Whelk Pot or 'Wellie' as it was known by the regular clientele. He made his way to the pub, which had a commanding view of the harbour and pushed open the heavy outer door into a small porch and then through a second door into the bar area. As a child, he had wondered why it was necessary to have the two doors set so closely together but having seen the way the cold wind off the sea hit the front of the pub in less clement weather, he was convinced that the extra level of insulation was essential. Inside the pub, Dave, the landlord, was leaning behind the bar reading a recent copy of the local paper.

"Morning, Alex, although it's a bit of a blowy one out there. Your usual?"

This was exactly why Alex liked being in the village; he had only been there a short time, and already some people knew his name, and the landlord knew what his regulars liked to drink. He understood that such behaviour made good business sense, but it seemed to make the place more personal. Without waiting for an answer to his question, the landlord pulled a pint of bitter and put it in front of Alex, who dutifully handed over his money and took the change which Dave had taken from the till behind the bar.

"Thanks, Dave," said Alex. "It's a bit miserable out there, but not a bad day for a brisk walk. Is that the latest copy of the *Gazette*? Mine hasn't been delivered yet."

"Yes. Norman drops me one in early. He always gets a copy to check how his articles have been produced. He still gets a kick from seeing his work in print and delights in pointing out to me just how he has contributed to this week's copy."

"Norman? The old guy who comes in with the Airedale?" asked Alex, who was pleased that his attempt to learn the names of locals was paying off. "So he's a journalist?"

"Our Norman likes to think of himself as the oldest cub reporter in the business, but as he's quick to point out, he is largely a column-filler. The local papers get their money from advertising, but they have to put in some bits of 'news' just to make it worthwhile for readers to buy the paper. Norman can be relied on to produce copy of some sort, and the income augments his teaching pension. It's become quite a local tradition to scan the *Gazette* and to try and identify what Norman has contributed to that edition."

Dave was distracted at this point by the sight of someone coming into the pub, followed by a rather scruffy Airedale Terrier.

"Morning, Slippers, have you got yourself a new dog?" asked Dave of the latest visitor to the pub.

"Looks like it," replied the newcomer. "I saw him sitting patiently outside, and I just assumed that Norman was in here. There's no sign of him in the street."

"He was in here an hour ago to deliver the paper," explained Dave, "but he didn't have Muffin with him then, so the scruffy mutt must have decided to come on his own again. Never mind. Norman will know exactly where the dog is, and he'll be along soon to collect him, and no doubt he'll stop for a drink. I've known men take the dog for a walk as an excuse to go to the pub, but Norman goes one step further. I'm sure he sends the dog to the pub as an excuse to follow him."

While all this was going on, Muffin sat quietly looking up at the bar from whence dog treats had miraculously appeared in the past. It would be true to say that Muffin was not the brightest canine in the world, and a less charitable description would have listed him among the thickest, but he was always happy in his own little world. He would stare for ages at absolutely nothing. If Norman threw an imaginary object into the air, then Muffin would wait expectantly for it to fall for a few seconds before sniffing all over the floor in search of the elusive missile. The cerebrally-challenged dog had a written pedigree that went back several generations through many breed champions, and his original kennel name had been very ostentatious, but within the family he had originally been called Jake. Norman's wife had quickly assessed the dog's intelligence level, and the name Muffin had stuck. The dog sat patiently watching the bar and occasionally glancing up at Alex and Slippers. Alex was intrigued to know why this new guest was called Slippers. It might have been seen as rather forward to just ask him, so he attempted to work out why he was so named.

"How's things going, Slippers?" asked the landlord. "Did you manage to eventually sort out old Ma Dawson's door for her?"

Slippers rolled his eyes upwards and shook his head before replying, "That woman! I must have spent hours over the last few weeks trying to sort it out. I told her she needed a new one and that it would be cheaper in the long run. If she'd been paying any other tradesman to do the job, it would have cost her two hundred quid, and it still wouldn't have been done properly. Anyway, I've done another temporary job. I think she only asks me round to have someone to chat with, and she keeps filling me up with tea and biscuits."

While this conversation was going on, Alex found himself trying to discreetly examine Slippers' feet. The old police brain was searching for some evidence to support his recent theory that the new customer's name was a reference to the kind of footwear he favoured. Perhaps he was ex-military and had been excused heavy boots because of some problem with his feet? Or perhaps he had some minor problem with his feet, and a podiatrist had insisted that he shouldn't wear heavy shoes? These solutions did not appear to stand up to scrutiny when Alex noticed that Slippers was in fact wearing heavy working boots. In the end, his curiosity got the better of him and he delivered what he hoped would not be seen as a nosey question.

"That's an interesting name you have there; mine's Alex. I was named after my paternal grandfather. Is Slippers a family name?"

Slippers looked at Alex and then burst into laughter. He had the kind of laugh that could drown out all conversations in a crowded room, and all Alex could do was to look on in bewilderment at how his innocent question had provoked such a show of mirth, which had also apparently amused the landlord.

"No, mate," replied Slippers, once he had stopped laughing, "I have an informal style of bookkeeping for when I carry out minor work within the village. I consider that many of my small jobs do not necessarily need to bother those nice people in the Inland Revenue, so I don't enter all of them into my tax returns. Why bother making life more complicated for them by submitting piddling invoices for every little job? Instead of complicating matters and wasting hours of my own time on paperwork, I will often suggest that a customer could give me a few pounds. So, if I do a job and charge 20 pounds, I might ask if they could slip me 20 pounds."

Alex was obviously still none the wiser, so the landlord had to slowly explain,

"If our friend here wants to charge 20 pounds, he might suggest, 'slip us 20 quid'. Slip us! That's how he got the name. As he suggests, it's part of an informal commercial system that operates around here. If you find you have some job that needs doing, then there is usually someone in the village who can do it for you. Slippers is an odd-job man, but the village is full of people who can turn their hands to all sorts of things. Slippers has a legitimate fencing business, but he's always willing to help out."

"If someone's prepared to slip him a few quid," added Alex to show he had at last got the message.

Throughout this conversation, Muffin had been sitting staring at the bar in his usual mindless way until the pub door opened, and he obviously recognised the newcomer. The dog ran over, his whole body appearing to be wagging in the way such animals do to show how pleased they are to meet a long-lost friend, even if they had only been parted for an hour or so. Alex recognised the new visitor to be Norman. Muffin stopped short of his master, who stood upright trying to look annoyed but soon gave in to the servile behaviour of his delinquent pet and bent down to stroke him.

"Good grief, Muffin!" exclaimed Norman. "You've been at it again, you little devil, haven't you?"

Muffin looked up sheepishly. As was always the case in his confusing life, the dog had no idea what he had done wrong, but he knew from the tone of Norman's voice and the fact that he had recoiled from the dog that something had upset his master.

"Has he been up to his old tricks again, Norman?" asked the landlord. "I don't know how he manages to find them this late in the season."

Once again, Alex had a reminder that he was relatively new to the village. It had taken him a while to get the cottage sorted out, and he had made a point of getting down to the pub a few times to get to know the locals, but he obviously knew little about the antics of Muffin. Alex understandably looked confused, which prompted Dave to explain.

"Muffin has a penchant for eating wasps. He just can't get enough of them. I would have thought there wouldn't be many about so late in the year, but if there is one, then that mutt will chase it, and he often catches them."

"Doesn't he get stung?"

"Every time," replied Norman, wishing to add to the explanation, "but it never puts him off. He just stands there smacking his lips and then goes searching for another. I thought it was just because he was thick and kept forgetting what wasps can do, but he obviously loves them. But then some people like to eat red hot chillies. I've got nothing against wasps personally, but I wouldn't mind him snatching the odd one if it weren't for the after-effects."

"After-effects?"

"Yes, his breath smells terrible after a single wasp. I mean really bad. He has breath that could strip paint, and he keeps finding them, and then he's so chuffed with himself and expects to be able to breathe all over me. Anyway, while I'm here, I might as well have a swift pint just to get rid of the smell of wasp breath. My good lady knew where the dog would be, and she knows full well that I will be obliged to stop for a pint by way of apologising to Dave."

"Very decent of you, Norman, and while you're here, I have to admit that I couldn't find any of your work in the *Gazette* this week. I thought you said you had a new feature."

"And we gentlemen of the great British press are renowned for our unimpeachable integrity. Check out page eight, and you'll find my latest contribution to the journalistic world. I'm rather proud of this one."

Dave flicked though the paper and scanned the said page. After a moment, he looked up at Norman and declared, "No. You sure you've got the right page? I can't see any of your work unless you provided the copy for the big advert for the last few days of that 'massive furniture sale'. No, it can't be that because they've been promoting that sale for years. I can't see you having done this small piece on the latest advances in computer technology; it took you months to learn how to make a call on your mobile. The report about recent trends in women's fashion doesn't appear to tap into your less than extensive knowledge of the subject either."

In desperation, Norman took the paper from the landlord and, with a triumphant gesture, indicated a column on the side of page eight. Dave looked at the piece being emphatically indicated, and Alex also strained to see what the mystery journalistic gem was.

"There you are!" said Norman with a suggestion of pride in his voice. "I've been telling the editor for years that it would be a good idea. We all know that small rags such as ours rely on advertising to make money, but the advertisers don't want to invest their money in a paper that nobody reads, so it's down to dedicated people like me to contribute things that the punters want to see."

Dave read from the indicated column, and a smile crept across his face.

"*Madame Estelle. International astrologist to the stars interprets your cosmic reading for the day.*"

Alex and Dave could not suppress a little laugh, and Alex was prompted to say, "But you're not a woman."

"Well spotted, Sherlock," replied Norman sarcastically. "You should be in the police."

Alex knew that the remark contained a degree of unintentional truth. He had made it a policy during his working life not to make it known that he was in the police. It made some people a little guarded in what they might discuss if they knew his true calling. He had no intention in his new home of hiding the fact that he had been in the police, but he had decided not to broadcast the fact.

"And it may come as no shock to you both," added Norman, "to hear that I know absolutely nothing about horoscopes, but we in the media world know that there are hordes of people who won't leave home in the morning without checking what the world has in store for them. All that talk about the position of stars and the moon is senseless twaddle to me. I don't pretend to be able to read star charts, but the odd mention of that stuff lends an undeserved credibility to 'my' predictions. All I do is trawl through past horoscopes from other papers and just reassign them to different star signs. It fills up a few column inches, and the public are happy. I'm providing a public service really, even if I don't know my Aries from my elbow."

"But isn't that illegal? You're conning the public," suggested Dave.

"Illegal? No, it's just a harmless deception. I'm giving the readership what some of them want to read. My nom de plume for the piece is likewise designed to impress a certain group of our more superstitious readership. The name sounds marginally more mystical than Norman Bliss. I never make precise predictions; if I told anyone that they were going to have a fantastic day winning millions of pounds on the lottery and it would be a good day to go in and tell their boss where to stick the job, it might cause waves."

Alex had taken the opportunity to take the paper and he read out, "*Capricorn. 'This is not a good day for making rash financial investments.*' I would have thought that was a bit of advice that should be heeded most days. What's your star sign, Dave?"

"I'm Gemini, can't you tell? We are thoughtful, dynamic, intelligent and great romantics."

Without bothering to comment on Dave's assessment of the Gemini character, Alex read out, "*Gemini. Take every opportunity to promote relationships by displaying your innate generosity to friends by buying them a drink.*"

"Rubbish!" protested the landlord. "It doesn't say anything of the sort."

"How do you know?" asked Alex before answering his own question, "Because you had read it. You couldn't resist a sneaky look."

"It proves my point that people do tend to read that sort of tripe even when they know it is just that," added Norman, "and in the past, I have churned out more than my fair share of such spurious column-fillers. Sometimes I do it out of boredom. There are just so many meetings of local interest groups you can report on before you feel the urge to add that little bit extra to spice the story up. It can lead to problems. When I left university, I had ambitions of being a journalist, and I managed to get myself a job on a very small provincial paper. It was in the days before most such publications were swallowed up into large media conglomerates. In those days, many young reporters worked on the small papers until they had a major story that they hoped would be picked up by the nationals who might go on to employ such promising young talent. My editor didn't help my chances of meteoric promotion. Like most young reporters, I was asked to cover the more mundane activities within the community. I reported on dozens of cases where local children had achieved something, or on the retirement of local dignitaries, or the success of some junior football team, or on any prosaic topic that involved groups of people. I would be sent along with Mick, a photographer who was as bored as me, with the instruction to get pictures with as many people in them as possible. The fact being that people liked to see themselves in the papers, so they would buy a copy and perhaps another to impress some relative. In the end, I got so fed up that I would make up my own stories."

"Surely that must be illegal?" suggested Dave.

"I must admit it became a bit of a slippery slope as I massaged the facts a bit. My report on the Middle Norton Horticultural Club's annual show seemed fine on the surface, except that there was no such club and no such village, and it's doubtful that any such club in the area would have offered a prize for the best crop of mangoes. Mick produced a rather good photograph of a selection of mangoes he took in Tesco, and it looked quite convincing as part of my report. For some reason, that one managed to get into the paper, and no one commented on it, which goes to show how little interest the general public have in a report of a minor event outside their area. Later, I heard a rumour that a big cat, a jaguar or some such, had been spotted in a local country park, so Mick and I took it upon ourselves to investigate. We spent most of our free time over the next week looking for the elusive beast but with no luck. In the end, I interviewed a lady who lived near to the park in the hope of getting news of a sighting, but she told us she'd seen nothing and suggested people might have been getting confused after seeing her friend's rather large black moggy. She pointed out the said huge cat, which was in her neighbour's garden, and we got a few photos of it in case we decided to run a story disclosing the truth."

"Not an unreasonable plan," commented Alex. "So did you run the story?"

"Not exactly," replied Norman hesitantly, "We thought about it but concluded that it would not be snatched up by the nationals, so we looked at it from a different perspective. We announced that we had seen what we took to be a jaguar that had been released into the wild by its owner, and my friend posted what was a deliberately blurred image of the perfectly safe domestic cat we had seen. With my somewhat sensational report, it caused quite a stir locally, with people being advised to avoid coming into contact with '*the Beast of Malton Park*' as we had named it. In the end, some over-zealous young park ranger learned the true identity of the animal. The photographer and I were given a real roasting by our editor, but he managed to convince the readership that it had been an innocent mistake, so we avoided being sacked. My job was relatively secure, but my chances of ever being sent to a major case were gone, so I did the dishonourable thing and went into teaching. I served a thirty-five-year sentence."

It was at this point that the trio at the bar were joined by Dave's wife, who he introduced to Alex by announcing, "And this is my lovely wife, Daureen, who is universally regarded as the brains of the management team as well as being the most attractive."

While the effusive description of his wife might have appeared somewhat over-the-top, it was delivered with obvious sincerity, and the way Daureen smiled at him showed that there was a very strong bond between the two of them. The landlady was an attractive woman who obviously took great care over her appearance. Some might have considered her a bit overdressed for her role within the pub particularly as she augmented her glamorous image with what might have been seen as an over-enthusiastic application of make-up. If anyone had ever plucked up the courage to criticize her, she would have explained that it was a part of the uniform she wore for her job, as was the carefully styled blond hair that necessitated her weekly visit to the hairdressers.

"Hello, you must be the gentleman who moved into the Cogans' place down by the old Post Office building," remarked Daureen. "How are you settling in? It must be strange being up here after London."

"It's still early days, but I'm enjoying the relative peace and quiet. The Cogans had left the cottage in wonderful order, and I haven't had to change much at all. I've just got back from a walk along by the harbour wall; it was rather bracing, but I loved it."

"You'd better make the most of the solitude," she explained, "in the summer, the place can be very busy if we get any fine weather. Particularly at the weekend, you can't move for Wessies."

"Wessies?"

"Visitors from West Yorkshire. Some days, this place can seem like Leeds by the sea."

"In that case," mused Alex, "I guess I was a Wessie as a kid when we came over from Wakefield for our fortnight camping holiday. If we are in confessional mode, I suppose I'm still a Wessie."

"Wessie Alex. It really suits you," said Dave with obvious delight. "Consider yourself duly appointed as such. We've adopted our own tame village Wessie."

Alex was delighted to be honoured in such a way. It was yet another small step to being accepted within the village he was pleased to call his home.

CHAPTER TWO

Alex was feeling rather pleased at the way his morning had gone. He had met a couple of the local residents he had only ever seen in the street before, and he had learned a bit about the way the local community got on. He was glad that his former job as a police officer had remained a secret. Would Norman have discussed his journalistic impropriety if he had known he was talking to a former police officer? Slippers would certainly have been reluctant to disclose his unofficial invoicing procedures if he knew Alex had been in the fraud squad. Alex had no intention of reporting every minor misdemeanour that he came across, but his new neighbours didn't know that, so it was best for him not to disclose too much about his former job.

When he left the pub, a cold wind was blowing, but the forecast rain had stayed away, so he decided to walk to the fish and chip shop. It had proved to be a convenient place to collect meals during the upheaval of settling into his new place, and he regularly chatted with Anita who worked there.

"Hi Alex," came the cheerful greeting as he walked into the welcoming warmth of the shop. "What can I get you today, my lovely? I've got some rather nice cod that came in fresh this morning."

Alex knew from previous chats with Anita that some of the fish she served in the evening might have been still swimming around that morning. There were very few boats fishing from Kirksea commercially these days, but some of the locals still managed to take their cobles out and get a few fish or crabs when they were in season. Alex looked up at the chalkboard to make his selection but knew he would settle for fish and chips, which he duly ordered. While he waited for his fish to finish frying, he chatted with Anita to build on his knowledge of the town and its people.

"So, are you local to the village?" he asked by way of a conversational gambit.

"Do you mean do I come here often?" she teased him.

In his youth, Alex would have been mildly embarrassed by such a reply, but he had known a lot of women in his time on the force, and he had become immune to some of their taunts and over-familiarity that he had been met with. His time in the vice squad had been an eye-opener for him as a young constable having to frequently question sex workers, so Anita's innocent comments held no fear for him, and he merely responded, "If I were 30 years younger and I didn't know that you had a large boyfriend, I might have been tempted to say that, but as a newcomer I'll content myself with finding out a little bit more about the village and how you fit in."

In his frequent previous visits to pick up what had almost become his staple diet from the fish shop, he had watched Anita flirting with most of the men who came in, whether they were teenagers or in their late eighties. Everyone knew she was harmless, and even the women who might accompany their menfolk were generally not offended by her banter, which was seen merely as a way to brighten up people's lives.

"OK," continued Anita as she deftly removed a large piece of fish from the oil and placed it in the heated tray above the range, "as long as you're not intending to whisk me off to the fleshpots of Bridlington, I guess I can tell you that I am indeed local. Born and bred in this little part of paradise. My dad is Gordon Loftus; he's a local builder. You've probably met him."

"I can't say I've had the pleasure yet, but I'm new to the village."

"Yes, I know. You moved into the Cogan place recently. My dad did a lot of stuff on their place when they were putting it up for sale. He's done up quite a few properties in the village since it became a popular place to retire to or buy a holiday home. A few years ago, you could hardly give some of the older properties away, but now they are definitely worth doing up, and it's virtually impossible for young people from the area to get a place."

Alex was once again struck by how some of the villagers seemed to know so much about him, but fortunately his 'guilty secret' as regards his former career had yet to become public knowledge. He continued with his 'interrogation' of the young woman in his quest to find as much as he could about his new home.

"Did you ever think of moving away?"

"My fella Tom wanted us to try and get a place inland near Wykethorpe," she replied as she skilfully wrapped his fish and chips. "It's a bit cheaper there, but it would have meant me having to travel into the shop each day, and Tom also has a job working for Dad in the village. The fact is that Wykethorpe is a pretty soulless place, and we never wanted to move there. Fortunately, we found a rather decrepit place up Main Street here and with a bit of financial backing from Dad and a lot of hard work, we've got it looking half decent. It still needs a lot doing, but we can live there and work on it when we can afford it."

"Yes, I can remember when my young wife and I moved into our first place in London. Even then, the prices were astronomical, and the mortgage was crippling. Our diet was pretty meagre at times, but we had the flat and, looking back, life was pretty good."

Almost immediately, Alex realised that he had broken one of the rules he had set himself. He had been determined not to give away any details of his previous life until the locals had chance to get to know him a bit.

Anita had seen this chink in his armour of secrecy, and Alex was not surprised when she innocently commented, "It would be almost impossible for Tom or me to afford separate places, but our joint income means we can just about manage to run our place and we are very happy. I guess you and your wife would both have to have had jobs to even think about a place in London."

It wasn't a question as such, but it was an open-ended 'fishing' statement and one that caused him some concern as to how best to respond. He couldn't just ignore it, and he began to realise that now he was in a corner, and he might as well disclose a bit more rather than be seen as being rude. If he wanted to be accepted in the village, then people needed to know what kind of person he really was, and hiding behind the 'mystery stranger' persona would merely put up barriers.

"Yes, we were lucky in that we were both working, and we even managed to afford to keep my old Morris Marina on the road. We were both new to our jobs and at the bottom of the career ladder, but we got by, and, yes, we were happy too."

"Is your wife going to join you up here then?"

Alex recognised that the floodgates had opened, and he was prepared for what he anticipated would be a deluge of questions, so he decided to pre-empt her as he went on to explain.

"Megan and I are divorced. She's staying on in London as she has a small business there."

"Oh, I'm sorry," said Anita at the thought that she might have intruded into his personal unhappiness.

"Don't be. It was a mutual decision. We'd had some very good years, but our careers kept getting in the way. The children,

Stephanie and Jessica, were grown and had lives of their own. There was no acrimonious court case, and the only question of custody was as regards the cat, and I let Megan keep that. I hated the little brute anyway. When I retired, it was always my dream to come back up here, but Megan had her business, so it was another reason to go for a divorce."

Anita then asked the question he had wanted to avoid facing for a while. "What line of work were you in?"

"The police." He waited for some sort of response from her, but she did not recoil in horror.

"Oh! My uncle Ted, that's Dad's younger brother, is in the police. He works in Whitby as part of the traffic police. What sort of line were you in?"

"I ended up with a rather boring desk job as part of the team investigating fraud. I played a very small part in some big cases. It was rather interesting for a while, but as we got more and more into cyber fraud, I realised I was ready to get out, so as soon as I could I took my chance and retired."

"Good for you," she said as she passed him his lunch. "Enjoy the rest of your day, love."

CHAPTER THREE

As he left the fish and chip shop, Alex felt quite pleased with the way Anita had reacted to his 'confession'. He knew that the efficiency of the village grapevine would ensure that most of the inhabitants would know a lot about his personal history very shortly, but he now recognised that he couldn't have kept his secrets for long. The very nature of true friendship necessitated a degree of openness, and he was pleased at the way his disclosure had been received. He had intended to take his fish and chips and sit on the harbour wall, but good sense prevailed, and he set off home with them.

As he let himself into his cottage, he was surprised to find his cleaning lady doing some ironing in the kitchen. He had forgotten it was her day to come in and felt glad that he had left the cottage relatively clean that morning. He knew that it made little sense to feel the need to tidy up before the cleaner arrived, but he did it anyway. Jean had obviously done some cleaning and was now busying herself with some ironing she had found to do. Alex was always impressed at the way Jean actively sought out things to do rather than sit around, and it took considerable persuasion to get her to sit down and have a cup of tea during her working sessions.

"Hello, Jean, I'd forgotten it was your morning. I'm just going to grab my lunch. I'm going to make a cup of tea. Please join me, I've got some of those biscuits you like."

"All right," she replied, "but I can't sit down for long. I'll just finish these shirts, and then I'll put the kettle on."

He hadn't the heart to tell her that he never bothered ironing most of his shirts, and he just let her get on. Ignoring her offer to put the kettle on, he took it upon himself to make a pot of tea before sitting down to his fish and chips. It only took Jean five minutes to finish ironing the shirts and put the ironing board away, and then she joined him at the kitchen table, having collected cups and the biscuits.

"I'm sorry, Mr Lucas, but I'm going to have to leave a little bit earlier today as I have to go into town to collect some items for my husband. He's been doing some work repairing a handrail down by the harbour, and he needs a few items from the builders' merchant. He's spent so much time on Ma Dawson's door that he hasn't had time to get away and collect the stuff himself."

Alex recalled some discussion about Ma Dawson's legendary door, and it prompted him to ask, "You aren't married to Slippers, are you, Jean?"

"Guilty," she replied as she poured their teas. "That would be my idle loafer, Simon. Why? Did you want some fencing work done?"

"Not at the moment, thanks, and please call me Alex. It's just that I was introduced to him earlier, and he mentioned Ma Dawson, and it sounded a bit of a coincidence when you mentioned her."

"That would no doubt have been in his 'office' down at the Wellie. He claims he has to go in there each day to meet his customers and to pay some of his taxes. To be fair, he does get a lot of his informal work through the clientele at the pub. He has the fencing business as his legitimate work, but if other little jobs need doing about the village, then he is keen to get them done on a less formal basis."

"If people slip him a few quid," interjected Alex with a knowing wink before asking, "Why does he pay his taxes in the pub?"

"It is generally known that not all of the slipped money is diligently declared on his tax returns, but he maintains that he pays so much tax on his beer that he is actually balancing the books. What he doesn't declare on his income tax, he pays on excise duty on the beer. He's a very moral person is my Simon. He has explained to me that my few pounds I get from my cleaning jobs don't need to be declared because it's not worth bothering those busy people in the tax offices. He has a firm grip on financial matters does my Simon, and likes to keep things simple. He pays tax on the fencing business because he says it's only fair that the revenue people get some of his money. He has some interesting discussions with our lad Clive, who insists upon declaring all his income for the tax people. I don't know where we went wrong with that lad."

Alex felt quite pleased that he was further developing his knowledge of how people fitted together in the social jigsaw that was Kirksea, and he was particularly happy to hear of Slippers' fencing business. Alex had previously noticed that there was some slight sign of rot in part of the steps in the small yard behind his cottage, and he also had vague plans of having a small, covered area built out there to catch the afternoon sun in the summer. He remembered the time back in Wakefield when everyone had contacts with tradesmen they could rely on. When he had moved to London, it was difficult to know which of the local firms to approach when a small job needed doing, and it took time to find a company that could be relied on to respond if there was some minor emergency such as when a radiator sprung a leak. He felt that he was slowly building up his contacts and beginning to feel more and more a part of the village.

"Thanks for the tea and biscuits, but I'll have to get on now," declared Jean as she took her cup over to the sink to wash it.

Clive took his tea through to the small front lounge; he didn't like to watch Jean at her work in case she felt he was scrutinizing her efforts. He had seen the results of her work over the last few days, and he knew she was meticulous in her cleaning. He had been pleased that he had taken up the estate agent's advice about retaining Jean. She had worked for the previous owners of the cottage, and Mrs Cogan had given a glowing verbal reference for her. He had tried hard to impress upon Jean that she should call him by his forename. He couldn't stand the thought of it being a master and servant arrangement; she was doing a job for him and he employed her, as he might have any tradesperson.

Alex pulled through the paper that was sticking through the letterbox and took it to his armchair. He briefly glanced at the main article on the front page that spoke of the litter that was being dumped on one of the more commercial local beaches. While it was undoubtedly a very important issue, it was hardly a major news item but rather one that the paper returned to when news was a bit thin on the ground. He turned to the page that offered 'news from the regions' and turned to the small article that dealt with the area around Kirksea. The article was not attributed to any particular writer, and Alex couldn't help but wonder if Norman had contributed in any way. The main big item reported was about the Kirksea beach angling competition, which had apparently taken place the previous week. He had been aware of one or two extra people fishing from the harbour wall at the time, so it had hardly been the highlight of the angling calendar, but the report stated that a Mr Graham Clark of Hull had taken the first prize of £200 worth of fishing gear from the sponsor having landed a one pound six-ounce whiting which secured him the prize for the biggest single fish as well as the prize for the heaviest total weight of fish caught by an individual.

Fascinated as he was by the fishing competition, he turned to page eight to check the new horoscope page. He couldn't help but chuckle at the banal advice being given, but he felt a degree of admiration for Norman's cheek.

It was at this point that Jean came in to dust and polish the lounge. Armed with her spray polish, she decided to start on the coffee table, which necessitated her moving the paper that Alex had discarded. "I see they've got one of those horror scopes," she commented. "Of course I don't believe in all of it, but it doesn't harm to check. I'm a typical Leo, and we tend to be sceptical."

She stopped her cleaning regime for a while and perused Norman's work before reading out loud.

"Leo. Venus plays a large part in your life over the next week. As a fire sign, you can expect to receive overtures of passion from a loved one." She put down the paper and commented, "They can't be a hundred per cent right every time. Unfortunately."

CHAPTER FOUR

Alex was out early the following day and went for his customary walk along the harbour wall. It was one of those warm late summer mornings, and the cold wind of the previous day had gone. It was approaching high tide; the sea was smooth, and the waves now only showed themselves as a regular light swell against the stone of the harbour wall. As children, he and Val would have been tempted to jump in and then, having felt the exhilarating shock of the cold water, would have swum frantically around in a vain attempt to make themselves feel warmer before clambering out and wrapping themselves in towels. Alex did not find the water enticing; his days of swimming in the harbour were long gone. He smiled to himself as he remembered the time in his early teens when he and a few other boys from the campsite had decided that it was a good idea one late summer evening to go in for skinny dipping.

It had been a particularly warm day, and the group of young daredevils felt it would be good to cool off with a dip in the harbour. None of them had their swimming costumes with them, but they thought nobody would be around to see them if they just went for a swim in their underpants. They piled up their clothes by the end of the harbour wall. It was at this point that one particularly adventurous individual decided that it would be good fun to strip completely. The others did not want to appear to be 'chicken', and so pretty soon they were all swimming about, carefree and clothes-free. They were having fun and failed to see a small group of girls approaching from the landward end of the harbour wall. By the time the boys were aware of the visitors, the girls were almost up to the spot where the clothes had all been piled up. It was too late for the boys to get to their clothes before the girls, and a general panic set in. The group of young swimmers decided that they would just have to stay in the water until the girls left. However, one of the girls spotted the clothes, which caused her to look over the wall, and she caught sight of the group in the water. Even in the fading light, it was possible to see that the boys were not wearing any clothes. That particular young girl, far from being shocked at the occasional sight of naked bottoms bobbing in the water, gave out a shriek of delight and called her friends over. For what seemed like an eternity to the swimmers, the girls jostled for good viewing points and set up a barrage of raucous laughter and whistles. Eventually, the girls tired of the game and wandered off, leaving the very cold group of swimmers to clamber out and frantically rush to put on clothes without the luxury of having a towel to dry themselves on. It wasn't the last time Alex experienced the joy of swimming without clothes, but he and his friends were a lot more careful about the location after that.

The incident had been extremely embarrassing at the time, and for some days after that, whenever he walked past a particular group of the girls on the campsite, they would snigger in a conspiratorial way and look in his direction, which had caused his parents to enquire what could possibly have been the matter with them. He felt that his feigned ignorance had not been convincing. He now remembered that in later years, some of those same girls had joined him and some of his friends to go skinny dipping, but they chose a secluded beach in a cove some distance from the harbour, and their activities were restricted to much later in the evening. The two groups kept a semi-respectable distance between each other in the water, but it was still great fun, and they always had the good sense to take towels to get dried on later. They would often light a fire on the beach and sit around well into the night, sometimes until dawn. The nights were cold, but the cloudless skies enabled a clear view of the stars and the meteor showers over the sea. He would sit cuddled up to his girlfriend of the time in front of the campfire and watch as it slowly died down, and then in the morning, they would pack up their belongings and trudge back to the campsite.

Eventually, some of the individuals paired off, but the romances didn't tend to last. Alex remembered one particular girl he had been very fond of – Lynda McGregor – he could still remember her name nearly 40 years later. He and Lynda were generally viewed as the couple most likely to stay together, but she lived in Halifax, which was a long way from Wakefield for someone who had no motorized transport. For a while after the holidays, he tried to regularly travel the 20 miles to her house on his bike, but the romance was eventually doomed, and they both moved on, but he still remembered the trip as he biked home from Halifax on the day they broke up; he had cried for the first time in his life. The break up had hit him badly, but his parents had failed to realise it and passed it off as 'puppy love'. Alex remembered the hurt, and when his own daughters, in their teenage years, had experienced the anguish of splitting up from their partners, he had refused to treat it lightly; love, at whatever stage in life, was to be valued and the loss of it can cause genuine grief.

Alex looked out to sea. He had always loved this view, and he loved the village. He never had any illusions about it going to be the same place he had visited as a child, and all the warnings from former colleagues about how he would be disappointed to go back were not true. He knew full well that returning would provoke all sorts of memories, and he was ready for that. He was a firm believer in his mother's advice, stating that the past can be a good place to visit, but you shouldn't try to live there. With this adage in mind, he decided to walk up to the village shop to buy some items for his lunch.

The shop retained one of those little bells above the door that announced the arrival of visitors, and it gave a friendly tinkling as Alex walked in. A young man, whose smart clothes were protected by a long utilitarian apron, got up from where he had been stacking some of the lower shelves and approached Alex with a welcoming smile.

"Good morning, and how can we tempt you today?" he enquired.

"I just need some nice bread and something for sandwiches for my lunch please," replied Alex as he looked around the shop. For such small premises, it seemed to hold mountains of stock. Alex made a point of using the shop for much of his domestic needs. Obviously, the business couldn't compete on prices with the big supermarkets, but it was reassuring to know it was there, and he did his bit to support it.

"We've just received a delivery from Caldwick's; their seeded loaf is delicious, perhaps with a nice bit of Camembert or even a mature cheddar? We've got an assortment of olives and some local tomatoes."

In his previous visits, Alex had got to know a little about the two young men who had taken over the shop. Brian, who was currently serving him, was a vegetarian, and it was clear that his suggestions for Alex's lunch included no meat options, although the shop had a selection of cooked meats in their delicatessen section. Brian was not an evangelistic vegetarian and never tried to push his views onto others, but he had a natural reluctance to recommend foods that he would not choose for himself. The co-owner of the shop was Colin, and he didn't share his partner's dietary habits. Alex couldn't help thinking how much the shop had changed since Mrs Appleby's time. He remembered her from his early holiday visits. In those days, the range of goods for sale was much more limited and lacked any of the products which back then would have been seen as exotic. Mrs Appleby had never stocked the likes of garlic, French cheeses and continental cooked meats. The nearest she came to foreign food was tinned ravioli that came in a thick tomato sauce or tins of chopped-up spaghetti, which appeared to come in the same sauce. When Alex and his family came camping, they tended to bring a large selection of tinned foods from home, which they augmented with a few basic items from Mrs Appleby's shop as the holiday wore on.

Alex took up Brian's suggestion of the seeded loaf and tomatoes but couldn't resist taking some cooked ham. While Brian was packaging some of the ham with ill-concealed disdain, Alex looked at the array of fruit and vegetables, and he was taken by two of the hand-printed labels. They clearly stated that the apples were 'orgasmic' and the cucumbers were not 'genitally modified'. Brian saw his amusement and explained.

"That's Colin's handiwork. He claims he's dyslexic, but I'm sure the big lump does it just to wind me up. I've given up arguing about it. It's not worth breaking up the happy home, and some of the customers are entertained."

Alex smiled and, having completed his purchases and resisting the temptation to buy any of the over-sexed food, he left the shop. As he walked back towards his cottage, he met Anita, who, it turned out, was on her way to open the chip shop for what she hoped would be the lunchtime trade.

"Hi Wessie," she greeted him.

"I see it didn't take long for that name to get around," he said in response to her cheery remark.

"Dad was in the Wellie last night, and Dave just happened to mention it," she explained. "You don't mind the name, do you?"

He didn't directly answer her question, but inwardly he was delighted to see that he was considered sufficiently local to have his own honorary position as the village's adopted tame Wessie.

"It could be worse," he confided, "when I was at school, my friends initially changed my surname of Lucas to Lukey. I rather hoped it would develop further and become 'Lucky', but no; for most of my secondary school years, I was known as Lucy. I was always rather big for my age, so I think that the fact that I didn't look a bit like a Lucy seemed funny to my friends. When I joined the police, I made sure I never took the name with me; it might have been difficult to display a sense of authority if everyone called me Lucy."

"I think you're right, and anyway, Wessie seems to suit you. You were right to drop the Lucy. What have you got planned for this afternoon? It looks as if it's going to be sunny; I hate it, having to work on the range in this weather, but you're free as a bird."

"I guess you're right, but to be honest, I sometimes think I will have to find something to do with my days. After a lifetime of being in a job with lengthy and often unpredictable hours, it was lovely to get up here and have none of those pressures. After a few weeks of what has effectively been a holiday, I suddenly find I want something to do. There's no way I would want a regular nine-to-five job for five days a week: I'm not a masochist. Some of my former colleagues have gone into security work, but I don't fancy that. The trouble is that police work doesn't have many civilian counterparts."

"You could be in luck. Living in Kirksea, there are always bits of jobs to do. Obviously, in the summer season, there are temporary jobs around, but throughout the year there are opportunities to earn a bit of cash, and it's up to you how much of it you pay tax on. Sometimes, it's a bit less formal than that."

"Less formal?" asked a rather bemused Alex, who could envisage a whole new world of illicit dealings opening up.

"Yes, the old barter system," replied Anita. "Dad uses it from time to time; if he's getting a bit snowed under with work and Slippers is having a slack time, he might ask if he can help out. No money changes hands, but it's generally seen that if Slippers does a half day's work for Dad, then Dad owes him half a day's work. Quid pro quo! It's not an exact science, but it does away with all that complicated tax stuff. Dave at the pub has no difficulty getting odd bits of work done for him, and many of the workers are keen to take their earnings in liquid form."

"Sounds fascinating," he remarked, "and at least some of it is almost legal.

"I guess the wish to have a simple life without excessive state interference goes back to the old smuggling days. At one point, there could hardly have been a family in the village that didn't benefit from avoiding what they saw as iniquitous levels of duty, and local folklore insists that many vicars in this area over the years had more than a few purchases of illicit goods where the tax had been avoided. Nowadays, it would appear that only the wealthier members of society can avoid paying taxes."

Anita was quiet for a moment as they strolled in the direction of the fish shop and then suddenly announced,

"If you are interested in doing the odd bit of work, I can put a few feelers out and let people know you are available. As it happens, I can often do with a bit of help in the shop; nothing too complicated like doing the frying. That job is taken by me and Nora. We split the shifts between us for the main part, but we are often short of people to prepare the food or to serve the customers. It would only take a while to learn the basics, and you could be soon doing a lot of the jobs.

We often have problems in the summer if Laura is on duty and gets a shout."

"A shout?"

"Yes. Laura does a few shifts for us. She's a member of the inshore lifeboat crew, and because we are so near the harbour, she's often one of the first there. If she happens to be on call, we can suddenly find we are down one member of staff. It tends to happen in the summer when we are packed with customers, and we find a couple of visitors have managed to get themselves cut off by the tide while walking along the beach. Most of the times the lifeboat is called out, it's for people who have no idea about keeping safe. If you are not too busy, you could drop in tomorrow afternoon; Nora will be there, and we can show you the setup."

"It's a date."

"On that subject, I must warn you that you are likely to go home smelling of chip fat, and it does nothing for your love life," she added with a cheeky grin.

"I think I can put up with that disadvantage for now, thanks, but if I find that my appearance in a white overall in the shop drives all the local ladies wild, then I may have to reconsider my employment status."

CHAPTER FIVE

After lunch, Alex was faced with what was becoming a regular dilemma: deciding what to do next. He had found little that interested him on daytime television, which he seemed to feel was full of adverts for household appliances he didn't need and advice on how he could build up his credit score so he could afford to buy them. Interspersed within these would be ads from companies advising him how to bet safely online, and if he lost the will to live after all that, there were other companies advising him how to arrange his funeral. There was always the pub, but he didn't want to spend every free moment in there. He eventually decided to allocate time to drawing up some plans for what he might do with the small walled yard behind his house. Many of the cottages in the village had such yards behind them and could be accessed from a narrow roadway that would serve a row of cottages. The yards had originally been used by the fishermen to store fishing gear, but now most of them were used for recreation or hanging out washing. Alex had previously formulated some very rough idea as to how he could put up a small, covered lean-to, like a sort of veranda. He spent a large part of the afternoon trying to envisage where he would put such a structure and making preliminary sketches in an old notebook. At the end of his deliberations, he came up with a plan; he would ask Slippers to build it. Alex's actions in the yard and trying to put his ideas on paper convinced him that he was not ready to take on the whole task himself.

Having taken a lengthy walk along the beach, it was five o'clock when Alex decided it was a reasonable time to nip into the Wellie for a pint. There were a few locals sitting in what he took to be their regular places around the room. Slippers was deep in conversation with a young couple that Alex had seen regularly around the village, and they all appeared to be looking at some plans laid out on the table between them. Slippers looked up just long enough to greet Alex.

"Evening, Wessie. I'll be with you when we've sorted this little bit of business."

Alex waved his acknowledgement and approached the bar, where he found Daureen was on duty.

"Evening, love, the usual, is it?" she asked.

"Yes, please, Daureen, and a packet of plain crisps. I'm starving."

"Dave can always fix you up a sandwich," she suggested, pointing to a menu and a price list on the end of the bar. "It's about all I can trust him to do in terms of meals and, to be fair, he's quite good at them."

"I can confirm that," said a man standing further down the bar, and then he added, "I'm Gordon Loftus, and unless my information is incorrect, you must be Wessie Alex."

Alex smiled at this repetition of a name he had become rather fond of, and he countered by saying, "And you must be Anita's dad."

"Guilty as charged, but most people in the village know me as Bricky Gordon. I did a bit of work on your place shortly before you moved in; it's a good, solid property. It's certainly in a lot better state than the three places I'm doing up in Barnard's Yard. In all honesty, they should have been pulled down years ago. They were primitive, and only the barest bit of work has been done on them over the centuries to just about keep them habitable. But they're some of the oldest cottages in the village, and it would be impossible to get planning permission to redevelop them completely. That's why the big building companies don't want to take them on. I get quite a lot of business doing them up in a style I call 'mock artisan'. Outwardly, they look largely unchanged, but internally they are all bells and whistles and comply with all current building regulations."

"I certainly like my place," added Alex. "It looks quaint from the outside, but it's certainly got all mod cons."

"It wasn't easy getting access to your terrace in terms of getting machinery and building materials down there, and I had to get Clive to move a lot of materials around the site by hand when we could have done with a JCB, but the finished job was good." Gordon paused for a while before continuing. "I gather that you might be looking for the odd bit of work? If you are, I can sometimes do with a hand if things get a bit hectic."

Alex inwardly marvelled at the speed at which the nature of his possible employment needs had spread and couldn't help but comment, "By hell! The internet has got nothing on the speed at which news spreads around this place."

"I just decided to drop in to get some chips for lunch, and Anita happened to mention it. No pressure, but you're a big lad and could probably shift some materials around on site if you felt like doing the odd hour, and it would be cash-in-hand."

"Of course, isn't everything done that way around here? Thanks for the information. I shall bear it in mind," replied Alex before ordering his lunchtime sandwich and taking a seat at one of the empty tables. He took a gulp of his beer and sat, taking in the view of the assorted individuals who had taken the opportunity for an early drink… Slippers was still examining some building plans with the young couple, and Bricky Gordon was chatting to Daureen at the bar. There was a rather smartly dressed man reading a copy of the *Gazette,* and it was someone he had seen on one or two occasions in the

Wellie. He had turned up on each occasion that Alex had been in the pub in the early evening. Each time he had come in, ordered a pint, drank it and then after about half an hour he would bid the other guests a good evening and leave. Alex could not suppress his old inquisitive policing habits. There was nothing sinister about the lone drinker, but it seemed unusual for someone to regularly turn up and have so little to do with the others in the room. The Wellie was a place full of gregarious individuals, and the lone drinker seemed slightly out of place there.

Alex was just finishing his rather substantial sandwich when Slippers came over and sat beside him.

"They're a lovely couple," said Slippers, nodding in the direction of the young people with whom he had been talking. "They're intending to move into the village soon. They bought the basic shell of a cottage further up the village some months ago, and they want me to do some of the internal work for them, but I've had to explain that I can't do the electrics and so I've given them details of a competent sparky. Sandy Carter will do a good job for them and won't charge the earth. They could be able to move in within a month if I can finish off the central heating. Once that's done, they can do most of the rest themselves in terms of the painting and decorating. It's moving to see how much in love they are. It reminds me of the time Jean and I were setting up our place. We worked for weeks at every opportunity to get that place sorted in time for our wedding. Many's the time we would still be there well after midnight, but I have to admit that we weren't working all the time."

Slippers sat back with a contented smile as he reminisced about his early days with Jean, and his recollections struck a chord with Alex as he remembered the blissful days of what his parents insisted upon calling his 'courting' days with Megan.

He genuinely thought she was a great 'catch' when he met her at a friend's wedding. She had looked beautiful in her long bridesmaid's dress, her flowing brown hair decorated with small white flowers. She had the general appearance of a fairytale princess, and he had been greatly impressed. He knew that he was seeing her at her best, and it was not the image she would portray all the time, but even after many years and in all sorts of trying moments, he never failed to appreciate how attractive she was. They had enjoyed doing up their flat, and moving in was a stellar moment in their lives when they could comfortably be together and move on from those intimate fumblings in his old Morris Marina. The two men sat in contented silence for a while as they enjoyed their separate happy memories.

Their contemplation was broken by the arrival of a middle-aged woman wearing what Alex took to be hiking wear. She had a well-worn olive cagoule, which appeared to have numerous pockets. This went down to just above her knees, where it met with a similar coloured pair of baggy waterproof trousers, and below that were the mandatory heavy socks, the tops of which were showing above a rather stout pair of boots. This was an outfit that had seen some wear, as had the wearer. The newcomer took off her woolly hat and shoved it into one of her many pockets before buying a pint at the bar and walking over towards Alex's table.

"Mind if I join you, Slippers?" she asked. The request was purely a formality, and she sat down at their table.

Alex tried to find the best way to describe her attitude and decided she was brusque, not a woman to be argued with, and probably used to getting her own way, and yet he felt a certain affinity towards her. She had a genuine smile and a natural jollity that made her appear to be on the point of laughing all the time.

"Hello, Chris," said Slippers, "I don't think you've met my friend Wessie; he's only been here a couple of weeks. Despite the name, he's a resident now, his real name's Alex, and he's living in the Cogans' old place."

"That would explain why I haven't seen you before," commented Chris. "I supervise students at the field study centre. The university have the old, converted chapel up at the top of the village, and various groups from the university come here throughout the year for two-week residential courses. The new term is about to start, so I've just arrived back to make sure everything is ready for the first batch of the little darlings. The rooms are let out during the holidays, and a number of people doing the coastal walk take advantage of getting a cheap room, and I like to check everything is OK after the holiday break. I have to get everything ready so I can explain the ground rules when they arrive. They generally see me as some kind of authoritative sergeant major figure, but they have to appreciate that working down on the beach can be dangerous. By the end of their two-week course, and particularly after our final night party here in the Wellie, they appreciate that I'm just an old softie."

"You don't live here permanently, then?" asked Alex.

"No, and I'm not even a Wessie, I live across the water in Lincolnshire outside of the university terms, but I find the locals here are quite civilized, and Slippers here does some maintenance work on the old chapel for us from time to time. Although it does annoy him a bit having to do the jobs on an official basis with receipts and the like. It complicates his bookkeeping."

"I don't mind the tax man getting his fair share of my earnings. The problem is that we might not always agree on what his fair share should be," reasoned Slippers.

"I love working here," confided Chris. "I've been supporting courses here for over 10 years now, and all the locals have been very welcoming. They don't even complain too much if the odd student on one of the courses gets a little bit over-exuberant after one of our end-of-course parties in here. There's usually at least one every term who decides to go for a swim in the harbour or to serenade the locals late at night; I think the beer might be a contributing factor. I quite look forward to the evenings when the students are given time to write up their daily logs, and I can sneak down here for a little refreshment; it's the only thing that keeps me almost sane. This is my little refuge, and I love it, which is just as well because there isn't another pub for miles and certainly not one that you could walk to."

"Yes," agreed Alex, "I'd often considered retiring here, and I'm glad I did."

"When I retire from the university, I had intended to look for a place here. I've got my little place in Lincolnshire, and I love it, but I spend a lot of time here, and I don't know many of my neighbours over there. Since my husband died some years ago, I don't have much reason to keep rushing back there, so I'm giving serious thought to moving up here before all the cottages are snatched up. I've had some informal chats with Bricky Gordon over there," she said, gesturing to the builder who was still chatting with Daureen at the bar, "and he's going to keep an eye out for me. I suddenly realised that I don't need to wait until I've retired, so I'm going to go for it now."

"Best of luck," said Alex, "I certainly have no regrets about my move here."

It was at this point that their attention was drawn to the arrival of a small group of men led by Norman and Muffin.

"I'd forgotten it was darts night," exclaimed Slippers.

"Darts night?" questioned Alex. "I didn't know you had a darts night."

"Oh yes, the darts team meet up regularly to practice here. We haven't been beaten in the pub league for over 10 years. Norman is our captain."

Alex was duly impressed but felt he ought to make one observation.

"I don't see a dartboard anywhere."

"No. We don't have one. We used to."

"So how do you practice darts without a board?"

"We don't practice darts; we practice dominoes sometimes, but generally we just get some drinking practice. There seems little point in training up a darts team when there's no competition."

"But what about the pub darts league?"

"There isn't one, hasn't been one for 10 years. We did have a thriving league, but most of the pubs have closed down, and many of the remaining ones have effectively become restaurants, and they don't want darts flying around. Some time ago, Norman wrote an article about the demise of the local darts league. In order to pad out his story, he wrote a few fictitious lines about how well our darts team were doing and pointed out we hadn't been beaten in years. Some of us felt we needed to help live out Norman's fantasy, hence the 'team' meets up to celebrate his journalistic talent. Obviously, this is the night for the men's team, but we do have a women's team who meet on a different night, and Bricky's daughter Anita is the women's captain."

"And Muffin is here as a member of the team?" queried Alex.

"No!" exclaimed Slippers forcefully, "he was useless at darts. He used to be the team mascot, but he couldn't cope with the intellectual demands of the role. We only let him attend for sentimental reasons, and because he can help Norman find his way home afterwards."

Alex looked over at Muffin, who had adopted his usual position by the bar in a trance-like posture, just staring into some sort of canine middle distance, which was only broken when one or other customer would give him a dog biscuit from the jar based on the bar. Not unreasonably, Alex suspected that not all that Slippers had just recounted was entirely true.

CHAPTER SIX

Alex had thoroughly enjoyed his evening at the pub, particularly when he was officially enrolled as a member of the darts team. Unfortunately, the ceremony had involved the drinking of a few beers, and when he arose the following morning, he felt slightly jaded. He could remember that, in his capacity as captain, Norman had made an elaborate speech to welcome the new member. The inauguration had taken some time as Norman went on extolling the virtues of 'his most illustrious friend', and he interspersed his ramblings with the exhortation to drink to 'Wessie Alex'. Each time the name was mentioned, there was a toast to his health. On that morning, Alex was doubting whether their good wishes had in fact improved his health to any great degree, and he decided to skip breakfast and go for a walk.

The sun was shining, but a wind was starting to pick up as he made his way along what had become his regular walk by the harbour. He was grateful for the freshening wind and soon began to feel more human. He smiled at the memory of his big night out; he had been made the centre of attention, and some of the amusement was at his expense but in a friendly way. He had met more of the local community in that one night than he had done in the previous two weeks, and a hangover seemed a small price to pay. Nevertheless, he was determined not to make it a regular occurrence.

Alex chose to alter his usual walk by turning down a small yard that he knew led to the inshore lifeboat station, where he found two young individuals who were apparently checking some of the equipment on the inflatable craft. He stood looking at the small RIB standing on its trailer and, not for the first time, felt a sense of admiration for the volunteers who went out to help others. Even though he understood that most of their turnouts were apparently to rescue visitors who had been cut off on walks down along the beach, he knew that sometimes they had to go out in quite rough seas to assist small fishing boats. Alex looked at the orange craft that would have been a welcome sight for anyone in danger and marvelled at just how small it was. He had seen the crew during practice exercises going out through a heavy swell and didn't envy them.

"Hi Wessie. Great night last night, wasn't it?"

Alex looked more carefully at the young woman who had addressed him and tried to remember exactly who she was. He estimated that she was in her mid-thirties, and she had a particularly lovely smile. He had met so many people at his inauguration ceremony the previous night, but suddenly it struck him who it was.

"Oh, hi Laura," he replied after a moment's delay, "I didn't recognise you dressed like that."

"I don't think the dress I had on last night would be entirely suitable for this job. I thought you put on quite a performance at Wellies with Norman."

"What performance?" he asked with some trepidation as he tried to remember if he had done anything outrageous. At police functions, he had been known to lead the community karaoke, very badly, and even to do some of his memorable disco moves, but, as far as he could recall, he had not been that drunk at the Wellie.

"Nothing outlandish," she replied, "but the banter you carried on with Norman kept us all amused, and the stories about your time in the vice squad were hilarious, particularly the one about your experiences with the streetwalker and the traffic cone. Who'd have thought a police officer could be so amusing?"

"I may have had a little too much to drink. It was just the sudden honour of being called to the ranks of the darts team, but you're right; it was a great evening, although I deny anything I may have said last night, particularly about that infamous traffic cone and its exotic owner."

"Giles and me laughed all the way home. Giles is my nearly fiancé. He doesn't work in the village; he does something in Hull. I don't have a clue what it is, but apparently it pays him a lot. We met at primary school, and we've been together ever since. He was the bald guy in the red sweatshirt you spoke to for a while about some financial scam or something."

Alex was reeling with this onslaught of information from Laura, who seemed to be able to talk without needing to draw breath and, if only to interrupt her flow, he looked to her friend and remarked,

"I don't seem to remember seeing you last night."

"No, I wish I had gone along now; from the reports I've had from Laura, it was quite a night. Unfortunately, I was on call for the lifeboat, so I wasn't able to drink, and I don't tend to enjoy just sitting in the pub with a soft drink all night. I'm Moira, by the way: I don't have a nearly fiancé at the moment, and I'm going to start saving up to buy a traffic cone."

Alex was starting to regret ever having done his traffic cone gig at the pub, but it had certainly made an impression, and he knew that disclosing another side of his character to his new friends, although not entirely intentional, had been a good idea. Moira was a little older than Laura, but she had evidently kept herself in shape with the lifeboat work. Alex felt that she was an attractive woman, and her gentle flirting flattered him. He stood for a while talking to his two new friends and then became aware that he was feeling hungry, so he said goodbye and set off in search of something to eat. He didn't feel he could cope with the pub, and it was too early for his appointment with Anita in the chip shop, so he headed off home and made himself a sandwich.

After what could have been breakfast or lunch, he took his plate and cup through to the kitchen and washed them up. As he stood at the sink looking out the back window at his yard, he once again experienced the need to do something to fill his life. He had made a start on finding some sort of employment, and he was extending his circle of friends in the village, but he still felt there was something missing. He enjoyed his walks around the village and on the beach. Both these activities gave him time for contemplation, but he was beginning to think it would be nice to share it with someone. He had begun to realise that his general inability to enjoy sitting and watching TV in the evening was partly due to having no one to share the experience with and, for a brief moment, he wondered if, despite all his new friends, he was lonely. It was only a fleeting thought, and he soon busied himself getting ready to go to the fish and chip shop.

Anita was busy in the back room of the shop when he arrived, and she beckoned him through.

"Hi Alex. Glad to see that you've survived last night," she said as she dried her hands on a towel. "I think that's one of the best darts nights we've had in the Wellie for quite a while. You certainly came out of your shell after a couple of pints, and you were a big hit with some of the women there; quite a stud!"

Alex knew he was being subjected to Anita's flirtatious flattery but felt pleased that he hadn't appeared to have upset anybody the previous evening. He was, however, keen to change the subject, so he announced, "It feels strange to be this side of the counter. It's really quite amazing that you manage to produce so much food from such a small space."

"We have to be efficient to get some of the orders out when it gets busy. We can't just fry up a lot of fish and chips overnight and store them for when the customers come in the next day. It all has to be freshly cooked. We can keep food hot for a while in the top cabinets above the fryer, but not indefinitely. We have to keep a supply of chips and fish ready to fry, and sometimes it gets hectic."

Anita carefully outlined the processes involved in the preparation of the food. Alex was particularly taken by the ingenious device for cutting the potatoes into chips. A potato went on the top plate, the handle was depressed and, like magic, the chips fell into the bowl below. This was one of the jobs he could do, but Anita explained that frying was a lot more than dropping fish into the hot oil. Alex was impressed by the skills required, and he was prepared to start with simple jobs like a general dogsbody, and he would strive not to get in the way. His induction training was halted when Anita's co-worker, Nora, arrived. Nora had the kind of general appearance that Alex would expect of someone in the food trade. She was a rather short woman in her mid-fifties and gave the impression from her figure that she was not averse to sampling the produce of her labours. Anita introduced Alex to Nora, and together they set about preparing food for the afternoon customers. Alex did what he could to help in the back room, and he was called into the shop at times to be introduced to those customers he had not previously met.

It had been a quiet afternoon, and Alex was convinced that his novice status meant that he had not been a great help, but his two tutors gave him simple tasks, and he felt some slight sense of achievement by the end of the shift. Anita explained that she would keep a tally of his hours and pay him at an agreed rate at the end of each shift. All three understood that his employment would be on an ad hoc basis depending upon the expected level of custom and which of the other staff were available. As he was about to leave, Anita took him aside and said, "Thanks for that, Wessie; now let me see, you've done four hours, so we owe you…"

Before she could continue, Alex protested, "You don't owe me anything. All I've done is a few simple jobs you could have done yourselves, as business has been so slow. The most useful thing I did was not to get in the way too much. On top of that, I've received some slight insight into how the shop runs. I should be paying you for the training."

"OK, but you may find that there's a couple of pints in at the pub for you, and thanks again. Now you'd better get home and wash off the cooking smells, or you may lose some of your manly attraction for all your women friends."

As he walked home, Alex felt a sense of satisfaction after his afternoon. He had learned something about the workings of the shop and even been able to help out a little bit. He had also met a few more of the locals and learned a bit about how they were interconnected. He had heard small snatches of gossip that had enabled him to paint an increasingly complex picture in his mind of how the village functioned. Most of the chatting had been friendly and often expressed support for someone who was experiencing difficulties, but there were the odd mildly spiteful comments, and Alex mused that even the most apparently idyllic communities have their troubles. He had been pleased to hear that arrangements would be made for a couple of pints to be available for him at the bar particularly because he recognised that he had just joined the ranks of those in the village that did not pay tax on every penny they earned. He did not feel like going to the pub that evening as he felt that he had drunk more than enough the previous night, so he headed straight home. The large portion of fish and chips he had been given at the end of his shift meant he wasn't hungry, so he contented himself with a cup of tea and a biscuit before sitting down to catch the news on the TV. He started to watch a depressing article that indicated that 25 pubs a week were closing, and he figured it wasn't surprising that the darts league had folded if so many pubs had closed. He switched channels and watched a re-run of an old crime drama. From his own career, he knew that the programme was hugely inaccurate about police procedures, but he watched it anyway. He remembered how Megan would complain when they watched such programmes, and he gave a running critique of the procedural inaccuracies, but there was no one to complain tonight.

CHAPTER SEVEN

When Alex left home the next morning, he was aware that there were more people around than he had seen for a while. The reason became clear when he stopped to have a chat with Norman, who was out walking Muffin.

"Typical!" said Norman, looking up and down the road. "A little bit of late summer sunshine on a weekend and the place is filled with visitors. I know the town needs them, and I've done my bit from time to time to encourage them, but sometimes it would be nice just to have a quiet life. It can be worse if there are any dolphins spotted off the shore because hordes of people turn up to catch a glimpse. Sometimes, you can hardly find a spot to stand on the harbour wall. It's particularly annoying when you know that dolphins aren't really rare around here; they can often be seen clearly just off shore."

"I'd forgotten it was Saturday. You can lose all track of what day it is if your week doesn't have the structure imposed by work. I gather our impromptu repartee went down well at the darts night meeting, and I must say I thoroughly enjoyed it."

"It was a bit of fun," replied Norman, "and it can often be those unexpected events that can be the most enjoyable; old Muffin here was beside himself."

Alex glanced at the dog, who was his usual pensive self and appeared completely uninterested in anything going on around him. Like some canine yogi, he appeared to be deep in thought, but Norman had often asserted that any meaningful thought would be impossible within a brain that was largely running on empty.

"Has he had any more wasps lately with this sunny weather?"

"Fortunately not, but he does keep an eye out for them. His brain is tuned in to detecting them. That, and his meals, seem to be only things that occupy what passes for his brain, but we love him," he said, bending over to roughly stroke Muffin. "Anyway, I've got to get home and study my star charts so I can give accurate horoscopes for my readers, and I'm working on a new venture. My professional pride dictates that I give considerable thought to all my projects, and this one's a belter."

With this enigmatic statement left hanging in the air, Norman and his hairy companion headed home, and Alex turned and followed the crowds down towards the harbour. The majority of the throng appeared to be made up of small family units. Sometimes, it would be parents escorting their children, and sometimes it was older couples who appeared to be taking their grandchildren. Many of the youngsters were carrying the obligatory bucket and spade, and some toted small shrimp nets that had obviously seen many such visits over the summer. Alex couldn't help but note to himself that many of the children would be disappointed at the fact that the tide was pretty high at the moment and much of the sand near the harbour would be under the water. Likewise, the rock pools they were longing to explore wouldn't become accessible for a few hours. He remembered how, as children, he and Val had learned to predict the state of the tide so they could plan their day in advance. One day he had been amused to hear a conversation between two teachers who were obviously taking a group of young children 'crocodile-style' on an elementary field trip. One young teacher had turned to the other and declared her disappointment as she stared out over the harbour at high tide and confided, "I don't understand it. Last time we came, there were rock pools here." It had amused Val and him, but they later realised that the party leader was contemplating taking a group of children out, and yet they had no idea of how the tide influenced accessibility to the beach. No wonder the lifeboat continued to have to rescue people who had managed to get themselves into dangerous situations.

As he approached the waterfront, Alex was intrigued by a figure sitting on a small camping stool who was obviously engrossed in sketching some area of the harbour. He had heard about a local artist who had exhibited some of her paintings in a number of galleries along the coast, and he assumed that this must be her. He approached cautiously. He knew that many artists working in the open air resented what they saw as the intrusive behaviour of strangers, and he didn't want to disturb her, so he just stood to the side of her and looked at the scene she was attempting to capture on paper.

Eventually she looked up at him and said, "You must be the guy who moved into the Cogans' place; I happened to be sketching nearby when you were moving in."

Far from resenting his intrusion into her day, she actually seemed pleased to have the company.

"Yes, I'm Alex," he replied, "I hope I didn't spoil your sketching when I turned up with my belongings; I know it took quite a long time because it was impossible to get the removal van close to my place."

"Not a bit of it. I was working on a commission for the owners of the place next to yours. I was not having a very good day, and I'm not doing too well today either, but it will all come together somehow. I'm Helen, by the way. What brings you to this little bit of Yorkshire paradise; is it a holiday place?"

"No, this is my new home. I took early retirement, and here I am."

"That's a coincidence," she exclaimed, "I took early retirement as well. From teaching."

Alex looked at her and estimated that they were of a similar age, which prompted him to casually ask, "Have you retired recently?"

"Not exactly," she calmly replied, "I got out of teaching over 30 years ago; I couldn't stand the job. There is the disadvantage in that my teachers' pension is about three groats a month, but I got out while I had some semblance of sanity, and I sell the odd piece of work which supports my red wine habit. I was doing quite well at one point and had a particularly good exhibition in Whitby, which brought in a few hundred pounds, so I felt I had to declare my earnings for tax. Unfortunately, the tax office assumed that I would make the same money every year, and my tax position became very complicated. I could have started claiming exemption for my materials, tools, travelling and work premises, but it was simpler to not bother. The tax office staff have enough on their plate without my piddling earnings to take into account."

"I seem to have heard that fiscal policy expressed by others here in the village," he commented with a wry smile.

"That's true," she admitted. "We do have our own little commercial community in a way. We're not communists but more sort of social capitalists. Sometimes, it might seem a bit anti-establishment, but nobody round here wants to man the barricades and cry '*Freedom for Kirksea*'. We just want a quiet, uncomplicated life. We pay our taxes, but we might not always follow the letter of the law. Anyway! Enough about political economics; do you fancy an ice cream? Young Simon has got his van out today."

"I know it might seem strange, but I haven't had an ice cream for years. I've walked past the van repeatedly over the last couple of weeks and never been tempted. When we came here as kids, we always rushed to get an ice cream. It always seemed to taste better than it did from the van that patrolled our estate in Wakefield."

He paused for a moment, remembering the way that he and Val would rush off to buy their first ice cream 'reward' as soon as they were able to get away from their parents on the annual holiday.

"Sounds like a good idea," he said, before adding, "My treat."

Alex watched as Helen folded up her stool and packed it in a large satchel along with her sketch pad and the small box containing her pencils. It was quite obvious that this was a well-practised routine, perfected over years of doing countless sketches outdoors. They walked the short distance to the ice cream van together, where Helen greeted the young man inside by name before stepping back to allow Alex to place his order. He asked for two ice creams and was met by the vendor's response.

"Would you like that in a tub or a cone?" And then he started to laugh.

It was at this point that Alex looked more closely at the young man. He looked different in his white outfit, but he was definitely one of the crowd who had been at the darts team meeting, and he obviously felt very pleased with himself to be able to allude to the traffic cone tale. Helen looked quizzically at Alex. She was obviously what appeared to be one of a very small number of the villagers who had not heard his account of his run-in with the sex worker and the infamous traffic cone. Choosing not to enlighten her there and then, he simply asked what she would like.

"I'll go with the cone, please, Alex," she said.

"Two large cones, please, Simon."

Rarely can such an innocent request have met with such hilarity on Simon's part. He dutifully filled up two cones and passed them to Alex, and, refusing the proffered money, he said, "No. It's on the house, mate. You've really made my day."

The couple took their ice creams and headed to one of the benches by the harbour wall. Alex waited for the questioning about Simon's hilarity, but none came. Instead, she looked at her ice cream and asked, "I hope this extravagant gesture isn't an attempt to worm your way into my heart."

"No, if that had been my intention, I'd have asked him to put a flake in it."

They both smiled and then sat eating their ice creams. He knew at one point he might have to explain the reference to the cone, but it didn't worry him. He realised that the infamous incident had made him the centre of a shared joke, but he knew that the locals were sharing his humorous, if somewhat embarrassing, incident. They were laughing with him and not at him, and he felt good about it. The couple finished their ice creams, and then Alex remarked, "You can't have been very old when you retired."

"No, I was 26, and I was actually doing very well in my career when I decided to hang up my chalk."

"So, you just decided to opt out?"

"Oh, I was never some sort of superannuated hippie. My escape from teaching was calculated. I had inherited a half share in a small property from my uncle, so I had a comfortable financial buffer, and I got fed up with being asked to do more and more within school. Admittedly, I had done very well and had a responsible post that paid well for someone my age, but appointing me to the post meant that the management team felt they could load every new initiative onto me. In the end, I just told them that I would take responsibility for the most recent educational hobby horse, but in return, I would have to discontinue working on some other subject that the management had previously felt was vital. It didn't go down well, so I got out and never looked back. Eventually, we sold my uncle's place, and I moved up here where the properties were ridiculously cheap, and I've never been tempted to move."

"We seem to have a lot of shared experiences. I too left a job as soon as I could because I no longer enjoyed it and the pressures were building up, and I also benefitted from moving from a relatively expensive area. Like you, I have no intention of moving from what you so eloquently call this little bit of Yorkshire paradise."

"I'll have to be getting a move on," she declared, "I've got to get a new angle on the harbour. Pictures of it always sell well in the holiday season, and I could just churn them out from memory, but I get so bored. I sometimes add the odd coble or a couple of crab pots to the picture just to break up the monotony for myself. When the weather is fine, I take every opportunity to get out and make preliminary sketches, which I can finish at home in what I grandly call my studio when the weather is less accommodating. Nice to meet you, Alex. I will no doubt see you again around the village, and perhaps you could then explain the hilarity of the ice creams?"

With this, she picked up her satchel and headed off in search of a new view of the village to sketch. Alex sat for a while, watching the holidaymakers making the most of what was likely to be one of the last relatively warm weekends of the year. A few of the children stood looking down at the sea, obviously waiting to get to the rock pools which were still inaccessible below the slowly receding water. He remembered the times he and Val had waited expectantly to get to the wonders of the rock pools and the number of times their visits to the pools had been curtailed as the incoming tide reclaimed them. He decided that when the pools were uncovered later that afternoon, he would go out to see them again. Meanwhile, he opted to drop in at the Wellie for a sandwich.

The pub had only just opened when Alex arrived, but the bar was fuller than it had been of late. The usual collection of locals was augmented by what were obviously holidaymakers, and it took him slightly longer than usual to get served.

"Hi Dave, any chance of a sandwich?" he asked.

"No problem, but there could be a twenty-minute wait," he replied before explaining, "Daureen is rushed off her feet, and the dishwasher seems to have gone on the blink. On top of that, young Pauline, who normally helps out, has gone to visit her mum in hospital and Alice, our usual barmaid, has called in sick. Do you want a pint while you're waiting?"

"I could help in the back if you like. I used to help out at the rugby club in London. I haven't got any particular skills in the area, but I can wash and tidy things up if it helps."

In reality, Alex had played quite a major part in the catering at his former rugby club once his playing days had passed, so he wasn't daunted when Dave replied.

"That would be great if you could just help us get over the initial rush."

Alex was taken through the bar area to the kitchen beyond, where Daureen was feverishly plating up sandwiches with assorted garnishes. Dave promptly explained that the cavalry had arrived in the form of Alex, and then he quickly returned to the busy bar.

"You're a godsend," remarked Daureen. "If you could just sort out that pile of plates and dirty cutlery, please, I'll try and get on top of the orders."

It wasn't easy to keep up any meaningful conversation as Alex energetically washed and dried a stack of plates and cutlery, and Daureen efficiently prepared a range of sandwiches while making numerous trips to the bar to deliver meals and then collect the empty plates. Throughout this mayhem, Alex couldn't help but notice that she remained her usual impeccably dressed self with not a hair out of place and no sign of any flaw in her make-up. Despite the obvious pressures, she appeared determined to put on a good show for her public. It didn't take him long to assess how the kitchen worked, and on the rare occasions that he got on top of the washing up, he would help out in other ways. After two hours, the kitchen duo was working like a team, and as demand eventually died down, Alex was able to return to the bar.

Dave brought over the sandwich that Alex had finally been able to order and put it in front of him, saying, "There you are, Wessie. That's on the house, and we've put a couple of pints in the pipe for you. That reminds me, Anita came in earlier and paid for two more for you, so you should be set up for a good session sometime. Thanks again for helping out."

Alex couldn't help thinking that if he did any more jobs at this rate, then he would have to take a holiday from work to fit in all the drinking time he would need. He finished his sandwich and headed towards the beach to check out the rock pools.

CHAPTER EIGHT

It was still quite warm as Alex made his way on to the beach and started to head out towards the rock pools. The dry upper regions of the sand were still peppered with small family groups, intent on packing as much as they could into their mini excursions. Further out towards the sea, he could pick out individuals exploring the rock pools that were now completely exposed, and he set out across the wet sand towards them. When he got within a few yards of the pools, the sand became increasingly wet, and Alex had to engage in the particularly ungainly act of taking off his shoes and socks. Having fortunately been able to do so without falling over, he shoved his socks in his shoes and carried them the last few yards to the first large pool. He stood for a moment, his trousers hastily rolled up, and recalled the number of times he had seen his father in such a state of undress. He couldn't remember him ever wearing a swimming costume or shorts, even on those rare days when it was particularly hot. His mother had similarly never worn swimwear and the only concession she made to informal holiday clothing was to wear a pair of baggy slacks occasionally.

Alex spent over an hour peering into the various pools. He was genuinely fascinated by the numerous life forms that resided in those temporary ecosystems. He chatted with a group of young children and shared their excitement whenever they discovered something new. He remembered when he, as a young lad from Wakefield, had first found this magical world to explore and how he and Val would compete to see what exotic creatures they could find. They had persuaded their parents to buy a cheap guide to the seashore, which they used to try and identify what they found in the pools or washed up on the beach. He regretted that he and Megan had never brought their daughters to such a place. Their family holidays had been abroad, and, while he wouldn't deny the value of the girls having spent time in France and Spain, he couldn't help the feeling that they had missed out by not having the chance to explore these rock pools.

All too soon, he was aware that the tide was starting to come in. The beach was a safe one in that the tide didn't rush in, and there were no deceptive gullies to catch the unwary, but Alex decided to set off back up the beach. When he arrived at the soft, dry sand near the harbour wall, he sat down to put his shoes and socks on and experienced the age-old problem of trying to dust the sand off his wet feet. He had never been fastidious about doing so as a child, and he remembered his mother's constant complaining about the amount of sand that had been carried in this way into the tent. Having removed what he hoped was most of the sand, Alex put on his shoes and socks and made his way up to the harbour wall. It was quite apparent to him that he was still carrying excess sand in his right sock, so he walked over to the bench he had previously shared with Helen and took off the shoe and then the sock from the offending foot. He sat, and after turning the sock inside out, he energetically shook it. In so doing, he inadvertently managed to shake sand over an elderly man who was sharing the bench with him,

"Ey up!" exclaimed the old man.

Alex apologised profusely and proceeded to put his sock and then his shoe on before explaining, "The sand gets everywhere."

"Tell that to the sphynx," suggested the older man enigmatically before adding, "I'm Bob, by the way, and you must be the young chap who moved into the Cogans' place. How are you settling in?"

Alex remembered seeing Bob briefly on one of his visits to the pub, and he was pleased to get to know more about this particular resident.

"I'm starting to find my way about the place, and I'm slowly getting to know a few people. It can be a bit daunting being in a new place with a lot of people you don't know, but I'm still pleased that I decided to move in."

"I've never had that problem as I've never left the village apart from my time in the army during the war. That was a typical bit of military genius; I'd made a career of going out to sea in my fishing coble, so the powers-that-be put me in the army and for part of my time I was in the desert, so my seamanship skills were rarely called upon. I gather you were in the police. You won't need those skills here; we're a very law-abiding crew."

"Of course, but it's not my business anymore. I'm sure if anyone committed some serious crime, I would want to do something about it, as would any other citizen, but I wouldn't feel obliged to spring into action every time some petty misdemeanour came to light."

Alex and the old man sat in silence for a while. The crowds of holidaymakers had started to disperse, and the seagulls were noisily searching for any edible detritus. In the harbour, a man in a bright yellow bib and brace oilskin trousers was preparing his coble to go out and check his crab pots as soon as the tide was high enough. As the young fisherman went about his routine, the old man watched wistfully before declaring,

"That's Neil, Ma Dawson's lad, getting ready to go out. If he's lucky, he might get a few crabs. I can remember when there were a dozen boats fishing from here, and on a good day in the season, they could bring in hundreds of crabs. Neil just has a few pots he puts out relatively near the shore, but he only does it as a sideline for a bit of beer money. If you ever wanted a crab, then Neil can help you out. It was more of a cottage industry in my day, and we went out a lot further into deep water. The rewards could be more profitable, but if the weather blew up a bit, we might not be able to get out to the pots for days, and sometimes pots would be damaged or lost. It was a tough life, but I miss it."

"How long ago did you stop fishing?" asked Alex, keen to learn more from this rich source of local history.

"It wasn't a sudden retirement. I was still going out in *Charlotte Rose*, my own coble, until I was over 80, but it was only pretty close inshore on days when it was calm. For a while, I crewed for one of the young lads, but it got to be a bit difficult. I had a touch of arthritis in my shoulder, and those crab pots are heavy if you have to pull them up by hand. In the end, I saw that, while I was still able to pass on the benefit of my local knowledge, I was not capable of helping with the manual stuff, so I finally came ashore and sold *Charlotte Rose* to a young guy in Whitby."

"*Charlotte Rose* is a lovely name for a boat," observed Alex.

"Yes, I named her after my wife as they had a lot in common; both were built for comfort rather than speed, and both were broad in the beam." The old man paused for a moment and stared out over the harbour before adding, "I really loved her, and I was quite fond of my wife as well."

Alex smiled and, in an attempt to keep the conversation going, commented, "The wind is starting to pick up a bit now." It was a banal comment, but the state of the weather was always a good fall-back conversation piece.

"Just a sea breeze," replied the old man, "not a proper wind. As kids, we loved it during the holiday season on those days when we would suddenly get a gust of wind out of nowhere that would blow some of the visitors' hats off. We looked forward to seeing one blow into the harbour and watching the owners in a state of despair. In the summer, we would swim out to retrieve the hats and return them to their owners in the hope of getting a few coppers for our efforts. In the cooler weather, we would have Lofty Oxtoby's little rowing boat ready just in case. At the end of the day, we would take our earnings and blow it all on sweets."

"Very enterprising."

"The winds around the harbour mouth can be fierce in the autumn, though. I remember the day that Mrs Weller, the vicar's wife, was down here during a particularly windy day wearing one of those old-fashioned bonnets. She had taken the precaution of tying it under her chin with the bow, but there was a sudden blast of wind, and the bonnet ended up 20 yards up Main Street, and Mrs Weller was still wearing it."

Alex looked over at the old man's wide grin and made a mental note not to believe everything that Bob told him in the future.

Over the next few days, Alex tried to establish some sort of routine in his life. He would get up at seven and watch the news on the television while making himself breakfast. He was determined to ensure that he had a good start to the day. After washing up his breakfast dishes, he would set about what he called his domestic session, which might involve checking if any washing needed doing or running the vacuum cleaner over the place. He was particularly keen to ensure that the house was tidy on the days that Jean was due to do her 'proper' cleaning. He remembered, when they had found it necessary to employ a cleaner, how Megan had always insisted on tidying up before the cleaning lady was due. Only after he had done his chores would he allow himself to go for his walk. He would avoid the temptation to have fish and chips for lunch every day but would often drop in to see Anita and Nora to keep up to date with what was going on in the village before going home to a light lunch. In the afternoon, he would spend time on his computer keeping up his correspondence or working on his family tree. The afternoon would later involve another walk before going home to dinner, which he would prepare himself. After that, he might feel justified in going for a pint at the Wellie or perhaps two if he became engrossed in a particularly interesting conversation with one of his growing number of friends.

It was a laudable plan and would have looked impressive on a large wallchart festooned with different coloured stickers, but the reality was somewhat different. By the end of the second day of the regime, Alex realised that he had burdened himself with a work lifestyle rather than one befitting a retiree, and he relaxed his own self-imposed rules a little. Almost as a gesture of defiance, he dropped in at the Wellie for a pint just before midday. He was pleased to see a number of the locals, and he made his entry to a number of greetings for 'Wessie'. He made his way to the bar where Dave was reading an article in the *Gazette* while Norman was standing attentively, obviously waiting to hear what the landlord had to say about something in the paper.

Dave broke off his reading to set Alex up with a pint and then announced, "You've got me again, Norman. I don't see your name attached to any of the pieces in here. I can see your Madame Estelle slot, but that's not new, so where's your new piece?"

"Page six, next to the picture of the scouts."

Dave reshuffled his paper to the appropriate page before looking up at Norman incredulously and saying, "*Uncle Duncan answers your questions?* So, you've set yourself up as an agony aunt now?"

"At the risk of sounding pedantic, I'm more of an agony uncle. It's a page designed to give men an opportunity to seek advice anonymously on the problems they face."

"But this is your first article to be printed," observed Alex, having perused page six, and as his police brain clicked in, he continued, "So how is it that you already have questions to answer?"

"Because I ask them," retorted Norman in an exasperated tone.

"And what happens if people write in with real problems?" asked Alex.

"Easy. I would just pass them over to Maureen, who occasionally does a similar article for women. She would relish getting a different sort of letter to that which she usually receives, and she could answer them in her usual accomplished manner. In the meantime, I've put together a few questions and some excellent answers for them. The editor keeps them in the 'filler' file and uses them as and when he has an edition that is a bit light on material. I've even concocted some cryptic answers to supposedly anonymous letters where I haven't even bothered to show what the original question was. You know, things like, '*Dear Water Lover. Your feelings are not unique, and you should not be reluctant to share them with your partner*'. Any time I have an odd minute, I can run off a few of those, and the editor can use them when needed."

"Is anything you write in that paper genuine?"

"It complies with the finest rules of journalism," said Norman, with feigned indignation. "If it helps sell papers and keeps people happy, then it's good journalism. And if it brings me in a little extra beer money, then it is first-rate journalism in my book."

Alex was beginning to appreciate that the village almost had its own economic structure, and the standard currency appeared to be beer money. Throughout the whole conversation, Muffin appeared to diligently follow what each person was saying in turn. A stranger might have assumed this was a clever canine who was hanging on every word the men were saying, but the truth was that Muffin was simply watching to see who would offer him one of the treats that Dave kept on the bar. Once the said treat was delivered, then Muffin reverted to blankly staring into mid-air. He might not have thought of much, but he thought deeply.

The dog barely looked up when Slippers entered the bar and ordered himself a drink. He took a large gulp and then sighed with gratification. Having noticed that the copy of the *Gazette* was on the bar, he pointed to it and said, "I see there's another report on that great big housing estate they're building on the edge of Wykethorpe. Another two hundred houses but no public amenities. It's par for the course not to upgrade the medical services, but the new estate has nothing, not even a shop. The development will be good for my business, though, because the builders insist upon surrounding all the back gardens with those flimsy six-foot high larch lap fences. It blows a gale over the tops there, and repairing those fences will keep me in business for years."

"You talk about the lack of amenities, Slippers," added Norman, "but pretty soon they won't have a pub in the village. The brewery is going to sell off The Prince as soon as they can; I read it in a report when I was writing about the demise of the local. That's another former member of the darts league gone."

"It could get a lot closer to home," confided Dave. "The Prince is an Atkins and Dodd house, and they own the Wellie here. I'm not disclosing any secrets in telling you that Daureen and I have had informal approaches from the brewery to 'float the possibility' of us buying the place, but after a bit of optimistic research, we were assured that we couldn't match their price. I suspect that offering the place to us was some kind of procedural necessity. The building is worth a small fortune if they can get planning permission for a change of use to sell it on as domestic housing. I bet they've looked into the possibility. Anyway, Daureen and I said we weren't interested, and they haven't been back to us."

CHAPTER NINE

When Jean next came to do her regular cleaning job at Alex's house, she presented him with an envelope and informed him that she had met Kevin the postman on her way to work, and he'd asked her if she would take the letter up to 'save his tired old legs'. Kevin was as fit as a butcher's dog and would regularly all but run around with his deliveries if he wanted to finish early, but as Jean pointed out, "He's not tired; he just wants to spend a bit of time with Nora from the fish and chip shop. Everyone knows that he calls round to her place a lot and it's not always to deliver the mail. I don't know why he continues the charade; they are both single and adults. Well, at least Nora's an adult, I don't think Kevin will ever grow up."

Alex smiled and chose to say nothing except to thank Jean for the delivery, but he was quietly pleased to get this further insight into village life. Turning down the offer of a cup of tea, Jean bustled off to get on with the cleaning, leaving Alex to look at the envelope in his hand. He recognised the writing as being that of his wife. For a moment he pondered what Megan would be writing to him for. She usually contacted him on his mobile or with a short email, so why had she sent a letter? He suddenly realised that he was doing something that Megan had often criticized him for; he was trying to deduce what was inside when the obvious solution was to open the letter. He carefully opened the envelope and started to read the contents.

Dear Alex,

I'm sorry to have to contact you in this way, but I couldn't get through on your mobile and I find emails can be a bit business-like when dealing with personal matters. The fact is that I felt I ought to let you know that sadly Dad has died. The girls have been informed and they are fine but obviously upset. Mum is soldiering on but I'm not sure if the whole thing has sunk in yet. We don't know when the funeral will be. We shall be ignoring Dad's frequently stated request that we put his remains out with the dustbin so it looks like we will be opting for a cremation. Knowing how well you got on with Dad I'm sure he would have wanted you to attend, as would all the family. I will give you further details as and when arrangements are made and we all hope you can make it. Sorry that this letter is so short, but I do have a lot of people to inform.

Love as always,
Megan

Alex sat for a moment as so many thoughts rushed through his mind. Megan was right to say that Alex had got on well with his former father-in-law, Josh, as he had with Megan's mother, Ivy. Josh had never been a well man and had been hospitalized twice with serious heart problems, and his death should not have come as a great surprise, but it was still a bit of a shock to Alex as the news came at him so suddenly. The relationship with Josh had been a strange one; they disagreed about politics, musical taste, which football team was best and just about any topic that came up, but they had somehow become firm friends, and their banter was never acrimonious. Josh and Ivy had both been deeply upset when Megan had informed them about the divorce, and Josh had rung Alex to try and convince him to reconsider, and even when the divorce came through, Josh kept in touch. Alex wondered how the girls would react to their grandfather's death. They had been brought up in London, but they had frequent mini-breaks in York with their grandparents, and they in turn were able to visit London once Megan and Alex could afford a place big enough to accommodate guests.

Alex was struck by the obvious friendly tone of the letter, and he reflected on the fact that few divorced couples enjoyed being on such good-natured terms. His immediate reaction was that he had to phone her and express his feelings about their shared shock, but he realised that he had no idea where his mobile was. He couldn't remember using it for a while. He only ever used it to keep in touch with his daughters and very occasionally with Megan. He had never been one to check his mobile regularly during the day to avail himself of the myriads of services it offered him, and he hadn't contacted his daughters for over a week, so it took him some time to find his phone, which for some reason he had placed in one of those 'safe places' which in this case was in his sock drawer. He checked and found the battery was flat, which explained why Megan had been unable to get through. He quickly put it on charge and determined to phone her later in the day. In the meantime, he decided that he would go out for a walk. He still found it difficult to stay in while Jean was doing the cleaning and to be thought to be watching how she carried out her work, but their relationship was becoming a little more relaxed, and she had even started to call him by his Christian name. Their tea-break chats were no longer rushed, and she was a valuable source of information. Jean always maintained that she didn't like gossip, but it did not stop her from sharing quite a lot of details about the activities of some of the villagers.

As soon as he stepped out of his front door, Alex was aware of the slight mist that hung over the village. He remembered the way the sea fret used to drift in as the warm air passed over the cold North Sea, giving the impression that the houses could be seen in soft focus. He made his way to the harbour wall and was not surprised to see Bob on his usual bench.

"Morning, Bob, it's a bit foggy today."

"And a good morning to you, Wessie, but you're wrong; this isn't fog. It's nowt but a bit of moisture in the air. Now, when I was a lad, we had real fog, fog that was so thick you couldn't see your hand in front of your face. It didn't just waft in gently; it consumed the village. People could be gone for hours just going out into the yard to try and find the privy, and heaven help anyone who left their doors or windows open. The fog would get in, and you couldn't see from one corner of the room to another. Of course, it had its advantages; if the fog was particularly thick, the old women would knit it to make those fancy fishermen's jumpers like the ones they sell in Whitby. It took three days' worth of fog to knit a small jumper. That's why they were so expensive. No, this isn't proper fog."

Alex had not unreasonable doubts about the old man's grasp of the meteorological history of the village, but his accounts were always entertaining. Being careful not to make any casual comments about the weather, Alex asked, "Is there anything going on in the harbour today? I thought I heard one of the cobles on the move earlier."

"Yes, that was Neil just checking on his crab pots. He was getting out early in case the mist built up. Mist and fog invariably come along with very calm water, but it can be frightening to be out there. It can be so easy to become disorientated. You can't see anything, and it is hard to make out where sounds are coming from. You can hear the waves if you are near them, but it's impossible to know if you are heading towards them or not. All the boats carry a compass, but from a couple of miles out, it takes a good navigator to locate the harbour mouth in thick fog.

Neil doesn't take any risks, and it looked like he managed to get a few crabs today. You could probably get yourself a couple if you had a word with him."

Alex declined the offer; he had vivid memories of watching live crabs being cooked by tipping them into a large pan of boiling brine. It had fascinated him as a child when he and Val had watched the process in the kitchen of one of the cottages, and for some months afterwards, Val had been unable to face up to eating crab at all. Alex knew that was the way to cook the crustaceans but still felt a little reluctant to dispatch them in such a manner. It would be fish and chips for lunch today from the chip shop.

Alex said goodbye to the old man and wandered off to pick up his lunch. He would see Nora in a new light now after Jean's comment. The shop was busy, and Alex had to wait in a short queue while Anita fried up a new batch of fish. In London, this might have seemed a bit of a chore for him, but it offered an opportunity to chat with friends, and there was usually someone in the shop he knew. He was taken with a notice chalked up on a board announcing that crabs were available, and alongside was a small pile of them. After his discussion with Bob, he rather fancied crab for tea, and when his turn came to be served, he selected one to take home with his fish and chips.

"Hi Wessie," Anita greeted him, "I was hoping to catch you. Could you possibly help us out for a couple of hours this afternoon? Nora has an appointment that's come up at short notice."

"No problem. When did you have in mind?"

"If you could get in about two, it would be a big help."

The arrangements having been made, Alex picked up his lunch and headed home. He grinned as he wondered if Nora's sudden appointment was in any way connected to the meeting she'd had with Kevin earlier. Jean was still cleaning when Alex got home, so he took his fish and chips into the kitchen and made a pot of tea for himself and Jean. She made a token refusal of the tea, claiming that she had a lot still to do, but he persuaded her to sit down for a while.

"The place looks fine, Jean," he protested. "Just sit down, have a biscuit and tell me what's going on in the village. I've got half an hour before I am due at the chip shop to cover for Nora; she's had to rush off this afternoon."

Like most people who claim that they don't listen to gossip, Jean was always happy to pass on any news of the people of Kirksea. It was never malicious, but she was not averse to disclosing some facts that might cause embarrassment in certain circles. On this occasion, she restricted herself to saying that she hoped Nora's situation wasn't too desperate while raising a knowing eyebrow. The rest of the news seemed to centre on the fact that someone had said the pub might be sold off, and there was a rumour that Bricky Gordon was going to build a block of luxury apartments on the site. Alex was impressed by the fact that a snippet of information about the pub's future being uncertain had blossomed in to a story of Gordon building apartments that would sell for millions. Alex restricted himself to saying that he'd not heard the rumour but that he couldn't imagine Gordon doing that, and shortly afterwards he left Jean to finish, and he set off for his afternoon shift.

Business was slow in the chip shop, and Alex spent some of the time doing what Anita called 'deep cleaning', so the whole of the preparation area was even cleaner than usual. Just when Alex thought he would be heading home, there was a sudden influx of customers. Among their number were a few young people dressed in cagoules and waterproof trousers that Alex took to be students from the field study centre where Chris worked. They had obviously been out doing whatever students do on such occasions, and they appeared tired and very hungry. It was nearly five o'clock when Anita gave him his 'beer money' and he headed home.

Even before he went for his shower, he checked his mobile had enough power in it and rang Megan's number. For a while, the phone rang unanswered and then he heard Megan's voice.

"Hello, Alex?"

"Hi darling. I couldn't take your calls earlier as my phone was flat. I'm so sorry to hear about Josh; it must have been a terrible shock. How is Ivy coping?"

"It's a bit like it is with all of us; it wasn't exactly unexpected, given his history, but it still seems to leave a big hole in all our lives. I've taken a few days to come up and stay with Mum, and the girls are being a big support to both of us. There seems so much to sort out, but the funeral directors have got most of it in hand, and it looks like the funeral will be late next week. It will be at the local crematorium. Following Dad's wishes, it will not be a fancy affair. He always insisted that he wanted the 'cheap as chips' package so we won't be having the black carriage drawn by four horses, and he didn't want any flowers to be slaughtered in his name."

"The dustbin lorry wouldn't take him then? Let me know the details when you have them, and I will make sure I get there. How are you keeping at the moment?"

"Everything seems a bit unreal, and there is so much to do that I hardly have time to sit and think through the situation. Fortunately, the business is ticking over nicely, and my partner Fatima is more than capable of running it on her own. I had been giving some thought to selling off my share to her and slowing down a bit, but all those plans are on hold for the moment so I can just concentrate on Mum. How are you settling in at your new place?"

"Despite all the warnings I had about making such a rash change to my life, I am extremely happy. My little cottage suits me perfectly, and I'm starting to meet some of the locals. They are a lovely lot of people, and it's a world away from London in so many ways. I still have my first winter to face up to, but I'm sure that my cottage and I will cope well. I'm loath to give advice, but in your position, I would let Fatima carry on the business, and I'd go off and do something else."

"You've no idea how attractive that proposition sounds at the moment. It's true that I'm earning a fair salary, but I hardly have any spare time to do anything with it."

"I find that I have a lot of spare time on my hands now, so I've even got myself work for the odd few hours a week. In fact, I've just got in from doing a couple of hours at our local fish and chip shop."

"You? Working in a chippie! The former Detective Inspector Alex Lucas is now working as a fish fryer?"

"Nothing so grand as that. I prepare some of the food and even get to serve it sometimes, but I'm not ready for doing the skilled aspects of the job yet. I also did a bit of work helping in the pub kitchen, and I have let it be known that I'm available for the odd unskilled job from time to time."

"You amaze me, Alex. After a successful career in the police, I just can't imagine you doing such jobs. Is the financial situation that dire?"

"First of all, I have to point out that the village did not have any obvious vacancy for an extra senior police officer. I don't do the odd job for the money but to give me something to do. It gets me out of the house, and I meet people. I don't want to sit for hours watching television or going on regular strolls around the village to fill my time. I've also become part of the local informal economy where people help each other out, sharing skills and keeping the money in the village."

"You have changed, Alex. Isn't there some questionable legality about your 'informal' system?"

"Perhaps, so don't mention it to any former police officers you might have been married to. I'm sorry, love, I have to go and get a shower to remove the smell of the chip shop. Please email me with any details you get of the funeral, and I will get straight back to you. Bye for now."

"Bye, darling. I'll be in touch."

Alex switched off his phone. It struck him just how easy it still was to chat with Megan, but it had been a 'friendly' divorce, and they had known each other for over 35 years. He couldn't help feeling some strange wish to get over to York to see her and support her through what must be a difficult time, but he wasn't sure how much his presence might be appreciated by the family. It had been a rather satisfying day, and he had a crab waiting in the fridge. Alex liked village life in Kirksea.

CHAPTER TEN

It was two days later when Alex received a short email from Megan informing him of the arrangements for the cremation. He was relieved to see it was scheduled for midday, which meant he wouldn't have to set off early in the morning, and he wouldn't be late getting back. He made a mental note to start the car up at some point before the day of the funeral, as it had been standing idle since the day he arrived. There had been no need to leave the village, so the car was in what had become a car park for the locals. It had once been an area set aside for fishing boats and much of the gear that went with them, but now it housed a collection of cars and a pair of old tractors that were used to move boats around at low water. Alex had been considering getting a newer car when he moved to the village, but he had been warned that the sea air was not kind to bodywork, so he had stuck with his old Volvo.

Alex sent a brief email to Megan confirming that he would attend the service, and he informed her that he would meet them at the crematorium. Having sorted out his correspondence, he decided that he needed to check on his outfit for the funeral. No mention had been made about there being a relaxed dress code, so he chose to go in one of his dark suits. He selected one and hung it on the front of his wardrobe to be able to inspect it. It looked fine, and he found suitable shoes and a plain white shirt to go with it. As he looked at the assembled outfit, he noted how it had effectively been his workwear for many years. It seemed alien to him now as he stood in his old jeans and casual shirt, and he felt glad to have left his old life behind him. Feeling pleased with this reaffirmation of the wisdom of giving up his old lifestyle, he decided to treat himself to a trip to the Wellie just because he could.

The pub was relatively empty. Daureen was rearranging the assorted bottles on the shelf at the back of the bar and taking the opportunity to clean them with a damp cloth before putting them back. Alex knew from his days at the rugby club that there was a lot more to running a pub than just pulling the odd pint and chatting to customers.

"Afternoon, Alex love, the usual? You've still got one in."

"Yes, please, Daureen," he replied while inwardly marvelling at the way the pub staff were able to remember exactly who'd had a drink pre-paid for them. He took his 'wages' over to a table and sat down near Norman, who was busily writing in a large notebook.

He was careful not to disturb his friend, but after a while, Norman looked up and said, "Sorry, Wessie, I was miles away, just sorting out another journalistic gem for the *Gazette*."

"Another work of fiction for your devoted readership?"

"It doesn't do to be cynical, Wessie. This one's almost legitimate. I'm just reminding my followers that this coming Saturday is the annual Saint Bodolv's Day celebration in Kirksea."

"Saint Bodolv? Never heard of him or her."

"Few people have heard of him. He's special to our area, the patron saint of whelk fishermen. It used to be a big thing with the annual church ceremony where anyone who had been fishing these waters for the previous 12 calendar months could demand a share of a bushel of whelks and a firkin of ale which were provided by the vicar. The last recorded full ceremony was in 1887, but there were only three requests to share the bounty, and so the tradition died out. Legend has it that Bodolv was a Danish monk who was sailing to Whitby on missionary work when he was shipwrecked just north of here, and he was taken in by a young woman with whom he lived, and he fathered six children until he saw the evil of his ways. As a penitence, he chose to live out the rest of his days in what is now known as Monk's Cave. Perhaps he was doing so to get away from six children. Who knows? It was here that he miraculously seeded the waters with whelk eggs, and we have them to this very day."

"Very interesting, Norman; so, what happens on Saint Bodolv's Day nowadays?"

"Oh, it's not the big event it used to be. The local fishermen don't bother going out for whelks much, and consequently it's hard to fill a bushel of the little gastropods, but a fair amount of ale gets consumed. On Saturday, Dave will line the bar with a string of whelk shells; he keeps them in a box in the cellar for the rest of the year. He'll also put out the plaque in front of the pub to remind everyone of the achievements of the great man. Quite a lot of people from local villages turn up, and the pub does quite nicely out of it."

Before Alex could question Norman further to establish just how much of the story was true, they were interrupted by Muffin, who had managed to sneak in when a new customer had entered the door. Once again, the dog was beside himself with excitement at finding his 'lost' owner and sat patiently by his master's side, waiting to be rewarded for his diligence.

"Has Edna forgotten to close the door again, Muffin? Or has she let you out on purpose to drag me back from the pub?"

A stranger observing this one-sided conversation and the way Muffin tilted his head from side to side attentively might have assumed that the dog understood every word. Many dog owners labour under such a misapprehension when talking to their own pets, but Norman knew the reality; Muffin was thick. Eventually, Norman went to the bar, and his trusty companion followed him dutifully to collect a dog treat.

As Alex sat reflecting on the story he had been told, he noticed Slippers had come into the pub, and Alex went over to speak to him. The two men chatted for a while before Alex said, "I was wondering if you could build a little veranda for me in my back yard, Slippers? I don't want anything too elaborate, just a small, covered area, a bit like an open-fronted summerhouse. I've put up simple structures in the past, but I will need someone who knows what they are doing. The other little problem is that I have no tools, so I thought I'd check how busy you are."

"Normally, it wouldn't be a problem, but our Clive usually helps me out on such jobs, and he's committed to working for Bricky Gordon. What I can do is draw up some plans and if they suit you, I could set on to the job and you could work as my labourer. I would then take your wages off the cost of the building. If you like, I could drop round tomorrow morning and look at the site?"

"Suits me. Tomorrow, Jean is coming round, so I could make us all a cup of tea, and we can share thoughts on the position of the veranda."

The following morning, Alex set about firming up his plans for the back yard. He found the notebook in which he had started some rough drawings and tidied them up a bit so they appeared more like plans someone might be able to work from. By the time Jean arrived, he had the kettle boiled and ready. Slippers arrived a few minutes later and was eager to familiarize himself with the layout of the yard before coming in to sit with Jean and Alex, who passed him the rough drawings. In between biscuits and gulps of tea, Slippers periodically went out to look at the yard and make measurements while scribbling in a shabby notebook. Jean drank her tea and had a biscuit but was obviously uncomfortable that she wasn't getting on with her work. After a while, she explained that she had to get on, and she went through to start in the lounge. When she had gone, Slippers broke the news to Alex about the proposed cost.

"I can't be exact, but I can see it being about £1,500 for cash. The problem is that wood is getting to be very expensive and it all needs to be treated. That makes up the biggest part of the bill. On top of that, you need good quality felt for the roof, guttering, downpipes and an assortment of fixtures. I can do it cheaper, and you would effectively have a two-sided shed, or I could go all bells and whistles and make it a fully glazed summerhouse, but that would obviously put your price up, and some official at the planning offices might find something to object to. In my experience, it is better not to involve officialdom. Think it over, and don't forget that you will do some of the labouring."

"I don't need time to think it over. If we can get something like my sketch, then I will be quite happy with the price, thank you. When do you think you might be able to start?"

"I've got a bit of slack time now, and normally I would have started on Saturday for you, but it's Saint Bodolv's Day, and I will be celebrating at the Wellie. I could do the work on Monday and Tuesday next week if you're available and weather permitting."

"Suits me fine. I have to go to a funeral in York next Thursday, but I'm free earlier in the week."

Having set up the deal, Slippers went off about his varied businesses, leaving Alex to realise that Saint Bodolv's Day might be a recognised holiday. The saint sounded an unlikely character, but many saints had equally incredible stories to support their canonization. Perhaps he had been wrong to doubt Norman? Alex's next task was to check the condition of his car, which proved difficult as he spent nearly an hour looking for his car keys. It struck him that he was not as dependent on his car as he had been in London. On the contrary, it was almost surplus to his requirements in his new life. Eventually, he found the keys in the knife drawer in the kitchen and didn't even bother trying to remember why they had ended up there.

Armed with the keys, he approached his car and opened the door. He turned on the ignition and was relieved to see the array of dashboard lights flick into action. The fuel gauge indicated half a tank of fuel; it was going well so far. He turned the ignition key further, and the engine spluttered into life, but only for a brief few seconds. When it came to car mechanics, Alex was no expert. He had displayed his full range of mechanical skills by just turning the ignition key, and now he was completely out of his depth. He tried again with the same brief response from the engine. He tried again, and the engine turned over repeatedly, but now with no flicker of life. He turned the ignition off and just sat and tried to figure out what he could do now. He was suddenly startled by someone tapping on his window, which he wound down to hear someone ask, "Having trouble starting? Perhaps I can help?"

The individual offering to help was a petite young woman who looked to be in her early teens and barely old enough to drive, but Alex was prepared to accept any help.

"Thanks," he replied. "The car has been standing for a while, and now it doesn't want to play. It nearly started but then just gave up the ghost."

"OK, can you just pop the bonnet?"

Alex was embarrassed to find that he didn't know where the release mechanism was, but the young woman patiently showed him where the handle was, and the bonnet obligingly popped open. She wandered over to a van parked nearby and returned with some sort of aerosol spray. She asked Alex to keep running the starter motor on her command and then leant under the bonnet and shouted at him to turn the starter on. He did so, and within a few seconds, the engine fired into life. Alex left the engine running and got out to speak to his mechanical saviour,

"Thanks for that, I'm Alex, by the way. What's in the can?"

"Hi. I'm Julie, and you're the guy who moved into the Cogans' place. The aerosol is just something we use on our big petrol lawn mower if the engine gets cold or damp. Spray it on the air intake and the engine starts better. Here, I'll show you."

Julie showed him where the aerosol should be sprayed and then said, "There's still a bit left in the can. You can keep it as we've got more in our shed. You ought to buy a new can as you will probably need it if your car is not run for a while and the weather is cold or damp, as it often is in these parts as we move into the autumn and winter months."

"That's very kind. How much do I owe you?"

"Nothing. You can buy me a drink in the Wellie sometime. In the meantime, I suggest you buy a new can of the starter spray pretty soon and consider putting some insulation around your engine if you are leaving it for any length of time. You can turn your engine off now if you like, but it may be a good idea to give the car a bit of a run to charge the battery a bit. I must go now. See you around."

As she drove off, Alex read the signage on the side of her van. Apparently, he had just been helped by Julie of Kirksea Landscape Gardeners. For the first time, he found himself 'in the red' in terms of the local fiscal regime; he owed someone else a drink. He thought for a moment about Julie's recommendation to take the car for a lengthy drive and decided that he might as well do so right away. The engine was still running smoothly, so he nonchalantly dropped the bonnet down and got in the car.

Alex was now faced with the question of where to go. He had never been one for driving tours, so he decided to just follow whatever route took his fancy. He wound his way up through the narrow streets of the village, and when he got to the main road at the top, he decided to head north, and then after a few miles, he took a left-hand turn towards the moors. After a short time, he found himself on a minor road with clumps of pink-purple heather appearing to extend for miles in every direction. He found a place to pull in off the road and parked up. He was careful not to switch off the engine, and he just sat for a while. He wanted to just sit and enjoy the tranquillity of the place and resented not daring to switch off the engine. He contented himself with marvelling at the spectacular panorama, and he couldn't suppress a smile when he reflected that all before him had been 'made in Yorkshire' and that some of his London friends would be surprised to see that it was not all dark satanic mills up here.

Eventually, Alex had to drag himself away from his little Shangri-La and continue his meanderings. He drove through small hamlets and along narrow roads with ill-defined edges bordered by the ubiquitous heather. It seemed to be a place exclusively populated by small groups of sheep that appeared to assume they had the right of way. Alex had been driving for quite a while when he decided that the car had been sufficiently refreshed and he could safely return to Kirksea. It was at this point that he discovered he was lost. He knew approximately where he was and headed in the general direction of the sea, being guided by the odd signpost pointing towards places he had vaguely heard of. It was this haphazard wandering that led to him passing through Goathland, where *Heartbeat* had been filmed. He had never been through what was generally known as Aidensfield, but it all seemed remarkably familiar as some of the entrepreneurial locals had dressed parts of the village as it had appeared in the television series. Driving on, he found himself back on the coast road, and he made his way back to Kirksea.

As he turned off the main road and descended into the welcoming familiarity of the village, he felt glad to be back. The car tour had been strangely enjoyable for someone who didn't particularly like driving, but it was good to re-immerse himself in the village he called home. What had once been just a place with happy memories was now a community of friends. He parked up his car in its allocated spot and set off on the short walk home.

CHAPTER ELEVEN

Saturday was the famous Saint Bodolv's Day, and Alex was mildly inquisitive to find out what was so special about it. He had never heard about it as a child, but then the family holiday had not been so late in the year, so the saint's day had never been part of his experiences. Alex convinced himself that such an auspicious day should obviously start with a good breakfast, so he set about making himself a rather large one. The meal proved very enjoyable, but the kitchen looked like a war zone. He remembered how Megan used to chide him about the fact that he could create a mess just by making a simple sandwich, and, looking around him, Alex had to concede that she had a point. It took him quite a while to tidy up the kitchen before he could do his regular circuit with the vacuum cleaner, and only then could he set out for his walk.

It was a bright, sunny day. He remembered that his mother would describe such conditions as an 'Indian summer' although such a season may only last a day. Approaching the Wellie, he was taken by a large sign next to the front door. It was a rather smart design on a piece of hardboard almost as big as the pub door and fastened by screws to the wall. It looked strangely permanent but hadn't been there the previous day. On it was a four-foot-high figure of a man in a monk's habit with a mitre on his head, which was surrounded by what looked like a goldfish bowl but which undoubtedly represented a halo. His right hand was raised in some sort of religious blessing, and in his left hand, he held three whelk shells. Underneath was the simple inscription.

Saint Bodolv of Aeskrik
AD626–AD692

The border of the sign was decorated with images of whelk shells entwined with seaweed. It was an impressive icon that further convinced Alex that the venerable character had been a real person. The room was unusually full, even for a Saturday lunchtime, and it took him some time to get to the bar and get served. While he was waiting and admiring the chain of whelk shells across the front of the bar, he picked up a sheet of paper from a pile which featured the same design on the front as the sign outside the pub. The fliers were in a box inviting patrons to take one, so he did so and took it with his pint over to a seat next to Norman, who had apparently left Muffin at home. Norman was engaged in conversation with someone else, so Alex took the opportunity to read the information on the reverse of his flier. The printed information on the paper gave the same basic information he had been given previously but included further details about the need to celebrate the saint's achievements.

He had barely had time to start reading it when Norman, having finished his conversation, turned and said, "Hi Wessie. I see you're getting the low-down on the great man. You can see why it's seen as such a big day in the village."

"I'm getting there, but why is today chosen to celebrate him?"

"There's no precise date for his date of birth or death, so it was decided that it should be the first Saturday in October. The flier is just to inform the uninitiated about him and to put in some background, like directions on how to get to Monk's Cave and the state of the tide that dictates when it's safe to access it."

"I see there's a mention of the Triple Whelk Ceremony. What's all that about?"

"Bodolv had his own special way of explaining the scriptures, and he allegedly used three whelk shells to represent the holy trinity: hence the design on the icon. Each year, one of Bodolv's acolytes eats three whelks here in the pub and then goes down and throws the shells in the harbour."

"Who are the acolytes?"

"Anyone who turns up on the day."

"And how do you decide which one performs the ceremony?"

"Whoever is daft enough or drunk enough to eat three whelks."

Alex had begun to suspect once again that Norman was not being entirely open about the origins of the legend, and having glanced down at the flier, he asked, "It mentions the appointment of Saint Bodolv's Knight and the saint's penny. How does that fit in, and what does it mean when it talks about the Bodolv love contract?"

Norman was starting to weary of so many questions and wanted to get on with his pint, but he patiently explained.

"The honourable post of Saint Bodolv's Knight is one that runs for a year. In view of the Sex Discrimination Act, we have to consider applicants from either gender as long as they meet the demanding requirements of the post and officially register their intention to stand. The reference to the penny will become apparent later. The love contract is simple and states that any couple who meet on Saint Bodolv's Day and subsequently court each other will have a lifetime of love together."

A thought suddenly struck Alex. He had met Megan at his friend's wedding, and that had been the first Saturday in October, and they were no longer together, so the Bodolv love contract wasn't entirely reliable. He looked around the room at any woman who might be deemed a future partner; if Bodolv was right about the romantic possibilities, he would have to be careful. The afternoon proved to be very enjoyable, and Alex had plenty of time to talk with several people that he hadn't had chance to chat with before. As the pub filled up, the noise levels increased, and suddenly a huge cheer went up, and the crowd repeatedly chanted, "Whelk, whelk, whelk." Then there was another cheer followed by some commotion as large numbers of the crowd headed for the door. Noting Alex's confused expression, Norman leaned over and spoke.

"It seems that young Tom has managed the whelks, and he's off to perform the ceremony of throwing the shells in the harbour. Anita may be proud of his efforts; it all depends on how sober he is when he gets home."

As the afternoon wore on, Alex was careful not to have as much to drink as he had on the darts night. He didn't want to risk disclosing too much of his past life and certainly nothing like the incident of the sex worker and the traffic cone. It was almost four o'clock when Dave rang the brass bell behind the bar, and when the chatter in the bar subsided, he announced:

"Ladies and gentlemen, fellow acolytes, we come to the appointment of this year's Knight of Saint Bodolv. As is the custom, all those wishing to be considered for this honourable title will be approached by Laura and asked to purchase your ticket, on which you will write your name before placing it in the box. Please have your Bodolv pennies available."

The general hum of conversations resumed, and Alex almost forgot about the cryptic message. He got on with his pint and the sandwich he had purchased. Half an hour later, Laura approached the table he was sharing with Norman and two other locals.

"Good afternoon, gentlemen," she said, "please have your pennies ready. Now, who's first?"

She looked straight at Alex and held out her collecting box while proffering a small white card. He was obviously confused, so Norman explained.

"You put your name on the card, and it goes in the box."

"But I'm not really up for becoming a knight."

"It's not a matter of choice. If you're here, it's assumed you will put your name forward. Then you put your penny in the collecting box."

"But I don't have a penny; nobody carries pennies these days."

"I hope not. Just put in what you like, a pound or a fiver, whatever, it's for the lifeboat."

Alex took out a five-pound note and put it in the box as directed before putting his name on the card and handing it back to Laura. Having collected from all those on the table, she smiled sweetly and went on to work the rest of the crowd, leaving a bemused Alex to ask Norman, "Now what happens? Once they've got all the names, do they have some sort of committee to decide who takes the title?"

"No. That would be open to corrupt activities such as bribing the committee, and anyway, we don't have a committee. We just draw a name out of the box so there's no chance of electoral malpractice."

"So how does that fit in with the legend of Bodolv?"

"It doesn't. It's just a way to make money for the lifeboat. This day brings in a lot of money for the village, and we like to pass a bit of the wealth to the lifeboat guys," explained Norman.

"Exactly how much of the legend is based on any facts?"

"Not a lot really. It's more like a sideshow. I invented Saint Bodolv as an April Fools' Day spoof for the *Gazette* some years ago, and some people were obviously taken in by it, so we decided to elaborate on the story a bit. Dave had Helen make up the sign to be put outside the pub each year, and he keeps his string of whelk shells to put out. I don't think that there are many of the locals who believe all of it, but it's a good excuse for a party. We decided to do it in early October to try and extend the holiday season a bit. Blackpool do the same; they have the illuminations, and we have Saint Bodolv's Day."

Alex couldn't help but think that he ought to have relied on his policeman's suspicions when he heard the story, but it had been plausible. Norman was a sensible man with a firm grip on reality, but occasionally he released his grasp and descended into a world of fantasy into which he would attempt to draw others. Alex's thoughts were interrupted by the sound of the pub bell being rung loudly, and he looked up as Dave began to make what was obviously going to be a serious announcement.

"Ladies and gentlemen, your attention, please. We now come to the most important part of this most auspicious day; the appointment of this year's Knight of Saint Bodolv. We have, as ever, attracted a large number of worthy applicants for this singular honour, and I call upon Laura to officially declare the appointee."

Laura approached a space that the eager crowd had cleared in front of the bar, and she carried the box into which she had encouraged applicants to drop their names. After a moment's dramatic pause, she plunged her hand into the box and withdrew a single card, which she read to herself before announcing:

"Ladies and gentlemen, fellow acolytes, it is my pleasure to announce that the spirit of Saint Bodolv has selected the following as his knight." There was another dramatic pause before she announced, "Alex Lucas, aka Wessie."

Alex sat in stunned silence. His name had been drawn out to announce him as the recipient of a title he didn't understand, and it was obvious from the way Laura was beckoning him that he had to fulfil some sort of role immediately. He rose slowly and approached Laura to the accompaniment of clapping and cheers, which he knew were more the result of the alcohol than any respect for the title that had been thrust upon him. Laura kissed him on both cheeks before presenting him with a whelk shell on a red ribbon, which she placed around his neck before stepping back. The room was now in silence, and he was faced by a crowd who obviously expected him to make some sort of acceptance speech. He naturally did not have a prepared statement to make, but he had to try, so he cleared his throat and started.

"Fellow acolytes. I can honestly say that I have never received such an award before, and I feel truly humbled and more than a little apprehensive at the thought of all the official duties that I shall be called upon to perform over the coming year in the name of Saint Bodolv. I have to admit that as a newcomer, I don't know all the details of the life of our venerated patron, but I'm sure that Norman will tell me – as soon as he makes it up."

To the sound of more good-natured alcohol-fuelled applause, he returned to his seat, proudly wearing his official regalia and went on to enjoy the rest of the celebrations.

CHAPTER TWELVE

Alex was determined not to over-indulge at the celebration, and he left while the festivities were in full swing. He still had his whelk on a ribbon when he entered the chip shop where Anita was busily serving.

"Hello, handsome," she greeted him. "I heard that you had been recognised for the fine, upstanding citizen that you are, and now, with your official badge of office, even more women will be throwing themselves at you. I must learn to control myself."

"Thank you for your restraint, but I must admit this whole Bodolv thing is a mystery to me."

"It's just a bit of fun and an excuse to party, but it does bring people into the village; Nora and I have been rushed off our feet. Laura didn't want to nip out, but it's good for her to be seen when money is being raised for the lifeboats. We probably won't have many visitors for a while now until the summer season starts again, except on the odd dry weekend."

"If you do have a bit of a rush, I'm available most of the time."

Having picked up his fish and chips, he headed home to eat them as the harbour was looking less and less attractive as an alfresco eating location as the autumn drew on. Once home, he ate his meal and then sat down to watch the television. It was sometime later before he awoke from an extended nap to see the last part of a documentary on some minor celebrity's travels through Peru, which failed to grab his attention, so he switched the set off. He was annoyed with himself for having fallen asleep as he knew that it would mess up his nighttime sleeping pattern. Megan wouldn't have let him fall asleep in the afternoon. The thought of her made him calculate that it was about 35 years to the day since they had first met at the wedding. He thought of her now as she faced up to the upset of her father's death. It may not have been a surprise, but it would have hit her badly, and initially she would have been on her own. Once again, he felt something like guilt at not having been able to be with her to offer some sort of support.

Slippers turned up promptly at eight o'clock on the following Monday. Turning down the tea he was offered, he guided Alex to a small van, some distance from his cottage, laden with the materials that had been selected for the proposed extension.

"If you can get this lot down to your yard," said Slippers, "I will just start the marking out."

With this, he picked up a large toolbox and set off for Alex's yard. Alex was impressed by the efficiency of his new builder. There was no idle chat; Slippers knew his job well and wanted to get on with it. Alex spent the next couple of hours fetching all the materials and then carrying out any instructions that he was given by the 'master builder'. The pair seemed to work well together with very little idle chat, and eventually, without bothering to stop to check his watch, he said, "Eleven o'clock, time for a break."

Alex set off to put the kettle on but found that Jean had already set out two cups of tea and a packet of biscuits. She obviously knew her husband's work routines.

"There you are, Alex," she said. "That will keep him going for a while. Now, I'll leave you to it and get on with the upstairs."

When Slippers came into the kitchen, he didn't seem surprised that the tea was waiting, and he sat down to help himself to a biscuit. He had obviously switched from work mode, so Alex ventured a bit of conversation.

"It was quite a celebration on Saturday. I had no idea that the day would be so eventful, and you can imagine my shock at being appointed the Knight of Saint Bodolv. What are the chances of me getting that honour in my first year here?"

"A nailed-on certainty."

"What do you mean? It was the luck of the draw, surely."

"Luck had nothing to do with it. We don't like to risk someone from outside the village walking off with such a prestigious title, so we keep it local."

"What do you mean? It was fixed?"

"I think that 'fixed' is a strong word. We merely arranged it so that the venerable saint's wishes were respected. In short, Laura palmed your card and then 'selected' it from among the others. After all, it's not as if there was any fabulous valuable prize at stake, but even so, we prefer to keep the selection process a secret. Over the last few years, a number of regulars have won, so we needed someone new. Anyway, Norman thought that you would be best equipped to carry out the ancient rites that need to be observed."

"What ancient rites?"

"I don't know, Norman hasn't invented them yet."

Alex didn't bother trying to find out any more about the honour that had been so feloniously bestowed upon him, but he had a feeling that he had not heard the last of his ceremonial duties.

Over the next two days, the two men worked well together, and by the end of Tuesday afternoon, Alex found himself to be the proud owner of a rather smart covered veranda which even had an electric point in it. This had been put in by Slippers' friend Sandy Carter, whom Slippers referred to as Sparky, and Alex had been happy to pay the electrician in cash and a promise of a couple of pints in the Wellie.

When it came to sorting the payment for Slippers, Alex explained, "As you might expect, I don't keep such an amount in cash in the house, and I'm sure you don't want a check, but as the job was arranged at such short notice, I haven't had time to get to the bank. I'm going over to Whitby to my bank tomorrow, and I can get you the money then. In the meantime, I could give you some on account. Perhaps 50 pounds and a couple of pints in the Wellie tonight?"

"There's no rush on the money, so just give me it when it's convenient. I'm sure I can trust a Knight of Saint Bodolv, but I will take you up on the two pints."

Despite Slippers' protestations that there was no rush for Alex to pay, he decided that he would go in to Whitby the next day to collect some money. He knew from experience that parking might be difficult, so he opted to go on the bus. He had previously checked on the bus times and knew that they ran every hour into Whitby. It had been his intention when he moved to Kirksea to regularly visit Whitby, but he hadn't managed to find the time. He remembered the days as a boy when he and the family had gone on daytrips to Whitby from Wakefield. He had loved walking around the harbour and doing all the things families did on such visits, with ice creams, fish and chips and climbing the steps up to the Abbey. There was the obligatory visit to the amusement arcades when Dad would mildly lecture the children on the evils of the money-grabbing machines while giving them a few pence to entertain them for half an hour. Alex had even tried eating a whelk once but decided it was not unlike chewing fishy rubber, so he had discreetly removed the half-chewed sample from his mouth and thrown it into the harbour. His dad always insisted on taking home some kippers, which he regarded as his special treat because nobody else in the family would eat them, largely because the whole kipper seemed to be made up almost entirely of head, tail and thousands of small bones. Every time they visited, they did the same things and ambled along the same walks, but it always seemed to have something different to offer.

The next day, Alex walked up to the main road above the village and boarded the Whitby bus, which arrived pretty much on time. As he travelled, he was impressed by the countryside they passed through. He liked to travel on the bus as it was possible to see so much more than when driving, and as he looked at some of his fellow travellers, he wondered if they always appreciated the beauty of the region or if it just became routine. Whitby did not disappoint. Alex went to the bank, drew out the money, and put it in his wallet in a zipped pocket inside his jacket. Having done the business of the day, he felt free to wander the town. He was almost in holiday mode again and soon found himself travelling the same route he had done with his family over 40 years previously, but there were subtle differences.

Walking along the harbour side, he passed the fish restaurant that he had always wanted to visit as a child, but family finances wouldn't stretch to such a place, and they had always had their fish and chips from one of the other vendors all of whom served first class fayre. Today, Alex paused for a second and then ascended the steps to the restaurant and waited a few minutes to be shown to his seat. He ate an excellent seafood salad and felt a definite sense of achievement at finally eating there. As he walked back along the harbour, he looked at the signs offering boat trips. Such an expenditure for a family of four would have been considered an extravagance, but now he could afford it. He checked the times and calculated that it would mess up his plans for the bus home, so he walked on. Perhaps some other time, he could tick the boat trip off his bucket list. He walked over the bridge to the shops offering Whitby jet jewellery. His dad had bought his mum a silver and jet ring there one year. It had been one of the few times in his life that he had shown such conspicuous affection for his wife, and she had always loved that ring. Val had inherited it and cherished it because she knew how much it had meant to her mother. Along with her wedding ring, she had worn it her entire life. Alex walked into what he seemed to remember was the same shop, and after some deliberation, he selected a silver ring set with a band of jet. The assistant put it in a small ring box and handed it to him, but as soon as he got it outside, he put the ring on his finger, the box in his pocket, and he walked off to the bus stop, but not before buying a new can of the miracle engine starter that Julie had recommended. Whitby hadn't changed much, but his circumstances had.

The first thing Alex did when he got back to the village was to seek out Slippers so he could 'slip' him the agreed cost for the building work. As was the custom, the money was passed over in a brown envelope, which Slippers casually put in his pocket without bothering to count it.

CHAPTER THIRTEEN

Alex woke early the next day, and he put on the clothes he had selected for the funeral. As he stood in front of the wardrobe mirror in his dark suit, shirt and tie, he was reminded once again of his days in the police, and he even felt as though his warrant card should still be in his pocket. He had decided to take the route over the moors to York as he had enjoyed his time meandering around there recently. Fortunately, the car started first time, and he set off on his way across the vast expanses of the North Yorkshire moors. It was an overcast day, but the massed ranks of heather seemed to glow with their subtle purple tones. He remembered his daily commute into London and questioned how he could ever have been so misguided to opt for such a lifestyle in a place with so little sky compared to the open splendour he was enjoying now, but then remembered that the move had been dictated as much by finances as by his need to move away from Wakefield. Both he and Megan had profited financially from their time in the capital, but at what cost?

He drove on through the Vale of Pickering and Malton before approaching the outskirts of York, and as he did so, he remembered the first time he had been invited to meet Megan's parents. He had only been to York once before on a school outing, which was memorable only because it had rained continuously all day. His memories were of driving around the city in a coach with 30 other children who were denied the promised picnic by the river and walk around part of the walls. The general atmosphere was not helped by the fact that one child had been sick and two others threw up in response. The visit to meet Megan's parents had been a lot more agreeable. Right from the start, he had got on very well with Josh and even with Ivy. They had welcomed him into the family and into their home, where he had stayed for a pleasant three days despite sleeping arrangements that dictated that he had to occupy a spare bedroom rather than share Megan's bed as had been their habit for some months previously. That apart, Josh and Ivy had been perfect hosts. They had a possible itinerary, which they discussed with the young couple, and a plan of visits was made. They did an extensive tour of many of the tourist sites and even enjoyed just walking around the old streets by the minster, so Alex had many happy memories of that and later visits to the city.

He parked up on the outskirts of York and checked the time. He was early, so he drove around to find somewhere he could have a coffee and a piece of cake before driving to the crematorium. He was still a little early, and it was before half past eleven when he arrived in the large car park. He had marvelled at previous ceremonies just how efficient the crematorium was. Funeral cars arrived at a set time. The coffin and guests went in one door, and the guests later emerged from another and all to a strict timetable, but despite this, the staff worked to ensure that each family of the deceased felt they were getting a special event. Alex was careful not to move to the crematorium door too soon as he would be in danger of attending the wrong service. The previous group eventually made their way into the building. It wasn't long before a number of fellow mourners left their cars and began to congregate in the porch by the entrance door, so Alex took it as a signal to be on the move. As he stood with the other mourners, he looked around to see if he could recognise anyone. No one seemed familiar, and he was conscious of the fact that he was being scrutinized by others to see how he fitted into the day. He realised that as he and Megan had spent so much time away from York, there would be few who might remember him, and he knew that their acquaintances from London would be unlikely to travel up so far on a work day. He saw one or two faces he thought he half recognised, but he was not so certain as to feel comfortable about approaching them. Most of those attending were rather elderly, and he assumed that they were probably friends or former colleagues of Josh or Ivy. He had a short conversation with an elderly lady who introduced herself as a neighbour of the deceased, and she seemed mildly surprised when he explained that he was Megan's former husband. Apparently, the old lady found it strange that one might attend the funeral of one's former father-in-law.

The funeral cars arrived right on time, led by the hearse. Alex deliberately hung back as Megan and her mother emerged from the first car, but he did risk a very discreet wave and a slight smile. Ivy looked very drawn and held on to her daughter's arm as they moved towards the hearse. He was expecting Ivy to have been badly affected by the occasion, but he was surprised to see how Megan was looking in some way fragile. She had always been so resilient and took life's knocks on the chin, but her father's death seemed to have hit her hard. He had to fight the urge to rush over and hug her because he knew her well enough to know she needed support, but he was still unsure how she would respond, and he didn't want to risk embarrassing her. His attention was then drawn to the second funeral car as Stephanie and Jessica got out, accompanied by two young men he took to be the partners he had heard about. As the main party stood behind the hearse, Alex felt it was appropriate to move forward and join them. He gave Megan a lengthy hug and somehow knew that she appreciated the emotional support before hugging each of his daughters in turn and shaking hands with their young men. The group stood in silence as the casket was withdrawn from the back of the hearse and shouldered into the chapel. As Josh had wished, there were no flowers, and this seemed a little strange as this very basic box was carried along. Alex was struck by the thought that the remains of someone he had known and even loved was in that coffin, and they were leaving this world with as little fuss as possible. As the casket was carried in, Alex had intended to hang back a little, but Megan clasped his hand and made it clear that she wanted him by her side at this time. They entered to the peaceful strains of 'A Summer Place', and Megan, with her mother on one arm, led him with the other to the seats at the front of the hall. It was not what he had intended, but he knew she appreciated his support. They took their seats as the music faded, and the celebrant started what proved to be a short service. After the introduction, the official pointed out that Josh had chosen much of the contents of the ceremony himself after explaining that his serious health problems meant that he knew that he wasn't going to live forever.

Alex glanced down at the printed order of service, which gave little indication of what Josh had selected. It gave brief information that readings would take place at particular points, and these would be interspersed by unnamed musical episodes. As the programme progressed, Alex could feel Josh's influence on the proceedings. There were, naturally, some moments of reflection tinged with sadness, and during these, Megan would squeeze his hand slightly as if to reassure herself that she still had his support. During other parts of the service were anecdotes showing Josh's almost irreverent attitude to death, explaining that due to his heart attacks, he had already had two innings during which he had been declared 'not out', but this time stumps had finally been drawn. The second piece of music was introduced as being one where Josh wanted to leave a message for Ivy. After a moment, the sound of Nat King Cole singing 'When I Fall in Love' filled the room. The beautiful sincerity of the lyrics had many of the congregation dabbing tears from their eyes, and Alex couldn't resist glancing towards Ivy. She had tears running freely, but she had a serene smile on her face. The service continued with a reading of a romantic poem by John Donne before Ivy got up to say a few words.

"Thank you all for coming today. Josh would be pleased to see so many had turned out, but the old whinger would probably have just tried to imply that he didn't want a lot of fuss. We shared over 50 very happy years together, and I know that is a luxury denied to many couples. During that time, we have been blessed with a daughter and two lovely granddaughters, and Josh would have been delighted to see so many of the family here today."

At this point, she smiled directly at Alex before continuing.

"Many of you may only have known Josh as a crusty old man, but he brought untold romance into my life, and they are memories I shall always hold on to. He was never keen on funerals, least of all his own, but he always loved a good wake, so he would be offended if you couldn't make it to our house after the ceremony to raise a glass in his memory."

Once again, Alex got the distinct impression that this last invitation was aimed specifically at him, so he smiled back at her. Ivy returned to her seat, and the celebrant went through the committal reading before the curtain closed around the coffin. As they waited to leave, the final piece of music started. Many of the congregation were more than a little surprised when they recognised the music as 'Je T'aime Moi Non Plus'. It was a song that had been banned in several countries because of its overtly sexual content. Ivy smiled. She knew it was Josh's ultimate comment on life; love is all important, and sometimes it is a good idea to shock people a bit to get the message over. In an attempt to reinforce his philosophy, Josh had arranged for a quote to be printed on the back of the order of service that simply stated:

"Those who love deeply never grow old; they may die of old age, but they die young."

The words were attributed to Sir Arthur Wing Pinero, and they had given the congregation an insight into what Josh felt was important. Ivy was secretly proud of him, even if some of her friends and neighbours might have been a bit offended by the choice of leaving music.

Alex knew that his absence from the wake would not be acceptable, so he felt obliged to put in a brief appearance. When he arrived, Ivy almost rushed over to kiss him and led him off to meet people. He had managed to grab a few words with his daughters after the funeral but hadn't had chance to meet their partners. Ivy introduced Stephanie's friend Roger, and then explained that Leon was Jessica's friend. In chatting with the young men, he found Roger to be quite an interesting and witty guy, whereas Leon was incredibly dull, and Alex could not understand what Jessica saw in him. He consoled himself with the fact that if the girls were happy, then he was, but he wouldn't be too sad if she moved on to someone with a little more life in them. Despite Leon hanging around, Alex quite enjoyed the buffet while restricting himself to a small glass of wine as he was driving. He was just explaining his appointment as Knight of Saint Bodolv to a bemused Megan when her mother arrived with an opened bottle, having apparently consumed some of it herself, and gestured to him that he might like a top-up.

"No thanks, Ivy, I'd rather not as I'm driving back tonight."

"Go on, you can stay here, then you can have a drink or two."

"That's kind of you, but I really have to go, and I wouldn't want to put you to any trouble," he explained.

"It's no trouble. You could share with Megan."

"Mum!" exclaimed Megan with horror. "We are not married anymore."

"So what?" asked her mother. "Stephanie and Jess are staying over in a hotel with their friends. You don't honestly imagine that they are going to have separate rooms, do you? Really, you can be so prudish, Megan."

For the first time in years, Alex was embarrassed. He could cope with sex workers and their traffic cones, but a former match-making mother-in-law was a different thing altogether, and he knew that Megan was also less than impressed with her mother's attempt to get her in bed with her former husband. With a sigh of resignation, Ivy wandered off to see to some of her other guests.

"I'm sorry about that, Alex, I think she may have had a little too much of the wine, but she didn't seem that drunk. Perhaps it's a reaction to the funeral?"

"No need to apologise, love. She means well, but I think she may be trying to get us back together because of her having lost Josh. Their marriage meant so much to them that she can't envisage a situation where two people who'd had a good marriage would ever want to split up. It's understandable."

"I guess so, but she did overstep the mark a bit."

"Yes, she called you prudish! It's obvious she doesn't know what went on in the old Morris Marina."

Megan looked at him with mock disapproval before commenting, "Mothers don't know everything, thank goodness."

In an attempt to turn the conversation on to some other subject, Alex looked desperately around the room and, seeing an empty dog's basket, he asked, "Wasn't Mandy invited to the party? She would have been in her element hoovering food up off the floor."

"No. That dog's a menace anywhere near food. Mum arranged for her to spend a couple of days with Mrs Howard. She often spends time there, and Mrs Howard spoils her rotten; she loves dogs. She's just set up what she calls a Doggy Hotel, which is her name for kennels. She has absolutely no idea about running such a place, but Mandy knows her and always settles well there, and it's convenient."

The wake went well, with everyone sharing stories about their interactions with Josh. He would have been pleased to see such conviviality and to hear the frequent outbursts of laughter. Alex was glad to have the chance to meet up with his family again, and before he left, he offered an open invitation for them to visit him. It was early evening as he set off for the drive home and already getting dark. As he drove, he reflected on the times after he had married Megan that he had visited her parents. He felt a little guilty in having to admit to himself that he had preferred their company to that of his own parents, but he put it down to the fact that, as an adult, he had never got on well with his father in particular and his mother always did as she was told and sided with her husband. It was one of the things that had attracted him to Megan; her strength of character. She was not prepared to be subservient in a relationship. Some might have seen her as too self-willed, but if she believed in doing something, she would show a terrier's tenacity. As he drove on over the quiet roads, he thought how much he had enjoyed his time with her and hoped she took up his offer of coming over to see him, although he appreciated that it was a long way to travel from London.

When he arrived back in the village, it had started to rain lightly. He locked up the car and set off on the short walk home. His initial intention was to go in and make himself a light supper as he was still not really hungry, having been plied with countless sausage rolls and similar buffet delicacies. He contemplated eating supper and then watching a bit of television before going to bed, but when he met Norman, who was on his way to the pub, he didn't take a lot of persuading to accompany him. The pub was particularly welcoming on what had turned into a rather wet, miserable evening, and Alex was pleased to collect a pint and sit down at a table with Norman.

"You didn't have to dress up for your new role," called out one of his many new friends in the pub.

"He means you don't have to dress specially now that you're a knight," explained Norman with a sly grin.

Alex belatedly realised that his business suit was not something the people of Kirksea had seen before, and he smiled before waving regally at the individual who had commented on the funeral outfit. He turned to Norman and explained.

"I'm surprised it hasn't got around the village that I've been over in York today for my former father-in-law's funeral. It turned out to be quite an enjoyable day, given the circumstances. The funeral service wasn't all misery and moping about; obviously, it had its downside, but there were a few laughs along the way. The party afterwards was good because I got to meet up with my former wife and other members of the family. As funerals go, it was good. How have things been back here today?"

"Much the same as usual. Pretty quiet."

Alex felt that the description of the day's events in Kirksea summed up a large part of its attraction for him. After a busy life dealing with all sorts of issues in his police work and coping with the manic traffic in London, it was refreshing to now be faced with the pleasing, unchanging routine of his new lifestyle. Nothing untoward had happened, and the same predictable uneventfulness would no doubt fill his diary for years to come. The only little issue that faced him now was how to get home without getting absolutely soaked. Bidding goodbye to some of his friends and acknowledging the wisecracks about his smart clothing, he left the pub. It was raining quite heavily now, and he pulled his jacket collar up in a relatively futile attempt to fend off some of the rain. He made his way as quickly as he could to the sanctuary of his cottage. He hung up his suit to dry and, looking at it, he hoped he would not have need to call on its services in the near future. The rain continued to beat down as Alex made himself a cheese sandwich and a cup of tea before heading upstairs to bed.

He had been asleep for some time when he awoke with a start as he became aware of a loud throbbing noise. As he looked around in his confused state, he saw the curtains at his bedroom window were illuminated by a display of bright flashing lights. His first thought was that there must be some sort of wild disco being held in the street outside. He was about ready to go and complain to someone about the interruption of his night's sleep when he looked out of the window to find the source of his irritation. He looked in the direction of the harbour and, through the pouring rain, he could see that the main source of the lights appeared to be hovering in the air just outside the harbour entrance. In the limited visibility caused by the torrential rain, it looked like some alien spacecraft had visited the village. As his brain shook off the last vestiges of sleep, he could make out the shape of what was a helicopter. He had seen the coastguard helicopter before, but when it was so low with all its navigational lights and its searchlight moving along the shoreline, it seemed so much bigger, and the noise of its twin engines echoed around the village. He looked down towards the harbour and could just make out the blue and red flashing lights of some kind of emergency service vehicles.

Alex was torn between going to offer assistance and not wanting to get in anyone's way, but decided he would go down to see if he could help in any way. Quickly putting on the clothes he had designated his foul weather gear, he headed for the harbour. As he approached, he saw that there was a coastguard's blue and yellow Land Rover and a police car. The senior coastguard officer was on his radio, and the police officer was sitting in his patrol car. There was already a small crowd gathering to find what the commotion was all about, but Alex went over to talk to the police officer. It turned out that the constable was a young man, and Alex could see that he seemed a bit overawed by the situation.

"Excuse me, Constable," said Alex, "I'm former Inspector Lucas. I don't want to get under your feet, but if I can help in any way, then I'd be pleased to do so; perhaps by seeing if I could rustle up some refreshments for the crew?"

"Very kind of you, sir. Some senior officers are on their way, and I'm just holding the fort. I should have gone off duty hours ago, but we've been monitoring this situation."

Alex knew all about the enforced flexibility of shift times, and he also recognised that he shouldn't ask questions about operational matters. After politely suggesting that the police car didn't need its blue lights flashing, he went over to the Wellie, where Dave was standing in the doorway trying to see what was going on.

"What's going on, Wessie?" asked the landlord, who had observed Alex talking to the police officer.

"No idea, Dave, but I know from experience that these guys are probably going to be here for some time, and they would love a hot drink and perhaps a sandwich. Put it on my tab."

"No need for that, I'll get something sorted with Daureen; she can't sleep through this lot."

Dave went in to let Daureen know of the plan, leaving Alex to introduce himself to the coastguard officer and to take orders for drinks. As he was doing so, an ambulance turned up with obligatory flashing lights, and he took their drinks orders as well. No sooner had he done this than a second police car arrived with a police chief superintendent and a sergeant. Alex began to wonder if it was the refreshments that were attracting them. It was apparent that the operation had demanded a full turnout of the appropriate services. After an hour of serving drinks and then sandwiches, Alex sat down for a rest in the pub, which had become an impromptu incident room. He talked to the police chief superintendent, and when he learned of Alex's time in the police, they shared experiences of their careers, and eventually Alex learned what had caused the upset to his quiet village life. Apparently, two walkers were doing the Cleveland Way. They had, quite correctly, informed a friend of their intention and their estimated time of arrival at a particular point. When they failed to turn up the previous evening, their friend notified the coastguard, who organized a search along the intended route. While there was no sign of them, they did find the man's mobile phone on a section of the walk that was very close to the cliffs, so the search was reclassified as urgent. Apparently, the Whitby lifeboat had been launched, the inshore boat from Kirksea had been scrambled, and even the coastguard helicopter had been brought in. Between them, the services had begun a systematic search of the cliffs and inshore waters in the designated area. Fears had been raised when the heavy rain had set in as anyone in the sea or even on exposed areas on land could well suffer from hypothermia.

Throughout the night, Alex helped keep up the supply of refreshments as radios crackled with messages passed between the various members of the search team. Alex couldn't help wondering if Laura was in the Kirksea boat. Whoever was in it would probably be wet and cold despite the gear they wore, and he was, once again, impressed by the commitment of the lifeboat people to turn out and put themselves through such discomfort and potential danger. It was approaching four o'clock when the coastguard officer took a call on his radio. He smiled broadly and raised a thumb to the others. The tension in the room fell away, and the team started to congratulate each other for a job well done.

Meanwhile, the coastguard was still in conversation with someone on his radio, and when he had finished, he announced, "Both safe and well," he paused before adding, "At home in bed. It seems that they were on the walk, and the weather was getting so bad that they decided to backtrack to their car and go home. He didn't phone his friend and let them know about the change of plan because he'd lost his mobile. When they got home, they were so tired that they dried themselves off and went to bed. It was only when their friend, in desperation, thought to try the landline that they were informed of the situation. Apparently, they say they are sorry if they caused any bother; so that's all right then! Never mind, we can stand down the search now and classify this as a very expensive training exercise."

The group slowly dispersed. Alex stayed and helped clear up before he left the pub, and he stood for a moment looking at the harbour, experiencing that mixture of feelings, exhausted but satisfied that he had played a small part in supporting the emergency team. As he set off home, he passed Norman, who was carrying out an informal interview with the coastguard officer. This would be one week at least that Norman wouldn't have to make up stories for the *Gazette*.

The rain had eased off, and Alex decided that it was probably too late to go back to bed, so having got halfway home, he retraced his steps down to the harbour and stood for a while just gazing out to sea. The first signs of dawn were just appearing out on the horizon, and he thought back to the days of his youth when he had sat with Lynda after one of their long nights on the beach. They had watched the dawn come up on several occasions, and Alex felt it was a particularly romantic time of day, but on a wet October morning after a sleepless night, the romance was less obvious. As he stood and experienced this nostalgic memory, he became aware of the sound of an outboard engine approaching, and within a few moments, the lifeboat appeared from around the harbour wall. Alex found it hard to make out exactly who was crewing the boat as they were dressed in their waterproof clothing, but he was pretty sure that one of them was Laura, so he waved to them, and they acknowledged his greeting. He felt glad to see them returning safely. Judging by the time it had taken them to get back, they must have travelled well up the coast. The sea was relatively calm, and the crew was never in any great danger, but it was good to see them back; any safe return to harbour was worth celebrating. He toyed with the idea of walking round to the lifeboat shed to help them but knew he would probably be getting in the way, and so for the second time, he set off for home. As he walked, he was struck by how quiet the village was. A few hours ago, this place had been the site of all sorts of excitement and drama, but it now seemed as if the village had just turned over and gone back to sleep.

CHAPTER FOURTEEN

Alex was determined not to go back to bed, so he made himself a cup of tea and sat in his armchair. The sound of his phone ringing sounded miles away, but as he slowly awakened, he realised that, despite his intentions, he must have fallen asleep. Fumbling to find and open his phone, he answered it and heard the familiar sound of Anita's voice.

"Hi Alex. Sorry to mess you about at short notice, but could you possibly lend us a hand over lunchtime? It tends to be a bit busier on Fridays, and Laura was out most of the night on a call, so she wondered if she could miss her shift today."

Alex didn't bother to explain that he had also had a bit of a broken night and, having agreed to be at the shop for eleven o'clock and being told that he was 'an absolute darling', he put the phone down. He checked his watch and found it was just after nine, so he had a quick shower and change of clothes before making himself a cheese sandwich for what must be his breakfast. It was all he could think of that did not involve any cooking. The walk to the chip shop helped Alex wake up a bit further, but the weather was still overcast.

"Hello, darling," came the familiar greeting from Anita. "Thanks for stepping up to help out. It appears that there was quite a lot of excitement in the village last night. Tom heard a commotion, but it didn't wake me. It seems that some muppets caused a panic by not ringing to tell their friends that they were safe, and in the meantime, all the emergency services were called out. I heard about it from Dad's brother, Uncle Ted, who had turned out with the chief superintendent. Mind you, all he did was sit about drinking tea and filling his face with sandwiches while poor Laura was patrolling up and down the coast in the pouring rain looking for people who weren't even in danger."

"So, your uncle Ted is a sergeant?"

"Yes, but how do you know?"

"I bumped into him in the Wellie last night. We shared a few sandwiches while they were monitoring the search and rescue operations. I saw the inshore lifeboat coming back later and thought it was Laura, but it's hard to tell when they have those protective suits on."

"So, you were up during the night as well? You must be shattered. You should have said when I called."

"No problem. You get used to irregular shift patterns and silly sleeping routines in the police; ask your uncle Ted. When all is said and done, we just sat about waiting. It's people like Laura who were doing all the work."

"Even so, you should have said. If you do feel tired, then you'll just have to go home. Nora and I can always manage."

"I'll be fine. I must have had over three hours sleep this morning. There were times when I was in the Met that I would have killed for three hours kip. My Megan would tell you how silly my work patterns were at times. She had a lot to put up with, bless her."

The shop was busy, as Anita had predicted, and many of the customers were keen to discuss the events of the previous night. Despite his attempts to play down his minor role in the night's activities, Anita kept explaining to customers that he had been there, and so there was a general interest in what was seen as his first-hand knowledge. When he finished his shift, Alex received his beer money and decided that he deserved to spend some of it appropriately. Normally, he would have gone home and showered, but he felt thirsty, so he headed for the Wellie.

The pub had more than its usual quota of customers that day as a group of tradesmen who had been employed by Bricky Gordon for a few weeks were celebrating an early finish. Their loud conversations and frequent outbursts of raucous laughter made it difficult to carry out his chat with Norman, but their presence in work clothes made him feel better about turning up in his.

"Quite a night last night," observed Norman. My report will please the editor when I put it in. We can pair it up with a piece advising people to let others know when setting out on such a walk and to let them know if plans are changed. I saw that you were rather pally with the emergency services."

"Not really. I just helped Dave and Daureen to provide refreshments for them. I know what it can be like on such occasions. As a young copper, I once spent six hours on duty, keeping people away from a crime scene without anything to eat or drink. I think my sergeant had forgotten to get a replacement to relieve me. I was hungry and thirsty, and by the end of my session, I was dying for a pee. All we did last night was to give some basic support."

"I guess that as a Knight of Saint Bodolv, you have to do good deeds like that all the time."

"I don't want too many nights like that during my year in office," commented Alex before changing the subject. "I see that Muffin's not with you. Is he grounded?"

"No, but he wasn't keen to come out tonight. Usually, as soon as I start to get ready to come out, he assumes I'm coming down here, and he's standing by the door. I think he may have a touch of arthritis as he hasn't been moving too well recently. I can't remember exactly how old he is, but he must be nearly

13, so he's getting on a bit. Mind you, he'd be up in a flash if he heard a wasp."

Their conversation was interrupted by the arrival of Bricky Gordon, whose entry was greeted by subdued cheers from the workmen around the bar. Bricky went over to the bar, and it was apparent from his gestures and what little could be overheard that he was ordering drinks for the entire crew. When he came over to sit with Alex and Norman, the situation was explained.

"They're a fine bunch of lads," said Bricky. "We've just about finished the cottages on Barnard's Yard, so I thought I'd hold a little topping-out ceremony for them. They've worked hard, and all that's left now is a little bit of tidying up on the site. There's little point in paying for them to come in on Monday, and they were hoping to start up on a new job, so I will just have to find someone to shift one or two items, and then the cottages will be ready for the painters and plasterers to move in."

Bricky looked at Alex as he made his comment about the need for a little casual labour.

"And I suppose you want a certain knight to ride to your aid for a few hours?" asked Alex.

"If you could, Alex; it should only take a few hours at most, and it will help me out."

"OK, when do you want me round?"

"It would move things on a lot if you could do it over the weekend. I can always see if Slippers is available if it's too short notice."

Alex showed his willingness to help, and arrangements were made for him to turn up on Saturday morning to meet Bricky on site. Having sorted out his temporary worker, Bricky declared that as Alex was now almost a part of the workforce, he must have a pint to join in the topping-out ceremony, and Norman could be an honorary member of the team and have a drink as well because of the occasional oblique references he made in the *Gazette* to the fine craftsmanship shown by a certain local builder in regenerating the area.

"I know the crew can get a bit noisy," said Bricky as he nodded in the direction of the celebrations going on at the bar. "But they do create quite a lot of business for Dave, and most of them are local lads as well."

Alex was introduced to the small gathering and found that they included a Crabby Stan, Splosher Dixon, Inky Pink, and Captain Susan. The latter was quite obviously a man but showed no objection to being called what one might have assumed was a girl's name. After a brief chat, Norman, Alex and Bricky returned to their table.

"I was wondering if everybody in this village has an alternative name," commented Alex.

Norman took a deep breath, and Alex prepared himself for what he suspected might be another fanciful, if not completely fabricated, explanation.

"It's rather like the convention in certain Welsh villages where many of the inhabitants have the same surname and a limited number of popular forenames. So, even a small community might have 10 inhabitants who go under the name Dafydd Jones. To differentiate between them, they have a series of individual nicknames sometimes, but not always, related to their profession, so you might have Jones the Fish or Jones the Wheel. In many of the local villages around here at one time, there were some large family groups, and over the centuries, as people didn't travel so much, you might find that a village might be made up largely of people from a small selection of families. In Kirksea in the early eighteenth century, most of the residents were either called Bedlington, Barnard, Cappleman or Leighton, so a local folklore grew up of using nicknames. In my grandfather's day, it was very common, and today there is still that tradition among some of the older families. But we've never had a Wessie before."

"On this occasion, he's telling the truth. He does it from time to time to keep us on our toes," confided Bricky.

"The name Kirksea itself is in fact of Norse origin," continued Norman. "Kerkar means craggy, and Cera translates as shore. Thus Kerkarcera, or Craggy Shore, became Kirksea."

"And that is complete rubbish," commented Bricky. "Which is what we have come to expect from Norman. But you can't fault him for trying."

After a disturbed night and then a busy afternoon in the chip shop, Alex was feeling a little tired and, refusing another pint, he went home. He had only been in a few minutes when his phone rang and, after a moment's hesitation, deciding whether he would bother answering at all, he picked up his phone and took the call.

"Hello, darling," announced the unmistakeable voice of Megan. "I wonder if it would be OK for me to bring Mum over on Sunday? She says that she's a bit embarrassed about her invitation for you to stay over after the funeral and wants to make sure she hasn't offended you."

Alex couldn't suppress a laugh before saying, "Of course I wasn't offended, surprised, yes, but nothing I can't get over. When did you have in mind?"

"It could take a while to get Mum sorted in the morning, but I think we could be in Kirksea by about midday. We thought it was a good idea to take advantage of the fact that Mandy's staying at the kennels, so it's one less thing to worry about. How will I find your place?"

"Drive down into the village, and just past the shop is a narrow alley to the right. Pull down there, and you will see a small enclosure with a couple of tractors and some cars, including mine. The area is for locals, but if you park in front of mine, you won't be blocking anyone else. It might be an idea to put a note in your windscreen saying you're visiting Wessie."

"Wessie?"

"It's a long story. I'll explain later. If I'm not at the car park, then the best bet is for you to walk down towards the harbour and drop into the Whelk Pot. It's the local pub."

"Sounds intriguing. I'll see you about twelve on Sunday then."

"Right, see you then, darling."

Having rung off, he sat for a while, planning out how he would entertain Megan and Ivy when they arrived. It was going to be a busy weekend.

CHAPTER FIFTEEN

When Alex arrived at Barnard's Yard the following morning, Bricky was already there and ready to show Alex what needed doing. Two things quickly became clear. First of all, Bricky was obviously a competent builder, as the cottages had all been finished to a high standard. Secondly, it was clear to Alex that it would take more than the 'few hours' that had been suggested as some of the builders appeared to have finished in a bit of a rush so as to get to the Wellie on time. By working hard and through what should have been his lunch break, Alex finally thought that the properties were in a fit state for the plasterers to move in, and he walked down to the Wellie for a very well-earned pint. As expected, Bricky was there, and he paid Alex by passing him some banknotes and informing him that he had a pint waiting. Alex had learned that such small transactions were carried out this way, but if larger sums were involved then the money would arrive in a 'pay packet' in the form of a brown envelope. Having checked with Daureen about the possibility of taking two guests in for lunch the following day, and explaining that he had friends who would be parking next to his car in the parking area, he headed off home to make sure that everything was tidy for his guests the following day. He knew the house was clean because Jean had been in recently, but he wanted to ensure that he hadn't left a mess anywhere. He knew it might be seen as farcical to go to such extents, but he had convinced himself that he wanted Megan to be reassured that he was coping in his new life, although he knew that his actions were essentially designed to impress her.

Alex was pleased to see that it was a dry if slightly blustery day when he awoke the next morning. He showered and washed his hair, had a shave and applied some of his more expensive aftershave before carefully selecting his clothes for the day. It suddenly struck him that he was getting ready as if for a first date rather than to see his former wife and her mother. He smiled at himself in the mirror in what he thought was a nonchalant fashion, realised it looked as if he was grinning inanely, shrugged his shoulders and went down to make himself breakfast.

Even after giving the cottage a final checking over, he was still ridiculously early, so he decided to go for a walk down to the harbour to pass a bit of time. It was refreshing to stand on the harbour wall and to feel the wind blowing in off the sea. It would have been an ideal day for a younger Old Bob and his urchin friends to collect hats from the harbour for unwary visitors. Alex and his sister had never liked days when the wind blew in off the sea as it usually meant that the water would become a little bit choppier, making swimming a little more challenging. Their father had never learned to swim, and he was always concerned when the children went in the water, and he restricted such activities to when the sea was calm. In later years, Alex loved to go in the water when there was a slight swell so he could feel the power of the waves lifting him up. He had even taken to swimming out some distance through the surf, almost as a sign of rebellion against his father's over-cautiousness.

It was still too early to meet his visitors, so he slowly sauntered up through the village until he came to the shop. The tinkle of the bell above the door alerted Colin, who came through from the back room to meet Alex.

"Morning, Wessie. What can we do for you today?"

"Morning, Colin. I've got some friends coming over, and I'd like to get something for sandwiches for tea in case they stay a bit longer. What would you suggest?"

"I've got some very nice German smoked ham," he said, in a conspiratorial way, while looking over his shoulder towards the back room. He knew that Brian did not like to think his partner was trying to suggest that customers might like meat products. In his attempt to keep the sale quiet, Brian gave the impression that he was selling some illicit product rather than a few slices of cooked meat.

"That sounds perfect," replied Alex in a similar whispered voice.

Alex took the opportunity to have a lengthy conversation with Brian about largely inconsequential matters just to pass a bit more time. Brian was generally keen to have a good gossip, and Alex had often found himself in lengthy discussions with the shopkeeper and found it difficult to get away, but this time it was Brian who obviously had matters to sort out, and Alex took the polite hints and left the shop. It was still not quite midday, but he decided to walk round to the parking area. He had shown the forethought to take his car keys, so he let himself into his car and took the opportunity to sit in comfort and wait. He considered putting the radio on but had no idea if that might drain the battery, so he sat in silence. After half an hour, he had read all the assorted booklets and leaflets in the glove compartment and carefully wiped over every inch of the dashboard and instrument panel with some wet wipes he found in his door panel pocket. He looked around at the other parked vehicles. He took the letters from the number plates and tried to assume that they were acronyms, and he would then interpret what they might stand for. He was so bored that he was on the verge of playing I-spy with himself when he saw Megan's car entering the parking area.

He carefully directed Megan to park in front of his car, and when she got out, he kissed her and then went to help Ivy.

"Hello, darling, I hope we're not late."

"No, I've only just got here myself," he lied graciously. "I thought it better if I met you here to show you the way. Did you have a good journey?"

"It was lovely," interjected Ivy," It's been years since I came across the moors. Josh and I used to travel over in his old Morris Minor before we were married. We had some fun in that old car."

"We had the Morris Marina, and we had some fun in that," added Alex.

Megan glared discreetly at him, but judging by the knowing smile on Ivy's face, it was apparent to him that some tacit cross-generational communication had taken place.

"Happy days," reminisced Ivy.

"Happy days indeed," agreed Alex.

Suddenly remembering something, Megan checked inside the car and placed a neatly printed card on the dashboard. Alex read the note, which, as he had suggested, announced that the occupants were visiting 'Wessie'. Megan looked at him and shrugged, and he felt obliged to explain his new persona as he walked his guests down to the pub.

The Whelk Pot was quite busy, and Alex acknowledged a number of his friends as he escorted his visitors to a table next to one occupied by Norman and his wife, Edna. Alex introduced his guests to Norman and his wife before going to buy drinks and order sandwiches for lunch. He was held up for a few moments, chatting briefly to Bricky and some friends at the bar, and when he returned, he found his little group chatting happily with each other. Alex passed over the drinks and sat down to rejoin his guests.

"Norman was telling us about the search and rescue operation last week," said Megan, "so this isn't always a sleepy little backwater. Norman tells us that you were up all night helping the emergency services."

"You must learn not to take Norman's journalese fantasies too seriously. He can sometimes believe his own hyperbole. He might make it sound as if I was single-handedly controlling a complex air-sea rescue operation, but all I did was help to provide tea and sandwiches."

"They also serve who only stand and serve," added Norman. "It was a gallant effort, sallying forth with cups of tea through the wild stormy night with no thought for your own safety while others were tucked up safely in their beds, oblivious to the life and death struggle being played out in their own village."

"See what I mean? Norman could describe the contents of a bag of crisps as if it were the greatest gastronomic treat ever produced."

Alex and his visitors enjoyed very substantial sandwiches and the opportunity to discuss how life was treating them all. Ivy and Megan both commented on how well Alex appeared to have settled into the village as he recounted some anecdotes about his life and employment status there. Eventually, Alex suggested, "Why don't I take the pair of you to have a look around the village before we go back to my place?"

"I'd love to see more," replied Megan. "I'm intrigued to find out what it is about this place that has had such a beneficial effect on you. How about you, Mum? Are you up for a walk?"

"I would love to, but my sciatica is playing up a bit. You two young people go ahead, and I'll just stay here and chat to Norman and Edna about what you've been doing. You can pick me up on your way back."

"If you're sure, Ivy," he said, "we'll not be long, and in the meantime, remember that Norman's accounts of what goes on in the village must always be subjected to scrutiny. His contact with reality can often be fleeting."

The wind was still blustery, but the weather was quite warm for the time of year as the couple headed towards the harbour wall and walked out to the seaward end. They stood for a while gazing out at the sea. The tide was quite high, and the waves were rather choppy. Alex thought that it would never have been a day when his father would have permitted swimming, but the teenage Alex would have been out there feeling the swell of the waves beneath him. His reminiscing was interrupted by Megan remarking, "You do realise that Mum has never had any problems with sciatica, don't you?"

"I thought I'd never heard her mention it, but then she was never one to dwell on her problems."

"She just wanted to give us 'young people' time to be on our own. I think that she is so lonely since Dad died that she wants to busy herself patching our lives up along the lines that she thinks are appropriate. She wants to play happy families with our lives because she can't rebuild her own. I know she means well, but she is starting to get little digs in at every opportunity. Just after the wake, Stephanie commented that she and Roger had been considering getting married at some point. It wasn't an official announcement or anything, but Mum's first comment was to the effect that it would be nice if her father could walk her down the aisle. I pointed out that if either of the girls ever wanted to be escorted in such a way, then I'm sure you would oblige."

"Naturally, it would be a pleasure."

"I thought so, but Mum's immediate response was that it would be so much better if we were still married. I've told her that we had decided to get divorced for very good reasons, and we had our own lives to lead, but she still finds ways to make her preference known."

"I'm sure that she will come to terms with it someday, love. Why can't you make subtle hints that she should get married and see how she feels?"

"I haven't gone that far, but I have suggested that she concentrate on her own life a bit, perhaps by getting out to see people. You'd have thought I was suggesting she started speed dating."

The couple stood in silence for a while, looking out towards the sea, before Alex broke the reverence by asking, "Does Stephanie have serious intentions about getting married to Roger? He seemed like a good match for her, and I got on with him very well. I can't say that I warmed to Leon much, but if he makes Jessica happy, then it's fine by me."

"Roger is a lovely young man, and I wouldn't be surprised if they did get married at some point. It might be something for Mum to concentrate her match-making skills on."

"And what about you? How are you getting on these days?" he asked.

"I have to admit that it's been difficult getting my life back in gear. The business is doing reasonably well, and as I said before, Fatima is running it on her own at the moment while I give Mum a bit of extra support. The evenings can be a bit of a drag when I'm in London. After work, I go home to an empty house, and it's difficult to develop any enthusiasm for cooking just for myself. I sometimes go out to that little French restaurant that we used to frequent, but it seems strange to be eating on my own. Martin, the young administrative assistant in the office, has asked me out for meals a couple of times, but it's difficult because he seems to be suggesting it as a date."

"You can't fault his good taste."

"Thanks, but it's no laughing matter. He's a nice guy and great to work with, but that's about it. If I do go out in my free time and choose to wear casual clothing, then people think I've 'let myself go', but if I dress up smartly, then it's assumed that I'm out looking for a man. You will remember that on our rare nights out, if we went somewhere such as Luigi's Bar or the Carlton Club then we would dress up appropriately. If I turn up at such places now in my best clothes, then some men seem to assume I'm touting for business. What wouldn't I give to have a place like the Whelk Pot near me?"

"I never thought of it that way. I'm lucky in that I can pop into the Wellie anytime they are open and be sure to find someone to talk to, and I'm consciously getting out to meet people during the day. I must admit that I would end up putting my boot through the television screen if I felt compelled to watch it all day long. I've also got my little beer money jobs that I've told you about. All in all, I've got a good life here. After 33 years of marriage, you get used to having company in the evening so I have to admit that life still feels a bit empty at those times."

"Thirty-four years," she corrected him, "but you have to admit that we didn't spend all our evenings together. You could never be sure to be back at a certain time, and even when you were supposedly settled for the evening, you might get called out for some reason. Likewise, once the business took off, my home life was prone to interruptions with deadlines or emergency meetings. Some months, we might only spend four or five evenings together, and the weekends were never sacrosanct either. I have toyed with the idea of stepping back from the business, but that would just give me more hours to fill. I thought about moving back up north myself, but I wouldn't want to move back to York. The city is magnificent, but not so much as it would persuade me to live on Mother's doorstep when she seems to want to spend all her time making veiled suggestions that you and I should get together. I wouldn't want to encroach on the girls' areas either, so for the moment, I'm stuck where I am."

"I can see it's a problem. Why don't you pull out of your business commitments and move near here? There's plenty of small villages near the coast up here, and the house prices are very attractive after London. If you do consider it, then

I would recommend you spend some time looking around a lot of places to see if they suit you."

"I did go and have a look at a place in Lincolnshire while the divorce was going through. It was a lovely village, and I stayed in a cottage for a week to check it out. The surroundings were beautiful, and it was wonderfully quiet after my London place, but there was nothing going on. There was no sense of community, and it was largely a dormer village for workers in Grimsby. There was no community centre or even a pub. There was a church, but as you know, I'm not a churchgoer. It wasn't so bad moving areas when the girls were little because I met other young mums through the school, but if I moved now, I feel I might be isolating myself. I even considered getting a dog for company if I did ever move! I think the experience of that village has given me cold feet about moving."

"That doesn't sound like you. You were always prepared to take on any challenge; that's why the business went so well. Don't give up on the move. I'm sure you can find somewhere; I did. Come on. We'll have to get back and pick your mum up. God knows what sort of rubbish Norman is telling her."

On the way back to the pub, Alex pointed out some of the features of the village to which he had become so accustomed. He stopped briefly to chat with Helen, who was trying to sketch the waves breaking outside the harbour while fighting the wind to hold her sketch pad steady enough to draw. Old Bob was in his usual seat, but Alex resisted the temptation to stop and be regaled with tall stories the old man could draw out from his unreliable store of memories, so their conversation was brief.

"Afternoon, Bob."

"Afternoon, Wessie."

The interaction was short but accompanied by smiles from both parties, and in a tone that gave some indication of an underlying friendship.

"Do you know everybody in the village?" questioned Megan. "We spent years in both our places in London, and we barely knew who our neighbours were for months. Even down at the Carlton Club, we were members for years, and yet we only ever got to know a handful of people. The folk here seem so much friendlier."

"In my experience, people are much the same wherever they are. The majority of people are basically social animals and like to mix, but the circumstances need to be right for them to do so; they need the places, the inclination and the time to meet up. In the village, the people are pretty much contained in a little bubble, so there is a sense of shared identity, and historically things were often desperately hard, so the inhabitants learned to help each other through the bad times. There are opportunities for people to meet up. We have a couple of local shops, the chippie and of course the Wellie. There is often something going on around the harbour to take an interest in, but most importantly, people make time to talk to each other. I don't want to give the impression that all is sweetness and light. There are disagreements of course, but for the main part, people feel the need to get on with their neighbours. I decided from day one that when I came here, I would accept the ways of the village and not try to bring my isolationist philosophy with me. It took a while, but I learned to be myself and to let people know who I am. Friendship demands openness, and people here are prepared to be seen for what they are."

"I never really thought of it before, but back home, life can be so hectic that we use our home to keep the busy world outside, but what we actually do is lock ourselves in so the sanctuary becomes our prison."

CHAPTER SIXTEEN

Ivy was obviously amused by something in the conversation she was having with Norman and Edna at the pub when Alex and Megan arrived back.

"Norman has just been telling me about your investiture ceremony here, Alex. Who'd have thought that my own son-in-law would have been knighted and had such an interesting career sorting out sex workers and their traffic cones?"

"You don't want to believe everything Norman tells you, Ivy," insisted Alex. "He's a general fount of misinformation in these parts. Besides, it was only one sex worker; I was on duty, and she wasn't."

Megan gave Alex a quizzical look but decided it was not the best time to go into this hitherto unknown episode in her former husband's career. She was struck by the fact that her mother still referred to Alex as her son-in-law. It was a title she did not wish him to relinquish, but she was only hiding from a fact she didn't want to accept.

"Do you want to come up and see my place?" asked Alex, eager to move the conversation away from the infamous traffic cone incident.

"To see your etchings?" quipped a rather giggly Ivy, who had obviously enjoyed an extra drink while she had been left in the pub.

Megan looked at Alex and shook her head despairingly at her mother's comment before suggesting, "I think it might be a good idea to get Mum a bit of fresh air."

Back at his cottage, Alex gave his visitors a guided tour, which did not take long. He was pleased that he had made sure everything was tidy. When he pointed out the fitted wardrobes in his room, he slid open the door to show the neat array of his clothes, which prompted Megan to remark, "Clothes in the wardrobe; was the floor full?"

He ignored this gentle criticism of his previous behaviour when he had been living with her, and he showed his guests into the smaller back bedroom. He had deliberately made up the bed rather than leaving it as simply a surface to dump things on.

"This is lovely," declared Ivy, sitting on the bed and testing it for comfort. "This would suit me down to the ground. I often tried to convince Josh that we should have a smaller place. Our house is fine for having family over, and people often talk about having a big dining room for the family at Christmas, but it's a big house to run and only use its potential for a few days a year. It's become particularly obvious now I'm rattling around there on my own."

The memory of Josh no longer being around obviously upset Ivy, and Megan went to sit with her on the edge of the bed and put her arm around her.

"Never mind, Mum. I know it must be hard for you, but you know Dad wouldn't want you to upset yourself, and I will stay around until you feel a little more settled."

"Thanks, love. I know he would have wanted me to soldier on, but after a lifetime together and sharing so much, I know that the void is still very much there."

Alex looked at the couple sitting on the bed. Megan was trying her best to console her mother, but he was struck again by the feeling that someone should be helping Megan. He wanted to fill that role but wasn't sure how to do it, so he said he would leave them for a while, and he went down to put the kettle on. It suddenly occurred to him that the smoked ham he had bought, largely as an excuse to fill time at the shop, was still on the passenger seat of his car. He wasn't too concerned as he had made sure that he had a range of food in for his guests, and he could pick up the ham when he escorted them to their car later. When the two women came downstairs a few minutes later, Ivy apologised for her show of emotion. He instinctively walked over and hugged her, saying, "Don't be daft. You've had a rough time; you're entitled to feel bad. Now just sit down, and I'll get you a cup of tea."

The fact didn't escape him that he could instinctively offer Ivy some comfort, but he felt the need to keep some emotional distance from Megan. They all sat and enjoyed a cup of tea together before Ivy insisted on doing the small amount of washing up that was necessary. As she stood at the sink, she looked out of the window and remarked, "What a lovely little courtyard. It really lends itself to some nice patio plants in big pots. It could look quite Mediterranean with a splash of colour on the walls. Is this a shed under the window?"

"No, that's the roof of the veranda I've had put up. I worked with a local handyman and only finished it a few days ago. Just leave the washing up to drain, and let me show you."

Alex took Ivy and Megan out of the back door and down a short flight of open wooden stairs to the yard, where he took an obvious pride in showing them the new addition to his home and explaining that it still needed appropriate furniture.

"I love it!" remarked Ivy. "With some of those nice wicker chairs and a little table, it could be quite cosy, and I see you've got electrics, so you could have a little heater and sit out even if it's a bit chilly. What's that little door at the back?"

"That just gives access to a space under the kitchen," explained Alex. "I'm told that some of the fishermen would keep some of their gear in there, but I just use it for odd bits of junk."

It was quite obvious that Ivy was very taken with the cottage and continued to give suggestions as to what she would do with it as she helped prepare a meal with Alex. She was obviously happy to be involved in such domestic activities. Throughout the meal, Ivy continued to express her love for the cottage and frequently made remarks implying that she would be keen to have one similar. She hadn't seen a lot of the village, but she had obviously fallen in love with it, and just as they were preparing to leave, she commented, "This would be a lovely place to come on holiday and to get a chance to meet more of the locals."

Alex wondered for a moment if this was some kind of a hint to secure a holiday at his place, but he realised that, if that had been her intention, she would have come straight out with it; she was simply daydreaming about some time in the future. He was pleased to think that she was looking ahead to better times when the grief had subsided a bit. She had something to look forward to in her life, and that signalled the very earliest signs that the agony of her loss was someday going to fade.

Eventually, Megan indicated that it was time to take her mother home as she felt that it had been a rather tiring day for Ivy. Despite the old lady's protestations that she felt fine and her obvious desire to stay in Kirksea longer, the trio set out on the short walk up to Megan's car. For the entire walk, Ivy made frequent positive comments about the 'quaint' cottages and the wonderful views and was obviously less than keen to leave, and having finally encouraged her to get into the car, Megan gave a sigh of relief.

"I thought we'd never persuade her to leave, bless her," said Megan.

"Yes, she was obviously taken with the place."

"I can't blame her. It's a lovely village, and you seem to have met a lot of nice people; I quite envy you."

"Yes, I'm very happy, but it's not too late for you to get somewhere for yourself; you could certainly make a success of it. Carpe Diem."

For a moment, the couple stood in an awkward silence, and Alex was aware that, not for the first time recently, Megan didn't look her usual happy, confident self, and there was a suggestion of vulnerability about her. This was not the confident, assertive Megan that he had known for many years. He walked over and hugged her and found himself saying, "Look after yourself, love, and remember that I'm here if you need me."

He hadn't meant to be so forward, but to his relief, she smiled and thanked him before getting into her car. He waved them off as they pulled out of the car park, and then he retrieved his smoked ham from his car and walked home.

Later that week, Alex's copy of the *Gazette* dropped through his letter box. He picked it up and took it through to the kitchen, where he casually put it on the table while he made himself a cup of tea before he sat down to glance at the headlines. "*Dramatic air-sea rescue operation in Kirksea.*" Norman had apparently been displaying his usual journalistic hyperbole, and Alex smiled until he read on. The village's own cub reporter had been exercising his usual facility for over-exaggerating, and Alex was keen to talk it over with his friend. After he'd finished his tea, Alex picked up his paper and walked down to the pub.

"Morning, fellow superhero," greeted Dave while pulling a pint for the new arrival.

"Morning, Dave," he replied, putting his copy of the *Gazette* on the bar.

"Norman's up to his usual tricks again. Never mind, drink your pint. You earned it last Thursday night, apparently, as did Daureen and myself."

"But he made it look as if the three of us oversaw a massive multi-agency rescue attempt while facing immense personal danger in the teeth of a raging storm. I don't need to remind you that all we did was provide refreshments. I know they were greatly appreciated, but it hardly constituted heroic behaviour. The way Norman was going on, you'd think we were up for some gallantry award. He even managed to get a photo of the Wellie and mentioned us by name."

"Never mind. Everyone in the village knows what he's like, and it will just get a bit of a laugh."

"Yes, but why did he have to describe me as the 'recently appointed Knight of Saint Bodolv?' Readers might believe I'm someone special."

"Don't worry about it. The people in the village will read between the lines and know it's not entirely accurate, and people from outside may be impressed or curious and come to the pub to check it out. We could always do with some extra custom, as the brewery is grumbling about the lack of business. Look on the bright side; at least Norman didn't mention the bravery you had previously displayed with the lady and the traffic cone."

"Where is Norman?" asked Alex. "He's normally in about now, isn't he? I'd hoped to have a quiet word with him."

"He popped in earlier to give me my copy, but he was eager to get home because old Muffin is still not very well. It was nice to see your two friends on Sunday. Ivy seemed to be having a good time chatting with Norman and Edna, and they were laughing a lot at times."

"Yes, she was very taken with the village and the pub, but I fear that her apparent jocularity is a bit of a way of hiding her grief over the loss of her husband. It was his funeral that I attended last week, and I'm not sure that the fact that he's died has sunk in yet. He was a great guy, was Josh, and we got on very well. It's not everyone that has the good fortune to have such good in-laws."

"I don't make a habit of listening in to conversations, but things that the old lady said now make sense. She was your mother-in-law? And I guess the younger attractive lady was her daughter; your ex-wife?"

Alex waited for what he expected would be the next question as to why he had ever split up from her. He had often asked himself the same question, but the landlord knew better than to pry into such matrimonial matters. Alex finished his drink, and having established that Norman was unlikely to come back, he headed for the door with a final bit of advice from Dave.

"See you later, Sir Wessie, and beware of autograph hunters and groupies now your heroic exploits have been disclosed."

Alex couldn't pretend to have been offended by the article, and in a way, he knew that the inevitable ribbing that he would get from his friends would be an indicator of how he was slowly being absorbed into the ways of the villagers. He had a delightfully uneventful week, during which he made time to go into Whitby again. He had nothing that necessitated such a trip. Nothing in particular to buy and no need to go to the bank or any other such business matters; he just fancied a day out, and the novelty of going to Whitby still seemed like a holiday. He wandered around the town with no particular destination in mind, as tourists often do. He read posters advertising the Whitby Goth Festival later in the month but decided it was not for him. He visited the Lifeboat Museum on the harbour side as he had done many times in the past and bought himself a souvenir mug. As he left, he looked out at the lifeboat anchored across the other side of the harbour and smiled at the thought that it was the same vessel that he had reportedly assisted the previous week, at great personal risk, during the 'dramatic' search and rescue operation. As he walked back towards the bus stop, he saw the men advertising boat trips. He didn't take up any of the offers, not so much because he was rushing to catch his bus but because the sea looked a bit choppy beyond the harbour entrance. Despite what Norman had reported, Alex was not a risk taker, let alone a hero.

As he returned home from his day trip, and even before he could make a cup of tea in his lifeboat souvenir, the phone rang. It was Megan with an update on Ivy.

"Mum is bright and cheerful much of the time, but things happen to remind her of Dad, and she becomes weepy. She thoroughly enjoyed her visit to Kirksea, as you probably gathered. It has given her something different to concentrate on, and if I'd given her any encouragement, she would have had her house on the market and been searching in your area. In her good spells, she talks about how much she enjoyed the pub and how lovely the people were."

"I suppose it's good that she has something to take her mind off your dad's death."

"True, but I'm having to try and persuade her that spending an hour in a pub is hardly sufficient confirmation that she ought to move to the village."

"It must be putting a terrible strain on you, love. How are you feeling about the situation?"

"I had to explain to Mum that I can't stay here indefinitely as I have to get back to work. It's not strictly true, as Fatima can easily run the business without me. The truth is that I don't think it's a good idea for us to stay together for weeks on end. We have a tendency at times to almost feed on each other's pain. If one or other of us suddenly feels down, then the other seems to almost key in to the grief. Neither of us is moving forward."

"Then you have to move out for both your sakes. It can't be helping Ivy to get back on her feet if she knows you're there to carry her a bit. The girls live quite close to her, so they can be there to give a bit of support. As you suggest, you need to get back to your life and find your own way to cope. Have you mentioned when you might be going back home?"

"Not exactly, but I have spoken in terms of my leaving 'in a few days'. Fortunately, she has Mandy back now, but that has been a bit of a mixed blessing. When we went to pick her up from the kennels, she seemed reluctant to leave, which upset Mum a bit. Then we got the dog home, and she started sniffing all over the house, which made us think she may have been looking for Dad, so that didn't help either. On top of that, both girls have been talking, albeit in general terms, about moving to follow their careers, and that makes Mum worry about being left on her own at some point."

"At the risk of seeming to be interfering, I really do think you have to look after your own health, love. The girls can keep an eye on Ivy, and I can call in from time to time to give a bit of support. If and when the girls move away, then we can always find some way through."

There was a lengthy silence, and Alex wondered if he had appeared to be bullying Megan about the way he thought she should deal with her life, and he began to regret his interference. When she eventually responded to his remarks, there was a slight quavering edge to her voice, and he knew she was more upset than he had realised.

"That's very kind," she said before taking a lengthy pause, "but she's not your mother, and it's not fair for you to have to get involved."

He was quick to respond before she could go on further.

"That's not the point. As far as I'm concerned, Ivy is family. I may not still hold the title of son-in-law, as she would wish, but she's been family for over 30 years. The fact that you and I are divorced doesn't mean that I suddenly stop caring for the people that were such a major part of my life for over half of it. I don't want to be seen as interfering, but I want to help."

"Yes. I know, and I appreciate it, but I think we need to think it through further when I feel a little more settled. Thanks for the offer, and thanks for your support over all this."

It was obvious to him that Megan was finding the conversation difficult, so he was not too surprised when she quickly drew the call to an end while agreeing that they needed to talk later when the emotional dust had settled. Alex tried to assess how the call had gone. He was concerned that he might have caused Megan some further distress, but he concluded that he had said what he felt was necessary, so if he had contributed to the complexities of her situation, it was only because he cared.

CHAPTER SEVENTEEN

Alex spent some time the following week making plans for furnishing his new veranda. He decided on a wicker-style sofa and matching chair, much as Ivy had suggested. He selected a small coffee table and ordered the lot online. He knew that getting any large objects delivered to the bottom of the village would be difficult, but that wouldn't be his problem. Jean was pleased to help out in planning the furniture for the extension but pointed out that alfresco living was not her choice in the colder months as winter was nature's way of telling people to stay indoors. Alex was surprised to see that the veranda furniture would be delivered the following week, and, in the meantime, he would make do with the two picnic chairs he found in the small cellar room under the kitchen. He sat out for a while one evening, but even with the portable electric fire he had put in, it was still decidedly chilly. Perhaps Ivy had been right to suggest glazing the structure.

Alex kept up his regime of taking a walk around the harbour most days and had even taken to occasionally visiting the rock pools at low tide, but he sensibly chose to wear wellingtons as the weather was becoming colder now. It was after one such excursion that he had returned to the harbour to find Old Bob sitting on his usual bench.

"Afternoon, Bob. By heck, it's cold out there on the sand."

"It's still quite mild, but we could get some snow towards the end of next month," commented the old man, "but we don't get the snow we used to. These days, if we get a dusting of snow, the country grinds to a halt. The trouble is that people are getting soft, not like in the old days."

Alex had begun to regret ever commenting on the weather, and he braced himself for one of the old man's dubious recollections of the climatic conditions of his youth.

"When I was a lad in these parts, me mam issued all us kids with bobble caps, not unlike the one I wear to this day. If the bobble was still visible above the snow line as we set off for school, then we were obliged to walk the 15 miles to get there, sustained on our journey by half a slice of cold toast and a herring each. If we were late for school, the head teacher, Growler Hoskins, would make us stand outside in the playground until lunchtime. This happened to my friend Eric during one period of particularly heavy snow, and his parents had to wait until the February thaw before one of the teachers stumbled across him, still standing rigidly to attention. Eric's parents were furious as they'd been keeping his dinner warm for nearly two months. Those were the days. Chilblains, chapped legs and mild hypothermia never did us any harm."

"Yes, I guess it must have been tough for you. I've never been here in the winter, but I expect it will get a lot colder than this."

"This is nothing, I tell you. It frequently got so bad just before the war that the village was completely cut off for weeks. The roads were all blocked, but we weren't beaten; we would walk all the way along to Whitby on the frozen sea to get our provisions."

As he wandered back up to the pub, Alex couldn't help thinking that Old Bob and Norman shared a similar facility for stretching the truth, but they were always entertaining. He was surprised to see that Norman wasn't in his normal seat, and he remarked on his absence when he got to the bar.

"We haven't seen him for a couple of days now," declared Dave. "He's normally in here by now to show off his piece in the *Gazette*. I see that his second Uncle Duncan advice column has got in. I guess there hasn't been any dramatic incident involving the brave citizens of Kirksea, so the editor might have been a bit short of anything interesting."

"I'm glad the search and rescue operation has faded into history. I don't know about you and Daureen, Dave, but I seem to have missed all the expected adulation after our big mention in last week's edition, although Slippers can't resist the odd dig."

It was at this point that the errant newshound came into the pub and approached the bar.

"Hello, Norman," said Dave cheerily. "The usual?"

"No thanks, Dave, I'll have a whisky, please."

Norman took his drink and uncharacteristically took it to his usual table without stopping to talk to his friends. After a while, Alex wandered over to join him and, by way of small talk, asked, "Muffin not with you? How is he keeping?"

"He's gone," replied Norman quietly. "He died last night. Edna and I hadn't felt able to leave him because we knew he was on his way out. He's gone now."

"I'm so sorry, Norman. We'll all miss him."

At this point, the few people who were in the pub fell silent as Norman's demeanour and limited snatches of the conversation made it apparent that something bad had happened and many of the regulars had been watching Muffin's steady decline. Dave came over and, without saying a word, placed another glass of whisky in front of Norman.

"He went at twenty past ten last night during my watch. He'd been sleeping most of the day, but at the end, he opened his eyes and looked at me. I think it was the first time in his life that he ever knew what was going on, and he was saying goodbye. I'm glad I was there."

Norman took a sip of his whisky and dabbed his eyes with his handkerchief before sitting up a little straighter to regain some semblance of composure before continuing.

"We all know he was not the brightest dog that ever drew breath, but he had a heart of gold. He seemed to sense if I had something bothering me, and he would come over and rest his scruffy head on my knee and just look up with that uncomprehending stare. He never knew what was going on, but he wanted to help. Some people don't appear to understand that losing a pet is losing one of the family. Edna and I didn't have any children, and Muffin was our family, not like some kind of child substitute but family, nonetheless. We've decided that we will never get another dog because we can't replace Muffin. We always said that he never had an evil thought in his head, largely because he never had any thoughts in his head."

After a rather protracted stay at the pub, Alex made his way home and was about to make himself something for dinner when the phone rang.

"Hello, Alex. I just wanted to let you know how things are going with Mum."

"Hello, darling, nice to hear your voice. I needed something to brighten up my day a bit."

"It sounds like you've had a bad day."

"You remember Norman from the pub; well, his dog died last night, and he's naturally a bit upset. A few of us had a drink at the pub with him, and I've only just got in. How are you and Mum coping?"

"Sorry to hear Norman's news. It was obvious by the way he talked about it that he loved his dog. We're slowly getting some of Dad's paperwork sorted. After his bouts of ill health, he was determined to leave things in good shape for Mum. All the details of his life insurance policies were written up meticulously, and we were able to inform the relevant companies and put claims in. What did surprise us was the number of bank accounts he had set up. We were aware that he had put all the money from the sale of his business into a bond, but they rarely drew on it. It was common knowledge that they had not been on expensive holidays, and Dad never spent a lot on cars. He seemed fixated on ensuring that he left Mum in a strong financial position, and he certainly did. He never trusted any of the financial institutions; hence, he had spread his money in small accounts over lots of different banks and building societies, and he never bothered Mum with the details. It's a veritable treasure hunt emptying drawers and cupboards."

"I remember when Val and I had to sort out my mum's finances when she died. There wasn't a lot of money as you will remember, but it still took months to sort it all out. Is Ivy a bit more settled yet?" he asked tentatively.

"The little weepy moments are less common now, but she still seems keen to move, and the discovery of quite a lot of unexpected money makes her think she has the cash to rush off where she likes. I think she may just want to move away from here with all its memories, but I've persuaded her to forget about that for the moment. She is still keen on moving to Kirksea because she loved the feeling of being part of a community. She saw how well you had settled in and assumed she could set up home there tomorrow and fit straight in. I've suggested that she has all her friends in York but, as she pointed out, she and Dad never had any extended social circle in the city. It's true that they spent most of their time together, and now he's gone, she can see little point in staying here. She's not convinced by my argument, but she's staying for now."

"And how are you coping, love? You seem to be spending so much time looking after Ivy, and I'm not sure that you appreciate how much strain that puts on you. Don't forget that you have your own grief to cope with as well."

"Thanks. I know it's been a strain on me, but as soon as I get Mum a bit settled, I can concentrate on myself. On that subject, I have told Mum that I need to get back to London and that I will have to leave on Sunday. I told her that I will ring every night, and I've alerted the girls to the fact that I'm going."

"And how did she take the news?"

"As I expected, she understood my position and knows it's the best course of action for all concerned. She admits she will miss me, but Mum was never selfish, and she knows she will have to stand on her own two feet."

"It's a hard thing to face up to, but it's true. I'll give her the occasional call to see how she is getting on and let you know how she is."

"Thanks, love. I'd better go now; Mum has got Jessica to bring her in a train timetable and is currently checking on the feasibility of getting to Whitby. I know it's good for her to have something to take her mind off Dad dying, but I'm worried she might go off and buy a place there. Dad always took care of the family finances, and now she suddenly has access to funds and control over what she does with them, I fear she could be like a kid in a sweet shop."

As the call came to an end, Alex had a sudden vision of Ivy walking around Whitby harbour, buying anything that the local traders could offer. He quietly chuckled at the thought that she might try to buy one of the cobles moored in the harbour or the entire contents of a seafood stall. He remembered the times he and Val had played '*If I had a million pounds*' on their visits to the town. Money had been tight when they holidayed as children, and they'd had a daily allowance for sweets, but that never stopped them of dreaming about what they would buy if they had lots of money. As they stood in front of the enticing trays of confectionery, they would announce their imagined shopping list. Their aspirations as to what to do with unimagined wealth had been unrealistically modest and was usually restricted to a few large chocolate bars and perhaps a whole tray of liquorice pieces. As he had grown older, he found he could afford all those things and more, but of course by then he had no interest in gorging himself on sweets. Ivy now had enough money to buy the entire contents of a sweet shop; she could afford to buy a number of sweet shops, but how would she choose to spend her money? It was an intriguing question but also a little frightening.

It had been easy for Alex to lose track of what day it was since his retirement as he hadn't got the rigidity of a work timetable to differentiate between days. Since he had moved to Kirksea, the relaxed atmosphere of the place meant that it was easy to just drift through the week and see what each day had to offer, but Friday had become a bit different as he was frequently called in to help at the chip shop as many of the locals still stuck to the ritual of having fish and chips on that day. He didn't have any sort of official regular shift, but Anita knew he was generally available. On this particular Friday, he'd had the luxury of 24 hours' notice that he would be required. It was late morning, and Anita was preparing the shop for the lunchtime customers. As it was quiet, she took the opportunity to introduce Alex to the secret alchemy of preparing the batter.

"This is one of the very important elements of frying fish properly," she explained as she finished mixing the batter with a large balloon whisk. "If you get this right and your fat temperature is correct, the results should be good. We can train you up, and at some point, you will be able to step in if Nora and I are busy. It's really not too complicated if you stick by the simple rules, but it takes time to get a feel for what's going on."

Alex felt a secret sense of pride that he should possibly, at some point, be considered reliable enough to work on the huge range. It might not appear a great honour to some people, but Alex knew how the locals and the droves of summer visitors valued good fish and chips. He had also observed that, while the range had a number of dials indicating temperature and cooking times, Anita and Nora rarely looked at them but preferred to rely on some indefinable affinity with the cooker, born of years of experience.

"It was a shame about old Muffin. Tom and I used to walk him on the beach when Norman was working. Muffin was scruffy, even as a puppy, and Norman never bothered to have him groomed in accordance with the pedigree standards. The breed details suggest that they are intelligent, but Muffin obviously never got the memo. He was a smashing dog, though. Norman used to sit with him down by the harbour. They would sit for hours, Norman thinking up some proposed article for the *Gazette* and Muffin just staring blankly into space, always wondering what was going on."

"Yes, he would sit in the pub like some Eastern mystic, but with nothing going on in his head at all. Some meditation methods instruct you at the beginning to '*clear your mind of all thoughts*'. Muffin managed that but never moved on from that stage."

Nora arrived, and the team set about serving the trickle of customers, which built up to the lunchtime rush before settling down in the afternoon. During one of the quieter sessions, Nora said, "Kevin the postman was telling me that the chippie in Wykethorpe is closing down. Apparently, the brewery managed to close The Prince down. It's supposed to be a temporary thing for some emergency structural work, but Ryan the landlord says it won't reopen. Betty at the chippie says that they get a lot of their business by being near the pub, so when it closes, there would be little point in keeping Betty's place open. This is all what the postman tells me, of course, and it's not official."

"He's a good contact to have," observed Anita.

"The best postie in the area," commented Nora.

Alex couldn't help wondering just how many of the local posties Nora had gone through in the rigorous selection process before deciding that Kevin was the best, but he chose not to ask and contented himself with a knowing look at Anita.

"It is a worry," declared Anita. "If the Wellie weren't here, it would ruin our winter trade, and, in the summer, we would no doubt take a financial hit."

"It would be a major loss to the village in so many ways," argued Alex. "Where else can people meet up in the village? My ex-wife was telling me that she stayed in a village down in Lincolnshire with no pub and no other community centres; the place was dead. I think we should all support our local pubs, and I shall lead the crusade by going to the Wellie this evening and making my own contribution towards keeping the place viable. I shall have one or maybe even two pints, just to help out."

"And you will be making this gallant gesture in your official role as Knight of Saint Bodolv?"

"Noblesse oblige, Anita. Noblesse oblige!"

"Oh, I love it when you talk dirty, Alex," she replied, fluttering her eyelashes.

CHAPTER EIGHTEEN

Alex was as good as his word, and he did go to the Wellie, but not before changing out of his work clothes and having a shower. Anita had been right about the lingering qualities of fish frying smells, and he felt much fresher as he strolled into the pub. There was no sign of Norman, and Slippers was also noticeable by his absence. Alex took his drink over to what had almost become his regular table, and he reflected on the fact that many of the locals appeared to have places they preferred to sit or stand. It wasn't a territorial thing, but it was very handy to be able to quickly glance around the room and see who was missing. Early Pete made his customary short visit, and there were a few tradesmen who appeared to be celebrating the end of their working week. He had been sitting for nearly half an hour when he heard someone asking if they may join him. It took him a while to recognise Chris from the field study centre. She was wearing a bright pink top and black slacks. She had obviously had her hair done, discarded her old hat, and even wore some discreet make-up. Gone were the familiar hiking boots, replaced by smart patent leather shoes with a slight heel.

Noticing his apparent confusion, she sat down and suggested, "Don't tell me; you didn't recognise me without my clothes on?"

"Not exactly what I was going to say but essentially correct. Is this some special occasion?"

"Not really, but I do like to put my civilian clothes on sometimes, and I had a meeting with Bricky this afternoon.

He was showing me one of the places he has in Barnard's Yard. It appears that someone gave backword on one of them, and he knew I was interested so, in a nutshell, I bought it. The paperwork will all have to be done officially and appropriate taxes paid. Bricky hates going through official channels because it takes forever and costs more, but he just has to grit his teeth and do it. In the meantime, he's letting me move in. It's a bit unusual, but we both trust each other, and all the monies will be sorted out later."

"Which cottage have you bought?"

"The one at the far end. I saw all of them and luckily, I preferred that one. It will be perfect for me. While I'm still working, it will be a short walk up to the centre, and when I retire, I will have a lovely cottage all set up exactly as I want it. I wish I'd done it years ago."

Alex was aware that some of the customers probably wouldn't recognise Chris and assume that he was bringing yet another woman to the pub, but he didn't care. Generating a bit of gossip was a public service, and anyway, he was having an enjoyable evening.

"A friend of mine lost her husband recently, and she is mad keen on moving here into the village after only one brief visit." Announced Alex before adding," I'm not sure if she's being a bit hasty. She's threatening to move away from an area she has lived in for over half a century."

"You made the decision to do much the same yourself when you moved here," she pointed out. "Do you regret the move?"

"No, but it was different in my case. I knew Kirksea when I came here on holiday as a child."

"And did you expect it to be the same after so many years?"

"No. I had expected it to have changed. A lot of my former colleagues warned me about the dangers of trying to chase a memory, but I wasn't naïve. I knew it would be different in some ways."

"But you chose to move here anyway, even when you didn't know what to expect? You made that leap of faith into what was, in effect, the unknown. It appears to me that your friend is prepared to make the same gamble."

"I never thought of it that way. Perhaps I should try to see things from her angle. If she wants to take the risk, then I guess I have no right to try and dissuade her. She may like it here, or she may regret it."

"In my experience, most of the things we come to regret in life are not necessarily what we did but rather what we didn't do."

As he strolled home that evening, Alex mulled over what Chris had said. He realised that, with the best intentions in the world, he was guilty of trying to make decisions for Ivy. He knew that she was currently under a lot of stress since Josh died, but was that an excuse, he chose to believe, for trying to run her life for her? While his and Megan's efforts were motivated by a genuine willingness to help, were they slightly patronizing? They claimed to want to support Ivy, but were they actually carrying her? The questions kept rolling out without any answers, but Alex felt grateful to Chris for getting him to see the situation from a different point of view, and he decided to discuss the matter when he phoned Megan the next day.

The following morning, as he stumbled out of bed, Alex was aware of a strange stillness around the village. Looking out of his bedroom, he could see that Kirksea appeared to be hiding under a thick layer of fog. Alex chuckled at the thought that it might be a good enough fog to warrant starting to knit one of the fishermen's jerseys that Old Bob told him about. Alex took his time over breakfast and then did some washing as he was determined not to ring Megan too early.

"Morning, darling. How are things in York?"

"Reasonably settled at the moment, Mum's in the garden doing a bit of pruning on the rose bushes. She says she wants to get the garden in order in case she might want to sell the house. She still seems set on moving. I've pointed out the dangers of moving to a new area, but she just soaks up my suggestions and responds with an inscrutable smile."

"I was talking to my friend Chris last night, and she got me thinking. We know we want what's best for Ivy, but can we be sure what is the best course of action, and do we have any right to try and dictate what she does with her life? My own conclusion is that we should try and encourage her to stop and think before jumping into anything, but if she still decides to go ahead with her reckless plans, then we make sure we are here to support her if it all goes wrong."

"I think you are right, love, but I have great misgivings about her moving to somewhere she doesn't even know."

"As Chris pointed out last night, I did much the same thing when I moved up here. Fond holiday memories are not a sufficient reason to move 250 miles north in the hope that it turns out to be what I want. I don't want to be seen as keen to move her, and nor do I want to be perceived as someone who stops her living her own dream."

"It's a valid point. She wants the move, and I know from past experience that when she sets her mind on something, she can be single-minded in her pursuit of it. Some might call it stubbornness, and I know that I've inherited some of those qualities."

"No. Not you, darling," he said with mock incredulity.

"Perhaps just a tiny bit," she said, giving a little laugh. "I think we have to wait and see how things pan out, but I guess we both agree that trying to fight her is in nobody's interest. I have to admit that I've found it difficult trying to argue about her going to Kirksea when I was so taken with it myself."

"Are you all packed and ready to go home tomorrow? I hope the fog has cleared for you by then."

"What fog? It's a lovely, crisp autumn day here; not a sign of fog. I'm ready to go and hope to set off early in the morning, around eight o'clock."

"I will give you a call before you set off just to check how things are going with Ivy."

The following morning, Alex woke early. He knew he had to make his phone call to Megan at an appropriate time before she set off back to London. She had declared that she would set off at about eight, so he calculated that he would need to ring just before seven. He made himself a cup of tea and read his copy of the local paper until he thought it was an appropriate time to ring Megan. Her phone seemed to be ringing for a long time before she eventually answered.

"Morning, darling," he announced in what he hoped was a cheery voice.

"Alex?" she replied in an apparently confused state.

"Where you expecting some other man to call and wish you bon voyage. I hope I haven't interrupted your preparations for the journey. I thought I'd better ring you early because I didn't want to miss you. How is Ivy this morning?"

"She's not up yet, but she was fine last night. We had a long conversation after what you'd said yesterday, and it seems we were right to assume that we mustn't appear to be bullying her. She was very reasonable, and she obviously appreciates that we are only trying to persuade her to take some time to thoroughly think through her decision about her future. I have to admit that some of her arguments were pretty hard to refute, and, as I pointed out before, if she does set her mind on it then she won't be easily put off."

Having wished her a safe journey and promised to keep in touch, Alex rang off. He had enjoyed his recent conversations with Megan, going over some of their shared memories, and he decided he must get back in touch with some other friends from the past. He went through a mental list of some of his former colleagues but recognised that, while he had enjoyed working with them, few of them were people that he would really want to keep in touch with. After some consideration, he decided that he really ought to reconnect with his friend Doug, who had been best man at his wedding. Yes, he must remember to contact Doug. He had made that resolution many times before and suspected that, once again, he would forget his good intentions.

His early start to the day meant that the morning seemed inordinately long. It being Sunday, he liked to go along to the Wellie for a pint at lunchtime, but the pub didn't open until noon. He busied himself doing some quite unnecessary domestic chores as Jean kept the house very clean. He did some washing and hung it up on a line he had strung across inside his new veranda and even found time to spend reading his most recent detective story. As usual, he quickly became frustrated by the fact that the storyline was hard to believe for him as someone who had served in the force, so he put the book down. He prepared a casserole for dinner and washed up the few items he had used before returning to his comfortable chair in the lounge. He remembered what life used to be like on Sunday mornings when he was a child. For many years, there was a routine where he and Val would be dressed up smartly, given a few pennies for the collection box and then sent off to Sunday school. This had seemed strange at the time as neither parent had any strong religious convictions, but sometime later, Alex realised that, for the sake of a few pennies, his parents had secured reliable child-minding facilities and ensured a quiet morning for themselves.

Eventually, he checked his watch and noted it was five to twelve. He put his coat on and sauntered off to the pub, only to find it was locked and still dark inside. Dave was usually punctual about opening times, even if closing times could be a bit flexible. After a few minutes standing around and frequently checking his watch, Alex was becoming a little concerned as to what might be delaying the opening, so he was relieved to see lights flickering on inside. After another couple of minutes waiting patiently, Alex knocked on the door. Eventually, he heard the ritualistic turning of the key and sliding back of the two large bolts on the door, and he saw Dave standing in front of him in the doorway.

"Morning, Dave. Having problems?"

"Problems?" queried the bemused landlord.

"Yes, you're a bit late opening up today."

"Late? You mean you're a bit early; it's only a quarter past eleven, and it's Sunday."

There was a moment of mutual confusion before Dave suddenly understood what was going on.

"Did someone forget to put their clocks back an hour last night, Wessie?"

"What kind of idiot would do that?" replied Alex as his oversight became apparent.

"Come in and take a seat now that you're here. I can't serve you until twelve, but you might as well wait in comfort. It's a good job we have an Early Pete in the pub, or you'd become Early Wessie."

Alex was pleased to have somewhere to sit and wait. He suddenly remembered his conversation with Megan that morning. No wonder she had initially sounded a bit confused; she was probably still in bed when he rang. The day hadn't started well. Alex was impressed at the way Dave and his wife went about their business of getting the pub ready for visitors. He knew from his days working at the rugby club that the landlord and landlady of a pub do not simply spend their time drinking and chatting to customers. The days are long and extend far beyond the limits of opening hours. Dave and Daureen worked incredibly hard in the pub so others could wander in and spend a few pleasant hours there, and few people appreciated it.

Alex had taken the opportunity to put his watch back an hour so he could watch as noon came and one or two customers came in. More than one of the new arrivals commented on the fact that Alex was early, and it was obvious that Dave took great delight in telling the newcomers about Alex's mistake, but he took it all in good heart. Being part of a community means opening up to others, and if that meant disclosing the odd failing, then so be it. He remembered his early days in the police when they enjoyed taking the micky out of each other. An outsider might have interpreted the general banter among the young officers as being cruel or insulting, but it wasn't. He had often observed that apparently disrespectful language among people who know each other can be indicative of real friendship, so the odd gentle taunt from friends was to be welcomed; it was a sign of belonging.

The pub hadn't been open long when Norman arrived, and having collected a drink, he came over to sit with Alex.

"Dave tells me you had a bit of trouble with your time-keeping today, Wessie," said the newcomer, who made no attempt to hide a wide grin. "Never mind, I reckon many of us have been caught out that way over the years."

"I wouldn't be surprised if my one tiny mistake made it to *News at Ten*. Dave certainly seems to be getting some mileage from it over there with Bricky. Let's hope some local reporter doesn't get it into next week's *Gazette*."

"That's a thought, but don't worry, I'm thinking of doing a bit about the local pet crematorium. My experience with old

Muffin has taken me into a whole new world I knew nothing about, and it will fill a few column inches if the editor wants it."

Alex had forgotten all about this snippet of conversation until a few days later when he was sitting in the pub in the evening, and Norman turned up with a small cardboard box, which he placed on the bar with the bizarre request, "A pint for me, please, Dave, and a whisky for Muffin."

The landlord looked confused for a while, but eventually he understood what was going on, and he pulled a pint and set it down on the bar next to a glass of whisky. Alex was intrigued and left his seat to join Norman at the bar, who explained, "I'm just going to take Muffin for a last walk," he said to Alex while nodding in the direction of the box.

"He liked to pop in here, so I thought I'd share a last drink with him before we have a wander down to the harbour. If you fancy a stroll down there, I'm sure Muffin would be pleased. Edna didn't fancy it; she's still a bit upset about it all."

"I would be honoured, Norman," replied Alex, and the two men finished their drinks before Norman picked up his precious box, and they left for the short walk down the harbour wall.

"Muffin loved it down here," reminisced Norman as they reached the outer end of the harbour. "When he was a puppy, we would bring him down at low tide, and he would race around like some mad thing on the flat sand. He never liked the sea for some reason and hated to get his feet wet. He was a scruffy little scrap of a thing with not an ounce of brain in his little head. As he grew up, he was always scruffy, and his brain remained in neutral all the time, but he was good company."

The two men stood for a while. The sea was calm, and inside the harbour there was barely a ripple on the surface of the water. It was as if the harbour itself was showing its own respect for the old dog. Norman reverently took a small container from the cardboard box and unscrewed the lid before gently pouring the contents into the harbour. Most of the ashes slipped down into the water, leaving only a faint dusting on the surface which, itself, eventually disappeared down in to the depths of the harbour.

"Goodbye, old lad," said Norman before carefully putting the jar back in the cardboard box and turning to walk back up to the village.

"The tide is on the turn now, so Muffin will soon be on his way out to sea, but at least he doesn't have to worry about getting his paws wet," declared Norman with just a trace of a smile.

Neither of the men felt like going back to the pub, so they walked on to their respective cottages.

CHAPTER NINETEEN

The following morning, Alex received a phone message from the company who were due to deliver his furniture for the veranda, indicating that the driver was on his rounds and due to arrive sometime between nine and midday. Alex resigned himself to the fact that he was housebound for the morning, so he decided he would use the time efficiently by cooking something a bit special for dinner. He raided his freezer and selected some rather nice-looking venison steaks. The packaging indicated that it was a meal for two, but he knew he would have no difficulty eating the entire contents himself, so he took them out to defrost. By eleven o'clock, he had prepared all the components of his meal and washed up all the utensils he had used. He decided to make himself a coffee as the delivery could arrive at any time. At half past four, he received a call from a confused delivery driver.

"Hello. Mr Lucas? It's Ronnie with your garden furniture. Sorry I'm a bit late. I had a bit of difficulty with the sat-nav. It took me to Kirkella for some daft reason, but I'm in Kirksea now and ready to deliver your order. Sorry if it's caused you any problems. I hate these bloody sat-navs. I was quite capable of getting lost without them."

"Where exactly are you now?" asked Alex, trying to hide his annoyance.

"I'm parked outside some kind of chapel, but the sign says it's a university."

Alex surmised that the wandering van driver was parked by the field study centre, and he gave instructions on how to get to the alleyway behind his cottage. It was a further 10 minutes before the van pulled up behind Alex's cottage, and he went out to open the back gate.

"Sorry about this, sir. My last drop was in Middlesbrough, and then I should have dropped in here, but the sat-nav took me to Kirkella. Apparently, there is a street in Kirkella with a similar name to yours. I know I'm a bit late."

Alex marvelled at the driver's understatement, but he looked so pathetic and had obviously had such an awful day that all Alex could say was, "So, you did Middlesbrough to Kirkella and then back here? That's almost a one-hundred-and-twenty-mile detour."

"It did seem a bit unusual as my next drop is in Whitby, but once something goes in the sat-nav, I just assume that the dispatch people know what they are doing. We prefer using addresses as much as possible, as postcodes alone can be confusing. I've learned that just one letter adrift in the area code can make a lot of difference. I once found myself heading to Dundee when I really wanted Derby."

"So, you went all the way to Dundee?"

"No. I'm not daft. When I got to Hawick, I knew there was a problem because our firm doesn't cover Scotland, so I turned back."

It was already starting to get dark by the time the furniture was unloaded, so Alex put it in the veranda for the night. He gave Ronnie a five-pound tip, not because of any professional skills he had displayed but out of sympathy. He had quickly ascertained that Ronnie had real problems with navigational technology and had serious doubts as to whether he would be able to find his way out of the village, but that was Ronnie's problem.

As Alex sat down to his venison steak dinner, it occurred to him that he had been waiting in for the delivery man for seven and a half hours, and he looked forward to receiving one of the routine surveys that would ask him how satisfied he had been with the service. The company would not be pleased to hear his evaluation.

The venison steaks were delicious, and Alex sat back in a self-congratulatory mood. He was toying with the idea of going down to the pub to see who was in when the phone rang, and he answered it.

"Hello, love," said a familiar voice, "I'm not interrupting anything, am I?"

Alex had to think for a moment to try and recognise the caller and then realised it was Ivy. She sounded quite like Megan on the phone. Ivy rarely spoke on the phone to him, and that's why it took him a while to place the voice.

"Hello, Ivy, there's nothing the matter, is there?"

"No, everything's fine, but I just wanted to let you know that I've planned myself a little holiday."

"Good for you. Where are you going?"

"I've booked into a hotel in Whitby."

"Whitby?" Asked Alex, trying to conceal the slight anxiety he felt. "When are you going?"

"This weekend. I'm arriving on Friday and coming home on Sunday, so I wondered if we might meet up on Saturday in Whitby?"

Alex was concerned that he might be being manoeuvred into something, so he didn't want to appear too enthusiastic.

"I'd love to Ivy. What are you doing about Mandy? Is she going back to the kennels for a couple of days?"

"No, Jessica has agreed to look after her. She's not going back to Mrs Howard's so-called Doggy Hotel after the last time."

"Why? Was she maltreated?"

"On the contrary, she obviously had the time of her life."

"So, what's the problem? Was she over-fed?"

"No, but Mrs Howard obviously knows nothing about dogs, and she let our Mandy 'play' with some of the other residents, so we now have a litter of pups to look forward to. The vet offered to terminate the pregnancy if I wanted, but I couldn't bring myself to let him do it. As a consequence of that, I will be busy with the puppies in early December so I thought I'd make the most of a quick break now."

"Puppies? Doesn't Mrs Howard know anything about the mating habits of dogs?"

"Not half as much as Mandy knows. We don't even know who the father is. It appears that she was 'playing' with a number of different dogs at different times during her stay, so we could end up with a complete pick-and-mix assortment. Shortly after she came home, I took her to the vets to have one of her regular jabs, and the vet pointed out the situation to me. I informed him what Mrs Howard told me about the other dogs being around, and he told me that, in view of Mandy's possible 'dalliances' with several dogs, she might produce puppies from any number of them in the same litter. It would appear that Mrs Howard had not been too diligent about obtaining any appropriate qualifications or a licence to run a kennel, and the vet says he will ensure that she won't continue to run the business until she sorts those little matters out. It's a shame because I know she wasn't doing it to make any great profit. She just loves dogs, and Mandy has always enjoyed her stays there."

"I'm not surprised if her last visit is anything to go by."

"She looks so happy, though. I can see her now just lying there in her basket, a picture of contentment. I know it's silly, and I know it will be hard work, but I'm actually looking forward to having the puppies around, even if it has screwed up my holiday plan."

"It sounds like your holiday plan isn't the only thing to have been screwed up. Have you told Megan about the forthcoming happy event yet?"

"I've just got off the phone from her. She was a little surprised, to say the least. I did offer her the pick of the litter, but she didn't jump at the offer. So many people I've met in the past have taken to Mandy and made comments about loving to have a puppy if we decided to breed from her, but I suppose it's different if you don't know exactly how the pups will turn out. I can't help trying to imagine what the outcome will be. Mandy is pure-bred red setter, but the genetic make-up of her puppies is a mystery at the moment, so it's anybody's guess what the little darlings will look like. Anyway, I can't stop here chatting all day; Mandy needs her dinner. I'm booked into the William Wouldhave Hotel. Give me a ring when you're sure you can meet me on Saturday. Must go now. Take care, love."

The phone went silent, and Alex sat for a moment, trying to assimilate what he had just heard, but he didn't have long to try and make sense of the whole thing when his phone rang again.

"Hello, darling," came a familiar voice, and this time it really was Megan. "I've just had Mum on the phone."

"Yes, I know. She's just informed me of her news."

"She told you about Mandy?"

"Yes, and about the holiday in Whitby. I'm still getting over the shock. She seems delighted about the prospect of Mandy's puppies, and I guess that will give her something positive to look forward to, but I don't know why she has decided to come to Whitby in November, and I'm worried about her announcing she's bought a place there or something."

"We both know what she's like, and we both know it's not our place to tell her how to run her life, but it's hard to stand on the sidelines and watch her doing something she might regret."

"Did she tell you she's invited me over to meet her on Saturday?"

"Not in so many words, but she did make some vague comment about how it might be possible for the two of you to meet up, and it's still quite obvious that she's set on moving. She has definitely been giving it a lot of thought, so she's not being quite as reckless as we might have feared. Her initial thought about moving was impulsive, but she has obviously weighed up the situation and still seems to favour a move."

"I'll get over to Whitby and see what she has to say because I suspect there is more to this visit than just to see the sights at the seaside."

The telephone conversation went on for some time. Alex liked to chat with Megan, and this was a better way to spend an hour than watching the television on his own. By the time he had finished washing up the few articles from his venison dinner, it was after half past eight. He momentarily toyed with the idea of nipping down to the Wellie, but he tended to be one of the early crowd in the pub, and he couldn't be sure if many of his regular acquaintances would still be in, so he made himself a cup of tea and went through to the lounge. The Gazette wasn't due until the following day, so he picked up the book he had started to read some weeks previously, but he couldn't raise any enthusiasm for that, so he just sat.

It was a dark October evening, and the weather had taken a turn for the worse. The rain was falling steadily, and he could hear it beating against the cottage window. He wondered how the original occupants would have occupied themselves on such an evening if the menfolk were unable to get to sea. Probably, they would have been mending their fishing gear. Alex couldn't see that as a meaningful way to spend his evenings as he didn't go in for a lot of fishing off the coast. Perhaps those jolly fishermen of the past would have hobbies making articles to sell to tourists? He had seen such items in the antique shops in Whitby, intriguing models of sailing vessels in whisky bottles. Alex examined such a potential hobby but conceded that, while he could open a bottle of whisky, and in time he could drink it, the model bit was quite beyond him. Once again, the question arose in his mind; was he bored, or was he lonely?

CHAPTER TWENTY

It was overcast on the following Saturday as Alex drove over to Whitby to meet up with Ivy. He had considered taking the bus but realised that it would place certain limits on the time he would be in the town. Also, because it was early November, he didn't anticipate any difficulty with parking, and this proved to be the case. He parked very near to the hotel and went in to find Ivy sitting in the lounge.

"Morning, love," she said as she got up to kiss him, "I bet you were a little surprised to hear from me during the week."

"A little, but a pleasant surprise, though. How is Mandy getting on now?"

"I know it's probably my imagination, but she appears to be wallowing in her new-found status. That isn't the main thing you want to know about; you want to know what I'm doing here in Whitby at the moment."

As usual, Ivy was not one for skirting around an issue, and she was certainly at an age when certain social niceties were not of prime importance. Alex knew that trying to be evasive was a waste of time with her, so he was open in his response.

"To be honest, Megan and I were wondering if you had come up to buy a place here. You seemed immovable in your determination to get over here."

"I can assure you that I haven't bought a place in Whitby, and I have no intention of doing so. I wanted to come over and see what the area was like, but more importantly, I thought it would be a nice place to talk some things over with you.

I know I can spend a lot of time on the phone to people, but it's not the same as a face-to-face discussion."

"I must agree that, paradoxically, the phone helps to bring people together, but it can also keep them apart. Like you, I prefer to be talking directly to someone. So, what exactly is it that you want to say?"

"As you know, Megan has been staying with me, and we've had lengthy chats, sometimes going on until the early hours, so I think she has come to understand my position as I do hers. I know that neither of you would presume to tell me what to do with my life. As Megan conceded, if either of the girls told her what she should do on such important issues, then her response would be brief and possibly profane."

"As would mine," conceded Alex.

"Precisely. I have given a lot of thought to moving. Even when Josh was around, we had talked about moving, but we sadly missed that chance. When I saw how you had settled so well into Kirksea, it made me appreciate that I am sitting there in York in a big house with very little contact with my neighbours. It's a beautiful city and offered plenty of things to see and do when we were younger, but when you are on your own, you can still do the tourist bit, but it's not so much fun."

"I know what you mean; you can be surrounded by crowds of people and still be lonely. But even in Kirksea, it is still possible to feel alone."

"I know you're right, but I was so taken by your village. I had to resist the temptation to try and buy a place there and then. I have thought it through now and looked at the idea very seriously to question my impetuous plans. I realise that I should ideally spend a long time thinking through the possibility of a move, but there is the inescapable fact that I'm now 74 and I'm not going to last forever. Josh and I should have moved 20 years ago but missed the opportunity, so I know I would always regret it if I didn't grasp the chance I have now. I do have one major reservation still, and that's why I wanted to talk to you."

"Reservation? You seem to have given a perfectly rational argument to support your plan to move, so what's the problem?"

"It's the fact that you live in Kirksea."

"But we've always got on well."

"It's not that I wouldn't want to live near you, but I don't want to be seen as interfering with your life. I don't have a good track record recently for keeping my nose out of family business. I know I've been trying to bring about some sort of reconciliation between you and Megan, and I know I've been less than subtle. I think we now all agree that we shouldn't try to tell other people how to run their lives. I know it could be awkward for the pair of you if I were in Kirksea and Megan came to stay with me from time to time."

"Don't worry yourself over that, Ivy. I certainly don't mind meeting up with Megan, and I hope she wouldn't be too annoyed to see me occasionally."

"Even so, I would rather forfeit the chance to move than be seen to be a nuisance. I would rather stay where I am than mess up your life or Megan's."

"Your presence in the village would not ruin my time there, and I'm sure Megan won't have any objections. You have obviously thought the whole thing through in far more detail than we might have expected, and if you want to go for it, then neither of us would stand in your way; we wouldn't dare."

"Thanks, love. Your understanding means a lot to me."

"So now we know how we stand, what do you plan to do?"

"The girls already know that I'm going to move somewhere, and I have talked about moving over here, but I will have to confirm that I intend to go ahead. I also have to tell Megan, and then I can make firmer plans."

"I must tell you love that properties in Kirksea are as rare as rocking horse droppings, so you could have a long wait."

"I know. I've been looking through sites on the internet, and there are very few along this coast at all. I wondered if you had any contacts in the village like that nice Mr Loftus."

"Mr Loftus? Oh, Bricky Gordon! You didn't waste any time getting insider knowledge when we left you in the Wellie, did you? I can mention it, but I know he just sold the last of three cottages he was renovating. That only came on the market because someone gave backword, and a friend of mine snapped it up. You have to be ready to push a deal through quickly."

"I can have my bags packed and ready to go in hours if needs be, and I don't necessarily need to sell my house first. We can discuss this further as we take a walk round Whitby if you're ready?"

"Raring to go! I love a stroll around Whitby, but what about your sciatica?" he said with a knowing grin.

"Sciatica?" She paused for a moment before explaining, "It's cleared up a treat; must be the sea air in these parts."

They both smiled and set out to explore the town. It might be argued that it wasn't the right sort of weather to walk around a seaside holiday resort. It was a slightly blustery day with a cold wind, but at least the rain was holding off. They walked out to the end of the West Pier, where they could now feel the full strength of the wind, and looked out at the sea. The water inside the harbour was deceptively calm and gave no indication of the power of the waves that they could now see were rolling in from the North Sea. Alex made a mental note that this was another day that a trip out in an open boat would not be an option for him.

The couple walked back towards the town centre and into the Lifeboat Museum. Alex couldn't recall how many times he had seen the exhibits, but they still fascinated him, and it was all new to Ivy. There was also the added bonus that they could shelter from the cold wind for a while before continuing their exploration of the town. They stopped for lunch in a pub near the swing bridge, and Ivy admitted that she was glad of the sit-down, having walked around most of the lower parts of the town.

"I'm on holiday, so this is my treat," declared Ivy. "So what would you like?"

"It has to be fish and chips for me, Ivy, thanks."

"Sounds good to me, and I'll have a small glass of white wine. Do you want a beer? Oh no, I forget; you're driving."

She thought for a moment and then, with a smile, added, "And I don't suppose you would take up the offer of spending the night with your ex-wife."

For a brief moment, Alex was baffled by this apparent non-sequitur but then remembered the embarrassing episode at Ivy's house after the funeral, and they both laughed.

Having finished their meals, they ordered coffees, and while they were waiting, Ivy stood up and holding her mobile phone, said, "I might as well give Megan a call now and tell her what we've been discussing. I'll just nip out and phone her."

"No need to bother going out. The room is empty apart from us, and I need to pop to the gents anyway."

As he left the room, he heard Ivy as she started to talk to her daughter in her usual cheery tone. He wanted to give Ivy time to speak to Megan alone so, after his brief visit to the gents, he wandered to the door of the pub and looked out over the water of the harbour. When he returned to the bar, as he expected, Ivy was still engrossed in her chat with Megan and it was obvious from the smiles and little laughs that the conversation was going well. Having seen Alex return, Ivy soon curtailed the conversation with a promise to ring again soon and explain things in greater detail.

"I gather that Megan wasn't too upset at your decision to move?"

"I'm pretty sure she was expecting it. We both know each other pretty well."

Alex couldn't help but feel a touch of jealousy about the way Megan and her mum shared some kind of bond. He knew that such feelings were not unusual, but he had never shared such links with his own parents, who had always appeared to be emotionally distant. They hadn't been uncaring but those special family links of love that many experience were not there. Even his sister Val had commented that she hadn't experienced any such connection, even with her mum. Once again, Alex was struck by the fact that he had always got on better with Ivy than his mother, so the thought of her living near him was not an unattractive one.

Alex and Ivy left the pub and continued along much the same route he had travelled recently, and he took her into the same shop selling jet where he had bought his own ring the previous month. Ivy was visibly impressed by the silver and jet rings and commented on the fact that he was wearing his and it looked very tasteful. Impulsively, Alex persuaded her to try on a ring, and when she said that she liked it, he bought it for her. At first, she had politely turned down his offer but put up little resistance when he insisted, so she kissed him and said thank you. As she walked out, she proudly wore her present, and he caught sight of her discreetly glancing at it from time to time as they carried on their tour. She showed that she was genuinely delighted, and Alex thought back to the days when he had given his own mother gifts. In retrospect, he knew that the tatty bits of models he had made at school had no great aesthetic qualities and even less monetary value, but when he had spent hours producing them, all he had ever heard was a comment of 'that's nice' before the precious model was consigned to some cupboard, never to be seen again. Even when he had saved for weeks from his pay for his paper round and bought her a bottle of perfume that he knew she liked, her response was less than effusive.

Alex had thoroughly enjoyed his time with Ivy, and when the time came to leave, he casually asked her what time she would be leaving the next day. She indicated that she would be catching a train in the late morning and changing at Middlesbrough before getting into York station in the afternoon, where she had arranged to be picked up by Jessica. Alex pondered the arrangements for a while and then suggested, "That means you will be travelling for hours. Why don't I pick you up in the morning and take you to Kirksea for a couple of hours before running you home? You might be able to have a chat with Bricky in the Wellie. He doesn't like to work on Sundays so he's usually there."

"That's very kind of you, Alex, but I can't possibly put you out like that."

"No problem! It's only an hour and a half's drive to your place. I could pick you up at eleven, we could have a saunter down to the Wellie for a couple of hours and still have you home before you would get home on the train. Give Jessica a ring and explain that she doesn't need to pick you up from the station, and that is non-negotiable."

He knew that Ivy would love another chance to look around his home village with the added possible bonus of talking to Bricky, and he wasn't surprised when she agreed. As they parted, he was aware that she was absolutely delighted at the way things had turned out on a day that she had initially expected could have been difficult. Alex was also pleased at how things had gone. He still had reservations about the speed at which she planned to move forward and suspected that Ivy had similar concerns, but if she was prepared to take that risk then he wasn't going to put any obstacles in her way.

CHAPTER TWENTY-ONE

When Alex arrived at Ivy's hotel the next morning, she was sitting in the foyer with her suitcase, obviously keen to make the most of her day in Kirksea. The couple drove over through heavy rain and eventually made their way to Alex's house, where they dried themselves after the walk from the car and had a cup of tea before it was time to walk down to the Whelk Pot. They were the first to arrive and Dave had only just unlocked the door.

"Morning, Wessie, morning, Ivy," he greeted them, "I see you've decided to wait until a reasonable time this Sunday. Now, what can I get you?"

"We'd like to book lunch, please, Dave, and, in the meantime, I'll have an orange juice, please, and what about you, Ivy?"

"After my partying last time, I think I'd better just have a tonic please."

"Is Bricky likely to be in today, Dave?" enquired Alex. "Ivy would like to have a chat with him."

"I'm surprised he's not here already. He's normally one of the first, but of course you beat him last week."

Alex felt obliged to explain to Ivy that he had been a bit early the week before because he had neglected to put his clocks back. They had been in the pub less than 10 minutes when Bricky turned up, and having picked up his pint, he came over to join them.

"Hello, Wessie, I gather you wanted to have a word with me."

"It was Ivy here; she's interested in moving in to the village and wondered if you knew of anywhere that might be available."

"Hello, Ivy, I remember now. You were here a while back chatting with Norman and Edna. Tell me, are you looking for a holiday place or permanent?"

"Oh, definitely permanent, or as permanent as any of us are. When I leave this place, it will be in a box, but not for a while, I hope."

"I'm very pleased to hear it. We need the holiday trade, of course, but it's nice to think someone wants to join our little community. That nice place adjoining Alex's is owned by Doctor Henderson and her husband who both work in hospitals in Leeds. They bought it six years ago as a holiday retreat, intending to spend a lot of time here, but in the last three years they've rarely been over apart from a couple of weeks in the summer and very rare weekends. They've become increasingly tied up with work and don't seem to have time to travel over. They don't want to rent it out, and they pay Slippers a few quid to keep an eye on it when they are not here. Some small coastal places are almost ghost towns in the winter, so we prefer to have permanent residents in our cottages. As Wessie will no doubt have told you, property in this area is hard to come by. A few years ago, you couldn't give cottages away, and there were a lot of pretty run-down properties, but recently a lot of the old places have been brought back to life as demand increased. I've done over a dozen and Slippers has worked on a few as well. The big companies don't want to get involved as it's difficult to get heavy machinery down here, and some of the restrictions put on certain properties means they can't easily convert them into the standard four-bedroomed detached where they can make a big profit. What kind of property would you like, ideally?"

"I like Alex's place. Down near the bottom of the village. I could get by with one bedroom but two would enable me to have the odd visitor. I suspect I want what everyone would want; a quaint former fisherman's house down on the harbour side."

"Places near the harbour are particularly rare and much sought after when they do become available. I managed to get three cottages a little further up the village, but they were snapped up. In fact, the last one sold very recently, and the new owner moves in tomorrow. She only secured it because she had the money ready when someone gave backward."

"I've got the funding ready to move in today," commented Ivy, "but I don't suppose it's as easy as that."

"Sadly, no. I can keep my eye out to see what comes up and let you know."

"What about the old building just up from here?" asked Alex. "The one with the tatty paintwork. I haven't seen any sign of anyone living there in the time I've been here."

"That's old Mrs Carson's place; number 30. She'd been living there most of her life. She stayed on after her husband died, but she found it hard to keep on top of the place. They had no children to help out. We rallied round to help, when she would allow it, but the place steadily got worse. She was fiercely independent and should really have been somewhere where she could have been cared for, but she refused to move. She died just over a year ago and all her belongings, including the house, eventually went to a distant niece down south."

"And isn't she interested in selling the house?" prompted Alex.

"She certainly is keen to get the money from it, and she put it on the market pretty quickly for a few months. It's been on and off the market with various estate agents since then."

"So why wasn't it sold immediately?" queried Ivy.

"Because the asking price was ludicrously high. I guess she'd heard about that sort of property selling well and made an estimate of its value based on the general prices in her area.

On top of that, she failed to take into account the condition of the place. It's not just a matter of flaking paintwork; the whole fabric of the place is rotten. The building needs stripping back to its basic structure and then starting again. It's not a case of sending a couple of guys in with paintbrushes. I became interested when I finished Barnard's Yard and was looking around for another project, and I gave it serious thought until I heard about the awkward owner and her unrealistic expectations about its value."

"So, it's a lost cause; Shame," observed Ivy.

"Nothing is beyond repair but in builder's terms this one would require the proverbial sharp intake of breath before calculating how expensive it would be."

"And what inflated price did this mysterious niece have in mind?" asked Alex.

"She started at 190,000 but dropped to 180 after a couple of months. Mrs Moser's son, Dezmond, who works at one of the estate agents who have it on their books at the moment, says they've not had any offers at all, and I'm not surprised."

"So, what would be a reasonable price for it if she was prepared to sell?" asked Ivy as she began to think through the issue.

"Difficult to say, because it's not like buying a plot of land and then working up from there. If the place is to be renovated, then a lot depends on the actual condition of the property and how much needs to be ripped out before you can start moving on to rebuilding. From what I've seen of comparable buildings in the village, like Barnard's Yard, I would have thought that the maximum she could expect to get for the place – despite the fact that it's one of the most desirable locations in the village – is 150,000, and I wouldn't rush to pay that."

"And what would it cost to bring it up to scratch?" asked Alex, pre-empting Ivy's response.

"Depends what level of build you want. A hundred and thirty thousand should see it done, but it always depends on what we find when we start ripping stuff out and what sort of finish you would want. It's all academic if the niece won't sell, though."

"But the place is a mess," added Alex. "It spoils the whole look of this part of the village. All the others in that row are very attractive, but number 30 looks almost derelict with weeds growing out of the guttering, and the tiny walled garden at the front is little more than a litter bin when some of our less welcome visitors turn up. It must drive the neighbours mad."

"It does. Even when Mrs Carson was living there, it was uncared for, but now it's just an eyesore. Mrs Moser lives in number 32 and her son, the estate agent, has tried to push the sale, but apparently the owner is having none of it. But she doesn't have to live alongside the mess. Early Pete said he would look in to it to see if anything could be done."

"Early Pete?" queried Alex.

"Yes, he works on the county council. He tells me that sorting out problems like number 30 are not strictly his department's responsibility, but when I said I might be interested in doing it up, he said he would have a chat with his colleagues at County Hall. He doesn't like walking past the place in its present state each time he comes down for a drink, so he's as keen as any of us to get it cleaned up."

"So, who is Early Pete?" asked Ivy, who was still getting used to the nicknames bandied about in the village.

"He's a regular at the pub," explained Bricky. "He visits most evening, stays for a pint and then leaves. I've no idea what he does at the council offices. He's a nice guy when you get to know him, but he tends to be quiet and keeps himself to himself. When he first turned up in his smart suit, some of the locals were a bit suspicious. Suits tend to be equated with officialdom, and we're not keen on officials poking their noses into our business affairs, but it turns out that it's just his working clothes. He says that he comes down to the village to keep his ear to the ground to ensure that the county council is working efficiently for the residents of Kirksea, but in reality, he just likes his evening pint. He has been a useful contact for me in the past when working with the planning department; a bit like a mole working in the council offices for me."

"And when do you think you might hear from this mysterious Early Pete?" asked Ivy as her interest in the vacant property grew.

"I only spoke to him recently when I had finished Barnard's Yard, but if you feel you might be interested in looking at the possibility more closely, I can have a word tomorrow; he tends to be in here most week nights. At the risk of sounding like a wet blanket, this is all very tentative and may amount to nothing."

"I know that, but I will say now that I am interested in the place and, as I said earlier, I'm fortunate to have the funds, even at the exorbitant asking price if necessary, and I would be pleased if you would take on the project if it goes through. What sort of timescale would you be thinking of?"

This time Bricky actually did take a long intake of breath before answering.

"There are so many variables. The sale, if it goes through, might take weeks, and when we did start work, it would depend on what we find needs doing. There's the matter of the weather; if we need to strip the roof, we could have delays if the elements are against us. All I can promise is that I would get the job done as quickly as possible, but it would be unkind to raise your hopes about it all being finished quickly, if we can obtain it at all."

"That seems reasonable. Please consider yourself hired and as I said the funding is not an issue. Obviously, I don't want to pay above the odds, but I must say that I'm keen to go ahead."

Having effectively finished their business, Alex and Ivy ate their meals which Dave had brought over and then spent a pleasant hour chatting with a number of the locals before Alex announced that they really ought to be getting on their way. As they walked back to Alex's cottage, he stopped for a moment with Ivy outside number 30. The building was certainly in need of a lot of attention. Ivy opened the dilapidated wooden gate and walked the few feet to the front door. In common with most of the doors in the village, there were no glass panels in it, so she moved to the window by the side and tried to peer in. The drab, worn curtains were partly drawn closed, and little could be seen of the room inside. She stood by the front door and looked out over the harbour.

"You do realise, don't you, love, that I've just committed to buying this broken-down shell of a building? I have no idea what it's like inside; I don't know the layout of the rooms or even how many bedrooms there are. God knows what is behind the place, but I'm delighted because of that."

At this point she swept her arm dramatically over the view to the harbour in front of what she hoped would one day be her home. Even on a rainy November afternoon, it looked good to her, so she could only dare to imagine what it would be like on a beautiful summer day once it had been renovated.

"I hope it works out for you," commented Alex. "With Bricky, you have a strong ally, and I've seen his work in my place and in Barnard's Yard; it's first class. Now come on, before we both get wet through."

CHAPTER TWENTY-TWO

Alex and Ivy both enjoyed the drive over to York, and he was pleased to note that she appeared to have given up on her futile attempts to get him back together with Megan. Jessica was waiting to meet her gran back from her mini-break and not entirely surprised to hear that she was hoping to purchase a cottage in Kirksea. The young woman seemed keen to learn as much as she could about the intended move and appeared to be in favour of the prospect. After an enjoyable couple of hours, Alex declined a second cup of tea and set off on his drive home. As he left the outskirts of York, he wondered how Megan would respond to the news of the cottage in Kirksea and assumed that Ivy would have been on the phone to her at that very moment. He knew that she would have her reservations about the haste of the move, but they both knew that Ivy had given a great deal of thought to the matter, and they respected her right to choose the course of her life. He was also convinced that Josh would have been delighted at the thought that she had chosen to make what appeared to be a radical decision and that she was making the most of her life.

As he drove into Kirksea, he was aware of a number of small fires and family firework displays in the newer houses at the top of the village. He had almost forgotten that it was November the fifth, but as he was locking up his car, the date was dramatically reinforced when the maroon went up down by the harbour to signal the start of the official display, which was run as part of a fundraising event for the lifeboats. He felt obliged to go down to the Whelk Pot, where he knew several events were going on to make money for what was regarded as a very good cause by the people of what had once been a thriving fishing community. He gladly bought some raffle tickets and waited around for the draw to be made. As Daureen drew out the tickets, there were cheers and occasional good-natured jeers as individuals collected their prizes. The pub was filled with people revelling in each other's company and, despite the fact that he'd had a very tiring day, Alex stayed on to the end. As he walked home, he reflected on the fact that he hadn't won a prize, but he didn't care; after all, he had 'won' the title of Knight of Saint Bodolv in the last draw, and he didn't want to appear greedy. The one other inescapable fact was that he had perhaps had slightly more to drink than usual, but he didn't have to work tomorrow, so he wasn't too concerned.

Apart from a feeling that he felt a bit slow to get started the following morning, he had no major ill effects after his evening of partying at the Wellie, but it was still a bit later than usual before he had finished breakfast and sauntered towards the shop. His journey was interrupted by the appearance of a removal van cautiously threading its way down the hill. He watched as it turned the sharp corner towards Barnard's Yard and almost held his breath as it achieved the manoeuvre with barely inches to spare at either side. He was reminded once again how the old part of the village had not developed with large lorries in mind, and he was very impressed by the skill and sheer nerve of any driver of a large vehicle who was prepared to take on the challenges it posed. It was obviously Chris moving in, and Alex reflected that, but for a couple of weeks, that could have been Ivy's place. She had missed that one, and he only hoped that she could get the property down by the harbour because he knew that she had set her heart on it.

Later in the day, Alex decided to treat himself to fish and chips. It was what could generally be classed as miserable weather, and he felt he deserved a bit of a treat. Anita was her usual cheery self.

"Good morning, handsome," she greeted him. "I hear you were out with yet another strange woman at the Wellie yesterday."

"That was no strange woman, that was my strange former mother-in-law. We're hoping she can move over here at some point."

"You want your former mother-in-law to live here? That is strange. One thing that's putting me off getting married is Tom's mother. I think she would be the archetypal mother-in-law. I get the distinct impression that everything I do just isn't good enough. She has even suggested in the past that I'm a bit flirtatious. I can't help it if my life is full of gorgeous men such as yourself."

"How could she possibly think that you were man-mad when you are simply fighting to get over your natural shyness? As regards my situation, I suppose it does sound unusual, but I always got on very well with my in-laws, and in any case, if Ivy really wants something, then it's foolish to get in her way."

"She'll be lucky to get anything here and the prices are ridiculous. If it weren't for my dad, Tom and I would never have been able to get our place on Main Street."

"We've told her not to get her hopes up, but she just loves the place."

"Are you sure she's not just keen to be near you? After all, she is merely an impressionable woman and knowing your reputation!"

"Once again, Anita, my sweet, I am impressed by your appreciation of my undoubted manly charms, but on this occasion, I feel Ivy finds Kirksea attractive for other reasons."

"While you are here, Wessie, is there any chance that you could put in a short shift today? We can manage, as it's likely to be a quiet day, but Laura had arranged to have today off after her involvement with the lifeboat fundraising last night, and Nora is not at her best. She is in, but the smell of frying fish can sometimes upset a stomach that is having some difficulty getting over the previous night's excesses. Nora and Kevin had a pretty heavy evening at the Wellie, and then she took him home for a nightcap. Apparently, the nightcap of choice was whisky, and it was a rather large nightcap."

"I feel her pain. Of course I can help out. It sounds as if she should stay well clear of food for a while, so send her home and I'll get my overall on. I did see her and Kevin for a while last night, but they seemed to disappear quite early. I guess the whisky was a greater attraction."

Anita and Alex exchanged knowing glances before she went through to the backroom where Nora was sitting quietly, and Anita persuaded her to go home. She didn't put up any resistance. The afternoon was indeed quiet, and Anita gave him an elementary lesson in frying fish. Following step-by-step instructions, he dipped a fillet of cod in the batter he had helped whisk and carefully lowered it into the hot oil. Then, following the guidelines from his new tutor, he timed the fish, turned it a couple of times and eventually lifted it from the oil with the slotted fish turner and placed it gently in to the warming cabinet with a sense of pride like that of a new father. He knew he was nowhere near the standard needed to keep a number of fish frying at once, but he had done it. It was his fish basking in the light of the warming cabinet. It was with this comforting sense of achievement that he walked home for a much-needed shower before heading to the Wellie.

He knew he was a bit late to the pub because he had caught a glimpse of Early Pete on his way home going up the village. Bricky was in the bar and he came over to see Alex.

"You've just missed Early Pete," explained Bricky, "but I've had a bit of a chat with him about number 30."

"Any luck with the council?"

"Nothing certain, but he has made one or two suggestions about possible ways we could move forward. Old Mrs Carson's niece faces being presented with a possible Empty Dwelling Management Order as it's been empty for over six months. I am reliably informed by Early Pete if the premises contravened the Environmental Protection Act, then the council might even consider a compulsory purchase order. These procedures are being considered, so at some point the niece will have to put a lot of work and money into the house to bring it up to a reasonable standard. It seriously weakens her bargaining strength, and I doubt she will want the fuss of having to pay out for repairs and the delay this would cause for a sale. I'm going up to explain the situation to the estate agent and point out that we have a potential cash buyer prepared to give her a reasonable amount straight away. If she has any sense at all, she will take the offer, but she's not shown much sense so far, given her obvious greed. We will see."

It was a couple of days later that Alex dropped in to the Wellie to discuss the contents of the *Gazette* with the landlord. Norman was usually there with his own slant on any contribution he had made to the current edition, and it could be an opportunity to discuss what was going on in the area with him. As expected, Norman was standing by the bar talking to Dave.

"I see you've got your edition straight off the press," commented Alex. "Anything of interest this week, or is it a week for Uncle Duncan or your Madame Estelle horoscopes?"

"Get behind me, ye doubters," declared Norman dramatically. "This week, I've had a real scoop. The ace reporter you see before you has come up with the inside story on the impending closure of The Prince in Wykethorpe. I have discovered that the brewery, Atkins and Dodd, have closed the pub temporarily but there's no plan to reopen it. Apparently, it's been up for sale in the trade paper. They've been trying to sell it for a while, but no one seems prepared to take it on. The county council are keen to preserve as many pubs as they can if they regard them as 'Assets of Community Value'. I haven't put it in my article, but the people of Wykethorpe don't seem too upset at the pub closing, largely because there's little sense of community up there. It's become another commuter town for workers in Middlesbrough. I got a nice little interview with some old chap in the town who wants to start a petition, but I saw little support for the idea, and I can see the site being bulldozed before Christmas."

"Nora at the chip shop was telling me about the rumours," declared Alex, "but they seem to be more than rumours now, so another pub bites the dust."

"Atkins and Dodd want to get out of brewing altogether," explained Dave. "They have aspirations to move into the leisure and entertainment industry. They sold the brewing side to a big company who still sell the famous 'Atkins and Dodd Yorkshire Ale' which we are obliged to sell, but it's brewed in London and tastes completely different. I've said before that the brewery have approached Daureen and me, so they've got plans for this place."

It was at this point that Bricky came into the bar and caught the end of the conversation about the closure of The Prince.

"So, they've eventually managed to close the place down," he commented. "It's been on the cards for years, but you might have thought that they would have wanted to keep it going; it's the only pub for miles. The Wellie is the nearest for the people of Wykethorpe. I've just been talking to Early Pete, and he says the council are keen to keep public amenities going, and I know they did what they could to keep the pub open, but there seemed little public interest in the issue. We were talking about another matter, and the council's general aim is to maintain the character of the area, which involves them being selective about what developments they allow. On a similar matter, could I have a quiet word with you, Wessie?"

Alex and his builder friend took their drinks over to a table away from the bar, and Bricky passed on the news about number 30.

"I went to see Dezmond at the estate agent's and pointed out that I knew the council were looking at the possibility of making a compulsory purchase of Mrs Carson's property. I may have given the impression that the procedure was about to start straight away, but Dezmond obviously knows the situation because the cottage is next to his mum's, and he realises that the property can't be just left to fall down. He seemed convinced that the vendor would be amenable to a lower offer as she was getting rather fed up with the thing dragging on and was keen to get her hands on the money. He rang her up there and then and explained the situation to her. We had an interesting three-way conversation with Dezmond relaying the messages between me and Mrs Carson's niece. To cut it short, she started with her 180,000 price, and I said that was impossible as the repairs to even make it habitable could be in excess of 130,000. I think she didn't fancy the idea of having to find that money before she could sell the property, so in the end, we settled on 120,000 for a quick sale, as I assured her that ours was a cash offer. It's a fair price, given the state of the cottage, and I'm sure Ivy would agree."

"I'm sure she will be ecstatic. I know that she would have been prepared to pay more, so thanks for your intervention. It will be all I can do to stop her from getting down here tomorrow with her old clothes on and ready to personally start the work. Are you sure that it will all go ahead?"

"I've signed to show our commitment, and Dezmond will do all the paperwork. It will take a while, but I am ready to get on with the work as soon as we get the green light. Obviously, I've had a lot of experience working with the local authority, and I'm well aware of the planning rules. All being well, I will submit plans that I know comply with all the local by-laws and building regulations and, because I know the council are keen to get that part of town cleaned up, it should go through on the nod. Let's hope so."

Alex didn't waste any time contacting Ivy to give her the news and, as he expected, she was keen to get over and see her new property. He did his best to explain that the deal was far from finalised, but she was obviously bubbling with excitement, and he could imagine her planning what she would do with number 30. He contacted Megan to let her know what the situation was with the property. She was obviously pleased with the fact that her mum was happy, but she still expressed some concerns at the speed at which Ivy was planning such a major move with what appeared to be very little thought.

CHAPTER TWENTY-THREE

The next morning, Alex woke to the sound of rain beating fiercely on his window, and he was pleased to note that he had no reason to go out in it. For a while, he lay in his bed revelling in that feeling of smugness, but after a while, he recognised that he had things to do or rather that he ought to be doing something. He took his time with his usual morning routines, periodically checking to see if the rain was easing off, but it wasn't. He thought that it was a good time to check if his veranda was standing up to the elements. He had stood for a while at this kitchen sink, watching the rain pounding on the veranda roof, so it seemed reasonable to check it inside. He waited until he felt the rain was slowing slightly and then quickly made his way down the steps into the yard and rushed into the veranda. It was perfectly dry, so Alex sat on one of the new garden chairs and watched the rain relentlessly splashing onto the yard, where it formed a shallow puddle before draining away down a grate in the corner. He sat there for some considerable time, partly because he was transfixed by the deluge but primarily because he didn't want to have to run the watery gauntlet of returning to the kitchen. Eventually, having fooled himself into thinking the rain was easing off, he made the soggy dash back inside.

As he stood in the kitchen, drying his hair on a small towel, he mused that this was not seaside holiday weather. There had been that occasion when the family tent had been hit by a deluge, but in general, his memories were of long, hot summer days. The truth was that both he and his sister had been determined to enjoy their time by the sea, so perhaps he saw it all with some sort of rose-tinted hindsight. He remembered the colleagues who had warned him about trying to revisit happy times, but they had been wrong; it was a cold morning in November, and the village was enduring atrocious weather, but he was happy to be there. For a while, he considered just staying in all day, but he needed some milk from the shop. He brought out his waterproof coat and his wellingtons and set off for the shop.

"Hello, Alex, I'm glad to see someone's braved the elements in this horrible weather," said Brian. "You're our first customer today, and I could do without a bad trading day after last night."

"Why, what happened last night?"

"Colin kept me awake all night; he's frightened of the thunder. We only had one little rumble, and that set him off. He just lay there listening to the rain and the wind, convinced that there would be more thunder. It was nearly four o'clock when I eventually got him to sleep. A fine strapping man like him, frightened by a little bit of rain."

"A lot of people are frightened by stormy weather; my younger daughter Jessica could never settle in a storm, and the merest suggestion of lightning would have her awake for hours until we could convince her the storm had passed."

"Colin is just the same. Cowering there under the duvet as if the house was going to collapse around our ears. He seems resigned to the fact that it's now just heavy rain, and he's catching up on his sleep. Lazy lump! It leaves me to do all the work, but I love him."

Alex was reluctant to leave the shop as the rain had not abated, but eventually, he put the milk he had bought into one of the large pockets on his waterproof jacket and went out to brave the elements. He reasoned that if he went home immediately, then he would not be tempted out again, so he headed straight for the Whelk Pot. When he arrived, he was not surprised to see that it was empty, apart from Old Bob and Norman. *What kind of idiot would turn out in weather like this?* he thought to himself. He laboriously took off his heavy waterproof jacket and hung it on one of the coat hooks by the door. Alex headed to the bar, but before Daureen could pull him a pint, he asked, "Could I possibly have a cup of coffee, please, love? I fancy something to warm me up a bit."

"Of course, Wessie. No problem."

While Daureen went into the kitchen to make his drink, Alex wandered over to sit by Norman and Old Bill, and he couldn't help wondering what fantastic stories about the local weather Bob was dreaming up now.

"Morning, gentlemen," announced Alex. "The weather is somewhat inclement today, but I'm sure that you've known it much worse in your day, Bob."

"Nay, lad," replied the old man. "I've known stormy weather with huge waves breaking right over this pub and receding to leave the bar full of codling. I've seen small boats from the harbour washed a mile up the beck by big seas, but this rain is something else. It's been raining heavily for nearly 24 hours, and it's showing no signs of stopping. It weakens for a few minutes now and then, but then it's monsoon-like again. The shipping forecast doesn't offer any hope, and even that lovely weather lady on the TV weather forecast is suggesting that this storm appears to have settled around here somewhere and no sooner does it move away than it turns back on itself, and we get another dose. It just can't make its bloody mind up; it's as if it comes in from the sea, swamps us and then goes out to sea to get some more water before bringing us another deluge. If this goes on for the length of time they are forecasting, then we would all have gills and webbed feet."

"It's strange weather indeed," added Norman. "We've had our fair share of storms over the years with huge seas breaking into the harbour, but this is just a constant downpour. Those people who dare to face the elements are scuttling around like drowned rats, but most of the villagers tend to just batten down the hatches and stay indoors. It will probably be dead in here tonight."

Having enjoyed his coffee, Alex was determined not to be beaten by a bit of rain, so he clambered into his waterproof coat, ventured out and set off in the direction of the harbour wall. The rain was still lashing down as he stood at the end of the wall, staring out at the sea, which was remarkably calm. There was a slight swell but not the raging tempest he might have expected in such a rainstorm, and he reflected on the intriguing complexities of the British climate. He wondered what his former colleagues would have thought of him, standing there in torrential November rain. They would probably have felt their warnings about his retirement were justified, but they would be wrong. He had never expected life in Kirksea would be a bed of roses, but standing there in torrential rain was infinitely more bearable than his daily commute into central London. He stood for a few minutes, as if to make some point, before wandering back home.

The rain continued for three days, with only short periods when it slackened off, and Alex spent pretty much all his time at home. He had hoped that his services might be required to cover his usual Friday lunchtime shift at the chip shop, but Anita had informed him that few people were prepared to go out to collect their usual meal in this weather.

He had a phone call from Ivy enquiring about any news on the property, but he'd had to tell her that he knew nothing further as he had not met up with anyone. It had become clear to him over the past few days how important the pub was as a place where locals could keep up with what was going on in the village, and without it, there was a sense of social fragmentation. Ivy had been a little disappointed, but she was happy to report that Mandy's pregnancy was going well, and the vet confirmed a date for the birth as being in the first week of December. Alex made use of his enforced stay indoors by making a series of phone calls to Megan and the girls just to keep everyone informed about what was happening in Kirksea. He was relieved when he awoke on Sunday morning to see that the rain had stopped and it was a bright, sunny morning, so he decided to get down to the pub at lunchtime to get up to date with the goings-on in the village.

It was shortly after noon when Alex arrived at the pub, and yet it was already quite busy. It was apparent that, after three days of being cooped up in their respective homes, many of the locals were determined to get out and socialize. Most of the regulars were there, but there were a number of people that Alex had never seen in the Wellie before. At first, he was a bit surprised but then realised that the pub was the obvious place to meet up. He bought himself a drink and wandered over to sit near Bricky.

"Afternoon, Bricky. You will not be surprised to hear that Ivy has been pestering me about when she can move in. I've told her that I will keep her informed."

"It's a good job we hadn't started in the weather we've just had," commented Bricky. "It would have been difficult sorting out the roof and any of the external structure. I've had some positive news from the estate agents. Young Dez tells me that the vendor has formally accepted the offer, and as soon as the contracts are signed and money is transferred, we can think about starting the renovation. We can't start until the conveyancing has been completed. As I don't see any need to alter the basic structure of the house, we shouldn't need any complex planning permission and, as I said before, I know all the current building regulations and the local development guidelines, so we should be able to crack on."

"That's faster than I'd expected. Ivy will be delighted."

"You will know from your own experiences that a lot of such sales are complicated by various chains of people who all need to synchronize at the same time, but we don't have that, and we have a cash buyer, which is a bonus. On top of that, we have to realise that Ivy has, in reality, bought the building 'as seen', so we won't be applying for an independent valuation. The only thing that is holding us up is the official conveyancing."

"And how long will that take?"

"There is a theory that it can be completed in as little as four weeks, but that is exceptional. A lot depends on whether any complications turn up on the searches. It has to be clear who owns the property and whether there are any restrictive covenants which might affect what the purchaser can do with it. I know I can rely on my solicitor to move on it as quickly as possible, and I think the vendor will be pressing to get her money quickly, but it can't be done overnight. In the meantime, Dez is going to see when he can give me a key so I can fully inspect the building. Perhaps Ivy would like to join us then?"

"I think she could be tempted to come over. As soon as you know when it's convenient, I will pick her up. Let me know when you want the purchase price transferred, and keep us informed about when and how you would like further money as the building work progresses."

Alex was delighted at the way things appeared to be moving rapidly on the sale, and Ivy was prepared to get on the next train to Whitby, but he convinced her that he would pick her up as soon as he'd heard from Bricky. Fortunately, neither of them had to wait long for news and on the Tuesday morning,

Alex found himself picking up Ivy from York and taking her to meet Bricky outside number 30. The builder gave the key to Ivy, and she stood for a moment and smiled broadly before going through the gate and placing the key in the door. She paused and looked back at the two men before turning the key and tentatively opening the door. Alex noticed that the room was relatively dark, so he instinctively went to switch on the light, but nothing happened, so he moved over to the window and drew the curtains back. The room was still laid out largely as the old lady had left it, with a few pieces of furniture directed towards a small television still standing in the corner. The rest of the house had a similar appearance of being recently vacated. The kitchen table was still adorned by a half-empty bottle of brown sauce, and the small bathroom had a selection of cheap toiletry products and a single toothbrush in a plastic beaker. It was apparent that the old lady's niece had quickly taken anything she thought might be of value and just left the rest for someone else to clean up.

While Alex and Ivy wandered around the house checking out the rooms, Bricky was casting his professional eye over the property. He poked at woodwork, took readings of the moisture content in various places and peered into every corner with the help of a powerful torch. All this time, he said nothing, so in the end, Alex had to ask, "What do you think, Bricky? How bad is it?"

"After a brief look at the place, I noticed there's some damp in the master bedroom, probably due to some blockage in the guttering. The back wall in the kitchen under the sink is also showing patches of damp. The roof needs checking over as there is some sign of movement, and in all probability, by the time you've sorted out bits of it, you might find you need to replace the whole roof. The stairs need replacing because there are signs of rot in the wood, but they are too steep anyway, so they would have to be repositioned. The window frames are pretty much falling to bits. The whole place needs rewiring, and it would make sense to put in an efficient central heating system."

"That doesn't sound too good," commented Ivy. "Do you think that you could do all that?"

"Compared to some of the places I've done up in the past in the village, this place is a palace," explained the builder. "The main thing is that the structure is essentially sound, and it can all be done. These places were built to stand up to hard wear. The torrential rain over the last week does not appear to have broken through anywhere. I can leave the layout as it is but perhaps add a small cloakroom under the stairs, and the third bedroom in the loft area needs to be properly finished off. If you wanted to make any major alterations, you might need planning permission. Just think it over and let me know what you want to do."

"I haven't moved house in years," commented Ivy, "but I remember it took months, so although I would love to move in tomorrow, I recognise that I will have a considerable wait, but that gives me time to plan exactly what I want doing to the place."

"I'm glad you're being realistic," observed Bricky. "It would be tempting to start work on the place tomorrow, but if the sale didn't go through then all we would have achieved would be to make improvements to a house we didn't own. When you have some idea what you want in the property, I will be more than willing to discuss it with you and get some formal plans made up."

"I realise that it's impossible to be precise," said Alex, "but when do you think the job might be finished, Bricky?"

"As you suggest, stating an exact date is out of the question. If we assume a six-week period to get the sale tied up, that would bring us to nigh on Christmas. The building work should take about four weeks, as long as we don't come across anything major that needs to be done, so that gives a very tentative finish date of around the end of January. If the conveyancing breaks local records and comes in at four weeks, then the building work could start before Christmas, but the holidays will delay things anyway. Think about moving in sometime in early February, and you shouldn't be far off."

Ivy was obviously pleased and a little excited to have had the opportunity to look around what she hoped would be her new home, and as Alex drove her back to York that evening, her conversation was largely about her plans for the cottage. It was certainly a topic that would keep her occupied for some weeks, and he was pleased to see that she had something positive to look forward to in her life. He had hoped to drop Ivy off and not to stay too long before getting back to Kirksea, but she insisted on him having a cup of tea and a bit of a rest before driving back. It was nice to see Jessica, who had, once again, been looking after Mandy for the day. Alex listened as Ivy excitedly described her cottage to her granddaughter, and he couldn't help feeling that the property she was describing was hardly the run-down shell of a place that he had seen.

Before he was allowed to go, he had to have a lengthy account of how well the vet had reported on the way Mandy was progressing. The dog was obviously pregnant by this stage, and Alex couldn't help but wonder how many puppies that bulge was enclosing and what sort of form they might take when they emerged. Mandy just looked supremely content, and in another three weeks the product of her happy holiday adventures would become apparent, and he wondered just how Ivy would cope with the event.

CHAPTER TWENTY-FOUR

Alex looked forward to Wednesdays and his visit to the Whelk Pot to check over Norman's contribution to the *Gazette*. There was really no need to meet at the pub to check the contents of the local paper because he knew it would be delivered to his cottage sometime during the day, but it was good to get the news directly from Norman. It had become a little tradition to meet up over a pint and find out what Norman alleged might be going on in the area. It had obviously been a slow week for news, and the editor had drawn on some of Norman's 'fillers'. Uncle Duncan's services had been called into action, and Madame Estelle filled another column.

Alex stood at the bar with Norman while Dave pulled a couple of pints.

"Check out the letters page," urged Norman. "Notice the approbation my work has elicited from one of my readers."

Dave quickly scanned the letters page before reading out some of the subjects covered in them.

"*The recent rains have made local football pitches unplayable.* Was the weather all your fault, Norman?"

"Not that one, Dave."

"*The amount of seagull droppings is an increasing problem?*"

"No; below that."

"I'm sure I wouldn't want to get below a seagull dropping problem," quipped Alex.

"You're both being deliberately obtuse," protested Norman. "Let me read it for you.

Dear sir,

I felt obliged to write and congratulate Madame Estelle on her most informative horoscope column. I have eagerly awaited her guidance each week and her forecasts are uncannily accurate. I am a Leo and last week she suggested that I should expect to receive some sound advice from a friend. That very night my neighbour said we ought to go to the Bingo so I went and my friend won the jackpot. My friend bought me fish and chips on the way home. I would have missed that treat if I'd ignored my friend's suggestion. Thank you Madame Estelle."

"Spooky!" commented Alex. "It must be a great source of satisfaction to know how much your work is valued by members of your readership. If you keep this up, you'll be appointed as Astrologer Royal."

"Thank you for your sincere appreciation of my worth, Wessie. I did, indeed, consider applying for membership of the Society of Astrologers. It was established in about 1647, so it certainly has some history to it. Unfortunately, it fizzled out in 1684 because it failed in its attempts to convince the scientific world of its veracity. There were some very sceptical people in those days."

"Never mind, Norman," said Dave. "We appreciate the diligent way you go about your work and value the contribution you make to the world of journalism. It's a pity that it's never the little man who gets the big prizes for journalism, or your trophy cabinet would be full of them."

"I fear we may be straying into the dark area of sarcasm, Dave, but I console myself with the fact that, deep down, you appreciate my efforts. I also contributed to the research on the closure of The Prince on page two. It doesn't make happy reading; the number of pubs closing is frightening. In order to get the local angle on it, I interviewed a representative of the local council. In reality, I had a chat with Early Pete, and he assured me that most local councils are very sensitive to the issue of the lack of social amenities in rural areas in particular."

"Yes," added Alex. "I was chatting with Bricky, who'd been talking to Pete, and he said the same thing, but if people are prepared to sit back and let the amenities be sold off, then the council eventually have to let plans to sell these places go through."

"The brewery haven't approached Daureen and me for a while," said Dave. "But I know they would love to liquidate this particular asset. The local rep from the brewery has told us as much."

The group fell silent for a while, even at the vaguest hint that the Wellie could join the legions of abandoned, boarded-up, or converted pubs that could be seen in so many parts of the country. Alex remembered the numerous TV programmes showing people who wanted to move out of the big cities into the countryside, and in so many cases the couples dreamed of having a traditional local village pub. Many people who made the move to the villages would be disappointed as their dream pubs were frequently converted to houses or torn down so that the site, including car park, could be replaced by half a dozen 'almost detached' houses. For many people in Kirksea, the Whelk Pot was their place to meet up. There was no designated community centre or large sports hall. Even the chapel had been sold off to the university for its outdoor activity centre, so where else could the villagers meet up? It was a depressing prospect.

The silence was broken by Norman, who asked, "How's Ivy getting on at the moment, Wessie? I gather she was over here yesterday looking at old Mrs Carson's place."

"She's doing remarkably well now, thanks. Of course, she still misses her husband, but the prospect of moving in here has given her something to plan for and look forward to. It also has the added benefit of taking her mind off trying to get Megan and me back together. She's looking forward to her dog having puppies after some promiscuous liaisons with one or more partners at the boarding kennels. I don't think she has any idea of the work they will cause, but it will give her something else to occupy her time."

"Edna and I still miss Muffin. It's daft, but in a certain light, there's a shadow cast across our kitchen floor, and at different times, both of us have stepped over it thinking it was the dog. He had a habit of just sprawling out on the floor, and he never had the sense to move if anyone approached. He assumed it was our job to avoid him. The great lump, but we still miss him. We've still got his feeding and water bowls and his collar. We'll get rid of them sometime."

Over the next few weeks, Ivy was in frequent contact with Alex as she attempted to find out what was going on with her cottage in the village, and he, in turn, kept Megan informed about how well Ivy appeared to be getting on. It was in early December that, in one of his regular chats with Megan, he learned that she was going to stay with her mum for a few days so as to be available when the puppies were due, and she was with her mum when Alex had a message from Bricky that the conveyancing process appeared to be progressing remarkably quickly. He suggested that it would be a good idea to meet up with Ivy to make more precise plans as to how exactly she would like the cottage fitted out. She had already decided about the room layouts, and Bricky knew how he would proceed, but the choice of finishing touches had yet to be finalised. Bricky suggested that Ivy met with him on site to discuss the details of the finish. Ivy was delighted at the prospect of visiting her cottage again, and it was decided that they should make the visit as soon as possible. Alex was a bit surprised when Ivy asked if he would mind if Megan accompanied her. Perhaps she had become aware that pressurizing him into getting them back together had been misplaced? He rang Megan to finalise the plans for the visit.

"Hello, darling. I've just had a novel request from your mum to ask if I minded you coming over with her to look at her new place. Of course, you are more than welcome, and I'm sure she will benefit from having someone to bounce ideas off. It just seemed an odd request after all her failed match-making ideas."

"Yes, I know what you mean. She hasn't mentioned us getting back together for weeks. I came up to be available when the puppies arrive. The vet seems to think it could be later this week or early next week."

"That will give her something to occupy her while the building work is being done. How are things with you and work?"

"I'm in the process of selling my share of the business to Fatima. Having seen how you appear to be thriving among the masses of the unemployed, I thought I'd give it a try. The paperwork is all with our accountants and solicitors, but in effect, I'm now on holiday, which will turn into retirement when all the paperwork is sorted."

"Good for you, love! I'm sure you will cope admirably with your new role. Welcome to my gang."

"I've already managed one decisive action. I've sold my car. It was linked to the company, and I could have kept it for a token amount, but I just didn't want it. As you know, I'm not an enthusiastic driver, and the drive up from London to see Mum was becoming more and more of a chore. There is a straightforward rail link to York, so I opted for that. I feel more relaxed than I have been in years."

"I'm very pleased for you. Who will look after Mandy while you're over here with Ivy?"

"Jessica has stepped up again, bless her. Ivy and I can catch the train to Whitby if you could possibly pick us up from there?"

"No need for you to bother with the train; it's quicker for me to pick you up. I can collect you at about 10.00, and then you will have plenty of time to look around the cottage with Mum before I get you back to York in the late afternoon."

"That's very kind of you, Alex, but you must let me treat you to lunch in that nice pub of yours."

After a lengthy conversation with Megan, he hung up and reflected, yet again, on how he always enjoyed speaking with her. He considered it to be quite natural, as they had spent so much time together, but he suspected that few divorced couples got on quite so well.

Later that week, Alex walked the short distance to where his car was parked. He had deliberately left himself plenty of time to scrape the frost from the windows before giving the engine a liberal spraying with Julie's wonder aerosol. The car was still a little reluctant to spark into life, but eventually he got it started and set off across the moors. It took a while for the heater to make the interior more comfortable, and then he travelled on in his cocoon of warmth as he passed through the frost-encrusted landscape. He had come to enjoy his drive through to York; whatever the season or weather, the views always impressed him. He couldn't resist a feeling of smug satisfaction as he calculated that, at that very moment in London, hordes of commuters would be facing the daily battle of getting to work through congested, polluted streets.

He was not surprised to see that Ivy and Megan were ready for him when he arrived, and after the mandatory cup of tea, they set off towards Kirksea. It was still very cold, and the weak sun had done little to dispel the frost that continued to embellish the landscape.

"Isn't it beautiful?" asked Ivy, glancing at the countryside. "Josh and I travelled this way a lot, as I said before, but we never came over this way in the winter time."

"I guess it would be pretty cold parked up in these parts in a Morris Thousand Traveller," commented Alex as he shared a sidewards glance with Ivy. They both smiled, and he drove on.

When they arrived in Kirksea, they wasted no time in making their way to the Whelk Pot, where Bricky was waiting for them. Having ordered lunches for later that afternoon, Alex, Megan and Ivy took their drinks over to where Bricky had been sitting and where he had left a number of letters and his little shabby notebook.

"I'm glad you could get here. The weather isn't ideal for travelling," commented Bricky, "but I thought it was a good time to share our ideas. I've had these letters from the vendors and the solicitors, so we are set to go ahead. We might be able to get some of the basic work started before Christmas, so I need to be sure of exactly what you want. It may sound daft, but I've had clients in the past who have approached me halfway through a job and asked me to change something completely. I shan't mention names, but I was working on one of the local cottages, and the owner decided she wanted a bath rather than a shower. It meant completely redesigning the upstairs, taking down a stud wall that my guys had put in, and then relocating it to accommodate the bath. The customer was paying for the extra work, but it completely screwed up my planning, and other jobs had to be put on hold. I don't like to disappoint clients by delaying the start or completion of their work. Little problems are unavoidable, but it's best that we all know what's going on."

"Makes sense to me, Bricky," agreed Ivy. "I found our last chat when we visited number 30 very useful. I find it easier to envisage things when I'm on site, but I would appreciate some guidance as to what may be possible, or otherwise, in the cottage."

"Fair enough. When we've finished our drinks, we can get straight down there. It gets dark pretty early, and there is still no electricity in the place, but these may help," said Bricky, pointing to two large torches.

"I thought it might be a good idea if Megan went round with her mum," suggested Alex. "I will stay here and wait for you to check the place out. The cottage would be a bit crowded with us all traipsing around."

The arrangements were agreed, and after putting all the documentation into a battered document case, Bricky picked up his trusty little notebook, and the trio set off on the short walk to number 30.

Alex sat for a while in the pub. His pint was enjoyable, but he knew he could not sit there drinking all afternoon as he had to drive his guests back to York, and he reflected on the fact that a pint often tastes particularly good when a second one is out of the question. As a young police officer, he had seen the tragic results of drink-driving, so he had never been tempted to have 'one for the road'. The pub was strangely quiet, so he decided to have a walk down to the end of the harbour wall, where he saw the familiar figure of Helen, who was attempting to do some sketching. She was perched on her little collapsible stool and muffled up in a large, padded jacket in an attempt to keep herself warm.

"Hi Helen, how's the sketching going?"

"Bloody awful! I'm wearing most of my wardrobe under this jacket, and I'm still freezing. I've got these fingerless gloves so I can feel my hands for drawing, but I can hardly feel my arms. Artists who go out in all elements must be made of sterner stuff than me. And look at the results; an uncoordinated chimpanzee could get a better likeness."

Alex looked at the proffered drawing and couldn't help feeling that it was a thousand times better than anything he could have produced in the most clement weather, but he restricted his comment to, "Perhaps you need a break?"

"I need a week to thaw out. I think I'll call it quits for the day and call in at the Wellie to warm up. I still enjoy a sneaky drink in the early afternoon when I consider that, many years ago, I would have been working at that time; it's almost an act of truancy."

"I've just come from there, but I came out to bravely stand up to the elements; it's a lot colder out here than I'd expected, so I think I may join you if that's OK?"

As they arrived at the pub, Alex pointed out the property which Ivy was buying, but they did not stand out in the bitter cold admiring it for long. Once inside, Alex bought himself an orange juice and a red wine for Helen.

"I've drawn the block of cottages that contains old Mrs Carson's place a number of times over the years," declared Helen. "But latterly, I've had to be a bit creative in my drawings because her place did spoil the appearance of the shot. I'll be pleased to see it brought up to the standard it deserves, and then I can draw it again, perhaps with a traffic cone outside?"

Ignoring the ill-concealed reference to his past, Alex just smiled and said, "I'll be pleased when it's all settled as well. Ivy is another refugee from the big city, just as we are."

The two of them chatted together for a while, and Alex started to become a little concerned that Megan and Ivy appeared to be taking a long time to look around the cottage, and the lunch he had ordered was due shortly.

Eventually, his visitors turned up, and he introduced them to Helen, who had to excuse herself as she was intent upon getting back to her cottage and making something of the sketch she had done on the harbour wall.

"I hadn't realised how cold it would be in the cottage," commented Megan, "but the place hasn't had any heating in it for years, and it's is far from draught-proof."

"We can get that sorted out for you," explained Bricky. "Those cottages were designed to fight off the elements, and by the time we've put in new windows and doors and some quality insulation, you'll soon be able to keep the place snug."

"You seem to have been a long time in there," commented Alex. "Did you find a lot of extra problems?"

"Nothing more than I expected," replied Bricky. "It took us quite a while because Ivy was clear about what she wanted, and I was able to get a lot more details of the proposed development than I get from some clients, and it's now in my little book along with more precise measurements. There's still bound to be issues we aren't clear on as we go on, but I can phone Ivy for clarification on minor points as we progress."

"It will look absolutely lovely when it's done, and the views over the harbour are wonderful, even on a day such as this," observed Megan. "I must admit that I'm quite envious, so if Mum changes her mind, then I'll take up the offer, Bricky."

"No chance," declared Ivy. "Go and find your own little bit of heaven."

Their discussion was interrupted by the arrival of their lunches. Alex hadn't realised how hungry he was, but then he recognised that he hadn't eaten since his early breakfast. The three of them enjoyed their meals and then stayed in the pub for a while, chatting with a few of the locals. It was a most enjoyable afternoon, Megan and Ivy enjoyed a few glasses of wine, but Alex stuck with his soft drinks. He was pleased to see how much his guests were enjoying themselves and was reluctant to call an end to the visit, but eventually he had to suggest that they should think about leaving.

CHAPTER TWENTY-FIVE

It was already starting to get dark as they left the pub, and the group set off for Alex's cottage. He had bought a small present for Jessica's birthday, which he had intended to take on his visit to Ivy's that morning. The present was still standing on the kitchen table where he had left it, so he gave it to Megan to pass on to their daughter. This small detour to Alex's place gave him an opportunity to show Megan his new garden furniture and to insist that his guests had a sandwich before they set off back to York. The truth was that he enjoyed their company and was reluctant to bring the visit to a close. They chatted about Ivy's plans for her cottage and Mandy's imminent puppies and before they realised, it was after eight o'clock. Reluctantly, Alex announced that they would have to be getting on their way, so they put on their coats and set off on the short walk to his car. It was bitterly cold by now, but it didn't stop Ivy from enthusing about the village houses and how beautiful they looked in the moonlight.

The car windows were covered in a thick layer of ice, and having encouraged his guests to get inside, he laboriously scraped the ice off. Then, in what he hoped would be seen as a purposeful, manly way, he took his magic aerosol, opened the bonnet and sprayed the engine. He then put the bonnet down and got in the car. He glanced and smiled at Ivy as he turned the ignition key, and then nothing. The engine gave no pretence of wanting to start.

"Perhaps you've flooded it?" suggested Ivy, who remembered that it was a phrase Josh used to offer when the car refused to start for her.

Alex picked up his can of aerosol spray, shook it vigorously, and gave the engine compartment a generous coating before quickly getting back in the car and turning the key again. The response was exactly the same as his first attempt. The car's inhabitants sat in silence for a while as the seriousness of their situation sank in.

"I'll have to contact the motoring agency," declared Alex, "and see how long they will take to get over here."

"But even if they can get you going, it would be a bit reckless driving over the moors to York tonight in a car that might let you down again," suggested Megan. "Mum and I can get a taxi to Middlesbrough and catch a train there."

"I'm sorry, love, but hailing a cab out here is not like London, and even if you got one, you could be waiting in Middlesbrough for ages and not get back into York before the early hours. By the time you got a taxi to your place, it would be time for breakfast. The sensible thing to do would be for the pair of you to stay over at my place, and then we can sort out transport in the morning."

"That's an interesting variation on the '*I've run out of petrol*' ploy; even Josh never resorted to that one."

Ivy's attempt at levity was wasted on Alex, who was already trying to figure out how best to cope with having two unexpected house guests. Megan saw that his plan was the best in the circumstances, and so the trio set off back for Alex's cottage. Ivy quickly contacted Jessica to update her on the situation and was glad to hear that she could stay overnight to look after Mandy. Fortunately, there was no news of any puppies, and Mandy seemed to be calm and unlikely to produce in the immediate future. Over a cup of tea, Alex outlined the emergency domestic arrangements.

"You can have the spare bedroom, Ivy, and Megan can have my room," he explained, giving Ivy a look that indicated that he did not want any suggestions about Megan sharing with him. "Jean has just washed all the bedding, bless her, so you should be OK. I've got a couple of pairs of pyjamas you can use. I only bought them for any time I was staying away in a hotel."

"In case the fire alarm went off during the night," added Megan, who knew her former husband's routine for going away.

"Exactly," continued Alex. "And I can sleep in my lounger chair. I never have any difficulty sleeping on it during the day, so I should sleep well on it tonight with my spare duvet. I've turned the central heating thermostat up, so we should all be warm enough."

"It's been rather an eventful day," commented Ivy. "So, if you don't mind, I will get off to bed now."

Alex was pleased that she hadn't added any rider to suggest that she was leaving the 'young couple' on their own. He showed Ivy to her room and found a pair of pyjamas for her. They both laughed as she held the trousers in front of her; they would certainly be a 'comfortable' fit. When he went back down to Megan, she was engrossed in something on her mobile. He was impressed to see that she was using it to search for transport details to get to York. He had never managed to understand that facility on his own phone, and he watched as she flicked through the pages on the screen and announced.

"There appears to be a bus that leaves Whitby in the early afternoon and goes to York, and if we caught that we could be back in York in a couple of hours."

"That appears to make sense. Anita at the chip shop will know a suitable guy to help get my car sorted out later; I hardly use it anyway, so there's no rush. I can go with you to Whitby on an early bus, and we could have a saunter about for a couple of hours before you catch the York bus."

"That seems like a good plan. Now, why don't you sit down and relax a bit?"

"It has been a busy day, so I'll be glad to get my feet up," he said before being struck by an afterthought. "I've got some whisky in the pantry; care to join me?"

"Why not? We appear to be marooned here, so we might as well make the most of it. After all, you're not driving."

Alex went through to the kitchen and returned with two glasses and a bottle of whisky, which he put on the coffee table before pouring a small measure for Megan and one for himself. She took her drink and then smiled, saying, "I remember these glasses; they were a wedding present from one of your colleagues in the police."

"I believe they were. I don't use them much as I rarely drink at home these days."

"I remember when you started in the fraud squad, you ritually had a large whisky when you got home in the evening."

"If I managed to get home in the evening. And I remember that when your business was just getting off the ground, you were glad of a drink when you got home to help you unwind when the pressure was building."

The couple sat and reminisced as they sipped their drinks. The house was warm, and the whisky helped promote a very relaxed feeling for them both. It was getting rather late when Megan paused before asking, "What happened to us?"

"We did, love."

"What do you mean?"

"We happened. We changed, or rather we stayed the same when circumstances changed. Life was tough financially when we got married, and when I was the sole earner for a while, we lived from one pay cheque to the next, and our credit cards took a hammering as well. I felt obliged to go for promotion and take on extra responsibilities to provide for the girls.

As soon as you could contribute, you did and worked yourself impossibly hard to get the business established. Even before the girls left home, we were comfortably off, and when they went, we were both earning relatively well, but we couldn't see that we were putting ourselves under a lot of strain to continue earning the big money when we didn't really need it. I've had time to think when I've been up here and I realise that, as long as you can get by, then that's enough. Just ask yourself, how often did we have quiet evenings like this together in the last few years of our marriage? On the rare occasions that we were at home together in the evenings, one or both of us would be too tired or stressed out, and our love life was not exactly fireworks for the same reason."

"I suspect you're right, but it wasn't always that way, was it?"

"No, but back in the Morris Marina days, we weren't worrying about the finances of bringing up a family. And in our first flat, life was tough, but it was exciting, a challenge, and we accepted the challenge and worked hard because we had to, but the work became the driving force in our lives, even when we didn't really need the money. We made our choices, and I regret my decision, but hindsight is no great help."

"We did provide a comfortable home for the girls, though, didn't we?"

"Of course we did, and I'm not suggesting we were driven by simple avarice, but perhaps we got the balance wrong. Would the girls have preferred to have more time with their parents? Sure, we took them on expensive foreign holidays, but my job kept me away from home for long periods on often unpredictable shifts, and I know how torn you were at times when you wanted to spend more time with them in the evening but you had paperwork to do. We weren't bad parents and I'm sure the girls didn't suffer, but we did, and I regret that."

"It seems so simple when you put it that way. When you consider that neither of us was brought up in affluent families, it's perhaps not surprising that we wanted to ensure we were good providers for the girls. But as you say, perhaps we got the balance wrong. However, it's an issue that I will have to think over at some other time because I'm bushed. It's been an interesting day, and now I'm off to bed. Goodnight, love."

As she walked past him, she bent over and kissed him. It was a gesture that Alex found very pleasing, and he smiled as he bid her goodnight and she made her way upstairs. As he sat with the last of his glass of whisky, he reflected on the fact that he had just experienced what a long-standing marriage should be about; a relaxed evening, sharing a few anecdotes about shared experiences and generally feeling comfortable in each other's company.

Alex sat for a while as he finished his whisky. After a heavy day and two or three glasses of whisky, it was hardly surprising that he was soon sleeping soundly, but just after one o'clock, he woke up to notice that the room was quite cold as the central heating had switched off. He remembered his intention to wrap himself in the spare duvet; the same duvet that he now recalled was in the top of the wardrobe in his room. He had no plans to risk waking Megan to retrieve the extra bedding he needed, and he certainly didn't want Ivy to hear him creeping into Megan's room in the middle of the night. However innocent his intentions might have been, Ivy would have been unbearable at breakfast with her innocuous but pointed remarks about people not sleeping well. Alex decided that he would have to put the central heating on, but when he got to the control panel near the boiler, he was reminded of the fact that the sum total of his knowledge about the system was knowing how to turn the thermostat dial. He could turn the thermostat to its highest setting, but it made no difference as the timer was set in the 'off' position. Lacking the skills to solve the problem, he found a less technical solution; he returned to his chair with his heavy coat and waterproof outfit that had been hung on the kitchen door. It took Alex a long time to get to sleep, and he was still asleep when Megan came down early the following morning.

"Morning, love," she greeted him as she gently shook his shoulder to wake him. "What on earth have you been up to?"

It would be fair to say that Alex had not slept well or long enough, and it took him some time to recognise what was going on. He still had his heavy coat around his shoulders, but his waterproof had long since slipped to the floor. He had the general appearance of some woodland creature emerging from hibernation, but eventually he was able to reply.

"I forgot that my spare duvet was in your room, and didn't want to disturb you or give Ivy the opportunity to see me sneaking into your room at dead of night, so I just covered myself with these clothes. I slept quite well," he lied.

Megan laughed and then explained, "Mum's just finishing in the shower and I've managed a quick wash. It looks like you could do with a shower to drag you back into the world of the living. Point me in the direction of the food, and I will try to put some breakfast together."

The domestic arrangements were somewhat ad hoc, but the trio were still able to catch the bus to Whitby, which deposited them there just after ten o'clock. Ivy took an obvious delight in displaying her knowledge of the town to Megan as they did a truncated version of the tour Alex had taken Ivy on. Ivy was particularly keen to show her daughter the small shop selling jet jewellery, and she reminded Megan that Alex had bought a ring there on their last visit. She proudly held out her hand to show off what had become one of her favourite pieces of jewellery and one that she had frequently made a point of showing to all her friends.

"Yes, Mum, it's lovely," commented Megan.

"Why don't you try one on," suggested Ivy. "They are such a simple design that they go with just about any outfit. I never take mine off."

After some encouragement from both Ivy and Alex, Megan was persuaded to try on one or two of the rings and eventually found one that she obviously preferred.

"We'll take that one," declared Alex decisively to the young assistant.

Megan had no chance to protest as Alex paid for the ring and the trio left the shop.

"You shouldn't do things like that, Alex, but it is lovely," she said, kissing him gently on the cheek.

"It's a birthday present."

"But it's not my birthday. It was last month; you missed it."

"I always forgot your birthday; and most of our anniversaries. The ring goes some small way to make up for the many hastily purchased bunches of flowers I bought from filling stations over the years. So now you are part of mine and Ivy's secret society," he said, holding up Ivy's hand with his to display their jet rings. "It's as near as we will ever come to being members of the jet set."

"Sounds like a pretty cool gang," declared Megan as she added her hand to the set displaying her jet ring.

"And before you ask, Ivy," added Alex. "That is not an engagement ring."

The three of them laughed as they set off for the bus stop, and Alex couldn't help but think that he ought to be getting some sort of special rate from the shop, given that he had been such a loyal customer.

Alex waited with his guests until the York bus arrived and then kissed them in turn and asked them to pass on the present he had purchased for Jessica's birthday, and to let him know when they got home. As he waited for his own bus back to Kirksea he reflected on the fact that it had been a very enjoyable mini-holiday. In fact, it had been one of the best days he had ever had in Whitby, and it had been good to feel part of the family again.

On his return to the village, Alex went straight to the chip shop to have a word with Anita.

"Afternoon, gorgeous, and what can we do for you today?" she asked.

"A bit of advice, please, Anita. My car finally gave up the ghost last night, so Ivy and Megan had to stay over."

"I heard the rumour about you secretly escorting two women out of your place in the early hours of this morning. I don't know where you get the energy," interrupted Anita.

"As I was saying. The car just wouldn't start and so I wondered if you could suggest a local garage that might come out and look at it. As regards my supposed attempts to disguise the fact that I'd had female visitors overnight, it would be futile to think such a thing could have gone unnoticed in the village. I might as well have broadcast the fact that they had been there."

"But a gentleman never tells."

"Thank you for your understanding, Anita; now if we could possibly get back to the issue of a mechanic?"

"Sure. Captain Susan, who works for my dad is also a first-rate mechanic. If he can't fix it then nobody can. I know he's hoping to start on a renovation job for my dad in the next few days, but he's probably available if you want me to give him a call?"

"Thanks, you're a darling, Anita."

"And you're a smooth-talking devil, Wessie. Hang on and I'll try and get him now."

By the time he had left the shop, arrangements had been made for him to meet up with the Captain the following morning at the car for a preliminary inspection. Alex knew better than to make any enquiries about the cost of any work because he knew that he would get a good deal. He also resisted the temptation to ask why the mechanic went under the title of Captain Susan. As long as he was as good with cars as Anita had suggested, then he could call himself whatever he liked. Alex knew that there would be no name on the invoice for the work anyway, as there would be no such paperwork, but he knew it would cost him more than a few pints.

CHAPTER TWENTY-SIX

Alex ensured that he was in plenty of time for his meeting with the mechanic. While he was waiting, he opened the bonnet; this remained the extent of his knowledge about car mechanics, and he just stood and stared at the block of metal in front of him. He was surprised by a voice behind him saying, "I see you've found the engine, Wessie. I guess that's the benefit of being a former detective."

Alex looked round to see Captain Susan approaching with a small toolbox and replied. "Morning, Captain. Yes, finding it wasn't too difficult but doing anything with the great lump is beyond me. It just doesn't want to start. It's been playing silly devils for a few weeks, but now it doesn't want to cooperate at all."

"This model is usually reliable, so it's probably something simple like your alternator. I'll give it a quick looking over and see what needs to be done."

The mention of an alternator had already taken Alex to a level of mechanical complexity that was beyond him, so he just stood around as Captain tapped and prodded. Occasionally, Alex was asked to switch something on or try to start the engine. It was bitterly cold and, after 10 minutes working over the engine, Captain welcomed the opportunity to sit in the car and share the flask of coffee that Alex had thought to bring along.

"Julie gave me an engine starting spray, and that seemed to help," suggested Alex.

"That can help in these cold, damp conditions, but it has its limitations. It's rather like the way WD-40 can solve a lot of problems and can get parts moving, but it's not a lot of good if the gearbox is snarled up."

"So, it's my gearbox?" ventured Alex.

"No. It's nothing like as serious. Your alternator has given up the ghost."

"So, it was the alternator as you first thought. Is it a big job, and can you do it?"

"It's not too bad on this model, and provided I don't find any extra problems, I could manage it in an hour to an hour and a half. I can get a supplier to deliver the replacement part tomorrow or the day after, if you want me to go ahead, and get it done before I'm due to start work on your Ivy's cottage."

"That's brilliant. I'd be delighted for you to do it."

As they sat in the car, Alex agreed to meet up with Captain later in the pub to arrange the purchasing of the replacement part. Before Captain closed the bonnet, he offered to show Alex what was involved. Keen to appear interested, Alex peered down at a small unit that the mechanic indicated on the front of the engine and watched as it was given a liberal spray from a can that even Alex identified.

"WD-40! Why are you doing that?"

"It will make those nuts easier to remove later," explained Captain, "and while I've got it off, I'll replace that little drive belt."

Alex felt a faint sense of pride that at last he knew a little bit about the attachment on his engine. He didn't know what it did, but he knew what it was called. Later that day, Alex met up with Captain in the Whelk Pot and learned exactly which parts were needed for the car. These were duly ordered over the phone with a promise that they should be delivered the next day to Captain's house. Alex was amazed at the efficiency of the service, and he gave his car keys to Captain so he could start the work as soon as the parts arrived.

"Thanks a lot, Captain, that's a great weight off my mind. I don't use the car much, but it's handy to have it available to visit family in York," explained Alex before venturing a question to his friend.

"I don't want to appear nosy, but your name intrigues me, and I couldn't help wondering how it came about. I assume you weren't given the name at birth?"

"I have to admit that it is a bit unusual," said Captain, "but it goes back to my childhood. My grandad was one of the last men who fished commercially from the village, and I loved to spend time with him around the harbour. It was my ambition at the time to become a fisherman like him, and he encouraged me to mess around on the boat with him; he showed me how the simple engine worked and let me work on it with him, doing routine jobs. That's where my love of engines comes from. I was kitted out with my own bright yellow oilskin bib trousers like a proper little fisherman. I must have been about six at the time and apparently, I told everyone I was going to be a captain when I grew up. Grandad's coble was called *The Suzanne*, after his mother, so I had the bright idea of decorating my oilskins with the name of the boat, and I appointed myself as captain. I didn't know how to spell the name of the coble so there, on the front of my oilskins, scrawled out in black using an indelible marker was my rank and the name of my vessel. My grandad always referred to me as 'Captain Susan' after that, and the name stuck."

"It makes perfect sense when you explain it, but don't people take the micky."

"They have done in the past, but it was all good-humoured fun. It was a bit like being in a gang if people shared nicknames. You're called Wessie locally, but it's just a sign of being accepted."

Alex had to agree with Captain, and he spent an enjoyable half hour in the pub before he felt the need to go home for lunch. As he set off home, he passed the cottage that was soon to become Ivy's new home. It was bitterly cold, but he took a few moments to stand and look at the dilapidated building. It looked less than inviting in its current state, but Alex knew that Bricky and his team would transform it within the next few weeks. Alex turned to look out towards the harbour, and he had to agree with Ivy's sentiments; the view, even on a cold, damp December morning, was very impressive. He only stood for a few minutes before briskly walking back to his own cosy cottage.

The car problem had hopefully been resolved, so Alex felt that he could settle down to a quiet afternoon and perhaps even read a bit of his latest book. He made himself a cup of tea and placed a couple of chocolate biscuits on the table next to his chair. Retirement was good. No sooner had he set out his snack than the phone rang.

"Hello, Alex," announced what he recognised as Megan's voice. "Since we got back, Mandy has been behaving oddly. Jessica told us that she had noticed some changes in the dog while we were away. She seems unsettled, the dog, not Jessica, and we wondered what we ought to do because the puppies might be imminent."

"Calm down, darling. So, why are you calling me?"

"You were in the police; you're used to dealing with emergencies."

"Thanks for your confidence in my abilities, but I have to inform you that in all my years in the force, I was never called upon to assist a dog in such a situation. And, to the best of my knowledge, dog midwifery has never been a prominent subject in the police inspectors' exams."

"I know, but you always responded so well if we ever had any emergencies to deal with, so you were the obvious person to call."

"I'm flattered, but I'm no expert. From my very limited experience of being around when my neighbour's dog had puppies, I can remember old Mrs Featherstone, the owner, being very relaxed about the whole thing and pointing out that most dogs, even with their first litter, are quite capable of getting on with it. We were encouraged to give the dog a bit of space and not to try and get involved. Mrs Featherstone was a very informed woman in such matters, but in your case, I would get in touch with the vet and get professional guidance."

"Yes, Mr Cooper, the vet, has been keeping an eye on Mandy, and he gave us a little brochure, but we just wondered if you had any advice."

"Contact Mr Cooper and let him know what stage Mandy is at, but don't worry. Remember that you've had two children yourself, and it was all very easy."

"Easy? Easy for some. When Stephanie was born, all you did was sit around playing with the gas and air, and when Jessica arrived, you were sitting in a sleazy little bar somewhere on observational duties. Admittedly, both girls were not complicated births, but I could think of more comfortable ways to spend a few hours."

"I bow to your superior knowledge of the subject, which only goes to show that you are at least as well qualified as I am to deal with the matter."

"Thanks for listening, darling," said Megan. "You just seem to have the ability to put things in perspective and take the drama out of the situation. Mum sends her love by the way and her thanks for your hospitality during our mini-holiday."

The couple chatted for a while, largely about the fact that the car was being sorted and that the mechanic was part of the team that would be starting on Ivy's cottage soon. Assuring Megan once again that Mandy would be OK, and after having asked to be kept informed about how the dog was getting on, Alex rang off. He thought for a moment that it was strange that he had been asked for advice on the state of the dog, but then he smiled broadly as he felt a strange sense of pride that Megan had shown such faith in his ability to help in the situation, and that she had turned to him when she felt the need for some support. His sense of self-satisfaction was short-lived when he remembered Megan's comments about his absence from the birth of their second child. He had indeed been in a bar when Stephanie was born, but she had arrived early, and Alex had not got the message about Megan having gone to the hospital. When he did get the news, he managed to get a colleague to get him to the hospital, but even with the blues and twos clearing the way, he had arrived too late. Megan had understood the situation and never made a big issue of it later, but Alex knew how deeply disappointed she had been that he had not been there. It had been yet another example of how his job had interfered with family life, and the memory always evoked a sense of regret in him.

The following day, Alex received another phone call from Megan giving an update on the dog's condition. There was no trace of anxiety in her voice as she reported that she had phoned the vet and he had reassured her that everything appeared to be going well with Mandy and the big day was not far off.

"I'm glad to hear that you feel more confident about the situation, love," commented Alex. "But if you need any further information on canine obstetrics, just give me a call."

"Thanks for that. By the way, thanks again for the lovely ring you bought me in Whitby. Mum keeps insisting we are twins because we have similar jet rings and Jessica also thinks it's lovely."

"My pleasure. It was a lovely day out in Whitby; it's just a pity that it was brought about because of the car problem, but

Captain thinks he might be able to fix it today if the parts turn up. I'll keep you informed. Meanwhile, love to Ivy and Mandy."

It was Jean's morning to do some cleaning, so Alex made her a cup of tea, and after a quick chat, he left her to get on with her work, and he walked down to the harbour wall. He still felt strangely uncomfortable being in the house while Jean was cleaning; as if he was monitoring her performance. The weather was particularly cold as he approached the harbour, so he was a little surprised to see Norman sitting on one of the benches there.

"Morning, Norman. Cold enough for you?"

"It is a bit parky, Wessie, but I can't stand being cooped up all day, and with the appropriate clothes it's not too bad. It can get a lot colder than this when the winds blow in from the east. Not all of Old Bill's meteorological reminiscences are lies. It's good to get down here and think. I concoct a lot of my news articles when I'm down here. I used to sit here for hours with Muffin; I would be thinking up some new journalistic masterpiece and Muffin would just be sitting. I still miss the old devil. Coming out for a walk without a dog still seems strange; you can walk anywhere with a dog and people just see a dog walker. It seems to justify you being out, but an old guy sitting on a bench in the bitter cold may be seen as odd."

"I've never had a dog. Our place in London was not the ideal place to have one, and the fact that Megan and I were out a lot meant any dog would have been left alone for a long time. We had a cat but I never really got on with it. How's the world of journalism going? Anything good this week to look forward to in the *Gazette*?"

"It's been a pretty quiet week. There're rumours of another pub near Whitby threatening to close, but sadly, that's not exactly news these days. Many areas in the north have even lost their social clubs. That's a sign of the times; people don't want to socialize in clubs anymore. They'd rather buy their booze cheaply from the supermarkets and then sit at home with their big screen television or some other home entertainment system while complaining that there's no sense of community anymore."

"Speaking of which, do you fancy a pint in the Wellie? We can do our bit to support the local."

Norman did not hesitate to take up the offer, but their stroll to the Whelk Pot was interrupted as they had to step smartly out of the way of a small white van emblazoned with signage to indicate it was from a company famous for delivering auto parts.

"They're going a bit bloody fast," commented Norman.

"Yes, I guess it might be the company delivering the parts for my car. There's no wonder they can offer prompt delivery with drivers like that."

In the pub, the two men took their drinks over to what had become their regular table. They sat for a while before Norman broke the silence by saying, "Merry Christmas, Wessie."

"Christmas? It's not Christmas yet."

"Two weeks today. I hated this time of year when I was teaching in the junior school. The big build-up towards the end of term. The kids were as excited and energetic as a bucket full of frogs, and some of the staff weren't much better. One teacher would have had a Christmas tree in her class from the middle of November if we hadn't all objected. The aim was to keep some semblance of a lid on the children's excitement, but there were all the additional things to arrange that meant normality and routine were things of the past. There were the children's parties, the carol service, Christmas cards to make for the children to take home for their parents, and, of course, the nativity play. It would be hard to think of anything more calculated to cause ructions at a time when the whole world seemed to have gone mad. Half the children seemed to want to be either Mary or Joseph and the rest didn't want to be in the production at all. We even had one lad who was offered the role of Joseph, but he was distraught because he wanted to be Mary because it was a smarter costume. Some parents made their disappointment very obvious if their little darling didn't get a big part, and there was always bound to be one girl in tears if she couldn't be the Virgin Mary. The only good thing about the production was the fact that something always went wrong. Some of the parents and staff would find it difficult to suppress their laughter, but Wendy Potts, the music teacher, took it all so seriously and was almost on the point of tears one year when fighting broke out in the tableau at the end when she was accompanying the choir on the piano as they were singing 'Silent Night'. When I got home on the last day of term, Edna would have a large whisky waiting for me, which signalled the start of my Christmas."

"So, you're not a fan of Christmas then?"

"I love it, but people will insist upon that old lie about Christmas being just for the children. It's a great time in the village. This will be your first Kirksea Christmas and I'm sure you will enjoy it. There's the big raffle which is drawn on the Saturday before Christmas. We all contribute a prize and then the Knight of Saint Bodolv draws the winning tickets from the hat, dressed in his ceremonial winter garb."

"Hang on a minute! I hold that highly esteemed post and nobody told me about my dressing up in a winter costume."

"No, you're right," conceded Norman. "That's because it only just occurred to me. You were the chosen one when your name was announced on Saint Bodolv's Day, so obviously, you'd be a natural for the Christmas job."

"But the Saint Bodolv draw was fixed!"

"True! It could be claimed that the outcome was predetermined, to a degree, but the Christmas draw is legitimate, so it's vital that we have someone of unimpeachable character, completely beyond reproach, to pull out the tickets. I'm sure that we don't need to look any further. You can pick the costume up nearer the day. Dave keeps it in his store room. It is what we in the garment trade describe as a 'one-size-fits-all' ensemble. To be fair, it never quite fits anybody, but I'm sure that your manly frame will do it justice. You may find the beard needs tarting up a bit, but otherwise you'll look the very acme of sartorial elegance."

"Beard? You mean I'm doing the Santa bit?"

"There you are. You're getting into character already; you'll knock 'em dead."

CHAPTER TWENTY-SEVEN

Alex was determined not to spend the afternoon in the pub; the company was good and it was warm, but he wanted to get back to his cottage and have a relaxing afternoon. As he passed Ivy's future home, he stood for a moment and looked at the forlorn cottage. He knew that Bricky and his gang would be starting the work on it the next day and wondered how long it would be before the site looked tidy. The early completion date had meant that the gang might be able to get 10 days' work in before Christmas, but Alex had no idea how far they might progress in that time.

When his phone rang just after two in the morning, Alex had a fair idea what it would be about. It took him a while to locate where the sound of the phone was coming from, but he found it in the bathroom and listened for the message.

"Hello, darling, she's started." Megan's excited tone left him in no doubt that Mandy had decided to do her mothering bit. "She seems quite unfazed by the whole thing."

"Good for her," declared a somewhat bleary-eyed Alex as he sat on the edge of his bed. "Has she produced anything yet?"

"No. Hang on, I think she's ready. Yes. She's done it. Oh, it's so sweet and now she's checking it over. I can't see if it's a boy or a girl. Yes, it's a little girl."

"Oh lovely," commented Alex as he tried to show great interest in the drama that was unfolding. For the next hour he was treated to a running commentary given by Megan and Ivy in turn. In the end, he managed to persuade them that they must concentrate on what they were doing and that he mustn't distract them from their duties. He suggested they could ring him later in the morning to give him all the details. As he checked his alarm clock, he noticed it was nearly half past three, and he knew it would take him a while to get to sleep.

The next time the phone rang, Alex was convinced that he had only just got off to sleep, but a glance at the clock showed it was seven o'clock.

"Hello, darling," said Megan. "I hope we didn't disturb you last night."

"Not at all," he lied before adding, "I had to get up to answer the phone anyway. How are things with Mandy now?"

"She's so clever. She's in her bed looking quite serene with her little family. They are so cute; their little eyes are closed, and they just seem to get about by wriggling, but they soon found their food source, and Mandy is such a good mother. She is quite content just lying there as they compete for milk. They are really so sweet that I could adopt them all."

"How many did she have in the end, and what are they like?"

"Three girls and four boy puppies, and they all seem fine. You can see Mandy's characteristics coming through strongly in some of them, but obviously they are not exactly red setters. They could turn out to be a bit of a pick-and-mix litter, but that will only become apparent over the next few weeks. I'm staying on with Mum now so I can help out, and the girls will no doubt want to get more involved as the puppies become a little more developed and need a bit of attention. Mandy doesn't seem to mind us being around the pups, but we don't handle them yet. Must go now, darling; we need to make some breakfast for us and to make up something for Mandy. Thanks again for your help. Bye."

It was clear that Megan's idea of ringing back later in the morning was not what he had expected, but he was glad to hear that everything had gone well, and he set about making his own breakfast. He had just made himself a cup of tea when he heard the letter box open. He went through to the lounge to see his car keys on the floor by the door. He quickly went out in to the street in time to see Captain a couple of yards down the road.

"Just brought your keys back, Wessie. The alternator went in a dream and it's working well."

"So, how much do I owe you?"

"We can sort that out in the pub some time; I must go now as we are due to start on your mother-in-law's place today. Catch up with me some time."

Captain set off for the harbourside, and Alex didn't have time to correct him about Ivy's mother-in-law status, but he had ceased to worry about it because Ivy still seemed to be family. He was determined not to keep Captain waiting for his money, so he made a point of walking down to number 30 later in the morning. The cottage looked much the same from the outside apart from a number of planks, ladders and trestles stored in the tiny front garden. The door was open, and Alex could see Bricky with his gang of co-workers in the front room.

"Sorry to bother you, Bricky," said Alex, "but could I have a quick word with Captain?"

"Thank God that's what you want. I was worried you might be coming to see if we had finished yet," joked Bricky.

Captain stepped outside, and Alex asked how much he owed him. The price seemed ludicrously low, and he told Captain that the same job done by his old garage in London would have cost four times as much.

"Yes, perhaps," explained Captain, "but don't forget that you paid for the parts yourself. My charges are going to be less than the big garages because I don't have the overheads;

business rates, the cost of running a large building and the like. I also cut down on the administrative costs such as all that bookkeeping malarky. Just slip me a few folding beer vouchers for the work later and we're quits."

"I had no idea it would be so cheap," exclaimed Alex. "I might even have the cash with me, and I don't like to owe people money, so I'd rather give it to you now if that's OK?"

He carefully counted out the required amount and then insisted upon adding another 'beer voucher' to compensate for the fact that Captain had carried out the work in the open air in freezing weather. Both men were satisfied with the transaction, so Alex let Captain return to what was obviously some kind of briefing with Bricky, but he couldn't resist waving to the builder and declaring. "Carry on the good work, Bricky. I'll be along later to see if you've finished."

Alex was determined not to go home and sit around watching TV because he knew that he would inevitably fall asleep and then be unable to sleep that night. He walked down to the harbour wall and out to the end. It was still cold, but the icy weather of the last few days had moderated. The sea was relatively calm, and he was reminded of the day that he had accompanied Norman to disperse Muffin's ashes from that spot. He reflected on the thought that a much-diluted Muffin was now likely to be spread over a large area of the North Sea and his spirit still probably wouldn't have the faintest idea what it was all about. Alex's thoughts turned to Norman; Muffin's death had hit him badly, but he was now getting over it and could laugh at memories of the dog's little idiosyncrasies and complete lack of brain power. His thoughts were interrupted by the arrival of Helen, who, for once, didn't have her satchel of art materials with her.

"Hi Helen," he greeted her. "Not sketching today?"

"Too bloody cold, but I couldn't sit about at home. I tried to finish off some work I did sketches for during the summer. I was completely uninspired and the work looked soulless and mechanical. I just felt the need to come out and get a feel for the place again. I love this spot at the end of the wall; it gives a lovely view up to the village. It sits there, a cosy haven embraced by the cliffs on either side of the valley with the cobles bobbing safely in the lower reaches of the beck, but if you turn your back on that, you have the vast expanse of the North Sea in all its ever-changing majesty."

"I never saw it that way before. It must be wonderful to be sensitive to such things. I just feel great standing here."

"Being sensitive with a romantic view of life is a mixed blessing, Alex. I sometimes feel driven by the absolute beauty of something, but I can rarely share that response with others in my work. It is a true blessing to experience a response to the beauty of the world, but it can be depressing if you try to share it with someone and you don't have the ability to do so. Your response is a better one, so just stand here and take it all in."

The couple stood in silence for a while, each engulfed in their own thoughts, before Alex broke the reverie by announcing, "You're right, Helen; it is bloody cold, but it beats the hell out of the pre-packed emotions offered by daytime television. Fancy a coffee?"

Helen didn't need any time to agree to the suggestion, and the couple walked up to the Wellie, where Alex ordered the coffees, and they sat down to warm through a bit.

"It's odd that there isn't anywhere in the village like a small café serving hot drinks," commented Alex. "But I suppose the Wellie covers that need."

"Yes, there hasn't been a café in the village as long as I can remember. There's little call for such a place in the winter and most of the day-trippers in the summer bring their packed lunches or grab fish and chips. The Wellie has always provided hot drinks. Let's face it; in the average British summer, holidaymakers are often glad of a hot drink."

The couple had a lengthy conversation which necessitated a second cup of coffee before Helen suddenly announced, "I was going to grab fish and chips for lunch and take them home. Do you fancy joining me?"

"Sounds a very attractive proposition, thank you. It will make a nice change."

Anita and Nora were obviously intrigued when Alex and Helen entered the chip shop together and he ordered fish and chips for two.

"There you are, gorgeous," she said to Alex as she passed him his fish and chips. "And I hope you enjoy it."

Alex was acutely aware that Anita's apparently innocuous comment was laden with potential layers of meaning, but he knew better than to explain that he was just having lunch with a friend. Anita's remarks had not gone unnoticed by Helen, and as she left the shop, she observed, "Anita never changes, bless her. In her mind she'll have us shacked up together by tomorrow. And I thought I was the romantic."

It only took a few minutes to get to Helen's cottage, and she efficiently sorted cutlery and condiments on the table. Placing the fish and chips on plates, she brought them over and set them on the table before apparently having an afterthought and adding, "I've got half a bottle of wine if you fancy a glass?"

"Why not? I feel like celebrating."

Helen brought two glasses and a bottle to the table and poured each of them a glass of wine before asking, "Celebrating what?"

"I guess I could legitimately be celebrating the start of work on my ex-mother-in-law's cottage, but, more importantly, this is the first time I've been invited into someone's home here in the village for a purely social visit."

"I'll drink to that," said Helen, raising her glass. "Apart from that, how are you finding life in the village?"

"I love it here. After a life where I appeared to be in competition with everyone; my colleagues jockeying for promotion, the traffic intent on messing up my day, and even pedestrians who blocked the very pavements I wanted to walk along, I got here and found that I could breathe freely and have a bit of space around me."

Helen smiled and then said, "There's a plaque on the pedestal of the Statue of Liberty which says, '*Give me your tired, your poor, your huddled masses yearning to breathe free.*' I think of those sentiments each time I come back to the village because I feel that sense of freedom every time. It might have been bloody cold down by the harbour today, but you could certainly breathe free."

After lunch, the kitchen was tidied and Helen suggested that they went through to the lounge at the front of the cottage. Alex observed that most of the cottages at the bottom of the village had broadly similar layouts, but Helen's had been decorated completely differently to his. Helen's lounge was a blaze of colour, with the furniture draped in ethnically patterned throws. The walls were largely covered in paintings and drawings, most of which were Helen's work. The one thing that he noticed was similar to his own lounge was that there were a number of chairs but only one of them appeared to be regularly used. One of the others needed to be cleared of a plethora of cushions and tapestry pieces before Alex could sit down. When you're living on your own, it is easy to become a creature of habit, he thought to himself.

The couple had a very enjoyable afternoon sitting and chatting about the way they had both managed to escape to

Kirksea. Alex recounted Norman's tales about the pressures of school Christmases, and Helen admitted that even after her own relatively short career in teaching, she could identify with Norman's views. Having been reminded that Christmas was approaching, Helen took it as an excuse to suggest that they might have a 'Christmas' drink together, and she produced a bottle of whisky. Conscious of the fact that it would be rude to refuse, and also because he was thoroughly enjoying the convivial atmosphere, Alex took the proffered glass.

"This is a very pleasant way to spend a winter afternoon," commented Alex as he swirled the whisky around in his glass. "The Wellie is a wonderful place to meet up, but it's nice to have this sort of relaxed ambiance to discuss things."

"We must, as they say, do this again sometime. I must admit that I've thoroughly enjoyed myself."

Eventually, Alex decided that he ought to be leaving. He put on his coat and was escorted to the front door. It was already quite dark as the winter evening had crept up on them. As he stood in the doorway, he thanked Helen again for a lovely, somewhat impromptu, afternoon and kissed her gently on the cheek.

"Evening, Wessie," came the unmistakeable voice of Nora.

"Evening, Nora," he replied dolefully before turning to Helen and saying, "What were the chances of that?"

"The locals will be getting more than fish and chips from the shop tomorrow," commented Helen.

The couple both laughed at the prospect of being local news, and Alex made his way home.

CHAPTER TWENTY-EIGHT

When he got back to his own cottage, he stood for a moment and looked at his lounge. It seemed very bare compared to Helen's. Some might charitably have described it as minimalist, others might suggest sparse or even Spartan. He hadn't bothered buying a lot of new furniture nor had he tried to personalize his new home. It had become a functional base from which to go out and explore Kirksea. He thought for a moment how much he had enjoyed his afternoon in Helen's cottage; it had been very comfortable, even cosy, but was that down to the furnishings or the company? The thought fleetingly crossed his mind that he might want to share his cottage with someone else at some point, but he quickly rejected the idea; he had tried the relationship thing, and it had ended in divorce.

In the pub the following day, Alex had his regular weekly update to see if Norman had managed to get anything into the *Gazette* that week and whether or not there was a shred of honesty in what he had written.

"Hi Wessie. Come to see my latest contribution to local culture?" asked Norman, brandishing the latest copy of the *Gazette*.

"He's excelled himself this week," added Dave. "It's his usual mix of fact and fantasy, and you often can't tell them apart."

"I can't wait to be impressed, Norman," commented Alex. "So what murky area have you been exploring this week?"

"Following my award-winning article last year on the haunted houses of the Whitby area…" started Norman.

"Award-winning?" interjected Dave. "What award?"

"I awarded myself a bottle of gin for the sheer brilliance of the text, but that's by the way. To get back to my current masterpiece, I turned my journalist's critical eye onto the subject of local superstitions, particularly those adopted by fishermen or sailors in general."

"Hang about, Norman," said Dave. "You've listed a number of so-called superstitions. You read them out, one by one, and Wessie will judge if they are true or if they are Normanisms."

"Very well," replied Norman. "How about this one, Wessie; it is unlucky to whistle on board ship?"

"I've heard that before, it's supposed to whistle up a storm."

"True. That's one to you. Next; it's unlucky to set sail on a Friday?"

"No idea, but I should think you made that up."

"No, it is a commonly held belief among trawlermen, who say it's better to sail on a Sunday. How about the suggestion that it's unlucky to have pigs onboard?"

"False."

"No. It's true. There are a whole host of animals that are held to be unlucky to have on ships, including rabbits. Do you think it would be deemed unlucky to step on to a boat with your left foot first?"

"No," replied Alex, who was beginning to tire of this game.

"Apparently you should step on with your right foot first. I go on to outline some of the other popular beliefs in my article. There is a whole host of people the fisherman must not come into contact with on his way to the boat, ranging from red-haired people to nuns and under no circumstances must he wear green! It may all sound very silly to others, but fishermen were preoccupied with their own safety and getting a big catch, so they wanted to avoid anything they might see as bad luck. Some ancient traditions are altered over time; it was always considered unlucky to rename a boat but if you wanted to do so, you had to make an offering of alcohol to the god of the sea. To this day, when large vessels are launched, an offering of champagne is smashed on the bows. When you have the pleasure of reading this week's offering, you will be delighted to hear that they are all genuine, commonly held superstitions. They are all true, and there isn't one thing that my detractors might call a Normanism."

"I told you, Alex," said Dave. "Sometimes his work is legitimate. It's quite unnerving."

"I only do it to give the conspiracy theorists something else to worry about," added Norman with a sly grin.

Alex stayed in the pub for a while, chatting with his friends, but his stomach was beginning to alert him to the fact that he was hungry. He was tempted by the ploughman's lunch on offer at the pub but calculated that the wait for it to arrive might necessitate the need for another pint, so he opted to go for fish and chips.

"Hi gorgeous," came the familiar greeting from Anita. "Did you enjoy your fish and chips yesterday?"

"As wonderful as ever," answered Alex, refusing to be drawn on the implied subject of his afternoon with Helen. "In fact, I was so impressed that I decided to try one of your lovely pieces of cod today, but hold the chips."

"She's a nice person, that Helen," added Anita, who was determined to stick to her theme. "She does some lovely pictures of the village, and her house is full of them, I'm told."

"I don't recall, but it's hard to concentrate on the surroundings when you're overcome by a love-crazed frenzy, but you're right; she is a very nice person, and we had a most enjoyable afternoon."

Realising that she was being teased, Anita just smiled and handed over Alex's fish. As he was about to leave, she suddenly asked, "I wonder if you could help out on Friday afternoon again? Nora and Laura were hoping to go to Whitby to buy one or two items for the Christmas do at the Wellie. I don't suppose there will be a lot of business here, but if you could be he around, it will enable the girls not to feel under pressure to get back here early."

"No problem; pleased to help out."

It was only when he left the chip shop that it dawned on him that it was really getting close to Christmas. Unlike birthdays and wedding anniversaries, Alex had never forgotten about Christmas and the need to buy presents for the family. Admittedly, his habit of waiting until the last minute to purchase gifts had often led to some panic buying, and his choice of presents was not always ideal. He had once bought Megan an expensive coffee-making machine and even managed to wrap it tastefully. Megan was appropriately appreciative on Christmas morning but in one of their later, less than amicable phases, she had pointed out that Alex was the only one who regularly chose to drink coffee at the time. This year he was determined to get it right, so he made up his mind to go into Whitby at the weekend to do some Christmas shopping and to arrange to visit York with presents early the next week.

As Anita had expected, trade was slow in the chip shop on Friday, but Helen was one of the customers on her way back from a sketching session down by the harbour.

"Nice to see you, Helen," said Alex, "and thanks again for a lovely afternoon on Tuesday."

"My pleasure," she replied.

"I'm glad to see someone's looking after our Wessie," interjected Anita, eager to get in to the conversation.

Alex ignored Anita's attempts to turn the conversation round to his social life and continued, "Any luck with your sketching today, Helen? At least the weather is a little less tiresome."

"It's not ideal, but I got one or two nice angles down by the pub. I wanted to get something a bit different because I always frame up a little drawing to go in the Wellie Christmas raffle."

"Thanks for reminding me; I'm driving over to Whitby on Saturday to buy some presents, and I must get something to put in the raffle."

"I don't like to be forward," said Helen, "but could I possibly grab a lift with you? I've got a few things I need to pick up before Christmas."

"No problem. I thought I'd set off in the early morning, so just let me know when it suits you."

"Thanks. You're a darling. I usually do such trips with Splodger, but he's busy working for Bricky this weekend; they're trying to get a move on with your mother-in-law's house."

"Heaven forbid that we should hold up the work, so I'd be delighted to stand in for him."

The pair arranged to meet up at nine on Saturday morning, and Helen left with her fish and chips. Anita smiled broadly and gave Alex a knowing look before saying, "She's obviously fallen under your manly spell, Wessie."

"Yes, I guess so," he said resignedly, "I put it down to the alluring smell of frying fish on my overall. You've been wearing this particular fragrance for years; you must be fighting men off all the time."

"It's true, but don't tell my Tom; he thinks I wear it just for him."

The trip to Whitby proved to be successful on many levels. Alex gave the car a trial run to prepare for his trip over to York, and he bought presents for the family and a special bottle of Whitby rum for the raffle. The best part of his day was having the opportunity to chat with Helen. Alex had forgotten how much he enjoyed the company of women; they offered a different range of subjects to discuss than an all-male group. He loved the camaraderie with the men in the pub, but women tended to be less guarded, more prepared to be open about their feelings and sensitive to the feelings of others.

When he got home, he rang Ivy and arranged to go over to York on the 21st to deliver his presents for the family because he knew that his daughters would be visiting Ivy over the holiday, and Megan was staying on to continue helping with the puppies. In a burst of efficiency, he set about wrapping the presents for 'his girls' in York. He couldn't claim to have shown any great originality in his choice of gifts; each of them was to receive Yorkshire gin, either as a bottle or as a selection of miniatures. He knew the gifts would be appreciated as gin was the drink of choice for the family. He pondered what to do with the prize he had bought for the Wellie Christmas raffle. He felt it had been a good choice as he had bought it from the lifeboat shop. He decided that there was little point in wrapping it, so he set it to one side to be taken to the pub later.

Late on Wednesday morning, Alex took his raffle prize offering to the Wellie and gave it to Dave to put with the collection of items to be raffled on the following Saturday. As expected, Norman was there with his early copy of the *Gazette*.

"Morning, Norman," said Alex. "And what delights are you offering this week?"

"I'm playing safe with this year's Christmas special after the response to my contribution last year."

"So, what exactly did you do last year?" asked Alex. "I wasn't here to enjoy it then."

"I ran a simple quiz about the stories and traditions surrounding the biblical accounts of the birth of Jesus. I saw it as a light-hearted look at how people remembered the nativity story. It was an attempt to get people to remember their early recollections of the Bethlehem birth, a sort of gentle nostalgia trip. I asked readers to state which animals were mentioned in the nativity story. What would you say?"

Alex took a sip of his beer and thought for a moment before declaring, "It's been a while since I went to a nativity play; work commitments meant that I seemed to miss all the ones my girls were in. Let me think; there was a cow and a few sheep that the shepherds brought. Then there was the donkey that Mary turned up on and the camels for the three kings, but I think they turned up a bit later."

"A pretty comprehensive list, Wessie, but not entirely correct. In fact, there are no references mentioned in the Gospels to any animals being present at the birth. Over the years, people have confused Christmas carols with scriptures. The song about Mary travelling on her little donkey gives us the idea that it was there, and the carol about the shepherds watching their sheep suggests that they were present. We are informed that 'the cattle were lowing' in another hymn, so nativity scenes the world over dutifully put a cow in the stable. There is no mention of a stable at all, but that was an answer to another question in the quiz. The modern depiction of the nativity mixes up folk tales, carols and images taken from Christmas cards to give us the image we have today."

"Interesting," said Alex, "I never really gave it much thought, but I've seen so many nativity scenes on Christmas cards and depicted in tableaux in public places that I just assumed it came straight from the Bible."

"Not an unreasonable point of view, but some of my readers last year became quite incensed because they assumed

I was attacking their religious beliefs, which I certainly was not. I had a good deal of correspondence on it and some of it was quite vitriolic. The fact is that a lot of the animals mentioned have a symbolic meaning, which is lost on the majority of people who attend their children's nativity play. The people who contacted me included some top-weight loonies who insisted that they 'knew' the truth because they had faith, and they inferred that I was some sort of servant of the devil just because I had published what was a biblical fact. This year, I will stay clear of controversy, hence my recent masterpiece on Yorkshire Christmas traditions on page three."

Before Norman could go on to extol the qualities of his most recent article, Dave emerged from the backroom with a large black bin liner, which he placed on the floor beside Alex, saying, "I gather that this is for you, Wessie. Look after it."

Alex couldn't resist looking inside the bag, and a glimpse of the fur-lined red material reminded him of his gig at the Christmas raffle.

"Oh, lovely," he said, with a complete lack of conviction. "Thanks for this latest honour that you have bestowed upon me, Norman."

"As the bard would remind us, 'Some are born great, some achieve greatness, and some have greatness thrust upon them'. I will leave it up to you to decide which category you fit in, Alex."

"I think I'm more sort of, 'some have greatness dumped upon them,' so thanks, Norman."

After a lengthy talk-through of the arrangements for Saturday, Alex picked up his bin liner and left the pub. Noticing that the door to number 30 was open, Alex walked over and looked inside, where he observed Bricky, who was in the process of trying to negotiate the position of a new staircase with a couple of his workers. Alex waited patiently while the team pushed and pulled the cumbersome article into place until Bricky announced, "OK, guys, that should hold it for a while."

"Hi Bricky. It looks like you've been having a few problems with the place. Have you come across any difficulties so far?"

"This sort of work always throws up some complications but so far this has been quite a straightforward job. You can see how we have had to relocate that wall to accommodate the staircase to comply with modern safety recommendations. I managed to get a quality staircase from another place I had worked on. It was tricky getting it in, but the lads love a challenge. It should be relatively straightforward from here. We're lucky in that we have a team who can cope with most trade requirements, and we can call on other local guys to do specific jobs."

"It looks a big job to me," observed Alex.

"It's always a bit of a mess knocking down the walls and stripping things back but when we start the process of building up from the shell it will look more like a house than a bomb site. We will be working till Thursday, tomorrow afternoon, and then breaking up for Christmas. We normally finish early on a Friday, so it made little sense to come in just for a half day."

"That's true," said Alex.

"The trouble is that this lot," he said, pointing to members of the team, "will want Christmas off, and then the idle bunch will have their eyes on a New Year break as well."

There was a chorus of boos and calls of 'humbug' from the team, who were regaining their strength after grappling with the staircase.

"To be honest, they are a flexible mob, and I've told them that if any of them want to get a few hours in between Christmas and the New Year, then that's fine."

"That seems reasonable, Bricky," commented Alex. "I'm sure that Ivy would love to get in as soon as possible, but she's realistic and thankful for what you and the team are doing. To be honest, she's got a lot on her mind since her dog had puppies last week, and they are keeping her busy. I'm going to see her tomorrow, so I can let her know things are going pretty well with the cottage."

"You can tell her that I will be in touch in a few weeks as we get to the choice of finishes around the place. You can also tell her that the stage payment she gave me has covered expenses so far, and I won't be needing any more for a while."

CHAPTER TWENTY-NINE

He set off early the following morning but the drive over to York was a bit of a disappointment to Alex as his view of the moors was spoiled by a heavy drizzle. The warm welcome he received when he arrived made up for the miserable drive, and he was quickly ushered into the lounge, where Ivy and Megan provided him with a welcome cup of tea.

"The puppies are having a morning nap at the moment," said Ivy, eager to let Alex know how things were going with Mandy's litter. "In fact, they tend to spend a lot of time sleeping or feeding. Anyway, how is the house getting along?"

Alex dutifully reported on the latest developments with the cottage and handed over the presents he had brought over.

"You've obviously done your Christmas shopping early this year," teased Megan. "But thank you. I'll give the girls their presents when they come over on Saturday."

The trio had a lengthy chat about the puppies, the state of Ivy's cottage and Alex's upcoming role as Santa Claus when Megan introduced her own bit of news.

"I think I may have sold my place in London," she announced, before explaining. "You know I talked about selling off my part of the business to Fatima; well, she has a friend who has apparently been trying to buy a place in my area for months and things sort of fell into place, and we are exploring the possibility of her moving in as soon as we have sorted out the price and all the legal bits. It's all been a bit of a whirlwind, but soon I may be jobless and homeless. Mum has said I can stay on here for a while until I get something sorted out, so I continue my search for somewhere for myself. It's all a bit scary but also exciting."

"Good for you, darling," he said before a sudden thought struck him, and he added, "What about the cat?"

"Obviously, given his response to dogs, I couldn't bring him down here on my visits to see Mum, so Satan has effectively moved in with the Turners from two doors down, and they are delighted."

Satan was the name Alex had given the cat when it first appeared in their lives as a stray. Alex was always doubtful if it had been abandoned or if indeed it had eaten its previous owners. It had never been a cat that liked to curl up on anyone's lap and would sometimes 'playfully' jump up and bite Alex's arm. This had often led to the cat getting impromptu flying lessons, but it still seemed to enjoy its little game while Alex didn't. He looked around Ivy's lounge and reflected on the fact that the brightly decorated Christmas tree would have been easy prey for Satan. The whole room had been tastefully decorated for the festive season, and for a moment, Alex was reminded of his own Christmases as a child. Their decorations had been less elaborate. The same rather tattered paper decorations were brought out each year and augmented by paper chains that he and Val had excitedly stuck together. The same much-loved ornaments were brought out of the cellar in their old cardboard box from which they were carefully lifted and hung on the tree. His dad had always insisted on a real tree and took great delight in ceremoniously bringing it into the house, where he would ritually wrestle with the string of lights while cursing at the fact that they had always been put away in a mess the previous year. There had been assorted greenery collected from the fields near the family home, fields long since lost to new houses. His memories were interrupted by Ivy's announcement.

"The puppies are starting to move about a bit. Come and have a look," she implored him.

In the utility room, just off the kitchen, Alex was met by the sight of Mandy laid on her side while a mass of puppies jostled to get the best feeding spot. Mandy looked serenely happy, occasionally giving one or other of her offspring a gentle lick. It was not easy to make out the details of what the puppies looked like. Their eyes had yet to open and their faces had that rather squashed appearance all young dogs do. As Megan had suggested in her early morning phone call, the young dogs seemed to have some natural resemblance to Mandy, but there were signs of some colour variation in a couple of them. The dogs were left to their feeding, and Ivy and Megan returned to the kitchen with Alex, where the women set about preparing a light lunch.

During a very pleasant afternoon, the group discussed, at length, the puppies and details of how they would affect Ivy's eventual move to Kirksea. The vet had advised Ivy that the puppies would need their first inoculations on the sixth of February, yet Bricky was still suggesting that the cottage could be ready two weeks before that. Megan bravely volunteered to stay with the dogs in York until a suitable transition could be arranged. In truth, she had no idea if she would have her own rented place by then. In the meantime, there was the problem of finding suitable homes for the litter. Jessica had been smitten by the puppies the moment she saw them and had singled out one that she had decided would be hers. She justified the decision to have a dog by explaining that she worked from home and would appreciate the company when her partner Leon was at work. Another of her friends had been looking for a dog for a while and was hoping to come over and see the litter when they were a little older. Ivy had always intended to keep one puppy for herself but that still left four to home. Alex was glad that it wasn't his problem. He was sorry to have to leave the convivial atmosphere, but eventually he knew he had to set off as he had a drive home in what was dismal weather. Having kissed goodbye to Megan and Ivy, and not before helping himself to a single stem of holly from the bush in Ivy's garden, he got in the car and set off home.

When he arrived back in Kirksea, he parked up the car and, after reflecting on how well that mysterious alternator apparatus had performed, he walked straight home. It was late, and he was tired, so he resisted the temptation to drop into the Wellie for a nightcap. When he got home, he took the presents he had been given by the family and arranged them on the coffee table. He then draped the single stem of holly over the array and stepped back to survey his efforts. As Christmas decorations go, it was pathetic, but at least he'd made the effort. While he was in this less-than-festive mood, he remembered the regalia he had been given to wear for the Christmas event at the pub. He sought out the bin liner and pulled out the costume. He tried on the outfit, only to find it was rather short in the leg while the jacket was more than generous, leading him to assume it had been made for a twenty-stone dwarf. He calculated that the lack of leg length could be concealed by tucking the trousers in his wellingtons, and a pillow under the jacket would complete the display. Norman had been right to suggest that the beard needed a bit of 'tarting-up'. It was essentially a piece of white gauze onto which had been stuck some cotton wool, some of which had obviously been lost during a previous outing. Alex found some cotton wool in his first-aid box and proceeded to stick it on the bare patches of the material using a powerful glue he had once bought to complete one of his many do-it-yourself failures. Apart from a bizarre combination of slightly differing 'white' beard areas, the result wasn't bad, but it took him ages to remove the bits of cotton wool from his fingers and the kitchen table.

On the night of the Wellie's Christmas special, Alex opted to change at the pub. He knew he would have looked a bit silly walking to the pub in his Santa garb. He knew he wouldn't look any less silly in the pub, but he felt he could cope with that. Clutching his bin liner, he strolled down to the Wellie. The Whelk pot was much fuller than usual, although it was still relatively early, and he had to pick his way through the throng to deliver his costume to Dave, who concealed it in the back room. Alex secured a seat next to Norman, and they struggled to have a conversation above the mounting noise of revelry. In the end, they just sat and watched the crowds. Alex was struck by the fact that there were many people in the pub whom he rarely, if ever, saw. There seemed to be party-goers of all ages enjoying the seasonal atmosphere. Laura was making her rounds of the revellers selling raffle tickets and eventually she confronted Alex, who dutifully pressed a ten-pound note into her collection box. Before she could issue him with his tickets, he protested, "No tickets for me, thanks, Laura."

"But you've put your money in now, Wessie."

"You may not recognise me in my cunning disguise later, Laura, but I will be doing the draw, and I'm not prepared to risk pulling out my own ticket. With my luck, I could end up with 10 top prizes and be very unpopular."

"Fair enough. I've just about coaxed as much money out of the crowds as I can, so the draw could be at about nine."

Alex sat for a while admiring the subtle seasonal decorations that adorned the room, and he was convinced that this showed Daureen's influence. By the time he was called to his 'dressing room', Alex was ready for his big turn. He recognised that his sense of confidence was not unrelated to the few pints he had enjoyed throughout the evening. He was shown through to the room behind the bar, where he struggled to put on his ceremonial garb aided by Alice, when she could be spared from her bar duties. Eventually, and with alcohol-induced confidence, he waited for his cue from the bar. After a while he heard the room next door go quiet, and then he picked out Norman's voice.

"And now, ladies and gentlemen, to oversee the drawing of our raffle is a very special guest who's flown a long way to help us out tonight, so please let's hear a big round of applause for him."

The door to the bar opened, Alex stepped out, tripped over some non-existent object, and all but fell into the room to rapturous applause.

"I see Santa has jet lag," quipped Norman.

Despite such an ignominious entry, the raffle went well, and Alex was pleased to see that the prizes were shared out between a large number of people. His duties completed, Alex returned to the backroom to the sound of loud cheers. Having discarded his costume, he returned to the party.

"You should have been here a few minutes ago," Norman greeted him. "We just had some clown dressed as Santa falling all over the place."

Alex just smiled and decided he had better slow down his alcohol intake, or he might start on his memoirs from his time in the vice squad again. After a while, the party was called to order and Daureen made an announcement.

"Ladies and gentlemen, we now come to our annual carol singing. We are pleased to have Helen to accompany us on the piano again this year, and Norman has been persuaded to join in with his violin. You should all have a copy of our songbook on your table, but Kevin has plenty of extra copies if you want one."

The said book was a collection of photocopied sheets stapled together to form a small booklet, and some of them had obviously seen many years of service. The carol singing was a strangely moving experience; a crowd who had recently been enjoying a high-spirited evening suddenly displayed a degree of reflective reverence as some of the quieter carols were sung. Alex was surprised at how accomplished the singers appeared to be; he knew nothing about the skills of singing in a choir, but the overall sound was rather moving. Daureen efficiently directed the singing, which ended with a rousing version of 'Oh Come All Ye Faithful.' At the conclusion of the performance, Alex made his way over to Helen.

"That was lovely," he commented. "I didn't know you could play the piano."

"Yes, I love to belt out the odd tune, but unfortunately my cottage does not afford the space for a piano. Dave and Daureen let me practice in here sometimes when the pub's closed, so I'm pleased to be able to support the carol service. I'm afraid I nearly messed up the last verse of 'Away in a Manger' again."

"Sounded great to me and very moving. It took me back to the days when I would go out carol singing as a boy with some of my mates. None of us had a decent singing voice, and we only knew a few verses from the odd carol. It's a wonder we were never charged with demanding money with menaces. So, what's your problem with the last verse of that particular carol?"

"I took a year out before going to university and worked as a classroom assistant in a school for severely disabled children. Despite the fact that favouritism was discouraged, I grew attached to a little girl called Tabatha; she had a range of complex health problems but was blessed with a lovely singing voice. I bought her a little doll and wrapped it up to present to her on the last day before we broke up for Christmas. The day before the end of term, we had the usual carol concert, and Tabatha was delighted to have been chosen to sing the last verse of the carol in question as a solo. I will never forget the words of that verse. 'Bless all the dear children in Thy tender care and take us to heaven to live with thee there.' In the darkened school hall and with a single spotlight on her, she sang it beautifully. On the following day, we learned that Tabatha had died during the night. I still have that unopened present, and though it's hard to play that verse, I do it in her memory."

Alex gave her a little hug before saying, "I can see why it's a difficult verse for you. Christmas has a sneaky way of turning up memories of previous years; some good and some not so."

The evening ended well as people prepared to leave. There was much kissing and hugging and exchanging of seasonal best wishes, and then the merry crowd dispersed. Alex stood for a while and looked out over the village. He noted that each of the houses had a light in the window, many of which were reflected in the still waters of the harbour. Norman had explained the tradition of leaving a light burning in a window over the Christmas season in memory of the fishermen who had not returned safely over the centuries. Next year, Ivy would be able to add her own light to the array.

CHAPTER THIRTY

Alex was not surprised to see that the New Year celebrations were also centred on the pub and culminated with the villagers standing outside as the maroon was fired at midnight. Not for the first time, Alex was struck by the feeling of community shared by the villagers; it was something he had never experienced in London.

The following day, the pub didn't open until midday. This information had been posted in the bar for a while, and it didn't seem unreasonable to allow Dave and Daureen a little bit of time to sort out the place after a very late finish the previous night. The pub was still empty when Alex arrived at one o'clock. Dave was not his usual bright and cheery self, and Alex put it down to a possible over-indulgence during the New Year celebrations, so he was shocked when the landlord announced, "I've got the letter I was expecting from the brewery; they've decided to close the Whelk Pot."

"They can't do that; the pub *is* the village."

"They obviously plan to," added Dave. "We got a letter through last Friday, but I didn't want to spoil the New Year party by announcing it then. Atkins and Dodd have made their intentions clear. They know Daureen and I can't afford to buy the pub, and they really just want to close it and get official permission to change its use. The pub was initially three cottages, so if you take into account the little bit of land behind, they could put quite a large development on here. Some building companies would love to get their hands on such a site to develop luxury holiday apartments and would pay the brewery quite a lot for the opportunity to do so."

"But surely the pub must have a preservation order of some sort on it," argued Alex.

"No, the nature of the building was changed when the three original cottages were combined to form the pub in the fifties. Since the brewery started hinting at selling off the pub, I've talked it over with Early Pete quite a lot; he says the local council would not want the pub to close because it's a valuable local facility, but they haven't got the funds to buy it and couldn't take the responsibility of running it either. In a mad moment of optimism, Daureen and I discussed the possibility of a bank loan to buy the pub, but the bank pointed out that we couldn't afford the repayments because the projected profits were just not big enough. This place is running on a shoestring, and some months we barely take enough to cover our outgoings. Obviously, all the number-crunchers at Atkins and Dodd have calculated that they could make more by just taking the pub off their books. They managed it with The Prince at Wykethorpe with little resistance, and they are ready to roll on to Kirksea."

As the afternoon wore on, a trickle of customers came into the pub and heard the news, and they in turn spread the word to others who came down later to get confirmation of what seemed an unthinkable situation. After a couple of hours, the pub had more than its usual quota of customers, and there was an appreciable degree of anger expressed at the thought of 'big business' threatening to tear the heart out of their community. The mood of the crowd changed gradually from one of fatalistic acceptance of the situation to one of fury at the thought that their beloved pub was under mortal threat. It was Norman who eventually summed up the feelings of those present.

"This can't be allowed to happen; I, for one, refuse to just resign myself to accepting the situation without a fight, and my personal contribution will be to ensure that the *Gazette* will run a campaign to show how much local resistance there is to the proposed closure. Other communities have rallied to prevent their pubs from closing."

"So, I'm told," said Kevin. "But pubs are closing in droves all over the country because people are choosing to opt for home entertainment and buying drinks from the supermarkets."

"It's true that there is a trend away from pubs," conceded Alex. "But the Wellie is more than just a pub; it's a place to meet up, to celebrate community events, to find out what is going on in the village. You will all know that I'm a newcomer, and I will say that I came here because I wanted to experience that feeling of being part of a community. I've experienced the isolation, albeit very comfortable, of living in an area where I hardly knew my neighbours. I had my privacy because I only ever let a few people into *my* world. Since I've been here, I have felt lucky to be among a lovely group of people, but I wouldn't have known how welcoming they would be if I hadn't gone out of my way to meet them. Many of my initial meetings were here in the Wellie. It has been my introduction to the village, and if it comes to manning the metaphorical barricades to stop the developers, then I will be there."

While this discussion was going on, Bricky had been listening attentively, and he announced, "As you know, I've done a lot of work in the village over the years, and I've had the odd run-in against companies trying to develop the place to support their own interests. There are a couple of points I'd like to emphasize. I am quite convinced that the council would not wish to see the pub close and would look favourably on any alternative. The other thing to bear in mind is that, although the brewery has a lot of money behind it, the last thing they want is any delay on the plans. They will want to push it through as quickly as possible because delays are costly."

The assembled group agreed to call a meeting the following Saturday in the pub, and to invite everybody in the village to get their views as to what could be done to halt the closure. Norman arranged to have informative invitations printed on fliers, which would be delivered to every home in Kirksea, and the delivery duties were shared out to a few of the assembled crowd. For the rest of the week the fate of the Wellie was the major topic of conversation for many in the village, and Alex noted that it wasn't just the regular pub-goers who seemed concerned.

On the morning of the proposed meeting, Alex went to the Wellie to help with the arrangements. It was difficult to predict how many would turn up, but he helped Dave line up the pub's chairs facing the bar along with a number of assorted chairs that had been brought down from a small storeroom above the pub. In front of the bar, and facing the rows of seats, were two separate chairs arranged behind a small table. The two men looked at the finished array of seating and wondered if they had been a little optimistic about the possible numbers of those who might attend. They need not have worried. By the time the meeting was due to start at one o'clock, the room was packed and people were still turning up. The rows of chairs soon filled up, and the sides and back of the improvised auditorium were all pretty full of interested villagers, and there was a constant hum of conversation.

Shortly after the designated start time, the two chairs at the front were taken up by Norman and Early Pete. Daureen obligingly rang the bell behind the bar, and the meeting quickly came to order as Norman stood up and announced, "Friends. Thank you all for turning up today. For those of you who don't know me, I'm Norman Bliss and my friend here is Councillor Peter Kerning who is here today to give us the local council's views on some of the issues. I'm sure that, like me, you can see the amount of interest there is in the future of the Whelk Pot; we are all concerned, so some of us decided to try and resist the planned closure of our pub. I must make it very clear that Pete and I do not represent any official local committee, nothing has been set up, we are merely here to offer a bit of advice so you can decide what you want to do. I give you Councillor Kerning to give a broad outline of the situation."

There was a polite round of applause as Early Pete stood up.

"I must say from the start that the local council do not like to see pubs such as this being sold off."

There was a loud cheer of support and when it subsided the councillor added, "However, the issue is a complicated one. The council cannot insist that these places are kept open. We are committed to doing what we can to stop the closures of what we call Assets of Community Value, or ACV's. It's a jargon phrase to mean that we appreciate that communities need such facilities to function at their best, but unfortunately councils don't have unlimited resources to buy up all the assets that businesses might wish to close down. All we can do is to try and protect places like this as best we can, if necessary, by putting administrative hurdles in their way. We can only do this legitimately if we know that the local community want to protect their resources."

There was another cheer from the assembled villagers.

"You will no doubt be aware," continued the speaker, "that another local pub has been closed. The council could do little about it because there was no sign that the local community really cared if the pub closed or not. I know from many years of visiting the Wellie that the people of Kirksea don't want to go down without a fight on this matter."

There was more cheering before the speaker continued, "I have spoken at length with Norman, and between us we have gathered a fair bit of background as to how any closure might be contested, but I must reinforce what he said; we are not here to run everything. For any fight to be put up, we must have the support of all the people of Kirksea, and we must try to ensure that each and every one of you has the opportunity to have your say. I now pass you back to Norman, who will outline a possible plan of action."

There was an energetic round of applause as Early Pete resumed his seat. When the applause and murmur of conversation had died down Norman took up the baton.

"Thanks, Pete," he responded before continuing. "I have been doing a lot of reading up on this subject for my articles in the *Gazette,* and in particular I've read case histories of communities that have successfully fought off pub closures, and there is a general pattern which seems to have worked for some. The first thing to do is to officially apply to the council for the pub to be deemed an Asset of Community Value. I hate acronyms, but it's simpler to call it an ACV. The best way to do this might be to apply as a Neighbourhood Forum made up of people on the electoral register. I've taken the liberty of getting the necessary form from the council. Whenever this is filled in, it must stress the social interest and well-being of the local community, stressing the pub is a recreational facility, perhaps by listing the social activities that centre on the Wellie. If the ACV status is granted, and I'm assured it will be, then it remains active for an initial five years, and it puts restrictions on what the brewery can do with the pub. They might try to get around it by applying for a change of use status for the building, but that will need to go through our friends on the council. The brewery might try to get around it with legal challenges, but that costs money and takes up time. All the red tape that we hate here in Kirksea could work in our favour if the brewery find it easier just to sell off the pub to the community. That opens up a whole new can of financial worms but that can be dealt with later. It depends what the village wants to do. In order to formulate that plan, we need an informal steering group to set out what we want. It should have a good mix of skills and experience, such as business management, accounting, and social media. We will also need someone with a legal background at some point. As I have been at pains to point out, I am not trying to run this group, but I suggest that anyone who feels they may wish to help on the steering committee could put their names and a brief outline of the skills they have to offer on a letter and pass it over to Dave. He can then arrange for the volunteers to meet up and select from among themselves who to have on the steering group."

There was a general murmur of approval before Norman offered individuals the chance to make their comments on the proposed closure. There were many anecdotal acknowledgements as to the way the pub served the village and a general enthusiasm to take on Atkins and Dodd. While there were no dissenting voices, there were a few comments emphasizing that the fight was not just to provide a place for a few people to spend their time drinking there. Alex became aware that the villages had divided views about just what role the Wellie should play, but there was unanimous support for the need to fight the closure. If the pub became community property, then there would be different perceptions as to what exactly it would be like. But at least there would be a pub.

Alex had been putting off informing Megan and her mum about the details of the pub's precarious position. When Ivy had phoned to get her regular update on her cottage, he had just mentioned that the brewery was interested in selling the pub, but now things were starting to move in Kirksea, he knew he would have to give her more details. After he had told her about the work the builders had done since the New Year, he broached the difficult matter of the pub.

"They can't do that!" came the vehement retort. "I love that pub. I was expecting to meet all my new friends there. I've already spent happy moments contemplating my short walk from my cottage to the pub. Surely, something can be done; I could pay for a solicitor to fight it. To hell with the cost, the Wellie mustn't close. It can't close."

"It's not a done deal yet, love," he said in an attempt to console her. "We are setting up a group of villagers to mobilize our opposition to the closure, and we've got the local authority to support us as much as they can. If the brewery is required to try and sell the property, then we will have to sort out a way to raise funds."

"How much would it cost? I'll buy it; I'll sell this place. I can't stand by and see the Wellie pulled down."

"It's not as simple as that, and you can't just go buying a pub. To foil the brewery, we have to show the pub is valued by the local community and we can use various procedures to push that idea. Our hope is that by delaying their development, they will decide to just cut and run, but it won't be easy."

"Well, you can rely on my support, darling."

Ivy passed the phone over to Megan, and he gave her as much information as he had in the hope that she might be able to console her mum a bit. In turn, he received a lengthy update on the condition of the puppies, which had changed considerably since he saw them. Megan excitedly reported how they were starting to explore the area away from their mother; they were playing with each other and had started on semi-solid food as the weaning process began. It was quite apparent that they were far more interesting than the little squidgy lumps he had seen. They were responding well to handling by humans and showing some signs of their individual characteristics, so much so that Ivy had already picked out the puppy she wanted to keep. They talked for a while, and he was pleased that the conversation ended on a happy note and they promised to keep each other in touch about events in their respective locations.

CHAPTER THIRTY-ONE

Over the next two weeks, a steering committee was set up to formalize plans to save the Whelk Pot. While a number of people had shown a desire to be involved in fighting the brewery, there was a reluctance among many to work on any sort of committee, but eventually a small group of residents was drawn together. Norman was determined not to be seen as the leader, pushing through some kind of personal agenda, but it became clear at the first meeting of the committee that he was perceived as a suitable chairperson. The other members of the group included people with a large range of experiences. Daureen's time at the pub, during which it was generally accepted that she was the one who looked after the administrative side of the business, meant that the committee could have some insight as to how the brewery managed their pubs. Anita was there representing local businesses, as was Bricky. Early Pete agreed to turn up as he was sure there could be no conflict of interest with his position on the council. It turned out that Giles, the man Laura had referred to as her 'nearly fiancé', worked for a firm of business consultants, and he was persuaded to join the group. Old Bob was there as a representative of the older members of the village, and Helen was a welcome addition to the committee to try and ensure a bit of gender balance. The group tried to persuade Alex to join, but he said that he was a newcomer to the village and, as such, not representative of any particular section of the community.

It was also a fact that Alex knew he would be very busy over the next few weeks, as Ivy's cottage was nearing completion, and the tentative date for moving in was less than three weeks away. In the meantime, Alex learned that Megan had said she would stay with the puppies in York for a week or so as they were not due for their first vaccination until the week after the moving date, after which they could be taken from Mandy. He was delighted that the homing process had gone quite well. Jessica and her friend had each chosen one, and one of Ivy's friends from the bridge club, who had only called in on a social visit, couldn't resist and she had ordered one. One of Ivy's neighbours, who had got on well with Mandy, was delighted to reserve another pup and the vet had managed to suggest suitable owners for the remaining two. It was going to be a busy few days for Megan, but she was pleased to do what she could to help her mum over the moving period.

When the day of the move finally arrived, Alex drove over to collect Ivy. While her house looked slightly different, it was clear that she had decided to take only those items she needed and those with a particular sentimental value. This had the extra advantage in that Megan would not be left in a house devoid of furniture. The removal van had left before Alex arrived, and he found Ivy and Megan entertaining the puppies, which by now had taken over the kitchen. Elementary house training had started, and Megan spent time encouraging the puppies to go out into the garden, but with all the excitement of a new visitor, there were the occasional leaks. It was a rather enjoyable, if short, stay until the time came for Ivy to say goodbye to Megan and leave by the front door.

Ivy stood for a moment by the door, and her eyes watered slightly as she declared, "It's been a good home to us over the years, Alex. As you know, it took Josh and me a long time, with a lot of hard work, to work up to this. We'd never have dreamed of having such a lovely place when we were newlyweds in our little council flat. I remember the day we moved in here; we couldn't believe our luck, and we were worried about how we would be able to pay the mortgage. We've done well, but I'd swap it all to have Josh back."

Alex and Ivy did not talk much for the first part of the journey, but by the time they reached Kirksea, the mood had lightened as Ivy became re-energised by the prospect of moving into her cottage. Arrangements had been made to meet up with the removal van at two o'clock, and Bricky had agreed to be around to meet the van outside the pub with keys for the cottage, so the removal team could check out the layout of the cottage. They had instructions to unload a number of boxes marked as needing to go in the kitchen in case Ivy was delayed for any reason. By the time Alex had parked up his car and walked with Ivy down to the cottage, the men were just unloading the first of the kitchen boxes, and Ivy quickly set about providing tea and biscuits. The removal did not take long as the men were extremely efficient and Ivy had not brought a vast amount of furniture with her. In negotiations with Bricky, a lot of the details in the cottage had been seen to. Ivy had ordered curtains, and Slippers had fitted them throughout. The small dining set she ordered had been placed in the kitchen, which had been fitted out with a full range of white goods. The furniture and personal items she had brought with her in a range of large cardboard boxes were placed in allocated rooms. The house would take some time to make it homely, but it was comfortable enough for Ivy to just walk in and get on with her new life. It was already dark by the time the job was finished, and Ivy gave the men a generous tip before they set off back to York. When they had gone, Ivy and Alex each settled in a pair of armchairs that had been randomly placed in the lounge area.

"It's been a hell of a day, Ivy, but you've done it."

"Yes, and I am very pleased to have got here. Josh would have been proud of me for doing it. I'm shattered and I'm tempted to make yet another cup of tea, but I think I'd much rather settle for a glass of wine at the pub. Come on; it's not far to walk."

Alex took no persuading, and after a quick phone call to inform Megan that the move had been completed, he walked Ivy the few yards to the pub. Ivy was greeted warmly by a number of the locals who had been monitoring the redevelopment of number 30. After a much-needed supper, Ivy was the first to mention the shadow hanging over the pub's future, and she made it abundantly clear that she was prepared to fight the closure and that she was not used to losing. She was eager to get all the details about the state of the plans to oppose the closure, and repeated her willingness to buy the pub herself rather than see it close. Bricky assured her that, while her enthusiasm and generosity were welcome, the steering group had already registered the pub as an Asset of Community Value with the county council, and that would make life a little more difficult for the brewery to close the pub and sell it to a developer.

Ivy was looking a little tired after such an eventful day, and she was pleased to allow him to see her to her door. The pair stood for a while outside the cottage, admiring the view over the harbour. It was a bitterly cold, clear night, and the lights of the cottages were reflected in the still water.

"It's just beautiful Alex. It's like the realisation of a dream. Who would have thought, just a few months ago, that I would be standing here outside my own cottage in such lovely surroundings? Thanks for letting me move in here, love."

"I made it clear at the time that I never had any objection to you moving in. Megan and I just wanted you to think it through, but we both knew that if you wanted to do it then you would, and it would have been pointless trying to stand in your way. The poor brewery don't know what they are in for if they try to close your pub. Anyway, it's freezing out here. Bricky has left the central heating on to warm the place through, so just go and settle in. I'll pop in tomorrow."

"Thanks again, love," she said before kissing him on the cheek and walking up to her new front door. She stopped and looked back at Alex before giving a little giggle of excitement and letting herself in. Alex set off towards his home, and it occurred to him that in future, whenever he went to the pub, he would walk past his former mother-in-law's cottage. Few men would be pleased by such a prospect, but Alex was delighted. When he got home, Alex made a lengthy phone call to Megan to assure her that her mum was settled and, in turn, he got a quick update on Mandy and the puppies, after which he decided to have an early night.

Alex made a point of getting to Ivy's place early the next morning as he knew there would still be a lot of lifting and carrying to do. When he arrived, Ivy was in the kitchen area enjoying a bacon sandwich and a cup of tea, and she insisted that she provided the same for him, and he was not inclined to refuse.

"Sorry I'm a bit early, Ivy, but I thought I would get here before you started humping all this stuff around on your own."

"Early? I was up at five and went for a walk along the harbour wall. It was very cold and still dark, but I just wanted to explore a bit. I've got rather used to waking early with a kitchen full of pups to see to. I do hope Megan is coping."

"I'm sure she can, but it won't be easy; Jessica will help a bit when she can, but she has her own life to lead. It's not been the best of times for Mandy to have had her little fling, but Megan is quite a woman."

"She certainly is. It's not been easy for her on her own the last few of years as the divorce has gone through. I sometimes think she regrets ever having gone through it."

"Stop it, Ivy love," he interjected. "We've gone through all that."

"Sorry," she said and then giggled. Alex realised that she had been teasing him, and he had risen to the bait.

"You are very naughty, Ivy. I often wondered where Megan got that trait from. In all seriousness, though, she has to arrange for the puppies to have their first jabs and then sort out the homing of them. It's a good job she's a very organized individual."

"We were lucky to find good homes for them all. They are absolutely adorable, but I'm afraid the pedigree line has gone to the dogs if you'll excuse the term. I can't wait to get Mandy and little Gordon over with me."

"Gordon? Because he looks like a Gordon Setter?"

"No; but I guess his darker colouring does give a superficial suggestion of a Gordon Setter. No, I named him after Bricky; he's been so helpful with all the issues surrounding the cottage."

"You sweetie! I'm sure Bricky will feel honoured."

"It could be 10 days or so before the dogs can join me. I've arranged for Mandy to be spayed before she comes here and then she can have a few quiet days to recuperate."

"I guess that you won't feel fully settled until you get the dogs over here with you?" suggested Alex.

"I suppose so, but I feel at home already, in a strange sort of way. When I woke up this morning and looked out over the village, even in the darkness before dawn I could pick out the shapes of the buildings and the dark mass of the water in the harbour. It was like being on holiday, and I felt rejuvenated."

The couple worked hard all morning, unpacking items and placing them where Ivy directed. It was obvious that she had put a lot of thought into exactly where she wanted her possessions to go. When she came to a large photograph of herself and Josh, she studied it for a while before putting it on the fireplace above her new wood-burner. Having arranged it just the way she wanted it, she looked at it for a short while and then in a quiet voice, said, "We finally made it to our retirement cottage, darling."

By midday, the cottage was starting to look more like a home, and it was Alex who declared, "I think that's enough for one morning. Do you fancy fish and chips? It will save cooking."

Ivy took no persuading, and the two of them put on their coats for the short walk to the chip shop, where they were met by Anita in her usual cheery fashion.

"Morning, gorgeous. I see you've got yet another lady friend with you. Still, I have to admire your stamina."

"Thank you, darling," he replied in similar manner. "But if you're making a play for me, you'll just have to get in line. I'm sure you know my friend Ivy; she's keen to try some of the best fish and chips in Yorkshire."

"We all know about 'Battling Ivy'. Dad told me how you were ready to roll up your sleeves last night and have a go at the brewery."

Alex glanced to see if Ivy was offended by the nickname but she seemed positively delighted, and she treated Anita to a short discourse on what she would like to do to Atkins and Dodd. Alex smiled at this latest sign that Ivy would fit in well in Kirksea.

CHAPTER THIRTY-TWO

Over the following week, Alex continued to help Ivy settle into her cottage and introduce her to the routines and some of the people in Kirksea. He found himself passing on snippets of information that he had only learnt of a few months earlier. At the same time, he made regular calls to Megan to ascertain how she was getting on with life in York. From his calls, it was apparent that she and Jessica had established some kind of routine and Stephanie had been able to help out at weekends, but it was obviously hard work.

As the time drew near for Mandy and Gordon to be delivered to Kirksea, Alex spoke frequently to Megan to finalise the plans. It was decided that he would drive over to York and return with the dogs and Megan, who would then stay with her mum for a couple of days. In his call on the evening before the planned visit, it appeared that everything was going well. Jessica's friend, who was the last to collect her puppy, was due to collect him on the following day, and then the entire litter would be accounted for. Alex was a little concerned when he arrived in York to find Mandy still had two of her puppies with her. He had expected the newly named Gordon, but there was an extra bundle of fur running around excitedly.

"I'm afraid that Jessica's friend, Seline, has found that she is due to leave the area to take up a new post," explained Megan. "She didn't want to mess us about, but she just couldn't cope with a puppy in the circumstances; she's been trying right up to the last minute to find a replacement home but was unsuccessful. So, we now have a spare."

"I'm sorry, Dad, I should have known Seline was a bit of a risk, but she was very keen."

"It's not your fault, Jess. We can get it sorted, but the first thing we have to do is to let your gran know what's going on."

Ivy was little surprised to receive a call from him outlining the problem with the extra puppy. He offered to keep it until it was possible to find a permanent home. Ivy would have none of it and insisted that she would prefer to keep the dogs together for the short term. Alex knew better than to try and argue, particularly as he had reservations about the practicality of having a young pup in his house. The problem facing him now was how to transport Megan and the dogs over to Kirksea. As Mandy had been spayed a few days earlier, it was important that she shouldn't exert herself, and the puppies were likewise not to be allowed to do anything too energetic. Mandy was encouraged to get on the back seat of the car and then her two puppies were lifted in beside her. The older dog had been a seasoned car traveller and appeared keen to get on with the journey, but it was a completely new experience for the young dogs, who bounded around excitedly. Eventually, they calmed down and looked out of the windows as Alex drove off with Megan beside him.

It was necessary for the puppies to have 'comfort breaks', which meant Alex having to stop in suitably quiet spots, off the main road, to let them sniff around a bit before performing. On the second such location, Alex mentioned that this particular parking place was one Ivy and Josh used to visit regularly on their days out before they were married.

"How do you know?" Asked Megan.

"Ivy pointed it out when I was taking her back to York that time."

"Oh! Of course. I'm not surprised they stopped here; it's such a beautiful view and so quiet."

"They would have appreciated the solitude, but I doubt they cared too much about the view."

"What do you mean?" she said, but after a short pause she declared, "You mean…"

"Yes, they were no doubt enjoying their own Morris Marina moments together."

"It never occurred to me that they would have been involved in that sort of thing," observed Megan. "I suppose you don't tend to think of your parents doing that before they were married."

"It's strange that every generation assumes that they invented sex. Your mum has a far greater understanding of such relationships than you might give her credit for. She pointed out at Josh's wake that she was fully aware that our girls were not staying in single rooms that night and, from the knowing looks that I share with her, I'm sure that she understands why we enjoyed going out in our old car before we were married. Nothing has been said, but we understand each other."

Having given the dogs time to empty themselves out, the couple re-joined the main road and resumed their journey to Kirksea. Megan sat in silence, smiling to herself from time to time as she reflected on her mum's behaviour, but by the time Alex next pulled over to let the dogs out, she was asleep. He was not surprised; she had been looking after the dogs for quite a while, and her nights had been frequently disturbed, so he let her sleep on.

Arriving back at the village, Alex parked the car up and they set off to meet Ivy. Mandy walked in a well-behaved manner, but the pups were keen to pull on their leads to explore this strange new place. As expected, her pets were all thrilled to see Ivy again, and she was surrounded by a frenzy of licking and tail-wagging dogs for a while before they could eventually be calmed down. Mandy was then content to sit quietly at Ivy's side, looking up at her adoringly while the pups explored their new environment. Alex had expected the cottage to be rather small to accommodate Mandy and Gordon, but the unexpected addition of a second pup, now unimaginatively called Spare, made it obvious that living conditions would be somewhat cramped, and Alex was pleased when Ivy suggested they all went for a walk.

The tide was out, exposing the hard packed sand of the lower shore as the three individuals, each in charge of a dog, walked towards the sea. It was tempting to let the dogs run free, but they had been advised not to over-exert the puppies, and Mandy was likewise not supposed to get over-excited after her operation. When they arrived at the point where the beck trickled into the water of the North Sea, it was obvious that Mandy was not keen to get her feet wet and nor was Gordon, but his brother was desperate to get into the shallow stream and pulled on his lead until Megan allowed him to have a little paddle. Alex wondered if Spare had inherited some genetic love of water from his particular father, as he seemed very much at home there.

The group walked for some distance along the shoreline, with the pups being keen to explore every item that had been deposited there. Eventually, the intrepid little band turned round and headed back to the harbour mouth, where they found Norman on his regular bench.

"Hi Wessie; I see you've got a full pack there," said Norman, leaning forward so that the dogs could sniff at his hand before he stroked each of them in turn and then asking, "What are their names? I know that she's the Mandy we've all heard so much about, but what about the other two?"

Alex introduced the dogs to Norman and briefly explained the reason for them having the unexpected extra puppy.

Norman was particularly amused to hear that the puppy Ivy had originally chosen was to be called Gordon, after Bricky. The group sat around for a while with Ivy taking the opportunity to say how much she loved her cottage and hated Atkins and Dodd. Norman was able to reassure her that the committee who were looking into the issue had high hopes that closure could be averted. Throughout the discussions, Spare was eagerly sniffing at Norman's feet.

"I suppose you can smell Muffin on my boots. I always wore them when I walked him, and he used to carry them off and put them in his bed if I wasn't careful," he said to the pup. Spare seemed to be impressed at being addressed personally, and he lifted his paw onto Norman's knee and gave a squeaky bark.

"I can't get out of the habit of talking to dogs," confessed Norman.

"That's weird; you wouldn't catch me doing that, would you, Mandy?" said Ivy as she turned to her own dog.

Eventually, Alex declared that he was starving and they ought to be thinking of a meal, so the group set off back towards Ivy's cottage, though Spare was reluctant to leave his new-found friend with the alluring boots. Back at the cottage, Ivy and Megan put the last touches to a casserole, and Alex was supervised in the routine of feeding the dogs. After their various meals, the entire household was comfortable. Mandy was sprawled out in front of the log burner with the two puppies asleep by her side while the human contingent found whatever comfortable place they could. It was once again apparent that three dogs could be accommodated in the small cottage, but only if the number of humans was restricted. After a while, Ivy made a suggestion.

"Why don't the pair of you nip to the pub for a while, and I will stay and look after my little friends? You deserve a break after all you've done to help me and the dogs. There's a programme I want to watch on the TV, and there'll be plenty of time for me to get to the pub when the dogs are a little more settled into the area."

Reassured that this was not one of Ivy's match-making attempts, Megan and Alex took up the offer. The Wellie was relatively quiet. Bricky was talking to Norman, who had obviously decided that he'd had enough of sitting out on the harbour wall on what was becoming a bitterly cold day.

"Evening, Wessie, evening, Megan," said Norman. "I was just telling Bricky that I've met his namesake."

"Yes, Mum was insistent upon calling the pup Gordon. She's probably got to know you quite well, Bricky, having phoned you several times a week while the cottage was being renovated. She can be quite persistent."

"No problem," he replied. "It's good to have a client who is clear about what she wants."

"Speaking of renovation work," said Norman, "we were just discussing what we might be able to plan for this place that would strengthen our dealings with the council. Bricky said that we could create a separate room downstairs by dividing up the existing bar area with a stud wall so that, in effect, what was the downstairs area of the end cottage of the three would be a separate room that could be used for all sorts of things. Bricky said it would be an easy job to reopen the front door to that cottage, thus creating a separate entrance, but we could put a door in the dividing wall so it could be accessed from the bar. We could even reinstate the old cottage's stairs to access the upstairs. That end of the pub is just a glory hole upstairs and could be closed off from the landlord's flat to create a small meeting room, or perhaps even two."

"Sounds interesting, but wouldn't it take a lot of room from the main bar?" suggested Alex.

"We've discussed it with Dave and Daureen, and they pointed out that the bar is rarely packed," replied Bricky. "If there's a big do on, like Christmas or Saint Bodolv's Day, then we could spread out into the new room we could create next door. We have to make the building suit many groups within the village to strengthen our case to keep the building as a community asset and be assured of the council's continued backing."

"I can see a lot of the regulars in the pub asking if the Wellie really needs separate meeting rooms," commented Megan.

"There will be those who don't want to see any changes," replied Norman. "But the fact is that we need to show that the building will serve different groups as well as being the village pub. In blunt terms, it's a matter of either accepting changes to the role of the pub or not having a pub at all. There will be conflicting views as to how the building should be used, but we all know that we are a group who are used to getting on with each other. There will be compromises, but I'm sure we can do it."

"So, what is the next step?" asked Alex.

"The steering committee have been tentatively working in a number of areas," answered Norman. "I've been using my connections with the *Gazette* to make people aware of the pub's position and to rally a bit of support from the readers, many of whom are dismayed at the prospect of losing yet another pub. With the support of the paper, we have arranged to put out fliers to the village members to inform them of our proposed plans and asking for comments. The one thing that has quickly become apparent is that it is a very complicated road that we have set out on. We need advice on legal and financial matters, and that may mean employing professionals. Laura's friend Giles has connections, and we could probably negotiate a good deal with him. The local branch of CAMRA has offered guidance if we need it, as they have a lot of experience of fighting pub closures."

"CAMRA?" queried Alex. "Aren't they just interested in getting people to drink real ale?"

"That's a big part of their brief, it's true," answered Norman. "But they are also concerned to ensure that there are suitable venues for drinking in, whether it be clubs or pubs, because they recognise the value of such places."

"It sounds expensive," said Megan.

"It is," agreed Norman. "The cost of the pub sounds very reasonable, even with the freehold. If you bought it at that price and then split it into three cottages again you would make a hefty profit, but to do that you would need to get a change of use order from the council, and our council would be very reluctant to issue such a document. When we buy the pub, and I'm sure we will, we have all sorts of financial issues to sort out. We need to pay someone to run the place, meet all the immediate running costs, business rates and energy costs, and we need to ensure that we have insurance for public liability as well as the building. It has to be constantly born in mind that squeezing a profit out of running a pub is not easy. If it were then Atkins and Dodd would hang on to their premises."

"Which begs the question as to where the money will come from," said Megan.

"Once again, the steering committee can only make suggestions," said Norman, "but, having looked at the possible options used by other groups such as ours, we would favour the selling of shares to local individuals and businesses. You can see the need for a specialist accountant to get the business off on a stable base and to carefully monitor it in the future. Potential investors should be aware that this project is never going to yield big profits."

"But at least we will still have the Wellie," asserted Alex. "And the brewery will escape the wrath of Ivy; God knows what merciless revenge she would have exerted on them if her pub had been closed down. We'd better get back and tell her how things are shaping up."

A cold wind was blowing in off the North Sea as Megan and Alex made the short walk to Ivy's cottage. Despite the biting wind driving odd flakes of snow onto the village, they stopped outside the cottage and looked out over the harbour together.

"Mum got it right, love," declared Megan. "This place is lovely. I'll have to go a long way to get somewhere as nice as this."

"I'm sure that you can stay with Ivy from time to time, particularly if you find yourself between homes at some time in the near future."

Alex smiled broadly, which caused Megan to ask, "What's so funny?"

"It was just that, on our first visit to Whitby, your mum effectively asked my permission to move into Kirksea because she was worried that I might be offended if you subsequently came to visit her here."

"And has it proved to be difficult?"

"I think you know the answer to that, love. As I tried to explain to your mum, the divorce was merely a way of ending an agreement; it was never about me not liking you or about us hating each other. So, I think I can cope with seeing you around."

As if to prove his point, he playfully kissed her on the cheek, which prompted the response, "Good. I'm glad I'm not a complete embarrassment to you; now we'd better get inside. If Mum sees us loitering out here, she will wonder what romantic escapade we are up to."

CHAPTER THIRTY-THREE

Looking out of his bedroom window the next morning, Alex was not surprised to see evidence of the previous night's snow. It was rather a pathetic dusting of white but probably enough to cause major traffic chaos if it had fallen in London. It was certainly not enough to impact on his plans for the day, which were to start with him helping to walk the dog pack. When he arrived later at Ivy's, the two women were ready for their walk along the beach, and the dogs were certainly keen to get out.

As they approached the harbour wall, they found Norman sitting in his usual spot, and he asked them if he could join them on the beach, explaining that it seemed to be largely a waste of energy to go for a walk without a dog. So it was that the four of them and the three dogs went down to the beach. The tide was on its way out, but it had receded sufficiently to leave a broad strip of wet sand. The beach was deserted, which was hardly surprising as the winds appeared to be blowing directly from Siberia. After they had walked a short distance, Ivy thought it was worth risking letting the dogs off their leads. Mandy walked sedately next to Ivy, but the puppies took the opportunity to explore parts of the beach. They never went far and kept returning to the group when Ivy called them back. This impressed Norman, who pointed out that old Muffin had never displayed that elementary sign of obedience, and in fact the dog had never heeded even the most basic commands. It was obvious during his time off the lead that Spare tended to walk next to Norman, and this was attributed to the allure of his old boots.

Within a short time, the party seemed to divide naturally as Ivy and Norman walked ahead with the dogs while Alex and Megan strolled along, some 20 yards behind. The sound of the wind meant that the two groups were not in earshot of each other, and Megan felt able to comment on her mother's situation.

"Mum seems to have settled in remarkably quickly to her new home. I suppose we should never have doubted it, but it did seem such a big gamble, particularly so soon after Dad's death. The dogs have been a great help to her."

"Yes, they are a handful, and I have serious reservations about her sharing that cottage with three big dogs, but it seems to have taken her mind off your dad's passing."

"Oh, the memories of Dad are naturally still there, and she makes frequent references to him, and particularly how much he would have loved Kirksea."

"Yes, it's obvious that she has been shaken by his death, but after over 50 years together it's not surprising that it left one hell of a void in her life. Few people are blessed with a marriage that lasts so long, and we should know. The dogs give her an interest, and now she has her crusade to save the Wellie, her life will be a lot fuller."

"We seemed to be getting on reasonably well when we were married, Alex, but I guess that wasn't enough."

"To say that we were getting on reasonably well is like saying we coped with it. I admit that I never appreciated the need to work on a relationship, and I guess that latterly we just wandered through matrimony, 'doing our time' until the children were off our hands. We had other things on our minds, largely our careers. I often think I could have coped with the split better if either of us had indulged in some extra-marital exercises or if there had been some acrimonious bust-up. To pinch an image from Eliot, our marriage didn't end with a bang, but with a whimper."

"I know what you mean, but I often wonder when the decline set in. Our friends thought we were made for each other and initially everything seemed great."

"It wasn't one particular event just an insidious crumbling away of our marriage. We must be grateful that we came out of it OK in the end."

Their conversation was cut short when Norman and Ivy stopped and started to head back towards Kirksea.

"The puppies have had enough exercise for now, so Norman and I are going to take them home. You two can continue walking if you like. Norman tells me Saint Bodolv's cave is about half a mile further. He knows a lot about Saint Bodolv."

"Largely because he made it all up," Alex whispered to Megan before declaring, "I think we'll leave that excitement for another day and get back to the village before we all freeze to death."

Ivy insisted that they all went to her place for a hot cup of tea and biscuits. The addition of Norman to the domestic scene only went to further prove that life with three large dogs in the cottage would be more than a little congested even after her present visitors had left. The dogs' presence in the lounge was a cause for concern for Megan, who expressed her reservations about her mum tripping over one or other of them. Norman recounted his own experiences of having to step over Muffin at times, even when he was actually just stepping over a shadow.

"Have you had any more ideas about the little chap's future?" asked Norman, pointing towards Spare, who had taken up his chosen position by Norman's feet.

"We were hoping that the young woman who gave backword would reconsider when she had settled in her new job," said Ivy. "She was heartbroken when she felt she couldn't take him. We couldn't bear the thought of selling him to just anybody, so hence, he has taken up residence by the seaside with me, and I love him to bits."

"I don't suppose you would sell him to me?" Norman said suddenly. "Edna and I are used to dogs, and even though we were determined not to have another after Muffin passed, we find life a bit empty. When I told her about Spare, she soon saw the sense of offering him a home; anyway, he seems to like me, or at least my boots."

"I'm sure the little mite couldn't hope for a better home," replied Ivy.

Norman leant over and gave his new puppy an energetic stroke before thanking Ivy and stating that there were a couple of points he needed to clear up.

"Would you be too offended if Edna and I changed his name, and what do you want for him?"

"All I want for him is a good home, and I'm sure you can offer that, but it seems unkind to just give him away as if he's not worth anything, so perhaps we could agree on you putting up a couple of wine tokens for me at the Wellie. I gather the usual currency is beer tokens, but I don't drink beer."

"He's worth a lot more to Edna and me, but it's a deal. What about the name change?"

"I think he deserves a proper name," replied Ivy, "not one that suggests he was just an afterthought. I'll sort out some of his puppy food, and perhaps you'd like to pick him up in the morning?"

Norman was obviously delighted with the way things had turned out and stated that he couldn't wait to give Edna the good news. He set off home with an extra spring in his step.

The next day, being Wednesday, was Alex's opportunity to discuss Norman's most recent offering from the *Gazette*. He enjoyed meeting up in the Whelk Pot with Dave and Norman to determine how much of the latter's journalistic contributions were factual and how much it may have owed to the writer's mischievous imagination. Norman was particularly pleased with this week's edition because he had made the front page.

"Look at this, gentlemen," exhorted Norman, holding up the paper to display the headlines which he read out, "*Kirksea villagers fight to save pub.*"

"Very impressive, Norman," conceded Dave after a while. "And you've even spelled my name right, although I have no recollection of the 'interview' you mention that you had with me."

"It's more of a summary of what we've discussed in the past, but I think you'll agree that it's more or less what you've said; I just gave it a little more emotional impact to get the public on our side. It's what we call journalistic license."

"It seems to read a bit like a Victorian melodrama," said Alex, who had taken the trouble to scan the article. "One might be forgiven for thinking that the wicked brewery bosses are going to mercilessly drive Dave and Daureen into the workhouse."

"Admittedly, I may have over-egged that particular bit of the custard, but I think you'll agree that the rest is pretty factual, and it gives the public some insight into the stage we are at with our fight to retain the pub. It's important that all the locals know what is going on with our campaign."

"I have to admit," said Alex, "that you appear to have summed up our current thinking pretty well without giving Atkins and Dodd any insight into our planning. Well done, Norman."

"Thank you, dear fellow. Changing the subject, have you told Dave about my new addition to the family?"

"I had no idea Edna was pregnant. Congratulations," responded Dave.

"Cheeky devil! Alex obviously hasn't told you about my new puppy. I'm going round to Ivy's soon to pick him up."

"I'm pleased to hear it. Are you going to train him up to come to the pub on his own like old Muffin?"

"I may be persuaded to bring him down after he's had his second jab so he can get a bit of pub culture. The Wellie was a finishing school for Muffin, but all he seemed to learn was where the treats were kept. It only took him 13 years, but he managed it. Speaking of which, could I pinch three of those little dog biscuits to take to my friends?"

"Why not? It's only the pub profits for the day gone. You'll have us in the workhouse before Atkins and Dodd do."

Alex couldn't resist the opportunity to accompany Norman to pick up his latest little friend. As soon as they entered Ivy's cottage, the dogs were obviously pleased to see their visitors, and they crowded around eagerly, wanting to be made a fuss of. Alex couldn't help noticing that Spare was particularly keen to greet Norman, and it was becoming obvious that it was more than the smell of his walking shoes that attracted the puppy. Perhaps it had been the way that Norman had responded to the little chap, particularly having heard that he had effectively been turned down by Seline. It had been the start of an obvious but indefinable bond between man and puppy.

"I've got some of his puppy food and his blanket to help him settle," explained Ivy. "Have you decided on a name for him yet?"

"Oh no! That's Edna's area of expertise. When she meets the little chap, she will no doubt come up with suggestions; the only thing I insist upon is that it mustn't be a name that I would be embarrassed to call out in public. Her mother used to have a Yorkie that she opted to call Woofsy. Whenever I took that dog for a walk, I insisted upon calling him Fang.

No one can argue that it was a stupid name for a Yorkie, but I was not going to sit in a pub where I had to call a dog Woofsy."

Norman was keen to get home and introduce Edna to their new family member, and pretty soon he was setting off with his bag of puppy goods in one hand and his new friend on a lead in his other. The puppy seemed completely unfazed by his sudden change of status, and he bounded along next to his new master as they disappeared up the road.

"I know it's silly, but I'm sorry to see him go in a way," admitted Ivy. "It's been the same with all of them. I'm glad I kept Gordon."

"You'll see plenty of Norman's new dog around the village, whatever they decide to call him, and pretty soon you'll be able to meet up in the Wellie or go for walks on the beach if your sciatica doesn't play up," added Megan mischievously. "Speaking of dog walking; do you fancy joining us for a walk down by the water, Alex?"

"I think my social calendar is not too full, so I would be delighted."

The truth was that he had thoroughly enjoyed the previous day's walk; he had enjoyed his conversation with Megan even though it had partly consisted of a dispassionate post-mortem of their marriage. At least it had confirmed the fact that, even after their experiences, they were good friends. It was a grown-up way to cope with the aftermath of the divorce, he kept reassuring himself. The walk proved to be enjoyable although it was cut short, by mutual consent, when it started to snow. This was real snow, and by the time the dog walkers had got back to the harbour, there was already a slight covering on the ground and no sign of the snow stopping. Alex suddenly had the image in his head that Old Bob had described of his legendry, and entirely fictitious, walk to school. In the short time it took the group to get to Ivy's, there was a full inch of snow. It was that white, unsullied snow reminiscent of those halcyon winter days portrayed on Christmas cards. Ivy stood for a while in what was now almost a minor blizzard, looking out over the view from in front of her cottage.

"Doesn't it look pretty?" she asked. "The covering of snow seems to clean everything up. I just love it."

"It does, Mum, but let's get inside before we lose the dogs in the snow."

By this time, the dogs had started to accumulate snow on their fur. They seemed completely unbothered by it, but Ivy conceded that they all ought to get inside.

"It's a pity it will all turn to slush at some point," said Ivy as she closed the door on the weather.

"It's a good job you weren't hoping that I could take you home tomorrow, love," commented Alex. "Did you have any particular thought as to when you might want to go back to York?"

"I had thought that I might stay on for a couple of weeks to help Mum get the dogs into some sort of regime, but I don't have any specific plans. It would be good to see that Gordon gets his second jab next week, but that's about all that I wanted to get done. As you suggest, it's a good job we have no imminent plans in this weather."

After the obligatory cup of tea, Alex declared his intention to get home before the snow got any deeper, and refusing the offer of lunch, he set off gingerly for his own home. It was the lack of fresh footprints in the snow that made him aware that few people had ventured out. As he passed the chip shop, he noted that there had been little sign of pedestrian traffic, so he called in to have a chat with Anita and to get some short respite from the snow.

"Hello, sweetie," he greeted her, "I didn't think you would be open today in this weather."

"Hi, handsome," she replied. "No, it's really hardly worth firing up the range, but some people have their traditions, and I don't want to let them down. If any of the local builders are working in the village, they like to drop in for their lunch break, so Nora or I try and be available. Nora is making herself available somewhere else, so don't expect any late post today. I hear Norman's got a new dog. I knew he wouldn't stick to his resolution not to get another. It's a bit like my boyfriend Tom after a particularly heavy night at the Wellie, who wakes up the next day and swears he'll never drink again. Norman looks lost without Muffin, so it was odds-on that he would get another."

"Yes, but I'm not entirely sure if he chose the dog or the dog chose him. They seem a perfect match; it will be nice to see them down at the pub when the puppy's had all his jabs."

"So, what's he decided to call it?"

"We don't know yet. Apparently, all big decisions like the naming of dogs are Edna's responsibility, so we'll just have to wait and see."

CHAPTER THIRTY-FOUR

Alex enjoyed his time with Ivy and Megan. It was like a mini-holiday. They took the dogs out for short walks each day in the snow despite a bitterly cold wind, and he enjoyed the shared meals at Ivy's cottage. He had to concede that it was preferable to always cooking for one and then eating alone. His enjoyment of the period was further enhanced by the progress being made to fight the closure of the Whelk Pot. After a period of consultation with the villagers, a management committee had been set up to finalise plans for attempting to buy and then run the pub. Alex found himself on the committee, partly because his former rank in the police added an air of respectability to the list of members. It had been decided that the initial attempt to buy the pub would be done by selling shares to local individuals and businesses. There were also plans to seek community development grants and to organize fundraising events. It was envisaged that the proceeds of all these money-raising events could be used to open a bank account and later to secure a loan if necessary. All of this meant that the committee had strayed further into the areas of officialdom that were so alien to some of them, but it was obvious that the purchase and running of the pub could not be done on an entirely unofficial level with money being passed around in brown envelopes and jobs being done without bothering the tax man too much. A number of the locals had shown their intentions to carry out any work on the pub at very competitive rates, and Bricky was already trying to envisage ways in which he could circumvent some of the official rules so that he might be able to work on the pub as cheaply as possible. Dave and Daureen had expressed their eagerness to take on the role of managers if the deal went through.

It was becoming increasingly obvious that the rescue of the pub was not as simple as collecting money and buying the building. Laura's friend Giles had agreed to give some guidance and, while she had been staying with Ivy, Alex had managed to persuade Megan to give some general advice. After all, she'd had considerable experience of running her own company. The following Wednesday, Alex was particularly eager to get his preview of the *Gazette* with Norman, who had done a follow-up article about attempts to buy the pub. The report seemed remarkably unembellished by Norman's standards but simply gave the facts about the ongoing attempts to prevent the pub closure. He had been demoted to page two because the front cover featured a full-page picture of Whitby under a considerable blanket of snow. It looked lovely, but the reality of getting around the village during the week had not been ideal, and the snow was still persisting.

"Never mind the *Gazette*," remarked Alex, "what about the name of the puppy formerly known as Spare? Has Edna made her decision?"

"Finally! We talked it through a lot, and eventually we went for Jake. It was Muffin's original name before his cerebral limitations became apparent and Edna changed it. The new Jake is so different; he's already shown more signs of intelligence in a week than Muffin did in his entire life. At this rate, Edna will soon want to change his name to Einstein, but I will resist."

"We look forward to seeing him here in the Wellie," said Dave, "along with Ivy's pair, and if they are as bright as Jake, it will make a nice change after some of the crowd we get in here."

"What about the darts team?" queried Alex. "Will Jake be able to take over the role of mascot?"

"The way he's developing, he'll be taking over as chairman," suggested Norman.

The snow showers had eased off, but there was little sign of any thaw as Alex carefully made his way to Ivy's cottage. He was pleased to get in out of the cold and gratefully accepted the offer of a cup of tea.

"I notice you've seen it," said Megan.

"Sorry! Seen what?" he asked.

"My Valentine's card from my 'secret admirer'. Mum never gives up. She's sent that and disguised the writing to suggest it's from you."

"I tell you, I know nothing about it. I didn't even know it was Valentine's Day," protested Ivy. "I just found it on the doormat this morning when I got up."

"You know as well as I do that Kevin the postie never gets here that early, Mum."

The women glanced towards Alex, who was looking slightly uneasy, and in unison they said, "Alex!"

"I may have been involved a little bit," he said unconvincingly before admitting, "I just thought it would brighten your day up a bit, love. You know I never missed Valentine's Day; wedding anniversaries and birthdays seemed to creep up and pass me, but I never forgot Valentine's Day."

The women laughed at his obvious embarrassment, and Megan kissed him on the cheek.

"Thanks. It was a lovely thought, weird, but lovely," she remarked.

"Norman and Edna have decided to call their new dog Jake," he announced in a desperate attempt to change the subject, and he went on to explain the reasoning behind the naming, but he couldn't help feeling that the women's minds were still fixed on his card. Later, while Ivy was out in the kitchen preparing lunch, Megan walked over, picked up the card and read out the scribbled dedication.

"*Love as always, from your secret admirer,*" she read out and then giggled before turning to the front of the card, which displayed a large red heart surrounded by cherubs, and she continued to read.

"*I give my heart and know it's true, my life is nothing without you.*"

"It was one of a very limited choice at the village shop, and Brian was keen to suggest it for me, having admitted that he'd bought the same card for Colin."

"It's a lovely sentiment," she said without much conviction.

"I know what you mean, but at least the dedication is genuine,"

"So, you see yourself as my secret admirer?" she said with a smile.

"I always admired the way you had a full-time job but still did a disproportionate amount of the housework and more than your fair share of bringing up the girls, but I effectively kept my admiration a secret from you. So, I guess that makes me a secret admirer."

It was at this point that Ivy returned from the kitchen, so Megan surreptitiously put the card back.

"This snow is nice to look at, but it makes getting around very difficult, and there seems no sign of it melting away. As soon as we have a bit of a thaw, we have the snow coming back," commented Ivy as she looked out of the window at the view over the harbour.

"Yes, it's been a predictable topic of conversation at the Wellie,." added Alex. "Even Old Bob admits that it's a bit unusual. He hasn't seen snow like it since 1963. It just seems to be persisting like you suggest, Ivy. We haven't had any great depth of snow, but it just doesn't seem to want to go. There is some good news about the pub's future; Dave has heard a rumour that Atkins and Dodd appear to be prepared to consider an offer from the village. It seems that they have acknowledged that fighting it would not be in their best interests. The obvious conviction within the village to fight the closure appears to have convinced them that it would be a lengthy process to try and obtain the site for any other purpose and that delay would cost them money. With the reluctance of the council to grant a change of use directive and the fact that we have secured a five-year moratorium on their plans by having the Wellie registered as an Asset of Community Value, the brewery have recognised that the Wellie closure will be no pushover. It's only a rumour, but Dave generally knows what's going on, and Early Pete has confirmed that the council are fully behind us. Even so, we've got to keep up our campaign to save our pub."

"I should think so," declared Ivy forcefully. "Nobody is going to steal my pub from me."

"Before you man the barricades, Ivy love," said Alex, "I'm hoping to get over to the vets tomorrow with Norman to get Jake's injections if the roads are clear. You had said that you would like me to take Gordon as well, so I could pick him up tomorrow if that suits you."

"That would be a big help, thanks," said Ivy. "And while you are there, you could ask about his little operation." The last part was delivered in a hushed voice.

"What operation?" asked Alex.

"Shush! You know the little…" She mimed scissors snapping together.

Alex winced visibly and nodded to Ivy. "I will look into it. Meanwhile, I'll pick Gordon up at about ten tomorrow morning."

The following day, Alex woke to bright sunshine. He was pleased that there had been no more snow, and having picked up Norman and the puppies, they walked up to the car. The road down to the village had been kept relatively clear of snow thanks to Captain, who had fired one of the tractors into action and, with a Heath Robinson-style snow plough attachment, had made regular trips up and down the road. The car started easily, and Alex carefully made his way to the main road, where he was pleased to see that the gritters had cleared the way towards Whitby. It was a strange driving experience as the clear, slushy road was bordered by some impressive, drifted snow. Slowly, Alex picked his way to the vet and the necessary injections were given. As directed by Ivy, Alex arranged an appointment for Gordon's 'little operation' and while they were there, Norman arranged for Jake to have the same procedure. The drive back to Kirksea was uneventful, and Alex delivered Gordon home to Ivy, who was delighted to be reunited with him.

"Megan will be down in a minute," explained Ivy. "She's just sorting out some of her packing, so she's ready to make an early start on Saturday. Are you still OK to take her back to York?"

"Of course. There's no need for us to set off early, so I thought I would be here at about ten."

"I've told her that there is no need for her to rush off, but she wants a bit of time on her own to settle some of the issues about selling her house. I know she's not keen to leave; we've had so much fun."

"I've got to admit that it's been a most enjoyable few days. It's been lovely to chat about old times, but I know that Megan wants to sort out her domestic arrangements; she feels to be in limbo at the moment and wants to get settled."

"Did I hear someone mention my name?" asked Megan as she came into the room and petted a rather excited Gordon, who was naturally delighted to see her.

"We were just finalising plans for getting you back to York on Saturday, love," explained Alex.

"Can't you wait to get rid of me?" she teased him.

"You know that's not true," he explained, "but you said you wanted to get back to sort things out. The weather forecast isn't ideal, but the main roads are clear, and the snow forecast for the weekend is quite a bit to the north of here and not expected to be heavy."

"Why don't the pair of you take the opportunity to nip out to the Wellie tomorrow, as it's the last day of Megan's visit," suggested Ivy.

Even though he had a slight suspicion that this was a last-ditch attempt at match-making on Ivy's part, Alex was more than happy to take up the offer but explained that he was working in the chip shop for one of his occasional Friday slots in the afternoon, after which he would need to shower and change before meeting Megan. He explained that his shift had been a last-minute arrangement because Nora had declared that she had a medical appointment.

"Medical appointment!" exclaimed Ivy. "She's probably playing doctors and nurses with Kevin."

Alex said nothing but inwardly reflected on the fact that it hadn't taken long for Ivy to pick up on some of the local gossip.

The following day, having finished his slot at the chip shop, Alex went home and had a lengthy shower to remove the alluring taint of eau de cod. He had a second shave of the day and applied rather too much of his best aftershave. Once again, he was struck by the thought that he was behaving more like someone going out on a first date rather than just meeting an old friend, but he felt rather pleased with his general appearance as he called for Megan, which of course was conveniently on the way to the pub. The moment Alex and Megan entered the pub, they were aware of a small group of people crowded around a display of notices on one wall beside the bar.

As Dave prepared their drinks, he explained the interest being shown in the notices.

"Bricky has done some drawings showing how the pub could be converted to accommodate different groups within the village, and Helen has produced some artist's impressions of what the building could look like, both from the outside and from the interior. I've been told that these are just possible ideas, and the committee would welcome any comments or suggestions for alternatives."

Alex and Megan wandered over to the notices and examined them closely.

"I must say that they look incredibly professional," observed Alex. "I didn't know that Bricky could produce such fine plans, and Helen's work is extremely professional. If Atkins and Dodd saw these, it would further convince them that we are serious."

"It gives people a chance to see what could be achieved," observed Megan. "Mum would be interested to see these, and now that Gordon's had his second jab, she will soon be able to choose a quiet moment and come in with the dogs to see what is envisaged."

"I'll get round during the week and come in with her to give her a hand with Gordon in case he's a bit over-excited at first; I think Dave's quite looking forward to meeting his new customers, and if they come in when Jake is around, then the pub will need an extra delivery of dog treats."

"It's a lovely pub in a lovely village, and I'm so glad she made it here. She's now threatening to buy thousands of shares."

"She must understand that while her financial support is appreciated, funding the Wellie must be a community thing, and there will be a limit on how much any individual can invest. Enough of business, I just wanted to say how much I have enjoyed these last few days. You must come over again when you've sorted your own domestic arrangements."

"Thanks. It's been a welcome break after the last few weeks with the dogs."

"You've been a big help to your mum, and she has appreciated it; Josh would have been proud of you, and I think you've done a marvellous job."

The couple enjoyed their evening together, and then, after bidding farewell to some of the regulars in the pub, Alex and Megan left for the short walk home. It was a cold night, and the sky was clear as they stood for a moment and looked out over the harbour.

"No snow clouds tonight," observed Alex. "It looks as though we might have a clear run tomorrow. I won't bother coming in as I want to get an early night; I don't want to be late in the morning. Give my love to Ivy."

He kissed her gently, and she headed off for the door, where she stopped briefly and blew him a dramatic kiss before going in to the sound of the dogs greeting her. Alex turned and set off home. It had been a good day and an entertaining evening, and he was tired.

As Alex walked to Ivy's cottage the next morning, he observed that there were some dark grey clouds hanging above the village, but he wasn't too concerned as the forecast had said they were due to head further north during the day, taking any few remnants of snow with them. He had taken the precaution of taking a flask of coffee with him in case they experienced any slight delay. Megan was ready with her case packed, and after kissing her mum and bidding farewell to the dogs, she set off with Alex to his car. The road out of the village posed no problems and the coast road was still easy to negotiate as the gritters had obviously been out. As they turned inland over the moors, Alex was relieved that the gritters had managed to keep that route clear of any appreciable amounts of snow, but he was slightly concerned to see that the flurries of snow had begun to fall again. They obviously hadn't heard the forecast that suggested they ought to be falling some distance to the north. As they drove on, the snow fell more heavily and the gritted surface of the road began to whiten appreciably. It didn't pose any problem as Alex was able to follow the tracks made by other vehicles. He felt pleased that he was in his trusty Volvo, and he reassured himself that it was a car capable of coping with Scandinavian winters. They drove on as the snow fell in larger flakes and the windscreen wipers were needed to clear a space to see the road ahead. All was going well until the small convoy he was travelling in were halted by the police. As the cars pulled forward in turn, they slid down their windows to speak to a young police officer who informed them that there had been an incident ahead where a lorry had managed to slide and block the road. The snow-covered officer directed the cars on to a diversion road. There was a large yellow sign with an arrow indicating that the cars should turn to the right. Each of the cars duly complied and drove on for some miles in worsening weather until a second diversion sign directed them to turn left. They continued along another minor road. The column of vehicles proceeded in convoy like a trail of marching termites, but there was no further sign of any planned diversion. As they went along, individual vehicles pulled off in various directions as their instincts selected a particular route until Alex found himself travelling on his own along a narrow road, with absolutely no idea where he was and with the snow falling heavily. He pulled over into what he surmised was a lay-by and pulled out his road map while silently cursing himself for not having had his sat-nav repaired.

"I just thought we'd stop here and have a coffee while I just check we are on the right road," he said nonchalantly, as if there was no problem. After all, what was there to worry about, being in the middle of the North York Moors in a minor blizzard with no idea where he was? After studying the road map, he established broadly where they were. They finished their coffees and Alex set off. He had established that there were three villages in the vicinity, and all he had to do was to run into one of them, and he would be able to fix his position and choose a route to York. The plan worked, but it was only after a considerable delay that he found himself entering Pickering from an entirely different direction to his usual approach. He re-joined his usual route and slowly made his way to Malton and then on to York, but it had added a considerable time to their journey. The snow was falling heavily as they pulled up at Ivy's old house, and they quickly scurried in.

"So much for the bloody weather forecast," exclaimed Alex. "If I'd known there was the slightest chance of snow like that, then I would never have set off. What should have been a journey of an hour and a half took us nearly five. Even the weather alerts on the radio gave no indication of how bad it was getting."

"Never mind, love," she said in an attempt to placate him. "We're here now, but I must admit that the journey only reinforced my reluctance to drive. You must be shattered; sit down, and I'll switch on the fire and then make us something to eat."

Alex was glad to comply, and he sank into a large armchair as the electric fire brightened up the hearth and soon ensured that the room was warm. He sat there, contemplating his situation. The most recent weather reports belatedly warned of extreme weather conditions with a number of roads closed and urging travellers only to undertake essential journeys. Much as he would have liked to be beside his own fire in Kirksea, there was no way he was going to put himself through that driving experience in a hurry. It only seemed a few minutes before Megan returned with a tray that she placed in front of Alex.

"There you are, love," she said as she presented him with an omelette and a cup of tea. "It had to be something quick because I don't know about you, but I'm starving. I'll just get mine, and we can eat in here as the central heating was turned right down while I was away, and the rest of the house needs to warm up a bit."

She disappeared to the kitchen, and as she returned, she reported that she had called Ivy to let her know about the weather situation.

"Mum says that the snow has started up again in the village, so you mustn't try to get back today."

"She can rest assured that I wouldn't risk that nightmare again. I'll see how things are tomorrow, perhaps in the afternoon if the major roads are clear."

The couple sat and ate their meal, and he suddenly remarked, "In all the time we were married, I never knew you to cook omelettes."

"No, but I've taken to making them occasionally. They are an easy meal, and I can vary them with all sorts of fillings. The truth is that I often can't be bothered to cook anything elaborate when it's just for me."

"Tell me about it. I frequently settle for something easy; I've even resorted to those ready meals at times. Some are quite good but others not so. Some of the ready meat pies are indeed soon ready, but the meat content is dubious in terms of quantity and origin. I have to fight the temptation to rely on Anita's fish and chips, but she has warned me that my status as eligible bachelor, if not local stud, would be in danger if I continued to bulk up."

"I like Anita, she's fun."

"Me too. She reminds me of you when we first married; before we grew up."

"Life always seemed so much more entertaining then before, as you say, we grew up," observed Megan. "It wasn't that life was easier then; on the contrary, as you've pointed out, we were financially insecure, and times were sometimes difficult, but we faced them together, and in retrospect I can honestly say that I enjoyed the challenges. Life is very comfortable now, but I often wish we could recharge that spirit of youth."

"Me too," he admitted in a rare candid moment.

CHAPTER THIRTY-FIVE

The couple sat and talked for hours until Megan observed that she was quite hungry and offered to try and find something for dinner.

"Good idea," said Alex, "but I've got a better one. Remember the little Italian place just up the road; why don't we see if we can get a table? I don't think many people would be daft enough to try and drive there this evening, but it wouldn't take us long to walk. I wouldn't put on a long posh frock, though."

"I don't think I've got one that would fit you anyway. I'll ring and see if we can book a table; I don't expect they will be packed out in this weather."

A phone call soon confirmed that, as expected, the restaurant was easily able to accommodate Alex and Megan, so she went off to change. When she arrived back in a rather smart dress and having taken the opportunity to put on some make-up, Alex couldn't help but feel somewhat under-dressed. Before they left, she put her smart shoes in a carrier bag and donned her wellingtons and a heavy coat for the walk through the snow to the restaurant. When they arrived in the foyer, the outer clothes were removed, and the wellingtons were discarded for the dress shoes. It seemed to Alex that Megan was like a beautiful butterfly emerging from a rather drab cocoon while he removed his coat to reveal his usual highly casual outfit. Looking at their reflections in the restaurants large mirrors, he was prompted to make an observation.

"You look like some fairy-tale princess," he remarked, "and I look very ordinary in my rags; I don't look worthy of escorting you to the ball."

"You look fine," she suggested, "and anyway, no one can see you in this subdued lighting."

The latter comment did little for his confidence, even though he knew she was teasing him. The room was, indeed, sparsely illuminated by discreet wall lights, and each table had its individual pair of candles. The aim had presumably been to try and create an intimate, even romantic ambiance, and Alex felt they had succeeded. A very attentive waiter escorted them to a table, passed them a rather large fancy menu and left them to choose their meals.

"An interesting accent," commented Alex after the waiter had gone off to see to one of the few other customers. "I wonder if he really is Italian. He seems almost a caricature of an Italian waiter."

"I don't care as long as the food tastes as good as the descriptions on this menu. Do you just want to stick with a main course?"

"To hell with that! I'm starving, and after a day like today we deserve to spoil ourselves, so let's go for it."

The meal was every bit as good as the menu had suggested, and they made their way heroically through from tomato bruschetta all the way to sfogliatella. In a moment of uncharacteristic extravagance, Alex had ordered a bottle of Barolo, not because he knew a great deal about Italian wine, but because the waiter had recommended it. As they finished the meal and were seeing off the last of the bottle of wine, a sudden thought struck Alex.

"You do realise that what we just paid for the wine is over twice as much as we used to spend on our weekly shopping when we first got married, but it was rather nice," he added.

"Yes, we wouldn't have dared set foot in a place like this then, and even when the financial constraints weren't quite so severe later on, we tended to go out to eat just to avoid cooking. We never went out for proper 'posh' meals much."

"I remember the little French place we used to frequent, but it was more of a café than a restaurant as such," he reminisced. "The waiter there insisted upon calling himself Anton and spoke with a strong French accent, but I found out he came from Barnsley and didn't speak more than a dozen words of French. Perhaps he thought that a strong quasi-French accent was more easily understood down south than a Barnsley one? I can't remember the last time we went out for a formal meal."

"I think it was that awful staff Christmas event that I organized. I had envisaged a civilized evening chatting with colleagues and their partners, but it turned out that there were three other staff dinners taking place in the same large room, and one of them had hired an entertainer for the event. Our group sat there trying our best to enjoy the 'all-in' Christmas package while that obnoxious comedian told filthy jokes."

"I remember the evening with brutal clarity. It was embarrassing because at least three of the women in one of the groups were sex workers with whom I'd had official contact in the past, and one of them insisted upon talking to me whenever I went to the bar as if we were old friends. I couldn't help noticing that even those ladies, who I had met in the course of my job didn't find the comedian funny either."

After dinner the couple chatted for some time. The restaurant was far from full and there was no pressure on them to vacate their table. It was only when the waiter had come over to ask if they wanted liqueurs that they realised it was getting late. Alex asked for the bill and there was a lengthy debate where each of them wanted to pay, but eventually

Megan insisted that she wanted to pick up the tab as Alex had endured such a lengthy drive to get her home. Alex consoled himself by leaving a generous tip, before they clad-up to head out and face the walk home through the snow that was still falling.

The house was warm now as Megan had boosted the central heating before they went out. She relaxed in one of the comfortable armchairs in the lounge while Alex sprawled out on the sofa.

Megan got up and walked over to her mum's record player, selected an LP from the rack and put it on the turntable. Soon, the unmistakeable sound of Fleetwood Mac emerged from the big old speakers. Megan turned the volume down to a gentle background level.

"Remember this from when we used to play it in our little flat and Mrs Talbot from upstairs used to complain about the noise?" she asked and then after a short pause, "I think I'll have a gin and tonic," she announced. "There's still some of Dad's special whisky in the cabinet. I'm sure he would like you to have some; you used to sit and share most of a bottle when you came over and stayed before we were married."

"Yes, they were great evenings, but I sometimes thought he plied me with whisky so I would sleep soundly and wouldn't creep off in the middle of the night to find your room."

Megan laughed and then sorted drinks for them both. She walked over to him with a drink in each hand and gave him his. She stood for a moment with her drink in her hand before sitting down beside him. He felt strangely uncomfortable. He could smell her perfume. She was relaxed and smiling; this was like it used to be when they were together a lifetime ago. They chatted about the times they had enjoyed together, and Alex kept asking himself why they had ever turned their backs on such apparently idyllic times. They had discussed it dispassionately before their divorce, and it had made such sense, but now he was having dangerous doubts. He wasn't sure if she shared his misgivings. Life had become safe and uncomplicated in Kirksea, but now here he was sitting with Megan, and she was obviously relaxed and happy, laughing at his jokes. Perhaps this is all she wanted from their relationship. Perhaps he was being ridiculously optimistic even to think that she might want to get back together; after all, it was she who had originally suggested a divorce. He looked at her attentively as she spoke of their joint past, but he could barely concentrate on what she was saying. He found himself staring at her lips. He wanted to kiss her; after all, he had kissed those lips tens of thousands of times in the past, but he knew it was probably irrational. He swirled the whisky around in his glass, but he was determined not to drink too much in case he did something mad like telling her he wanted her back.

While the evening was apparently relaxed, Alex didn't feel comfortable. A superb meal, the familiar music, a fine whisky and good company shouldn't have made him feel unsettled, but that company he was enjoying was provided by his former wife. Eventually, having taken a large gulp of whisky, he reluctantly declared, "I'm sorry, love, but I'm absolutely shattered, and I hope to be able to get off back home tomorrow if the weather isn't too bad. The major roads are generally kept clear in all but the worst weather, and I don't like leaving your mum in the village with the snow around and with those two dogs to look after."

The last part was a bit of a lie because he knew that Ivy was quite capable of looking after herself, and there were plenty of people she could turn to in an emergency, but by professing his concern, it appeared to support his decision to get back home.

"OK," she said, expressing slight surprise at his eagerness to brave the road back so soon, as well as his apparent sudden change of mood. "The bed has been made up in my old room. I'll sleep in Mum's."

The atmosphere at breakfast the next morning contrasted markedly with that of the previous night. The couple were polite but strangely reserved and this relationship continued throughout the day. Shortly after lunch, he kissed her gently before getting in the car and setting off for home. There were some light flurries of snow as he drove along the road home, but the roads were thankfully relatively clear, and he had no hold-ups. Having parked up the car in Kirksea, he walked down to Ivy's cottage to check how she was. The dogs were naturally keen to see him, and once they were settled, he sat in Ivy's lounge and waited for what he expected would be veiled enquiries about his stay overnight with Megan, but none were forthcoming. He assumed that she saw from his demeanour that there had been no rekindling of the romance. He certainly didn't feel any different. He had, for one glorious evening, allowed himself to dare to think that things could be different, but he had chosen not to risk embarrassing Megan by admitting that he knew he still cared deeply for her. He consoled himself with the fact that they were still friends, and he would see her from time to time when she came to visit Ivy, although he had been disappointed at her relative coolness when he had left her that morning.

"I gather that you've had a bit of a tough time," observed Ivy.

"Tough time? Oh yes, the roads were a bit tricky, but we would have been OK if we hadn't been re-diverted. The trip back today wasn't easy, but the old car just soldiered on. We had a lovely meal at the little Italian restaurant near your old place."

"Is that Poco Formaggio?" she asked. "It's a lovely place. Josh used to take me quite often. It appealed to his romantic side. We had some wonderful evenings that started there; in fact it was the last place he ever took me to."

She paused for a while, recollecting the happy evenings she had spent with Josh.

"Has Megan got any further with her house in London?" asked Ivy. "I know she's keen to get herself established in a place of her own. She's more than welcome to stay in my old place for as long as she likes, but I know she wants to move on and get on with her life."

"It all seems to be slowly moving on, but you know how house sales can drag on. I don't suppose that much has happened here in sleepy Kirksea?"

"There was quite a party in the pub on Saturday night. It was a very impromptu affair; a lot of people were discussing the proposed development of the place. Bricky was outlining his possible plans for the Wellie, and someone asked why it couldn't become a wedding venue to extend its versatility. Norman explained that it was possible to have the building registered as such, and then in a moment of rash romanticism, Tom said he would love to avail himself of such a service, and he proposed to Anita."

"And then, what did she say?"

"She accepted. I think she was swept along, as much by the romance of the proposal as by the couple of glasses of Pinot Grigio she'd consumed but I'm sure she won't regret it. Some people are obviously made for each other."

Alex was pleased to note that her last remark did not seem to be another comment on his and Megan's lack of relationship, and he was intrigued to know how Ivy had managed to gather so much information.

"It seems like I missed quite a night, but how did you get to find out so much?"

"Living so near the Wellie means that most of the pub-goers go right past my door, and if I happen to be coming or going with the dogs, I can have a chat with whoever. As well as that, Norman sometimes drops in for a cuppa so the dogs can socialize a bit. Bricky also drops in briefly from time to time to see how we are doing. They really are a wonderful crowd in the village here."

"I'm out of the village for a couple of days, and all sorts of things happen."

"That's not quite all. Norman has been trying to get the views of the owners of holiday homes to get their support for saving the pub. Most of them value the pub when they are here, and it makes the cottages a lot more desirable to rent out if they can advertise that the village has a pub. He has obtained promises from most of them to buy shares in the pub, so the coffers are swelling. As you've pointed out, I'm not allowed to buy up all the shares I might want, but I've agreed to buy my maximum allocation. Norman was a bit disappointed that he couldn't get any support from Dr Henderson and her husband, the people who own the cottage next to yours. They are known to be very wealthy and might have contributed a lot to the fund. Apparently, they have decided that their work commitments mean they can't get here often enough to warrant keeping it up, so they decided to put it on the market."

"That will be snapped up quickly. It's one the best locations around here, being next to mine."

"You're right, love, of course, but even if it hadn't enjoyed such a prestigious position, it wasn't going to hang about. In fact it was bought yesterday, even before it had officially gone on the market. It just shows how lucky I was to get this place."

Alex was impressed with the speed at which Ivy had managed to get her finger on the pulse of local life; within a matter of weeks, she seemed to know everything that was going on, and he was looking forward to meeting up with Anita to check how she was feeling after somewhat rashly accepting Tom's proposal. He didn't have to wait long because she was sitting in the Wellie with Tom when Alex dropped in that evening.

CHAPTER THIRTY-SIX

Alex went over to where Tom and Anita were sitting and announced to her, "I gather that congratulations are in order. I leave you alone for a couple of days, and you run off with some other guy."

He kissed her and then shook Tom by the hand, congratulating him on his good fortune.

"You couldn't expect me to wait forever, Wessie," she explained. "I really thought that you and Megan would get back together, hence my current choice. Tom knows he got me on the rebound, but he's happy with that."

"She never changes," observed Tom. "It does seem strange being in here now; it's the place where I proposed, and I hope it's the place that we will get married. We are just starting to think about wedding plans, that's to say Anita is starting on wedding plans. Norman seems to think the sale should go through before August, so we could have a summer wedding. With a bit of luck we could become a practice run for future events here."

"I'm very pleased for you, Tom, and thank you for taking on the challenge of Anita; I shall certainly feel a lot safer going in to get my fish and chips knowing that she's under some sort of control."

"Not much chance of that, Wessie," admitted the younger man. "She'll always be a bit feral, but that's why I love her. To be honest, she has to have some spirit to take on her future mother-in-law; I don't want to appear biased, but my money's on Anita."

The following Wednesday, Alex made his customary early appearance at the pub to get a preview of the *Gazette*. Bricky was standing at the bar with Dave, and the three of them chatted about recent events in the village and particularly about the snow which seemed reluctant to leave. Just when the snow was appearing to thaw out a little, another flurry would blow in and redecorate the village. Their conversation was dramatically interrupted by Norman, who burst through the doors dramatically, waving his early copy of the *Gazette* and shouting to the gathered drinkers.

"Ta-Da! Hold the front page! Norman does it again."

"You seem pleased with yourself, Norman," commented Dave. "What fantasy have you been reporting now?"

"It is undoubtedly my greatest journalistic achievement yet, a possible prize-winner, evidence of my talent for all to see. Check out the front page and rid yourselves of any doubt as to my ability."

"You're pleased about something, aren't you?" suggested Bricky, taking the proffered paper and reading out the headlines. "*Local pub saved by villagers.*"

"Is that official, Norman, or just a bit of wishful thinking? I thought that the issue was still under discussion," queried Alex.

"I managed to meet up with a Gervais Taunton, one of the directors of Atkins and Dodd, it turns out that he used to go to my school, and we had a couple of brandies at a pub I knew he frequented. He more or less admitted that they were apprehensive about getting embroiled in any protracted fight to develop the site of the Wellie, given what they knew of the council's opposition to such closures. I suggested a way that they could come out of it smelling of roses rather than being seen as the villain of the piece. If they were able to hold onto the pub for their own plans, they appreciate that it could cost tens of thousands in legal fees, and it would take them years to block our purchase of the place. After all that, their 'corporate image' would be tarnished, and it wouldn't help them gain future planning consent as they moved into other commercial developments. I pointed out that I could report the issue in a favourable light for the brewery, and so we produced a statement which my friend had ratified by the managers of Atkins and Dodd. The resulting press release appears in the second paragraph."

"Here it is," pointed out Bricky. "*A spokesman of local brewing company, Atkins and Dodd, has announced that they are delighted that the villagers of Kirksea have agreed to take on the running of the Whelk Pot. The brewery are always pleased to support such local ventures and pledge their support to make a smooth transfer of ownership, and they hope to work closely with the new owners in the future to ensure the pub continues to provide a valuable service for the village. We wish the new owners well.*"

"I've worked with that band of users for years and have to say that sounds even less credible than your usual fairy tales, Norman," commented Dave.

"Admittedly, I wouldn't buy a second-hand car from any of them, not even Gervais, but we have it in print, and so they must be seen to be cooperating with us."

"Well, for the first time, I think your imaginative journalism has served the village well, Norman, so, in my capacity as Knight of Saint Bodolv, I would like to buy our little group a drink. Oh, to hell with the expense, Dave, let's have one each."

There followed a rather lengthy celebration, which only broke up when Bricky declared that he had to check up on a couple of jobs that his men were working on, and Norman went off to walk Gordon. Alex took the opportunity to stop off at Ivy's place to pass on the good news that had been reported in Norman's article. Ivy was euphoric and insisted upon opening a bottle of wine and toasting the Whelk Pot. After a while, she calmed down, and the pair sat in armchairs with their glasses of wine.

"Look at me sitting here drinking wine at this time of day on a Wednesday," she exclaimed. "But I don't care. That pub means so much to me already. I couldn't be happier."

Alex knew that wasn't entirely true, but he was pleased that she made no attempt to allude to his relationship with Megan. He would have been the first to admit that her absence from his life was something that he deeply regretted, and he had loved having her around for the previous couple of weeks, but that was obviously the only kind of relationship she wanted, and he would content himself with that.

His thoughts were disrupted by Ivy suddenly announcing, "In this recent cold weather, Mandy has not been keen to go out, particularly when it's snowing, and I can't find her warm coat. I thought I'd brought it with me, but my memory's not as good as it used to be. I think I may have left it in the utility room in York. It's an awkward thing to post, so I'll have to wait for Megan's next visit."

"No problem, love, I can nip over and pick it up. We can't have Mandy being cold, and she needs to get out for her exercise, as does young Gordon. I've got some work to do on the negotiations for the pub and the insurances, but I can go over on Saturday as long as the snow doesn't get any worse. Is there anything you want taking over or collecting?"

"No thanks, I feel terrible asking you to go all that way, but I hate to see Mandy shivering."

"I'll pop in again on Friday in case you think of anything else you want."

Alex managed to clear up some of the insurance issues about the pub and met up with Norman on Thursday to check on how the sale of shares was going and to formulate some application forms to try and secure some community development grants. He felt that things were progressing steadily, and by the time he turned up at the chip shop on Friday afternoon, he felt he had achieved quite a lot.

"Morning, gorgeous," came the usual greeting from Anita. "I'm sorry that I had to spring that on you about Tom and me, but you couldn't expect me to wait for you forever. Anyway I was sure that you would settle with Megan. I was naturally jealous of Helen, but I thought you'd get over that. It appears my female intuition let me down."

"Never mind, I forgive you, but how do you expect to get on with Tom's mum?

"Badly, at least at first. She is very caring and tends to smother him, but if he can stand up to me I'm sure he has the backbone to show his mum that she can't interfere with our lives. My parents wouldn't dream of trying to run my life. You obviously struck it lucky with your in-laws."

"I guess so. Ivy has tried to help Megan and me get together again, but she has seen the inadvisability of trying to interfere, eventually."

On the Saturday morning, Alex checked that Ivy didn't want anything transporting to or from York before setting off. The intermittent snow flurries had continued through the week, although the roads remained relatively clear, but the weather forecast had warned of the danger of icy roads, so Alex drove very carefully. He was thankful of the advanced driving courses he had taken with the police, and he had taken the precaution of taking a flask of coffee and a shovel in case things got particularly difficult. As it turned out, he had a relatively uneventful journey, and it took him only a few minutes longer than usual because the roads were relatively empty of traffic. When he arrived at Ivy's old house, he was met by Megan, who was her usual pleasant self.

"Hello, darling," she greeted him, and he was pleased to hear that endearment, so he couldn't have offended her too much.

"Nice to see you again so soon, love. I assume your mum's been in contact to explain my sudden return."

"She said that you were coming over but was a bit unclear about why. To be honest, Little Gordon was having a good old yap playing with Mandy, so I couldn't hear every word, but she mentioned some dog equipment."

"Yes, poor old Mandy is feeling the cold in this extreme weather and is missing the warm coat she needs for walks. Ivy says it's in the utility room."

"Utility room, are you sure? I haven't seen it in there, and I cleaned up thoroughly when the puppies left. Perhaps she put it out in the shed; I've never seen it since I've been here. Never mind; I've made some lunch, so let's have that and we can search for the coat later."

Megan led him through to the kitchen where she had laid out a meal for them, and he was delighted to see it was salade nicoise, one of his favourite meals.

"This looks lovely, and so do you, by the way. Is that a new dress?"

"Thank you. No, it's one that I bought for work. It's a bit dressy for casual use, but I suddenly realised that I don't need a wardrobe full of smart work clothes as I'm no longer working in the office. Do you like it then?"

He restricted himself to saying that it was very nice. What he wanted to say was that she looked beautiful, and the cut of the dress accentuated the fact that she still had a very attractive figure. He wasn't going to let the conversation go off in that direction.

"Would you like a small glass of wine with your dinner, I know you're driving but…" She suddenly stopped and giggled.

"What's so funny?" he asked, somewhat bemused.

"It's just that I remembered that it was here in the kitchen that you turned down that glass of wine from Mum, and she suggested you should stay over and sleep with me."

"OK, I will have a glass of wine, but that's all, thanks."

Megan looked away for a moment, and he suspected that he had embarrassed her, so he quietly got on with his meal and changed the subject.

"If Mandy's coat isn't in the shed, have you any idea where it might be?"

"Absolutely no idea. You know what Dad was like for carefully putting things away. He hated clutter, so it could take a while to find it. When we were clearing up after his funeral, we found items in the strangest of places, including all those bank account details. We'll have a good look after lunch."

After a most enjoyable meal, Megan found the correct key, and the pair of them went down the side of the house to the shed. The snow had started to fall again. It was only a light scattering, but the path down to the shed had not been cleared, and there was an accumulation of some five inches of snow. It was a large shed, and when Megan opened the door it was obvious that Josh's dislike of clutter in the house did not apply to the shed, which was a mass of domestic debris piled high.

"This could take some time," observed Alex as he set about sorting through the assorted junk.

He was right, particularly because Megan kept stopping to pick up cherished items and to tell him about the memories they brought back. It was starting to get dark, and the shed didn't appear to have any fixed lighting, so Alex suggested that they find a torch. This proved to be of little use because dark clouds were beginning to fill the sky, and the shed only had small windows, so it soon became very difficult to see what was among the badly-stacked piles of discarded household items.

"Perhaps you should ring your mum and see if she can make any suggestion as to where it could be? It's getting dark, and those clouds are a bit menacing, so I don't want to be leaving too late."

Megan went off to find her phone, and after a final few minutes searching fruitlessly, Alex went in to join her.

"Did she have any further suggestions as to where it could be?"

"No, afraid not, but she did have some alarming news about the weather on the coast. Apparently the snow is back with a vengeance, and a lot of the local roads are reported as being almost impassable. She was most apologetic about sending you out in such conditions."

"The clouds look ominous here, but there are only slight flurries of snow. It shows how weather conditions can vary over a very small area. I remember that day when Kirksea was smothered in fog but it was lovely day for you here."

"Mum says she would feel terribly guilty about you attempting to get back in such conditions and all but begged me to persuade you to stay over until things improve."

"What's the French for déjà vu?" mused Alex.

"Sorry, love."

"It's not your fault. And it's not as though I have anything to rush back for. Find me the number of that nice restaurant; my treat this time."

And so it was that the efficient young waiter later greeted the sophisticated-looking woman and her scruffy companion and showed them to their 'usual' table. Megan confessed that she was not particularly hungry, so they restricted themselves to a starter and a main course with another rather nice bottle of Barolo. The restaurant's seductive atmosphere soon had them feeling relaxed, and it was over two hours before they felt inclined to return home. Back in the house, Alex was careful to sit in one of the armchairs rather than on the sofa where he had felt so vulnerable the week before. Megan declared that she fancied a gin and tonic and, without asking, she brought him a glass of what he knew to be Josh's special whisky. She then selected an album to put on the record player and came to sit down on the sofa. The sound of the group, Bread, drifted into the room from the two ancient speakers.

"I think these are some of the most romantic songs ever recorded," said Megan, before sitting in silence for some minutes listening to the lyrics being carried by the gentle melodies. "We used to listen to some of these when we were just married, and I still love listening to them."

Alex listened in silence, deliberately trying not to be seduced by the music. When the first side of the record finished, Megan got up and took her glass into the kitchen to fix herself another drink, and she brought the whisky bottle back and replenished his. She then went and turned the record over before returning to the sofa. After a while she patted the seat beside her as an obvious invitation for him to join her. He was faced with a real dilemma. Although he surmised that all she wanted was his friendship, he knew that he would be tempted to ask more of her and risk upsetting her and ruining their existing relationship. But if he didn't take up the offer of a seat by her side, then she might assume that he was being rude. As all this ran through his mind, she patted the seat next to her again and smiled at him. He felt he had no choice, so he took his drink over and sat beside her. All his feelings of the previous week ran through his mind. He was sitting close to a woman he still found very attractive; he could smell her intoxicating perfume, still felt the desire to kiss her, and all this was going on to a background of romantic songs. Megan noticed his sudden tenseness and was concerned.

"What's the matter, love?" she asked.

He knew he couldn't avoid the issue this time and tried to explain.

"I have to get something cleared up here and now, love," he said while trying to appear decisive. "I have been thinking that our decision to break up might not have been the best one we ever made. I certainly don't think we got it right, and sometimes when I see how we both still get on so well, I suspect that you have your reservations. To be blunt. Do you think we should start again?"

There was a lengthy silence before she gave her answer.

"I can see your point of view, love, but there is one major problem," she said, and then, after a short pause, she explained her concern. "It's just that I don't know where you are going to find a Morris Marina at this time of night."

It took a brief second for her response to sink in, and then he put down his drink, relieved her of hers and kissed her. This was not the polite, gentle kiss of mere friends but that of a couple who both accepted that they were meant to be together. After a while, he pulled back from her slightly, smiled, and then kissed her again. This simple but mutually enjoyable routine went on for a time before it was Megan who announced that it had been a long day and they ought to get to bed. She headed upstairs, and Alex followed her into the bedroom.

"So I'm back in your bedroom for the second time in a week; I only wish you'd joined me last week."

"I wish I had. I have a little confession to make. Last week I had only made up the one bed, hoping I could entice you to join me. The bed in Mum's room hadn't been prepared, so I had to start sorting it out after you'd gone to bed. If you hadn't made your dramatic announcement tonight, then I would have had to do something to draw you out of your shell. I was beginning to be afraid that I would have had to slip into something particularly diaphanous and flaunt myself in front of you, and that would not have been very dignified."

"Perhaps not entirely dignified but very attractive."

The following morning Alex woke early, as had become his habit, and looked over at Megan beside him. She was sleeping soundly, and he just looked at her. She appeared every bit as beautiful to him now as she had been as that bridesmaid he had first met. He was elated by the fact that they were together again, but his joy was tinged by a certain sadness that they had missed so much time when they ought not to have been separated. It was barely light, but he chose not to turn on his bedside light as he didn't want to wake Megan, and he walked over to the window and pulled back the curtain just enough to be able to look out on the garden. Never had he been so pleased to see that it was snowing. It was a pretty pathetic shower but enough to convince him that a trip to Kirksea was inadvisable. He readily conceded that he would take any excuse to stay longer with Megan but knew that at some time he would have to leave. As he stood by the window, he heard Megan moving about back in the bed.

"What are you doing, love?" she asked in a sleepy voice.

"Sorry. I didn't mean to wake you, but I just wanted to check the weather. It's still snowing."

"Good! So you're not going anywhere. Come back to bed."

Alex was in no mood to disobey her, and he climbed back into bed. He was aware that Megan had soon fallen back to sleep, but he couldn't. He lay there trying to formulate some sort of suggestions to put to Megan about their future plans. It was complicated. The practical solution was for them to stay together in York, but they had both admitted to being taken by the charms of Kirksea, where he only had a small cottage. Was it to be the heart or the head that determined where they ended up? Was he prepared to give up his little dream cottage and the community he had grown to love in his village? Megan had already expressed an interest in moving to a little cottage somewhere like Kirksea, but they both knew how difficult it would be to find such a place. When all was said and done, they'd managed in a tiny flat together before the girls had been born and compared to that, his two-bedroomed cottage was a palace. Even with these complex issues rattling around in his head, Alex did eventually fall asleep again, and when he awoke, Megan was gone. Quickly throwing on Josh's old dressing gown, he went downstairs to find Megan cooking breakfast.

"I'm afraid I'm a bit disorganized this morning; it was rather a hectic day yesterday," she explained.

"I guess it was. It had an awful start, but the ending more than made up for it," he said with a smile as he gently pulled her away from the hot plate and kissed her passionately.

"I'd forgotten what you used to be like in the morning," she said. "I guess I could get used to it. But, just for now, could I please prepare your breakfast?"

"I need to talk to you about that," he said.

"What, molesting me while I'm cooking?"

"Not exactly, but we need to know where we will be living. My main standpoint is simple: I'm not going to let you out of my life again. I know you have no great affiliation with York, so I guess you won't feel any great desire to live here."

"I won't let you go again. Couldn't I move in with you?" she asked.

"I would love that. As far as I'm concerned, sharing my home with you would make my little bit of heaven even better, but it's a tiny cottage," he explained.

"Our original flat in London was not much of a step up in size from the Morris Marina, but we were happy."

"I was hoping you'd say that. To be honest, I'd live in that old car as long as I was with you," he said before kissing her again.

"Steady tiger, we have to eat, you know."

"OK, if you insist," he said before remarking, "I must admit that you are a lot more amenable than you were over breakfast last week. The atmosphere was decidedly chilly."

"Sorry about that, darling, but I was in a strange state of mind. My inability to coax you into bed the night before made me feel rejected. I was disappointed because I felt you hadn't found me attractive. I had convinced myself before then that you wanted to get back together, but your lack of action convinced me we had no future together, and that was a depressing prospect."

"We managed to almost mess things up between us because of our fear of showing our feelings for each other, and I'm not going to make that mistake again," he said before kissing her again.

After breakfast, Alex addressed the next issue.

"Shouldn't we ring your mum and explain that I'm bringing an extra passenger back with me?"

"I bet she's already figured it out for herself. I know we accused her of interfering, but I think she had appraised our relationship long before we had. And, I'm not sorry to say, she was right. I'll ring her soon and break the news to her; I suspect she might be quite pleased."

CHAPTER THIRTY-SEVEN

Ivy expressed delight at the news and graciously did not suggest that she had been right all along. As Megan and Alex drove out of York, the roads were completely clear of snow, but he was steeling himself for the expected worse conditions over the moors. He had taken the precaution of refilling his flask with coffee, and he was confident that he would be able to fight his way through to Kirksea. As it turned out, the roads posed no problems, and even the last part of the journey into the village was clear. Captain had obviously been diligent in his snow-clearing duties.

When the couple arrived at Ivy's house, they were greeted by two very excited dogs and one equally euphoric Ivy.

"It's fantastic news," she exclaimed. "I'll put the kettle on. No. To hell with it, let's all go to the pub for a celebratory drink. It can't be every day that one's former son-in-law starts dating one's daughter."

"What about the dogs, Mum?" asked Megan.

"They can come too. It's about time that they had some pub training. It shouldn't be too busy over Sunday lunchtime."

The pub was, in fact, rather busy. Anita, Tom and their respective parents were just finishing a lunch to celebrate their engagement, and Norman had obviously decided to give Jake a taste of pub life. The three dogs greeted each other excitedly but then settled down by the feet of their owners. Alex collected drinks for his party, but before he had time to sit down, Anita came over and kissed him before surprising him with a comment.

"Congratulations, gorgeous," she announced. "It's lovely to see you together at last, and it's about time."

Alex looked over at Ivy, who seemed genuinely surprised.

"I never said a word, honestly. I haven't spoken to a soul since Megan rang this morning."

"Nobody needed to tell me. It was obvious the minute you walked in today. You are comfortable together and obviously can't hide your love. I've been working on it for weeks now. I knew you couldn't get together while I was in your life, Wessie. Why else do you think I took up Tom's offer of marriage? I knew if you realised that I was not available, you would look elsewhere. I'm not bitter, though; the best woman won."

"Thanks for your magnanimous gesture," replied Alex. "I only hope that life with Tom will help you get over your terrible shyness."

"I'll keep up the therapy," she replied. "But I have more immediate issues. Now you're no longer the most eligible bachelor in the village, who will take on the title? So far, Old Bob is the only contender; it's not a strong field."

Anita walked back to her party, nodding to them as she approached. They, in turn, raised their glasses in the direction of Alex and Megan.

"No need to make an official announcement in the *Gazette*; the whole village will know by tomorrow evening," observed Alex. "And I'm not complaining. I want everyone to know how lucky I am."

With this, he leaned over and kissed Megan before becoming aware that most of the customers in the pub appeared to be watching. He didn't care and raised his glass to his many friends.

"Don't worry about Mandy's coat," said Ivy. "It turns out that it was in a cupboard in my current place. I'm sorry that I sent you all that way by mistake."

"How strange! But there's no need to apologise, Mum," said Megan. "It seems to have turned out all right in the end."

It was at this point that Bricky came over to have a chat and to congratulate the happy couple.

"The snow seems to have cleared relatively quickly after the heavy fall yesterday," commented Alex. "Captain must have been working all night to clear it."

"What snow?" remarked Bricky. "We've had no more than a few flakes over the last couple of days."

Alex looked over at Ivy, who shrugged her shoulders and, with feigned wide-eyed innocence, replied, "I may have exaggerated the severity of the weather because I didn't want to risk you having an accident."

Alex leaned over and kissed her while saying, "You're a very naughty lady, Ivy, but I forgive you."

The group enjoyed a lengthy afternoon in the Wellie, during which they learned how well the process of purchasing the pub was progressing, but eventually they returned to Ivy's cottage and began to sort out their domestic arrangements. There was no doubt that Megan was to move in with Alex, but Ivy was quick to point out how small the cottage was and wondered how they would cope.

"It will be a bit of a squeeze," conceded Alex, "but it's bigger than the first place we had in London."

"Yes, it was rather pokey, as I remember," agreed Ivy, "but you could always buy the place next door to you and knock through later if you wanted."

"Lovely plan, Mum, but this is not Kirksea Monopoly, where properties come up all the time."

"That has become very obvious when trying to buy this place," agreed Ivy. "But you could try having a word with the owner to see if it's available."

"It's a bit difficult when you don't even know who the owner is. I've never met the Hendersons."

"I know who it is," said Ivy, and after a brief pause, she announced, "It's me. When I got the news from Norman that it was about to come on the market, I immediately offered the full price, and the sale is underway. Before you start, quite rightly, saying that I'm interfering, I must point out that I bought that house as an investment, and if you're not interested, I could sell it very quickly. Quite simply, I can't lose."

"If you are prepared to sell it on again, then it would make good sense for me to use some of the money from the sale of my place to invest in the one next to Alex. We always have the option to knock through at some later date if we want to or to rent out my new cottage. Thanks, Mum. You're a darling."

"It is very much my pleasure to help out a bit, but only when you want me to. My scheming days are over, not that I would ever own up to having played any part in you two getting back together. Josh would have been so happy. Here we are together in this lovely village with a pub that has bucked the trend and now appears to have a good future ahead with a supportive clientele. It's a little Yorkshire paradise by the sea."

"The most important thing I've learned," commented Alex, "is that the only thing that can improve paradise is sharing it."

ABOUT THE AUTHOR

Born in Hull in 1949, I spent many happy days of my teenage years in a variety of places on the East Yorkshire coast. From the age of fourteen until I went away to college, most of my school holidays and many weekends were spent with friends in a converted railway carriage at Tunstall. Such improvised holiday homes were popular in the postwar years. It proved a wonderful place to spend my study leave from school as I approached my GCEs, but little revision was undertaken, and this was reflected in my exam results. It was in those far-off days that I took my first tentative steps into the wonderful, if sometimes painful, world of love and romance, and my affinity with the coast is supported by those memories. After I married, we spent a lot of time by the coast, and when our children were young, we rented a cottage in Robin Hood's Bay for holidays. Certain elements in this story reflect my love of the area and the slower pace of life it can offer.

www.ingramcontent.com/pod-product-compliance
Ingram Content Group UK Ltd.
Pitfield, Milton Keynes, MK11 3LW, UK
UKHW040618120925
7862UKWH00001B/9

9 781836 151135